Boughs of Evergreen

A Holiday Anthology

VOLUME ONE

A collection of stories
celebrating the holiday season
in all its diversity.

Beaten Track
www.beatentrackpublishing.com

Boughs of Evergreen: A Holiday Anthology (Volume One)

Published 2014, 2015 by Beaten Track Publishing.
Edited by Debbie McGowan and Shayla Mist.

All stories are copyright their individual authors as indicated herein.
See pages following for individual copyright information.

Cover Design by Noah Homes.

A CIP catalogue record for this book
is available from the British Library.

ISBN: 978 1 909192 89 8

Beaten Track Publishing,
Burscough. Lancashire.
www.beatentrackpublishing.com

Boughs of Evergreen
A Holiday Anthology

Boughs of Evergreen is a two-volume collection of short stories celebrating the holiday season in all its diversity. Penned by authors from the UK, the USA, Scandinavia and Eastern Europe, these are tales of the young and the not-so-young from many different walks of life.

Themes of family, friendship and romance take readers on a journey through some of the major holidays, both past and present, including Thanksgiving, Advent, St. Lucia Day, Hanukkah, Saturnalia, Winter Solstice, Yule, Christmas and New Year. In each we find at the very least hope, and often love, peace and happiness.

Proceeds from sales of this anthology will be donated to The Trevor Project. The Trevor Project is the leading national organization [USA] providing crisis intervention and suicide prevention services to lesbian, gay, bisexual, transgender and questioning (LGBTQ) young people ages 13-24.

For more information, visit: www.thetrevorproject.org.

TABLE OF CONTENTS

Eve was always an outsider. So different from everyone else, she never made friends easily—until the day she met Anna, a totally mysterious girl who seemed almost too good to be true. A few times over the years they had found each other, and then Anna would disappear, leading Eve to conclude that she is an imaginary friend—a perfect girl she had created in her own mind to help ride the wave of difficult teens and other troubles in life. But what if Anna is real? Could they still be friends? On Christmas Eve they might just discover that the magic and love they've found can be held onto all year round.

It's a cold, desperate December when a young girl flees home, in search of food, shelter and the real Santa Claus. Stranded in George and Josh's hometown, she discovers that the spirit of Christmas can be found in the most unexpected of places. Includes the story of The Little Match Girl, by Hans Christian Andersen.

Simon is counting the days to Christmas, not because he likes the Holidays—no, he hates them. He dreads every single holiday ever created, but Christmas it the worst. As if his dad's drunken snores and his mother's faked Christmas spirit isn't enough, his sister has decided to celebrate Christmas elsewhere this year. The stress and anxiety drive Simon crazy. When he is introduced to a work colleague's son, Hannes, he mistakenly believes he's been set up on a blind date. Even after Hannes sets him straight in his assumptions, he keeps seeing signs that shouldn't be there. Is Hannes lying when he says he isn't interested or has the Christmas stress finally driven Simon mad?

Cade Bishop is finally on the mend from a traumatic event that happened almost five years ago. That healing didn't really start until last April, when he met Alan Troxler. Alan has problems of his own, but he's noticed over the last eight months that the more time he shares with Cade, the more easily he's able to put his troubles to rest. They're traveling together to Asheville, North Carolina to renew a Christmas tradition that was an important part of Alan's past, and to introduce him to Cade's parents—one of the few worries he hasn't been able to let go.

KISS ME AT KWANZAA

Coworkers and cubicle mates, Ishmael "Ish" Cutter and Adan Flores might come from different backgrounds but they have a good number of things in common. The biggest one? They each have a secret crush on the other. This holiday season they are both single for the first time in thirteen months. No boyfriends or clingy ex issues—maybe it's time for Adan to make his move? He formulates the perfect plan and invites Ish over for his family's Kwanzaa feast...but will he have the courage to make the first move or will this holiday season be one to forget?

LION'S HERO

Eight nights to fall in love. Ari has a mission: meet and fall in love with a man chosen for him by God. The catch: he only has eight nights to complete it—the eight nights of Chanukah. Gabriel has a test of faith. Reaching out to a young man, he finds himself confronted with the unbelievable. Believe, and the Festival of Lights may herald a miracle.

ONE NIGHTSTAND

Doug's not good with one-night stands, yet in the early hours of Christmas Eve, he returns home with Kirk—a good-looking guy he met at the club. Nestled together in the kitchen of his New England cottage, sipping hot chocolate and watching the snow fall, Doug wishes there could be more to this casual encounter. It's a feeling that stays with him as he heads off to a frantic day of work at the mall, swamped with last-minute holiday shoppers...the last place he expects to find something magical.

SHINY THINGS

At sixteen, Nathaniel Avery was shipped off to live with an aunt in hopes of quelling a budding relationship between him and another boy. Ten years later, a frantic call from his younger brother and his father's failing health, brings him back home. Just weeks before Thanksgiving and the most important day in Vincent Cooke's career, he nearly collides with the grown version of the boy he never really forgot. Will a gallery renovation, the holiday season and the art of a mad genius help them to rebuild a friendship and rekindle a romance?

THE BARD AND HIS BOYFRIEND: A TALE OF HOLIDAY HOMECOMINGS

Seth is a member of an ancient clan of druids that have existed for over 5,000 years. The rituals they perform at the changing of the seasons keep the very fabric of reality from unraveling. But as he goes home for the Winter Solstice, all Seth can think about is the huge fight he had with his boyfriend before he left school for the holiday break. Much to Seth's surprise, Alejandro decides to follow him home to apologize. When Seth decides to tell him the truth about his heritage, Alejandro has to make a decision. Seth and Alejandro must work together to make sure that wherever they are spending the holidays—they are home with each other.

A FRIEND
FOR CHRISTMAS

J P Walker

First Meeting

My story begins, as many do, a long time ago. A good twenty-two years into the past, when I was just five years old and lost in, what seemed at the time, the biggest playground I had ever set foot in. It was my first day in a large primary school and I was holding my *Teenage Mutant Ninja Turtle* doll closely to my chest as if it were bullet-proof. My scuffed-up trainers that still had lights in the heels were slowly guiding me amidst the huge crowd of kids, running and shouting and playing in every direction I looked. I had a feeling then, in the pit of my stomach and working its way up through my chest and, I'm sure, into my eyes, that I couldn't put a name to way back then. Now, however, I know it was loneliness.

I was a very shy kid. I would much rather have sat at home under a tree in our large garden, reading a book—or making childish attempts at writing one—than outside with other children. I had no friends, other than Raphael in my arms, that is. In that playground, I was the only little girl not running or skipping with a band of other little girls, and, for the first time, it bothered me.

As I continued to walk forward and be continuously bumped into and almost knocked to the floor, I moved with purpose, toward a group of girls sitting cross-legged on a patch of grass, with their dolls and what appeared to be a small tea set. I clutched Raphael even closer to me, tugging at the ends of the red bandana covering his eyes. As I approached, I saw them notice me and begin whispering to one another. I stood in front of the small group and smiled at them all, with their perfectly plaited hair, knee-high clean white socks and sparkly shoes. No one smiled in return. They looked at my short, scruffy blonde hair, my face, which probably had dirt smudges on it, my *Batman* T-shirt, shorts, and then down to my light-up trainers. They knew I was different, and obviously that meant I was not worthy to play with the plastic tea set.

One girl got up. She was in my class, and I had already noticed on this first day how much influence she held over the others, who all stood and watched from behind her. Again, feeling that nervousness set in, I smiled and even offered a small wave to them. Again, it was not returned.

While my arm was up, the girl in front, Natalie, grabbed Raphael from me, sniffed him and declared, "He stinks! He smells like poo!"

Of course, the other girls laughed at me and pointed. Other kids saw what was going on, and soon a large group was pouting, and laughing, and began calling me 'Poo Head'.

I wanted to cry. I wanted to run away and hide from them all. But for some reason I stood and took it for a full two minutes, clenching my fists against my legs, and feeling my eyes narrow at Natalie. Something inside me snapped. I stepped forward and pushed her as hard as I could, with everything I had. She fell to the floor on her bum and let out a yelp.

Immediately the laughter stopped, and there were gasps throughout the playground. I looked around at their faces and then stepped forward again, bent down and picked up Raphael. Quickly turning around, I stomped off, away from them all, knowing even then that I was never going to have any friends other than Raphael. So I hugged him tighter to me and went in search of a good hiding place. I could still hear the whispers of shock as I walked away. I kept my eyes down, concentrating on my shoes so I didn't really know where I was going. But I found myself at the entrance of a small hut at the edge of the play ground, near to the road the school was on. I looked around. No one was watching me now, and there wasn't anyone nearby, so I opened the door and stepped inside.

It was small, cramped space, with small chairs stacked one on top of the other, and a few desks along the wall. The room was dusty, with cobwebs dangling from the ceiling, and it smelt of pencils and paint, but it had a few windows, so it wasn't too dark. As I stepped further in, I could hear someone whispering—another little girl or boy. I saw someone with their back to me in the corner, hunched over and muttering very quietly. I felt scared, though only a little, because I was also very curious, and even in my meagre five years on this planet, my curiosity would win out my fear, every time.

"Hello?" I called out as I stepped forward again.

Whoever it was spun around quickly, and I saw it was a little girl. She had very long brown hair falling past her waist, and was wearing a dark shirt with a pattern on it. Her big brown eyes looked shocked that someone else would be here. She slowly walked toward me, and I saw in the corner behind her a blanket, a half-eaten sandwich and some books, one of which was left open on a page.

She wasn't looking at me in an angry way for intruding on what was obviously her private spot. in fact, she looked a little relieved and inquisitive. She was taller than me, and while my face was covered in smudges and I had kind of dark skin, she was very pale, and flawless. She took me in: my outfit, my face, my hair, my doll, and as I prepared myself for the onslaught of insults and meanness and steeling myself to push her over, she suddenly said excitedly, "Hi! My name's Anna. What's yours?"

"Ummm...I'm Eve," I replied cautiously.

She had a big smile on her face as she held her hand out to me. I looked down at the hand and then back at her. She kept smiling, so I slowly took her hand and we shook.

"It's nice to meet you, Eve," she said. She released my hand and stepped back.

"Who were you talking to?" I asked, setting down Raphael on a nearby desk.

She looked at me with a frown, but then recognition seemed to hit her. She giggled and walked over to her corner, picking up the open book and handing it to me. I looked down and saw it was one of my favourites, *Meg and Mog*.

"I'm trying to learn to read," she said with a shrug.

"OK... Do you go to school here?"

Anna shook her head and began nervously twiddling a piece of hair between her fingers. "I don't go to school."

"So why are you in here?"

"I like it here," she replied cryptically. I looked around again and thought how much I liked it there too.

Just when I was going to ask her more, the bell rang, and I saw all the kids from the playground running for the doors, I looked back at Anna, and said, "I have to go." She nodded and I walked to the door, picking up Raphael. As I reached out to the door handle, I asked, "Will you be here tomorrow?"

She nodded, and I smiled and waved. She waved back.

I ran into the school with a sense of happiness. I had made a friend.

The rest of my day in school went rather slowly, I remember, with no one speaking to me, and Natalie and her friends continuing to whisper mean things loudly enough for me to hear. I wanted to tell them I didn't care and that I had made a friend named Anna and she was nicer than all of them. But instead, I avoided them and carried on feeling excited about seeing Anna the next day. When the final bell rang, I ran outside with my *Ninja Turtles* backpack on both

3

of my shoulders and Raphael in my arms. My dad was at the gates, standing taller than the majority of mums, and even other dads. I sprinted past the other kids in order to get to him, and my dad, as he always did, ran toward me. As soon as I was in reach, he scooped me up and spun me around so that I felt like I was flying. When we both got dizzy, he set my feet on the ground and gave me a big grin, which I returned. He had thick blonde hair combed to the side and green eyes that always twinkled. I ran a hand down his face to feel his stubble and he stuck out his tongue at me, crossing his eyes to make me giggle. He stood again and we left through the gates, hand in hand.

"How was your fist day, kiddo?" he asked, as we strolled toward home.

I thought back on the whole day and remembered my one bright spot.

"I made a friend, Daddy. Her name is Anna and she's really nice, and she was hiding in a hut in the playground, and she says she doesn't go to my school, but she is learning to read, and she likes *Meg and Mog*, and she said I can go back and see her tomorrow, and she's really tall."

"Whoa, Evie! Breathe, sweetie!" he joked at my enthusiasm, which made me giggle again.

"So you made a friend, hey? That's wonderful. Did you just meet Anna today?"

My head went down and I shrugged, remembering the sadness I had felt for a lot of the day. Suddenly we stopped walking, and my dad knelt down to look at me. Sighing, he lifted my chin up with his fingers, so I could look him in the eyes. I felt tears welling up, now that I was with my dad, my protector, my very own Batman. I let the tears fall, and he gathered me in his strong arms and held me tight as I cried. We stood that way for a few minutes, and then he gently pushed me back so I could look at him again. Retrieving a hanky from his pocket, he wiped my eyes and under my nose. He smiled at me gently, I smiled in return to let him know I was OK.

"It's OK, Evie. You're very, very special, and you're going to make lots and lots of friends. But please remember, sometimes it's better to have one really, really good friend instead of lots of friends who…well, aren't as good? You understand?"

I nodded at him. I actually did kind of understand. He nodded and we continued to make our way home. It was only a short fifteen minute walk from the school, and my dad pointed at aeroplanes in the sky. We tried to find fairy tracks in the grass and on the trees, or Big Foot tracks in the mud. I was utterly convinced Big Foot lived with fairies and angels at the bottom of our garden.

When we reached our house, my dad opened our little gate for me, and I waved to the gnomes that sat in our little front garden. My dad had spent so long making the garden look pretty with lots of different coloured flowers and stepping stones. I stood in front of our bright red door and waited for him to open it with a key. As soon as he did, I ran through our little house and into our tiny lounge. It was painted a pretty shade of red, and Dad had placed twinkle lights around the fireplace, with a thick colourful rug covering the hardwood floor. In the corner was a bookcase filled with books my dad would read to me at night, or he would encourage me to read to him. I was actually pretty good at it for my age. I stood in front of the bookcase, searching and quickly found what I was looking for: a few *Meg and Mog* books, the cover illustrated with the funny-looking witch and her little cat. I smiled and put them by the door so I would remember to take them to Anna the next day. My dad was in the kitchen already making dinner. He made a lot of use of the worktop space by the window so he could keep an eye on me as I played outside with Raphael, defeating evil wherever we found it; namely, Button, the neighbours' cat.

My dad worked very hard through the day, doing odd jobs for just about everybody we knew. He was a gardener, plumber, carpenter, electrician, light bulb changer, personal shopper and, a few times, a doctor or a vet. He was everything to everyone and because he was capable of so much and still made sure he picked me up from school everyday and spent time with me each night, he was my hero. My very own Batman.

After eating tea with my dad at our little dining table, with more twinkly lights surrounding us and a candle on the windowsill, and after my dad helped me have a bath and to put my favourite *Ninja Turtles* pyjamas on, I was tucked up in bed. My room was pale green—my favourite colour—with only enough room for my bed, a wardrobe and a tiny desk. But again, it felt special to me. More twinkle lights were around my bed, my bed sheets had stars and planets on them, and above me were glow-in-the-dark stars, so I could look at them as I fell asleep. My dad sat on the edge of my bed and looked over to a picture I had on my wall in a small wooden frame. It was of him and my mummy. They had their arms around one another and they were smiling. They were very different in looks—my dad, blonde with pale eyes and skin, my mum, almost Spanish looking, with olive skin and long, flowing dark hair. A look of sadness came across his eyes, but it only lasted a moment, because then he smiled at me.

"What story would you like tonight, Eve?"

I ran through a few options in my head—*Knights and Dragons, Ghosts in the Park, Trolls in the Attic*—they were all original stories my dad would concoct for me each evening. I pondered for a few seconds and then finally said, "I would like Mummy's story, please."

"Again?" he asked in fake shock, hand to his chest dramatically. I giggled and nodded, snuggling a little further into my bed. He nodded and took a deep breath.

"Once upon a time, there was a beautiful young woman. She had long dark hair and dark skin. Her eyes were almost black, and yet they shone like stars. Her name was Isabelle. One day, Isabelle was sitting in a park reading a book, with many more stacked next to her, when a handsome prince came and sat down. The prince was a clumsy sorta guy, and he knocked coffee over Isabelle and her books. Isabelle was very mad at first. She yelled and pointed at the mess she was in, while the prince kept saying, 'I'm sorry, I'm sorry.' But by that time, he felt very silly indeed."

I giggled at him. That was always my favourite part of the story.

"Soon, though, Isabelle stopped being mad and instead, smiled at the prince and they began to laugh together, until their tummies hurt and they couldn't breathe. After that, Isabelle and the prince fell in love, and just a year later they got married. Isabelle became pregnant with a wonderful, beautiful, incredible baby girl." As he said these words, he touched my nose with his finger, making me smile at the warm words. Then, he looked a little sad again, so I grabbed his large hand in my tiny one, encouraging him to continue.

"The prince and Isabelle felt they were floating on the clouds, they were so happy and in love. They bought a small house with a red front door and started getting ready for their daughter to be born. Isabelle had a very big bump by then, where their baby was growing. On Christmas Eve, while they were decorating the biggest tree they could find and listening to songs on the radio, she said her tummy hurt and that she needed to go to the hospital. So off they went, ready to meet their daughter.

"After a long time in the hospital, Isabelle was pushing their little girl out but it was making her very weak. Finally, our amazing little girl was in the world at 11:55 p.m. on Christmas Eve. Isabelle was still very weak and doctors were doing everything they could to make her better. The prince held the baby up for Isabelle to see and she said, 'Her name should be Eve.'

"The prince agreed it was a perfect name. Isabelle held her daughter for a little while and said she had given birth to a beautiful star that was so bright and stunning she couldn't look at her for too long. She decided she needed to be a star as well, so that she could watch over Eve from the heavens.

"After giving Eve and the prince a kiss, Isabelle fell asleep. She travelled up to heaven and when you look up, kiddo, and you see the brightest star up there? That's Isabelle...that's your mummy, and she loves you very, very much. You can always talk to her. She may not always answer you, but she is always with you, as am I, the prince. The end."

I squeezed my daddy's hand and felt myself growing sleepy. He leaned forward and placed a kiss on my forehead, his whiskers tickling me as he did so.

"Goodnight, Evie. I love you," he whispered.

"Love you too, Daddy," I replied sleepily.

My eyes closed and I heard him lightly stepping out of my bedroom and turning the light off. When I opened my eyes again, the stars above my bed glowed brightly. There was a big one in the middle of the rest. I whispered, "Night, Mummy. Love you." And fell asleep.

The Hut

The next morning, I was so excited to see Anna again, I think I awoke a good hour before my dad, and got myself dressed, putting on a T-shirt with a nice car on the front, jeans and, of course, my shoes with their little lights. I wiggled my feet slightly to see them illuminate the floor around me. I ran to the bathroom and used my toothbrush that looked like a cat and washed my face with my 'magic' blue soap that foamed a different colour when it was wet. Then I ran downstairs and sat on the couch with Raphael. We watched a *Ninja Mutant Turtles* video for the hundredth time, though with no less enthusiasm than the first time. Soon after, I heard my dad moving around upstairs, the floorboards creaking so I could easily guess which room he was in and what he was doing. From the bedroom, back to the bathroom, to the bedroom again, and then his feet brought him downstairs, dressed in his dirty work trousers with splashes of paint and dust on them, and a shirt in pretty much the same state with the sleeves rolled up to his elbows. When he reached the bottom of the stairs, he smiled at me and waved sleepily, before going into the kitchen to have his coffee and make our lunches.

I always loved the lunches my dad prepared for me: chicken sandwiches with the crusts cut off, my favourite crisps, a chocolate bar and a cheesy snack. I hoped Anna liked some of these things too, as I wanted to share my lunch with her today. Once lunch was sorted, and Dad finished gathering his tool bag and other bits he needed, I grabbed my *Ninja Turtles* backpack, and we left for school. I was walking a few feet in front of my dad, but as we approached each road he grabbed my hand to keep me at his side. It was already warm at that time in the morning and my dad commented how hot it may be by lunch-time, reminding me to use the sun cream I had in my bag and try not stay out in the sun.

We reached the school gates, and he knelt down and gave me a warm smile. We hugged tightly before I went running into the entrance of my classroom. As I entered and went to put my bag on the peg with my name next to it, I stuffed Raphael into it, telling him I would come back to get him later.

The morning went very slowly, without any nasty incidents, but also without any friendly chat. I just worked by myself, building a rocket out of a toilet roll tube and straws, with my teacher occasionally bending down near my desk and asking how I was getting on. As I looked around and saw everyone else working in happy groups and laughing together, I actually felt sad. But I told the teacher I was fine. She smiled at me and patted my hand. I realise now she was a special kind of teacher who understood the embarrassment of forcing someone to work with me would be far worse than just allowing me to carry on at my own pace.

Finally, it was lunch-time, and all the boys and girls in my class were excited, but I'm sure none more so than me. I practically flew into the 'coat room', grabbed my bag, and sprinted to the hut in search of Anna. I reached the creaky door and I yanked it open and there she was: my new friend, sitting on an old desk, swinging her bare and dirty feet back and forth. She looked as if she had been waiting for me. Her wild-looking hair flowed around her, and she wore a dark skirt and girly shirt. I realised then how different we were from each other. I was always called a tomboy, whereas Anna was clearly more of a girly girl.

As I walked in, she smiled and jumped from the desk to envelope me in a hug, which I greedily returned. Stepping back I asked, "Are you hungry? I brought my lunch for us to share."

Anna began chuckling. I looked at her confused. I thought she was laughing at me and it hurt. But then she stopped and said, "I brought mine to share with you."

We smiled at each other again and sat cross-legged on the small rug in the corner of the room. Facing one another, we ate our lunch and I told her about the rocket I'd made, and about my love of reading and making things. I also regaled her with tales of the *Mutant Ninja Turtles* and a few of *Batman*. I told her about my dad and how funny he was. She told me very little about herself, she just listened to me. All she revealed was what I already knew: she didn't go to school and lived nearby, but she wouldn't tell me where.

"You haven't told anyone I'm here, have you?" she asked around a mouthful of chocolate. "I could get in to a lot of trouble."

I swallowed my chocolate nervously. I didn't want to upset her. But decided to be honest. "I only told Daddy, because I was sad I hadn't made any friends, and that the girls had been mean to me, and that you were my real friend, and that you like *Meg and Mog*, like me, and that you don't go the school, but I was going to help you read, and that you had long brown hair, and that you had no shoes but I didn't care 'cos you are loads better than the stupid girls in my class, and..."

Suddenly, I noticed her laughing at me and I realised I sounded silly saying all of those words at once, so I laughed too. We were rolling around holding our tummies because they hurt with our incessant giggling and we both had happy tears down our cheeks. As our giggles subsided, my new friend took my hand and made me look into her sparkling brown eyes. "It's OK that you told your daddy, Eve. But you can't tell anyone else I'm here. You promise?"

I stared back into her eyes and I knew it was a proper big promise she needed. I looked down at our hands and manoeuvred them, so that our little fingers were locked. "I pinky promise I won't tell anyone else about you, Anna."

8

She smiled. "I'm your secret, Eve. OK?"

Our little fingers were still locked very tightly together. I said, "OK."

For the next few months, I visited the hut every day at lunch-time and I helped Anna learn to read. I told her about Mum being a star, and she showed me maps of the stars and planets, pointing out which star she believed to be my mummy. I told her all about the adventures of the *Ninja Turtles*, *Batman* and *Superman*. She told me she walked around barefoot because she liked the feel of dirt and grass between her toes. I told her I had no other family but my dad. She never told me about her family, or where she lived. Over the weekends, I would think of things to show or tell her on Monday, and through school holidays I was always a little lonely without her, even though my dad would ensure we had fun. He never had a lot of money to take me away or go on extravagant days out, so we would pack up picnics and go for long walks to find adventures, or he would take me for a drive in the car just to the beach or a local forest to explore.

The seasons changed, and it became colder with each passing day. In the middle of December we were about to have our two-week Christmas break from school. On the last day, I went to the hut with a small parcel in my hands; I had made something for Anna and wrapped it in bright purple paper, with Dad's help. I was excited to give it to her and tell her to have a 'Merry Christmas' and how much I looked forward to hearing all of her stories when we saw each other again.

I was wrapped up in a big fleece and hat that were both cream coloured and made me look like a walking cloud. I didn't mind though, because I was warm. I opened the door to the hut and found Anna sitting in the corner. She was wearing a dark hooded sweater with the hood up over her head and gloves that looked too big for her hands. She smiled wide as I walked in and rushed to me to give me a big hug in welcome. When we parted, I held out the present to her.

She looked at the present and then back at me, with an even bigger smile in place now. Taking it from me, she studied the paper—I knew purple was her favourite colour. She gently started to unwrap it and reveal what I made for her. It was a bracelet; Dad had shown me how to make friendship bracelets and helped me make this one for Anna. It was a weaving of purple and green, with a small silver star at each end. Anna started crying and threw herself at me in a hug. I was utterly baffled. Did she like it? Did she hate it?

She backed away from me and slipped the bracelet over her right hand. There were tears falling from her cheeks and chin, but she was smiling.

"I have to go away, Eve," she said quietly.

"OK. Will you be back after Christmas?" I asked, full of hope.

She shook her head and made a small sobbing sound. "No. I won't be coming back."

I started crying along with her, my first real friend. We were sharing a mutual pain and we hugged again. I held her so tightly I feared I may break her. When we parted I asked, "Where are you going?"

"I can't tell you, I'm sorry. It's a secret."

I nodded, it didn't really matter anyway. She wasn't going to be here. That was all that mattered. She pulled me over to her rug in the corner and fiddled with the bracelet on her wrist. I was very happy I had given it to her as a way to remember me.

She took my hand. "I need you to pinky promise me something, Eve." I nodded and she continued, "You need to make some *real* friends, have some fun while you're at school."

I must have looked as shocked as I felt. "You're my *real* friend! The girls here don't like me, Anna. Please, don't leave me all alone!" I pleaded with her, crying again.

This made her start crying again too. We hugged for a long time. It had started snowing lightly outside, and the windows became fuzzy. When we parted again, it was getting so cold that we could see our own breath in the air. I knew our time was running out. I could feel the impending shrill of the school bell.

Anna quickly wrapped her little finger around mine and whispered to me, "Promise you'll try? I don't want you to be alone."

I looked into her big brown eyes and a thought occurred to me. "Can you pinky promise I'll see you again?"

Her eyes fell to floor and she shook her head, then looked up and said with a renewed brightness, "But I can pinky promise that I will try to see you again, if *you* promise to try and make new friends?"

I nodded and squeezed our little fingers together tightly. The bell rang. I stood to go, feeling utterly lost. Anna put her hand on my shoulder and placed an envelope in my hands. It was covered in sparkles and colourful stickers with the word 'Evie' scribbled on the front. My friend had tried very hard to write my name.

"Merry Christmas, Evie," she said.

"Merry Christmas, Anna," I replied.

Then I walked out of the hut, away from Anna and into the cold outside.

Second Time Around

During that first Christmas break, I was very miserable. My dad was constantly asking if I was OK. All I did was shrug and nod. When Christmas Eve came, we followed our usual tradition—putting on new Christmas pyjamas, watching *The Muppet Christmas Carol* and eating whatever we wanted. Because it was also my birthday on Christmas Eve, he always gave me small presents, often hidden around the house, but I was always more excited about Christmas than I was about my birthday.

The next day I ran down our stairs, excitedly shouting, "Merry Christmas, Daddy!" to wake him up, and as I entered the small but heavily decorated living room, there it was, the most beautiful thing I had ever seen: a bright green bike, with shiny images of the *Ninja Turtles* on it. The handles were black and sparkly, as were the stabilisers on either side. There was a basket on the front with a wrapped present inside. I couldn't wait. I screamed, and jumped, and clapped as my dad stood watching in the doorway. I ran to him and hugged him as hard as my little arms would let me. We took it outside and I rode around the empty streets in my PJs, while Dad made us breakfast. It was a truly magical day.

Back in school, I was determined to keep my pinky promise to Anna, so the first day I slowly walked around the playground, without Raphael. I didn't want him being picked on again; he'd done nothing wrong. I was beginning to wonder if I was invisible, when suddenly, a very scuffed football rolled to my feet. I looked up and saw a gang of boys a little older than me, looking expectantly, so I kicked it and it went straight to the boy I was aiming for.

He was a tall, lanky kid, with floppy hair in his eyes and glasses that seemed too big for him. Phillip was his name, but when his foot stopped the ball easily and his friends were badgering him to return to the game, he surprised them all and me, by kicking it to me again. I returned it again, just as well as I had before. He waved me over. The other boys groaned at the prospect of a girl playing with them but, as it turned out, I was good at football. I was faster than most of the boys, I could kick the ball accurately and, in a lot of cases, I got it further than most of them too. The next thing, they were arguing over who had me on their team, and it was one of the best lunch-times I remember at that school. We high-fived and they patted me on the back before we went back to classes.

This continued throughout all of the schools I attended—the guys and I having a laugh and playing at lunch-time and then in the local parks, as I got older. My dad was thrilled I had friends. He didn't mind at all that they were all boys, and he was also very pleased with my love of football.

=*Eleven Years Later*

So there I was, sixteen years old and a key part of the girls' football team for the high school. I was still not the tallest girl in school, though thankfully also not the shortest. I kept my blonde hair short and my skin had an all-year-round tan which I was pleased about. I had lots of friends—the girls on my team, the boys from their team—and generally everybody said 'hi' to me as I walked the corridors or entered classrooms. I wouldn't say I was very popular; just well-known for my athletic achievements.

I walked home on my own—I had since I was twelve years old. A few girls from the team walked with me through the gates, but from there, we went in separate directions. One girl always walked a bit further with me, because we lived near one another. Out of all the girls and other friends I'd made, she was my favourite. She was roughly the same height as me, with red hair, cut into a bob long enough for her to tie back. Her skin was paler than mine, though that was often the case, and she had really big bright blue eyes. Some people called them freaky, but I liked them. Her name was Jamie and she was a really good footballer. She was really funny, and we liked a lot of the same movies, and music, and TV programmes. She always told me funny little jokes as we walked and made me giggle. Sometimes, though I've no idea why, we would hold hands as we walked. It was nice to hold hands with a girl who was a friend, I often thought. It didn't feel strange at all. In fact, it felt more right than holding a boy's hand—much softer and more comfortable.

When we were near her house, we parted ways and hugged tightly, again. This was a nice part of my day. I continued walking and for a brief moment, I thought of Anna. She had entered and disappeared from my life so abruptly I sometimes couldn't believe she was real. Was she an imaginary friend? I didn't really believe so, but as I'd grown up, I'd had my doubts.

I reached home before Dad; I often did now, but that was OK. He didn't need to escort me from school anymore, so would sometimes work a bit later. I used my key to open our front door, always painted brightly—Dad never allowed it to become dull—shrugged off my back-pack and went through to the kitchen. I reached into the fridge and pulled out an already open carton of orange juice, gulping down the rest of the contents and closing my eyes as I felt the cool sweetness pass down my throat. I hadn't realised how thirsty I was. As I placed the carton back on a shelf in the fridge, I noticed the multi-coloured friendship bracelets on my wrist, all different colours and designs, and again, I thought of Anna and the bracelet I had given her the last time I saw her.

Shaking my head to clear my thought, I headed upstairs, taking the steps two at a time. I walked swiftly into my room. It was still the same shade of green and still had my twinkly lights and stars on the ceiling. I wasn't sure I would ever be willing to give those up. On my small desk now sat a laptop and a work lamp for studying, and my walls had football posters and musician posters scattered around. The picture of my mum and dad was still on the wall by my bed. I went to my wardrobe and reached around the top shelf under my semi-folded jumpers to find what I was looking for.

I felt it touch my fingers, slowly pulled it from the shelf and sat on the bed, laying it on my lap. There it was: the envelope Anna had given me when I had last seen her, still with the stickers and glitter on, and still unopened. I didn't know why I hadn't opened it. I guess I was afraid that whatever was inside would prove I made her up, that maybe I gave myself the envelope? Or it would offer me closure to the enigma of the little girl I thought about every day. My fingers ran over the opening, still stuck down with a heart sticker, sealing it shut in the middle. I was so tempted—as I had been a million times—to rip it open, but instead I quickly shoved it in amongst my clothes again and slammed the doors of the wardrobe shut. I shook my head in hopes of ridding some of the memories, turned and ran downstairs to make dinner for Dad and me.

He came home just as I was finished making spaghetti Bolognese. He gave me a hug and kiss on the cheek and sat at the table, tired and starving. As we ate, I told him about my day, and he informed me a wealthy family had moved to the outskirts of our town; they wanted to hire him to do all sorts of renovations to their new home. People were always talking about my father's work, so I wasn't at all surprised they wanted Dad. He told me they were a really nice, though slightly reclusive, family, and he was looking forward to working in one place for a while.

After dinner, I gave him a kiss and ran back upstairs to do my homework. As I tapped my pen against my notepad and my eyes glazed over at the words in my history textbook, I found myself grinning at a joke Jamie had told me about one of our teachers. She sometimes couldn't make it to football practice because she did extra studies, but I really hoped that she would be there the next day. Jamie was the smartest girl I knew and had high aspirations for her future. I really admired that about her. I admired pretty much everything about her. And I thought her eyes were just beautiful. As this line of thought continued, I realised something terrifying and the smile slipped from my face…

I had a crush on her. On Jamie. A girl. A girl like me. We're both bloody girls. Shit.

Now what?

I got very little sleep that night because of my new self-revelation. A million and one questions ran through my head: *does this mean I'm a lesbian? Am I a freak? What would Jamie think about me if she found out? What if other people at school find out? God, what if Dad knows? Should I tell him?* And so it went on.

The next day at school, I saw Jamie leaning against a wall, talking and smiling with another girl. They were laughing at something one of them had said and leaning toward one another. I felt and realised I was jealous. Jamie saw me, her big blue eyes wide with concern and she waved gently at me. I ran away—actually turned and sprinted toward the field we practised on. Once I was far enough away, I fell onto the grass in a bit of a heap and crossed my legs. It was October and, though it wasn't too cold, I did wish I was wearing a jumper, as my bum soaked up moisture from the grass. I shut my eyes and allowed myself to feel the low, hazy sun on my eyelids in a brief moment of peace.

"Eve?"

I opened my eyes and saw Jamie, the sun behind her illuminating her red hair, her eyes still full of concern. She tucked some hair behind her ear and smiled at me. Suddenly, my stomach filled with butterflies and my hands began shaking. She was gorgeous and now I felt nervous around her. Damn, I had a crush on her, for sure.

"Jamie… Hey," I said, trying to sound light.

"You OK?" she asked.

"Never better. Just enjoying the sun, and the grass, and there's a little fog over there, ya know, before we have to go to our first lesson, and I have to see Mr. Phillips at lunch-time about that exam, and so I won't get a minute to chill, and then we have practise after school. Are you coming to practice?" I stopped and took a big deep breath. *Just kill me now.*

I looked down, slightly embarrassed that I'd rambled on like that. I heard her giggle. "Yeah, Evie, I'll be at practice."

I just nodded and then, thankfully, the first morning bell saved me. I got up and brushed the grass from the back of my legs, cringing when I felt just how wet my jeans were. I was going to be cold all day. We smiled at each other and simply waved as we went our separate ways. As I walked around the side building of the school, something caught my peripheral vision. I peered back at the small, static caravan-looking thing that had been used for lessons in the past but now it was just for storage. And there, in the dusty window, I saw a familiar figure. I stopped dead and just stared, funnily enough not at all scared, even though I could very well be looking at a ghost. The ghost waved excitedly at me. I looked around and saw pretty much everyone had gone into their lessons so I walked over.

I yanked the door open and was immediately attacked by cobwebs. I quickly wiped them out of my hair and tried to shake them all away. The door slammed shut behind me, making me jump and stumble against a bag of hockey sticks leaning on the wall near the door. I started to fall and a hand grabbed my arm and steadied me. I felt faint. Anna's big brown eyes were staring right into mine. My feet were firmly back on the floor, but she hadn't released my arm. Her eyes were full of light and life, her hair was still the longest I'd ever seen, only now it was a slightly lighter shade of brown. She was a fair bit shorter than me, and her pale skin was flushed around her cheeks. I looked her up and down. She was wearing a long, flowing skirt that hugged her hips and a top with spaghetti straps. And the girl was still barefoot. On instinct, I raised a hand to her face and felt her soft skin beneath my fingertips. She smiled wide at me and my obvious disbelief.

"Are you real?" I asked in a whisper.

"Does it matter?" she replied.

It didn't matter. I threw myself into her arms and we held onto one another so tightly. I felt such a rush of emotion. I wanted to laugh, and cry, and collapse simultaneously. We stayed that way for a while. When I released her, we smiled at one another. She raised her hand and removed some more cobweb from my hair. Then I noticed it: she was wearing the friendship bracelet I had given her so many years ago. I beamed at her and felt tears of happiness threatening to fall.

"What are you doing here?" I asked. I could hear the awe in my voice.

"I came to see you, Eve," she said and then shrugged, as if it happened all the time.

"Are you going to school here?"

"No, I'm just here for you... I don't go to school. How have you been?"

I just stared at her. It were as if we were old friends who had merely bumped into each other coincidentally. She hopped back onto a nearby table and her legs swung from the knee. She was looking at me expectantly waiting for me to answer, though I was having serious issues putting a sentence together in my head, let alone having any luck of it leaving my mouth. I looked everywhere but at her. I even closed my eyes and shook my head, certain that when I opened them she would be gone. But when I did open them, not only was she still there, she was grinning at me, obviously amused by my behaviour. Running my hands through my short hair, I took a deep breath and levelled my eyes with hers. They were still the warm brown I remembered, but they seemed a little darker now. She was still grinning and patiently waiting for me to gather my bearings. I silently thanked her for that.

"I'm doing really well, thanks. I'm on the football team, have lots of friends. Dad is still working hard, but doing great. I've been fine...since you left." I don't know why I said that last bit, why I felt the need to add it, but I had, and now it was out there. The grin fell from her face immediately. I took a step toward her.

"Why did you leave? Where did you go?" I asked her.

She looked down at the floor and then suddenly back to me. I could see it all in her face. She was fighting with herself, whether to tell me everything or keep me in the dark.

"I'm sorry, Evie. I can't tell you. Please believe that I want to, I really do. But I just can't."

I nodded and smiled. To be honest, it didn't really matter. All that mattered was she was here now. However, that familiar feeling began to creep in. *What if she disappears again? What if I am imagining her?* She was looking at me curiously, and I realised I hadn't spoken in a while. Maybe I was going crazy. Was there a way to check? Damn, I still wasn't talking to her. I was talking to myself. *Damnit. Say something!*

"Ummm… I understand. I won't ask again. I'm just happy you're here."

She gave me a huge smile and I blushed. I went over and sat next to her on the table, and she asked me all about my life now. She wanted to know everything, so I told her everything—about how I made friends, like I'd promised her all those years ago. That seemed to make her happy.

We spent all day in that static room. I didn't care at all that I missed a day of school. It was just wonderful, talking, laughing and feeling once again. It was the strongest connection I had ever experienced with another person. We shared our packed lunches and she'd even had the good sense to bring a flask of hot tea with her. Toward the end of the day we were both thankful for that.

I heard the last bell sound for end of school, and saw everyone filtering out, wearing their jackets and heading home. I looked back at Anna. She seemed sad. I really didn't want to go. I was scared she wouldn't be there tomorrow, that I had created an older Anna to help with the teenage years. I grinned at myself. I was cracking up. I knew I had to go to football practice and then home, and make dinner for Dad. And I was sure Jamie would be waiting for me to walk to the pitch with her. I looked down at Anna's feet—they must have been freezing. How would she get home? I hoped she wasn't walking.

"It's OK, Eve," she said. "You should go home."

Startled from my reverie, I looked up from her feet to her face. She wasn't fully smiling, but her eyes were twinkling. God, she was beautiful, so beautiful in fact, I *must* have made her up—created the perfect girl to be my friend.

I went toward the door slowly, then turned back to her. I had to know.

"Will you be here tomorrow?"

"Would you like me to be?"

I nodded shyly.

"Then I'll see you tomorrow, but at lunch-time, OK?"

I smiled and then laughed. She was right. I couldn't spend all day away from school and with my imaginary friend, if that's what she was. I flew through the door and down the small steps, sprinting toward the gate to find Jamie. I heard someone shout my name. Turning, I saw Miss Seymour, telling me football practice was cancelled because it was supposed to rain soon. I nodded and ran off, feeling a little happier and well and truly buzzed after my wonderful day with Anna, but knowing I couldn't tell anyone about it, just in case I was crazy.

I found Jamie waiting for me, leaning against the gate. She looked pleased to see me, though also kind of worried, and asked, "Where were you today?"

"Oh… Ummm… I wasn't feeling well, so I was in the nurse's room most of the day. But I felt better after lying down." Damn, I hated lying.

She appeared relieved and nodded her head to indicate we should start walking. We were strolling along, my hands deep in my pockets because I was starting to feel cold. A wind had picked up through the day and was causing goose bumps to erupt all over my body. I glanced at Jamie. Her red hair was blowing in the breeze and she had to keep removing it from her eyes and mouth, while she filled me in on what I had missed during the day—nothing much, as I suspected. Then, as we stepped under a big tree near her street, without warning she placed a hand on my arm and turned me to face her. We were standing close to one another and she began running her hands over my arms in an effort to warm me up.

"You're freezing, Evie. Why didn't you bring a jacket?"

I was too lost in the sensation of her hands against my arms to answer. I felt strange and it was warming me up greatly. I felt my cheeks begin to burn, my heart rate picking up. Suddenly we were looking at each other. Her bright blue eyes were looking all over my face and then resting on my lips. I took her in. She was looking up at me slightly because of the height difference, and for the first time I noticed faint freckles across her nose and under her eyes. We were only inches apart. I felt drawn to her, the butterflies were back in the pit of my stomach and, without realising, we were moving toward one another slowly. Her hands had ceased rubbing my arms and were now resting near my hands. I turned them upward, in hope she would grasp mine, which she did.

In that precious moment, I realised something incredibly important: it was OK to have a crush on Jamie, because she felt the same. I wasn't a freak and there wasn't anything wrong with me. Yes, I was a little different to many of my friends, but Jamie and I were the same, and that filled me with hope and a sense of freedom so profound I almost began crying. However, it also filled me with a more pressing need to kiss the girl in front of me, to thank her for this wonderful moment.

Our faces were inching closer as the wind whipped around us, her hair blowing against my cheeks and neck, tickling me slightly and making me grasp her hands a little tighter. We kept our eyes open, looking at one another so closely. I think we both feared the other may be frightened, though now I know that was not the case. Our lips touched so softly the first time I barely felt it, though it sent the most intense shock through my body. Before I could recover, Jamie pressed her lips to mine again but more firmly, and held them there for a few seconds, which turned into a few more. We stayed that way for a while, our lips softly, yet firmly pressed together, too nervous to do anything else and also afraid to break the tender connection.

We felt rain drops falling onto our faces, and the water was so cold it shocked me, so it must have done the same to Jamie. Those few drops quickly became a steady fall, and we stared at each other, giggling at the romance of it all—'first kiss in the rain'. Jamie stopped laughing and came close to me again, resting her forehead against mine. It was cool and damp from the rain, and yet this move made me feel warm all over.

"Eve…was that OK?" she whispered to me, her voice sounding so small and insecure.

"Yeah, Jamie. It was more than OK," I whispered back.

We smiled at one another, and then the rain began to beat down on us harder. We parted company with a quick peck and ran in opposite directions. As I ran home, cold and wet from the rain and wind, my clothes sticking to me and my shoes squelching, I couldn't help but think to myself what an amazing day it had been. Seeing Anna again and sharing my first kiss with a girl who not only did I really like, but insanely enough, she liked me too.

I had huge difficulty sleeping that night. I could barely lay still. I couldn't stop thinking about the kiss, and seeing Jamie the next day. Was she my girlfriend now? Would we kiss again? I certainly hoped so. Also I was excited about seeing Anna again and wondered if I should tell her about Jamie. It would be very nice to tell someone about it. When I finally fell asleep, my dreams were filled with images of Jamie, and Anna, and the rain.

The next day, I had the brains to wear a warm jacket, and I snuggled deeper into it as I saw my breath against the cold air. When I reached the end of my street, Jamie was waiting for me, a bright purple scarf around her neck with matching gloves, and a huge smile on her face. She waved to me. I was so nervous by the time I reached her that I kept my eyes downturned, watching my feet shuffle slightly. I didn't know what to do, but luckily for me, Jamie wasn't as nervous. She leaned forward to kiss me quickly, took my hand and started dragging me in the direction of the school. I was grinning like an idiot. At school, we released our hands and acted as friends would, though I kept catching her eye and we smiled knowingly at each other.

As soon as the lunch bell rang, I sprinted toward the little caravan to see Anna. When I reached it, I found her standing by a window, wearing a long, dark, warm coat. She looked so beautiful and peaceful, watching other kids running around, unaware of her existence. If she even existed. I was bursting to tell her my news, that Jamie liked me, I'd had my first kiss and I felt more normal than I had ever felt before. But when she turned to acknowledge me, her brown eyes twinkled with excitement, and, for some reason, I didn't want to tell her. I just wanted my 'Anna time', to take her all in.

"Hey, Eve. Cold isn't it?"

I walked further into the room, nodding. We sat together, sharing bits from our packed lunches, and chatting about the books I was reading, what I was learning in many of my classes. She told me that, thanks to our lessons when we were younger, she could read and write much better and had continued to learn. That pleased me. I still saw no shoes on the girl's feet. She must have been so cold, especially in this weather.

I really enjoyed talking with Anna. We would have friendly debates on things we mildly disagreed on, which wasn't much. We laughed more than I think I ever had, and she talked with such passion about artists and authors and movies she loved, it was hard not to be swept up in her excitement.

Everything went on like this for a couple of months, leading up to the Christmas break. Jamie and I continued kissing and holding hands as we walked to and from school. We occasionally went to see a film or have a cup of coffee together, though, for the most part, we were content in our little world of kisses and cuddles. She made me happy.

I saw Anna every day at lunch-time and, whenever I was with her, I felt more than happy—I felt whole. A very scary notion, as I had at this point utterly convinced myself that she wasn't real. She was always barefoot, even in December. She never gave me details about herself or her family, her address, her past, her present, her birthday. Nothing—like a ghost. For that reason, I didn't tell anyone about her, and just continued to enjoy my little crazy universe that was the static caravan near the back of the school. It infuriated me at times, for if I had made Anna up, I should be able to see her when and where I wanted. But I never did.

The day we were due to start our break from school for Christmas, it was bitterly cold, and rumours of snow were flying around. Jamie and I were on the football field saying goodbye. She and her family were going away to stay with relatives over the break. She gave me a football keyring with my name engraved on it; I gave her a purple hat to match her scarf and gloves. We hugged and I squeezed her tight. I was really going to miss her. She quickly looked around and then leaned in to kiss me. It was soft and tender and made me miss her already. We promised to call each other, and then she ran off to get her ride with her parents. It was after school and I figured I'd try my luck and see if Anna was in our secret place. I hadn't gone at lunch-time, wanting to spend it with Jamie. I felt bad about that, but surely forsaking lunch with a fake friend in favour of a real girlfriend was acceptable?

Everyone was leaving school, whooping and hollering because it was the break. Lots of kids were singing Christmas carols at the top of their voices. I loved Christmas, it was always just me and my dad, and I wouldn't change it for anything. This year I had saved all of my pocket money to buy him a nice jacket. It was very warm with lots of pockets. The jacket he had was full of

19

holes and far too small for him, and I couldn't wait to give him his present. But first, I needed to wish Anna a Merry Christmas.

I walked into the small room; it was so cold the windows were partly frozen, and I found Anna, standing and waiting for me. She looked furious. I had never seen that look on her face before. Her eyes were hard and cold, and even though she was shorter than me, there was a power oozing from her that almost scared me. I gently closed the door and looked at her questioningly, waiting for her to say something. She just kept glaring at me angrily.

"Anna? Are you OK?" I asked quietly.

"Where were you?" she asked, not a hint of warmth in her voice.

"I spent lunch-time with a friend who's going away," I replied, beginning to get angry myself. How dare my imaginary friend be angry with me.

"You mean your *girlfriend*?" she retorted, a new edge to her voice. Not cold or angry, but sad.

I lowered my gaze. I couldn't look at her. I hated being the cause of any sadness in Anna, but I didn't know how to fix it. She was upset I hadn't told her about Jamie. Taking a deep breath, I dared look up at her and saw unshed tears in her eyes, though she was trying as hard as she could to keep the mask of anger on.

"Yes, Anna. Jamie is my girlfriend and has been for a couple of months. I'm so sorry I didn't tell you. I was just enjoying our time together so much, and I don't really know why I didn't tell you but it doesn't matter, because I won't see you or Jamie over the Christmas break, and you could disappear at any moment, like last time, so why talk about Jamie if that's the case?" I prattled on. Like an idiot.

Anna now had a hint of a smile on her face. She always found my rambling amusing. But the smile didn't stay in place for long. Soon she looked sad again. I thought she was upset because I had kept a secret from her. I felt horrible…until I remembered that she had kept countless secrets from me. I barely knew anything about her, because I had made her up.

"Wanna tell me why exactly you're so upset?" I heard myself asking in a harsh tone.

Now she was mad again at my tone and, I presumed, at my obliviousness to whatever it was that had her knickers in such a twist. It was not like she had any reason to be jealous of Jamie. Anna wasn't my girlfriend, she was in my head. This whole conversation was happening inside my head, so technically I was arguing with myself. This train of thought forced me to squeeze my eyes shut and shake my head in a feeble attempt to rid the unwanted craziness. When I looked up, Anna was close to me. I hadn't heard her move. She was staring straight into my eyes, and hers were so full of pain it almost broke my heart. We both took deep breaths and ended up smiling at each other, tears gently falling. We both obviously hated arguing with each other. She reached up and wiped a tear from my cheek with her thumb. Her touch was so soothing, it immediately righted my world again. I couldn't care less if she was imaginary, I needed her.

"Are you seeing Jamie on Christmas Eve?" she asked quietly.

"No, I'll be with my dad," I replied, a little confused by her question. She nodded and then backed away from me, leaning against a table and looking at her feet.

"Think maybe you have an hour for me? Meet me here?" She asked so softly that I stepped forward and strained my head toward her. My dad and I were always together on Christmas Eve. But when I looked back into those big, beautiful eyes, dark and hopeful, I conceded and agreed to see her. Suddenly, I found myself wrapped in a bear hug, and we were soaking up the feelings from one another. We parted and I don't think I had ever seen her so happy. She looked like a little girl, not a young woman of almost seventeen years old.

"OK. Can you be here as soon as it gets dark? Which is what? Around four-thirty-ish?" she asked excitedly.

I nodded and smiled at her exuberance, feeling the same level of excitement at the prospect of Anna planning something for me, especially for Christmas. Then she pushed me out of our new room, telling me she had lots to plan and needed to get on with it. We only had six days until Christmas Eve. I laughed at her and allowed myself to be banned from the secret place, looking forward to coming back. As I walked home, I couldn't stop smiling.

Over the next six days I was fidgety, impatient, and at a loss as to what exactly was going on. I was allowing my imaginary friend to lure me away on Christmas Eve. Surely this wasn't good? Or was it? Maybe 'Anna' was my escape from home, school and even Jamie, though I didn't consciously feel I needed an escape from these things. Regardless, I thought it only polite to bring my made-up friend a present on Christmas Eve. So I walked around a few shops a couple of days before, but I couldn't find anything good enough for Anna. The girl was positively magical; nothing about her was ordinary or boring. Everything about her was special and beautiful. Again, this convinced me she wasn't real. No one that amazing could ever be real.

After a couple of hours, I was growing weary and a little despondent, but then I saw it. In the window of a small quirky jewellery shop, was a gorgeous hair grip with a stunning butterfly atop, in shades of purple and pink, and even though it was rather girly, it was also a little dark looking and mysterious. I immediately pictured it in Anna's hair and smiled. It was perfect. I walked in with confidence in my choice, and walked home holding it in my pocket to ensure nothing happened to it.

On Christmas Eve, my dad woke me up early with breakfast in bed and a birthday card. He always did something a little special for me as part of my birthday, but he always knew I preferred Christmas. He and I went for a long walk, and the morning frost was still around. It was the enchanting time of the morning, when it was no longer dark, but the sun had yet to rise. The grass crunched beneath our feet and our cheeks were red. I looked to my dad. He was still the tallest and strongest man I had ever seen, though his hair was a little less blonde and had a few grey strands. I noticed that as I got older he seemed a lot less tired. I figured that was because I started learning to take care of myself and he had less to do.

As we walked across a field under the bare branch trees, we found a small winding path that reminded me of my childhood, going fairy and goblin hunting with my dad. I took his hand and squeezed it. He made every day wonderful. I was so incredibly lucky to have him. We reached a bench that faced down a hill, more fields and trees below us. My dad reached around into his backpack, pulled out a flask filled with hot chocolate, and a small plastic container of shortbread biscuits that he had made for us. It was perfect. We were both warm and cosy in our large woolly coats, scarves and hats. My gloved fingers were wrapped around the small cup of hot chocolate he had poured for me and, as I sipped from it, thoroughly enjoying the sweetness and warmth as it filtered down my throat, I cast my eyes to my dad. He was looking out at the view, holding his cup with one hand, the other holding a biscuit. Our breaths were more visible with the hot liquid lingering in our mouths. He looked at me, smiled and winked. I felt so special, so loved. I leaned my head against his shoulder and we both watched the sun come up over the hills. It felt as if we were the only two people in the world.

"Happy Birthday, Evie. Love ya, kiddo," my dad whispered.

"Love ya more, Dad," I replied.

We walked a longer route back, enjoying the exercise and fresh, cool air. When we arrived home, my dad lit a fire, we put some really comfortable clothes on and we watched one of our favourite Christmas movies, *Home Alone*, and laughed at the antics unfolding on screen.

Around four-ish, I noticed the sky beginning to dim. Looking to Dad, I saw he was now engrossed in a *James Bond* movie that he'd stumbled upon.

"Dad?"

"Mmmm?" he responded, tilting his head toward me without taking his eyes off the screen.

"Would you mind if I went out for an hour or so? I have a gift I need to drop off to a friend." I said it rather timidly. I didn't want to upset him.

He turned and smiled. "Of course I don't mind, kiddo, I'm glad you have friends to visit at Christmas." He sounded genuinely happy for me. I jumped up and gave him a giant hug and a kiss on the cheek. He hugged me back and patted my shoulder. He smelled of Christmas—I didn't know how, but he did.

Fifteen minutes later, I had changed into jeans and a nice jumper that was also warm. I had a leather jacket and scarf on, and a pair of simple earrings.

Anna's gift was tucked in my pocket, and I was so excited to give it to her. As I walked back to the school, I marvelled at the abundance of Christmas lights donning all of the houses. It was beautiful and bright, and just so merry I couldn't help smiling and feeling at peace.

I came through the back entrance of the school, where there was a gate leading to the football pitch. It was easy to jump over, which I did, and then walked to the static caravan. It was a little dark, but I could see the room in front of me. Anna had the lights on, and the curtains closed. As I grew nearer I could hear a chorus of "Silent Night" filtering through, and I grinned, already feeling a little giddy about entering.

When I did, I almost fainted. Anna stood in the middle of the room. There were no desks or chairs or dusty, unwanted things, just brightly coloured rugs and cushions all over the floor. Around the windows and hanging from the ceiling were hundreds of twinkling lights, all white and yellow. In the corner was a small tree, decorated almost perfectly, with green and blue baubles and tinsel. Somewhere a CD player brought forth festive songs. Amazing as the room looked, my attention was on Anna. She stood there staring at me, her hair down and brushed straighter, smooth and shiny. She was wearing a little make-up, making her brown eyes appear bigger and darker. She was wearing a long, black dress, her arms bare and the neck line rather low. She still wore no shoes, but I noticed a small anklet with charms, and the bracelet I made for her was on her wrist. Real, imaginary, good, bad—whatever else this woman was, she was, above all, stunning. I could barely breathe as I stepped further into the room, I was drawn into the wonder of it all. It was almost too good to be true but, as if drawn by a magnet I walked toward her slowly, and as soon as I was close enough to smell her perfume, I knew it was good, true and magical.

"Is this OK?" she asked, moving her arms to indicate the room.

"OK? Anna this is perfect!" I said, leaning down to hug her. She hugged me in return, and another slow Christmas number came on. Without realising it, we were swaying to the music, holding one another. Even though she was shorter than me, we were a perfect fit. I breathed her in, everything was just incredible. Her hands smoothed circles on my back and mine began to do the same. This was, without a doubt, the best Christmas Eve I had ever had and I never wanted it to end. I heard her whisper, "Happy Birthday, Evie," into my ear, causing me to shiver and hold her closer.

As I held Anna close, I could feel our hearts almost touching, and then suddenly, Jamie came to my mind—her smile, her hugs, her lips…I abruptly backed away from Anna, my eyes stinging with tears that made the twinkle lights blur in front of me. When I dared look at her, I could see hurt and confusion.

"What's wrong, Eve?"

23

I laughed and held my head in my hand, brushing my hair from my forehead. How did I answer that? She went under the tree and pulled something out, holding it in front of me. It was a small, silver gift bag. I took it from her and smiled. But I didn't want to open it.

"It's OK. You have to wait until tomorrow anyway," she said, trying to sound casual.

I could only nod. She grasped my hand and tried to make me look at her. I closed my eyes and kept my head down. Her hand was on my chin lifting it up, everything about her was so soft, yet so strong. I opened my eyes and gazed at her. Her eyes were pleading with me for something, anything, to let her know everything was OK. I was falling, her hand still on my face, but now her thumb brushed across my cheek, sending tingles everywhere. My hands moved to her waist, feeling the smooth fabric of the dress beneath my fingertips and she gently pulled me forward. Then Jamie appeared again. I jumped back and started pacing. I was insane. I had to be. I was having an argument with my made-up friend about my feelings for her.

"Damnit, Eve! What is wrong?" she yelled at me, watching me pace.

"I have a girlfriend, Anna! She is lovely, and sweet, and funny, and really likes me, OK? This isn't right. It's not fair!"

"You don't think I really like you? Is that it? I think you're gorgeous, Eve. I think you're wonderful, and funny, and strong. You don't think I'm nice and sweet, and all that other bollocks?"

I laughed again. This was getting ridiculous. Truly insane.

"I think you're bloody perfect! You're magical, mysterious, beautiful, and you understand me better than anyone ever has. But that's the point isn't it?" I said dejectedly.

"What's the point?"

I slumped against the wall and began praying she'd disappear. I closed my eyes and then reopened them. No such luck. She was in front of me, her perfume invading my senses, her breath tickling my face.

"What's the point?" she asked more quietly.

I took a deep breath, preparing myself to say the words out loud for the first time.

"The point is, Anna, I can touch Jamie and hang out with her at school. I can hold her hand and take her to the movies. Because she's *real*. And you're not." I closed my eyes and waited for her to be gone. Again, no dice.

"You don't think *I'm real*?" she screamed.

"Well, what should I think? You're like a bloody ghost! I only know your name and your favourite colour and other insignificant crap. If you want me to believe you're real, bloody prove it!"

I tried to move away, but she held me there, pinned against the wall with her body and before I could attempt to push her away, her mouth was on mine.

24

I thought I had been kissed before, but, my God, was I wrong. This was a kiss all-consuming—souls crashing, hearts screaming passion, friendship, and everything else possible in between. I pulled her to me dangerously close. I feared I may even break a rib. I wanted to consume her, keep her inside me forever and never let go. Our lips stayed locked, fitting perfectly, and I was already addicted. We kept going back for more, clinging to each other, she was still pinning me to the wall and I should have felt trapped, but I felt freer than I ever had. I was flying and crashing at the same time, her lips and tongue so soft and hot, and wonderful. We were moaning, and panting, and crying. This was heaven. I could never imagine anything better.

We eventually broke apart, needing to breathe. She rested her forehead against mine. I could feel our hearts pounding, and her deep breaths against me. She laughed breathlessly and whispered to me, "Merry Christmas... Eve," and smiled.

I laughed along with her and let my hands roam across her back. This was my new home... *Anna* was my new home...

My eyes shot open. What the hell was I thinking? I needed to get home to my dad, and phone Jamie, and finish my Christmas. I pushed her from me and bolted for the door, leaving her gift to me on the floor, and still with my gift for her clutched in my hand. I ran out into the cold, panic truly taking a grip on my heart, as she screamed after me, her voice full of pain and anguish. I carried on running into the darkness. The magic of Christmas Eve was gone.

The Gift of Reality

When I arrived home that Christmas Eve, my face was ice-cold. The tears had frozen to my cheeks and I was panting from the panic-ridden sprint. Immediately stripping off my jacket and scarf, I frantically wiped my face to get rid any evidence that I had been upset. Walking into the living room with the best smile I could muster, I found my dad still sitting there, and the *James Bond* movie coming to an end.

"Hey, Evie. Did you have fun?" he asked.

I nodded and sat on the sofa. We watched a few more Christmas films and we talked about Mum. Dad always talked about her a lot on Christmas Eve, being the anniversary of her death. God, I missed having a mum. I needed a mum now more than ever. I bet she'd have wonderful and insightful advice for me that I would have followed without hesitation to make everything OK again. I could tell Dad was missing her. She sounded amazing.

We stayed up as late as we possibly could, but he was exhausted from working so hard, and I was emotionally and mentally drained from the evening's events, so we went to bed. It didn't matter how tired I was, I couldn't sleep. All I could think of was Anna, my dream girl, and Jamie, my real girl. I really liked Jamie; I felt happy when I was with her. She made me smile and laugh, and we had so much fun together. I liked kissing her and holding hands very much. It made me feel tingly and warm. But it just didn't compare with whatever it was I felt with Anna that night. I was utterly consumed by my feelings, to the point where I didn't know where I ended or she began. I had never felt that close to another person—and not just physically. It were as if we were made for each other, literally. Anna was my other half, my soul mate, and when she kissed me I was on fire, yet at peace. God, I missed Anna. I kept thinking of her lips, her hair against my arms and how beautiful she looked in the dress. As soon as I ran away from her I felt empty and, deep down, I already knew I would continue to feel that emptiness unless I was with her.

But you can't fall in love with imaginary friends, can you? To love and desire something so greatly when it wasn't real must surely be a tell-tale sign of insanity. I couldn't possibly carry out a relationship with Anna. I couldn't introduce her to my dad, or invite her to parties, or take her out for meals. She only existed in that small room, in our secret place. I would never see her anywhere else and that would make having a relationship impossible. Besides, I was with Jamie, and I could do all of those things with her, if I wanted to, though now I felt so guilty that I didn't feel for Jamie what I felt for Anna. Maybe I would, given time.

I eventually fell asleep and woke to my dad singing "I wish it could be Christmas Everyday" at the top of his lungs and bouncing around downstairs. Immediately smiling, I ran down in my pyjamas and socks to join in.

It was another great Christmas. My dad loved his jacket, and he had bought me a new pair of football boots and a bag to carry my gear in. We lounged around, eating and watching great Christmas TV. Jamie called me that evening, but we only talked for about ten minutes; she had lots of family around her. It was nice to hear her voice and I was once again excited that I'd see her soon.

Yet all through the Christmas break I kept thinking of Anna. I didn't return to the secret place. I needed space to think and I doubted very much she would be there anyway.

We returned to school, and Jamie was waiting for me to walk with her and gave me the biggest hug and a small kiss. She was so happy to be with me again. I was happy too, but it wasn't the same. I probably convinced her and I kept telling myself if I was with Jamie long enough, maybe I would feel everything for her that I felt for Anna. I just needed to give her more of a chance, more time.

At lunch break, curiosity got the better of me and I went to the static caravan room to see if she was there. Not surprisingly, she wasn't, and there was no evidence left of our encounter. Everything was back to normal. I breathed a sigh of relief, yet felt despairing.

Things continued like that for a long while. This was my last year at the school and I wanted to make the most of it. So I worked very hard in my studies, I played some of the best football I had ever played, spent time with friends and especially with Jamie. We did a lot of stuff together and we always had a blast. We had been seeing each other for about six months and it was nearing the end of the school year, so we decided we wanted to go away together after our exams.

We agreed to come out to our parents and introduce each other to our respective families. I was very nervous about telling my dad. The man was my hero and I never wanted to disappoint him in any way. One Sunday afternoon, he took me for a walk around a lake, and he was pointing out different trees and how long they took to grow. I could've listened to him forever. We sat on a patch of grass and nibbled cheese and crackers he had brought with him. I must've been fidgeting and appeared nervous, because I suddenly felt his hand on mine. I looked up at him and saw nothing but understanding.

"What's up, kiddo?" he asked softly.

"Ummm…OK…well… What you're about to hear may shock you. I've been trying to figure out the best way to tell you and it's not easy at all. I mean, not because it's you, because I can tell you anything and I know that. Really I do, it's just that this is possibly the most important thing I'm ever going to say to you and I wanna get it right, and I'm so scared of upsetting you, Dad. Please don't be mad at me, and this isn't anyone else's fault it just...is..."

"Evie!" he interrupted, while struggling to stifle a giggle.

Damn rambling. "Dad..." I held my breath and it came out quick. "I'm gay."

I was still holding my breath. Dad just stared at me, no disbelief or acknowledgment; just a blank stare. I finally released my breath and looked back at him, questioningly, waiting for a reaction. He put his rough hand against my cheek and said, "It's OK, kiddo. I kinda figured that out a while ago."

"How?" I asked, a little shocked at this news.

"Well... When you were nine, I asked if you wanted to get married when you grew up and you said, 'No, Daddy. I'm going to play football and I don't see the point in boys.' That was my first clue. And then, when you were thirteen and you said your friends all had boyfriends, you once again told me, 'I don't see the point really.' But I've noticed over this last year you've been out a lot more and talking on the phone a lot with your friend Jamie?" He gave me a grin.

I blushed from the top of my head to my toes. This was so embarrassing.

"It's OK, Evie. I'm glad you're happy, and I would love to meet her." He pulled me into a hug. My God. My dad was awesome.

So a few days later, I introduced Dad to Jamie and, as I had predicted, they loved each other straight away. The three of us spent the day together, laughing and eating. I, in turn, met Jamie's family, which I found rather daunting considering there was six of them—her mum, dad and three younger sisters. But they were all lovely and life was pretty near perfect.

I did really well in my exams and was accepted to a college to begin sports science and teacher training. I wanted to teach and coach football. Jamie also did well and wanted to be a doctor. We knew we would end up in different places soon. She was going straight to university and it was four hours away.

The summer before she left, we went on a five-day trip to Greece and it was the most fun I think I have ever had. We hung out on the beach, went for long walks, enjoyed every sunset with a bottle of wine and kisses. It was also during that week that we made love for the first time, and it was everything I hoped it would be, for both of us, I think. We made love a lot and each time felt special and exciting. I will always have the fondest memories of that trip, the colour of the water, the soft sand, the blue skies, glorious food, and Jamie in a sexy bikini.

But once we got back we had to prepare for the inevitable. Jamie and I weren't in love. Still, breaking up was heart-breaking, but we knew a long-distance relationship wouldn't work, and decided to end things on the wonderful high of the trip and try to remain friends. Even though I was devastated, I knew it was right. Jamie was my first and had opened my eyes to a world of hope and possibilities. I don't think I would ever be able to adequately thank her.

When I started college, I stayed with Dad, both to save money and because I wasn't quite ready to leave yet, which I think he was secretly pleased about. When I turned eighteen, my dad told me he had met someone. Her name was Carol and she worked as a nurse at the local doctor's. She had treated his hand after a fall a few weeks before and they had been talking ever since, but he wanted to check with me before he asked her out. I was so honoured he asked my permission that I squealed in delight and said of course he should go for it. I was so happy he had met someone.

I went to college and university, and my dad and Carol became an item, though they took things very slowly, as she was divorced and my dad a widower—it was three months before I met her, and I liked her immediately. It helped that she knew a lot about football. She was in her forties, with sandy hair and trendy glasses.

. . .

I graduated university and got a job teaching physical education at my old high school. It happened by chance, but I was secretly thrilled to spend each day in a place that held so many fond memories. I moved into a flat by myself, close to the school and not far away from Dad, though it didn't stop us both crying on moving day.

I really liked my little flat. It had two bedrooms—I used the smaller room as a study—and it had huge windows, so it was always filled with light. I painted my bedroom a dark blue, with black and white photographs of me, Dad, and friends hung on every wall. The picture of Mum and Dad sat on my nightstand, and I kissed it every night. I kept my twinkle lights around the ceiling, and my glow-in-the dark stars above my bed, just as my dad had done for me when I was little. It made the room hold that magic of my childhood for me.

Each Christmas Eve, I couldn't help but think of Anna. I hadn't seen her since that last Christmas in high school, and concluded that I no longer needed an imaginary friend/love interest kinda thing. In the move, I'd lost the envelope she'd given me when we were five, and I was sad about that, but I tried not to think about it too much, concentrating on the good things—the real things. I'd had Jamie and happily moved through life with friends and other brief relationships—nothing serious, though. I didn't really have time and I was content in my life. I had friends who were also teachers and we often socialised together. I saw Dad and Carol whenever I could. I was happy.

One night in late October, I was in a gay club about twenty minutes from our town with a guy from work. His name was Max and if I wasn't gay I'm pretty sure I would've fancied him. He looked like a rugged supermodel and he was one of the nicest men I had ever had the pleasure of knowing. He had travelled to the UK from Australia for university, and decided to stay. He taught history and the kids all adored him.

Not surprisingly, Max had a boyfriend, Pete. They had been an item for four years, and I often envied them when I saw them together. Pete was just as good looking, though a little more clean-cut than Max, and whenever they were together they appeared totally in love and ecstatic to be in one another's company. It was a beautiful thing to be witness to.

It was Thursday evening, generally known as 'Women's Night', but my favourite boys came along to help me chat someone up. I had to laugh—they were so loud and crude sometimes, totally not my style. I wouldn't say I was shy, but I certainly didn't like making a spectacle of myself in order to gain attention. I don't think I particularly stood out from the crowd. I always kept my blonde hair short; I only ever wore minimal make-up and dressed very casually, always jeans and a T-shirt or top. I exercised constantly so I felt in good shape and slim—I was taller than most of the women and definitely darker. I thanked my mum for my olive complexion and my dad for my light green-blue eyes.

I spotted someone I knew in the crowd—an attractive blonde with killer legs, dancing with a few people. She saw me and waved. I'd seen her around and been introduced, but I couldn't remember her name. Suddenly, one of the boys came to my rescue as she sauntered toward me.

"Beth," Max whispered in my ear.

I smiled at her and said her name in greeting.

"Eve, really nice to see you here. Are you alone?" She looked around for another female. I grinned and shook my head, looking around also. But then, my throat and chest constricted. The door to the club had just opened, and through it walked my dream girl. My magical, mysterious, beautiful imaginary friend, Anna.

I stared at her, tried to place my drink on the bar, again and again, but I kept missing. I was too far away, so Pete grabbed it and placed it down for me. I was sure they were all looking in the same direction. Anna seemed a little lost, out of place. She was scanning the crowd, looking for someone. She still had her long dark hair, though now it was cut into a fresh, modern style with a fringe. Her pale skin was tinged with make-up. I couldn't see her eyes clearly, but I could see she was wearing a white tank top and a long leather skirt with black high heels. Black heels were, from that moment, my favourite shoes. They made her taller, more confident, more of a woman.

I wondered if I was the only one who could see her. Why was she there? I was fine now, I didn't need my made-up friend anymore. I was a bloody grown-up, with a job, and a flat, and friends, and casual flings.

Suddenly, Beth next to me waved, and Anna started approaching. What the hell? Shit, she was still walking toward us, Beth was acknowledging her. Double shit.

Then Anna saw me, and I watched the shock come over her face. The utter astonishment almost made me laugh, but I was sure my face had the same expression. She reached us and gave Beth a kiss on the cheek, but her eyes never left mine. We just stood there, in the noisy club, with witnesses, staring slack-jawed at one another.

"Anna, this is Eve. Eve this is my friend, Anna," Beth said.

I could hear the smile in her voice, but couldn't look away from the familiar brown eyes taking me in. Before I could stop myself, I asked, "You can see her?"

Anna smiled and the group around me laughed. I sounded like a lunatic. Marvellous.

Anna came forward and tentatively wrapped her arms around my waist. My arms automatically went around her and my nose buried in her hair. God, she smelled good. But the hug ended far too quickly.

"It's so good to see you, Evie," she said, loudly enough for me to hear over the music.

I couldn't speak, I merely nodded. She was real. It was all real. I wasn't crazy, I hadn't invented the perfect girl. The perfect girl actually bloody existed. I wasn't pining for something that could never happen. I had destroyed it before it could. I suddenly felt light-headed. I looked away from her and at the boys. They seemed to be finding the whole exchange amusing. I turned back to Anna, now looking concerned. I ran. I brushed past her and headed for the door to get some air.

As soon as I was outside, I leant against a wall and kept my head down, taking deep breaths. This couldn't be happening. I had no idea what to do next. I felt like an idiot for running away, but it was all too much. The door opened and I felt a hand on my back. I knew that hand, even with my eyes closed. The hand that could wipe all my troubles away with one touch, soft, strong and caring. I stood straight and felt it fall from my back, immediately missing the contact. Turning, I saw her, arms folded over her chest to keep warm.

"What are you doing here?" I asked.

"I was getting a drink with Beth," she stated matter-of-factly.

"Do you live here?" I asked.

"Yes, but a bit further away from the town. I don't like a lot of noise. I have a cottage, with beautiful gardens and a purple front door." She was smiling. I couldn't help it; I smiled too.

"That's the most you've ever told me about yourself," I said. She nodded, but looked sad.

"I'd like to tell you everything, Evie, if you're willing to listen. I'm sorry. I know I've no right to ask this of you after keeping so much to myself. But I really want you to understand why I was away so long."

I didn't hesitate, I nodded and started walking inside, hoping she would follow. She stopped me with a cold hand on my forearm.

"Not here. Want to go somewhere quieter?"

I nodded and smiled.

We walked a little way, to a small pub with hardly any patrons and very low-volume jazz music in the background. It was warm and cosy. I took a seat and Anna offered to buy drinks. I watched her at the bar, leaning her elbows on it and speaking to the barman. She was so beautiful I couldn't look away from her. This whole night was just so weird. Seeing her interact with other people was strange. Seeing her out of the rooms we used to share, and seeing her as such a sexy woman—the whole thing had me thrown for a loop.

She walked back to the table carrying our drinks, a white wine for me and a rum and coke for her. We each smiled and took sips. I watched her lips as she drank, enjoying a lovely flashback and grinning to myself.

She placed her hand over mine and took a deep breath. "Wow, it is good to see you. I've thought about you a lot, Evie."

"Same here," I said, and squeezed her hand before she released it.

"OK. So have you heard of William T. Bennett?" she asked.

I thought for a second. It sounded familiar. "The millionaire who built a business from a shed in his garden?" I asked.

She grinned and said proudly, "He's my father. He began building computer parts and programmes when he was sixteen, and created a very successful empire. He and my mum run several businesses together and help countless charities."

I nodded. Yes, I had heard of them.

"Well, when I was born they were thrilled. My mum was told she couldn't have children and they had everything else. All they wanted was me. So when I came along, they were so happy. But when I was three months old, I was kidnapped. Someone came into the house, took me away and held me for ransom. Apparently, they were from a desperate family in need of money and went to those lengths to get it."

I gasped. I hated the thought of anyone taking or hurting Anna. Her poor parents. I took her hand again, almost crying.

She gave me a reassuring smile. "I don't remember it, obviously, and as soon as they had the money, they took me home. Not a scratch on me. They'd had me for less than two days, and they'd fed and bathed me. I even had new clothes. But after that, my parents became super overprotective. I wasn't allowed to leave the house, I couldn't go to school and had bodyguards almost twenty-four-seven. But when I was five, I was walking through a wooded area near my house with my favourite bodyguard, or Watchman, as I used to call them. His name was Kyle and he was huge, but very kind and gentle. He let me wander a little further away, ensuring he could still see me and keep me safe. I stumbled across the hut near the school…and met you."

We smiled at the memories of our first meeting. I caught movement and saw her fingers stroking over the friendship bracelet I had made her. It was now a much duller purple, I wondered if she had ever taken it off in those eighteen years, and was about to ask, but then she spoke again.

"My parents' paranoia came back with a vengeance and we left again just before Christmas. We travelled up to Scotland and stayed there until I was eleven, and then we stayed in a small town in Wales until I was sixteen. That's when we moved back here—the place my parents said felt most like home. I was home-schooled by the best tutors money could buy, and my parents had me take self-defence and martial arts classes. After our last… encounter…" This made me look at the dark wood of the table in shame, and guilt swept through me. She placed her hand under my chin and brought my eyes up to meet hers.

"It's OK, Evie, really it is. It must've been a very tough and confusing time for you. I understand." She was looking straight in to my eyes. Those beautiful big brown eyes were taking me in and trying to transfer a message of truth. I nodded and wrapped my fingers around her wrist to move her hand away from my face. It was just too much. I felt overwhelmed and yet calm.

She cleared her throat and continued, "Well, after that, I told my parents I wanted to go to college and university. They were totally against it, wanting me to continue having private tutors at home, but I felt I had experienced so little of life. You were the only friend I had ever made and I was almost seventeen, for crying out loud."

I chuckled. After all the friends I had made, I felt the same.

"Anyway, they eventually relented, so long as I agreed to attend somewhere close to wherever they were living, call them every day and have a tag inserted into my palm."

I must've looked surprised, as she held out her hand for me to inspect. There was indeed a small faint scar in the middle of her palm. I ran my finger over it. It felt smooth. I grinned when I noticed her tremble from my touch and she quickly withdrew her hand from me, shaking her head. She must've been feeling the same thousand emotions I was.

"I studied philosophy and sociology. I loved it, and now I help kids with learning difficulties or challenging behaviour. I teach them patience and understanding, which in turn helps them with their studies, and to manage their anger toward teachers and other children."

I smiled at her. That was indeed a worthwhile job and I felt immense pride. It must have shown in my eyes because she lowered hers bashfully.

After she had finished telling me everything, I took another sip of my drink and kept watching her. She, too, was carefully watching my every move. Perhaps she was waiting for my response to everything she had said. But I couldn't really think of what to say. The only thing running through my head was how happy I was she was here—real and gorgeous and not imaginary. Before my mind could catch up with my mouth, the words flew out. "I'm just so happy you're here, Anna. I don't care how or why. Just don't leave me again."

She blinked back tears. I doubted she'd been expecting that. But then, neither had I.

"I won't. Maybe now I'm back, we could try a friendship again? Start over?" She was grinning shyly at me.

God, she was beautiful. I looked into her eyes, the deep brown, sexy-as-hell eyes, and felt my heart rate increase. Anna had the power to reduce me to a nervous teenager almost incapable of thought or speech, and yet I felt invincible in her presence, as if I could conquer the world if she asked. She was looking straight back at me. I noticed her breathing was growing laboured. A familiar ache began to burn within me. My dream girl was close enough to kiss and it was totally overwhelming. This onslaught of emotions rendered me powerless. I could see it all over her face—she was feeling the same as me. I drank in her fair skin, her perfect lips and flowing hair…she wanted me too, and yet, as I looked back to her eyes, I saw them pleading with me. We needed to start again and get to know one another properly, before anything else could happen. I leaned back a little, giving us both some space, and took a deep breath. She did the same and we both smiled.

"I'd really like that, Anna," I said, feeling positively elated at the evening's turn of events. "You are, without a doubt, the best friend I ever had. Let's try to have that again."

She nodded and we fell into an easy chat. I told her about Dad and Carol, how happy I was that they met, and that he had someone to look after him. I told her about school and the football teams I coached. She told me some more about her job. It sounded so difficult at times, though she assured me the rewards outweighed the troubles. I believed her. She talked about her parents and how they lived nearby and she still had to call them every day. It amazed and amused me—twenty-five years old and still having to check in everyday. Then I started to laugh and admitted I still called my dad everyday too, though it was more to check on him than the other way round.

We talked for a good couple of hours, about everything we could think of, until we realised we were the last people in the pub. I glanced at my watch: it was almost midnight. We were shocked by how much time had passed and both had work the next day. Smiling, we stood and swapped phone numbers. She promised to call me the following afternoon, after work, so we could get together over the weekend. We shared a quick hug at the door—too quick for my liking—and then I walked to a taxi rink and she to the bus stop. She wasn't allowed to take taxis anywhere.

She did call me the next day. We went for lunch that weekend and for a long walk around the woodland near her home. She showed me her beautiful cottage. It was just as she'd described it—cosy and elegant—and it was wonderful being there with her. It had a lovely big fireplace that she loved to use in the winter, as well as big, comfy chairs and lots of light wooden furniture and tables. It seemed the perfect mixture of almost cluttered and almost minimal.

Over the weeks that followed, Anna and I saw each other almost every weekend, and began speaking on the phone pretty much every night, just to talk about our day. On the rare nights we couldn't due to family or work commitments, I realised how much I missed her and would have trouble sleeping without hearing her voice first. I took her to meet my dad and Carol one Sunday and we went to a pub for Sunday lunch. We all laughed and talked a lot, my dad kept regaling Anna with tales of my childhood antics and silliness. I was mortified more than once, especially when he told her of the time I was convinced I was Superman. I'd jumped from a high wall thinking I could fly, instead spraining my ankle and ripping my cape. I blamed the cape for my inability to fly. It clearly wasn't the right one. Anna laughed at everything he said, and kept looking over at me with a warmth that filled me with happiness.

We would go for long walks, and one time she took me along the coast to show me the beach house her parents occasionally used. It was mid-November, and it was freezing, but she had come prepared, with a blanket and hot chocolate in a flask. We sat huddled together closely, sharing the blanket. Because it was so cold and no one else was there, we felt the need to whisper. It felt magical; having her body so close to mine sent shockwaves along my arm and leg as they brushed against her. I was beginning to wonder if she was feeling the same. Was she attracted to me? Did she think I was pretty?

The week after we'd had our trip to the beach we'd agreed to try a new Chinese restaurant that had opened near my school, but she called that Saturday afternoon to tell me she had to cancel. I was more upset than I think I should've been.

"Why can't you come?" I asked, pouting.

"I'm so sorry, Evie, but I'd made plans in the week and I totally forgot about them. I'm truly sorry. Oh, stop pouting," she admonished with a chuckle. How she could tell over the phone, I don't know, but it made me chuckle too.

"OK, OK. So what are these plans? Got a hot date?" I asked, still giggling. Silence.

"Anna?" The fear started creeping in. She exhaled deeply and sighed.

"A friend from work has set me up with his sister."

I didn't know what to say.

"I don't want to go, Eve. If we'd made our plans first, I wouldn't be going at all, but I already said I would, and she'll be expecting me…" She trailed off.

I swallowed the huge lump in my throat and found my voice. "Don't worry. I hope you have fun," I said, trying to add a smile to my voice. It was bloody hard.

"I'll call you tomorrow?" she said.

"Yeah, sure. Tomorrow," I said and hang up. I felt sick. What now?

I pottered around my flat, unsure what to do with myself. I went to the kitchen and poured myself a glass of wine. What was wrong with me? I had no reason or right to be jealous. Anna wasn't my girlfriend. She could see whomever she wanted, do whatever she wanted, with whoever she wanted. We'd still be best friends. Right?

My mind strayed to wondering who she was out with tonight—probably a tall, gorgeous supermodel with lots of money, working as a brain surgeon and curing cancer in her spare time. They were probably talking and laughing, holding hands, hugging, maybe even kissing.

OK…stop it.

I squeezed my eyes shut and set my drink on the counter. Screw it—if Anna could go out on the pull, so could I. I went to my bedroom on a mission. I flung open my wardrobe and looked at my clothes, grabbing whatever I could find, intent on dressing up and going to a club. But halfway through putting my jeans over my feet, I felt exhausted and drained and instead just flopped back onto my bed, jeans around my ankles, shirt unbuttoned and hair a disaster. I laid my arm over my eyes and tried to stop thinking about Anna.

I've no idea how long I stayed that way, but I'd fallen asleep and woke with a start to the sound of someone knocking on my door. I quickly jumped up, forgetting I had my jeans around my ankles, and face-planted my hardwood floor. My chin hit the deck, making me bite my lip. Whoever was outside my door was now knocking continuously. I scrambled from the floor, pulling my jeans up the rest of the way as I went. I buttoned them as I reached the door and yanked it open to find Anna on the other side. She looked at me, concerned.

"Evie? What happened?" she exclaimed as she walked into my flat. I stared at her in confusion. Why was she here? Why was she worried? Why was she looking at me so strangely? Why was she focusing on my shirt?

Glancing down confirmed why; it was still undone, and Anna was staring at my black bra. I pulled my shirt tight around myself, trying to cover up. She took a step forward and raised her hand to my face. I couldn't move, her thumb was reaching closer, it was near my lips. I focused on her face, her eyes glued to my mouth. Ow! Her thumb pressed against something painful, and when it withdrew it had blood on it. I reached up with my fingers… *Oh yeah. I fell.*

I explained, "When you knocked, I was asleep. I fell over on my way to the door. You startled me." I wandered off toward the kitchen, Anna trailing behind me.

"Oh, I'm so sorry, Evie. Are you OK?"

I turned to answer, but was stopped short by how gorgeous she looked. Her dark hair was tied up, with a few strands falling over her face, her make-up made her eyes seem bigger and brighter, and she was wearing a tight purple dress and those black heels. They were good heels. I could see her calves, smooth and powerful. Her cleavage was showing a little at the neckline of the dress... I moved up her long neck, her chin, glorious red lips, delicate nose, to her eyes...they were twinkling. Blushing frantically, I turned from her and resumed damping a towel with cold water to apply to my face.

"So...how was your date?" I asked. I hated asking, but needed to know.

"Urgh," she said, bending to remove her heels. I turned back as she was taking her earrings out. "Awful. She was very...masculine. Not that I have a problem with that, I'm just not into it. She wasn't shy in letting me know where she wanted the evening to go, and kept rubbing her feet against my legs. On our first date! A blind date!"

I laughed, and again...my pesky mouth took over. "Well, have you looked in a mirror, Anna? I don't exactly blame her."

She blushed at my statement and sat on the small sofa patting it. She wanted me to sit next to her. I did, instantly enraptured by her perfume. The memories and feelings came rushing back. I closed my eyes and squeezed the towel harder against my lip, allowing the pain to distract me from her proximity.

"Does it hurt?" she asked. I knew she was looking at me, even though I had my eyes closed. I slowly opened them. The vision of her took my breath away.

"Yes. Yes, it hurts," I whispered.

"I'm sorry you got hurt."

I shrugged. I hated cryptic talk.

"I missed you. I would've much rather been at the Chinese restaurant with you tonight. Trying everything on the menu," she confessed. I smiled. That made me feel a hundred times better. Glancing at a clock above my TV, I saw it was only nine-thirty.

"Are you hungry?" I asked.

"Starving. I couldn't eat a thing with that woman pawing at me."

"Well, I'm pretty sure that place delivers. Want me to order some stuff?"

"Sounds like heaven. Do you have anything more comfortable I could wear?" She indicated to her dress.

Damn, that was a fine dress.

I nodded and ran to my bedroom to get us both some large, comfortable clothes. She used the bathroom to get changed, while I ordered the food. She emerged, looking adorable, in a pair of my track bottoms and one of my T-shirts. Due to our height difference, the clothes were far too big for her, but I couldn't help thinking how much the look suited her. We sat on my sofa, ate Chinese food, drank wine and laughed until our sides hurt. It was one of the best nights of my life.

After that, things carried on as normal. Anna didn't go on any more dates, and we were seeing a little less of one another in the run-up to the Christmas break—schools are so busy just before a holiday season. But then I would have a whole two weeks off, and lots of time with my dad and best friend.

The last day of school was crazy. I couldn't wait for it to be over, and once it was, all of us teachers and the kids were ecstatic. The day had been filled with Christmas-themed games and songs and I was completely into the spirit of Christmas by the end of it.

Anna and I wouldn't see each other for a few days. She was staying with her parents, but promised to swing by my flat first to pick up the presents I had for them. However, I was going to spend Christmas Eve and Day with her, because Carol had surprised my dad with a short Christmas holiday. I was thrilled she was so good to him and I knew he needed it.

I rushed home that afternoon and found the presents. My flat was heavily decorated with lights, ornaments and tinsel. I loved twinkle lights the most; I always had. Turning off the main lights so that it was dark with just twinkles filling my home—that was a huge part of Christmas for me.

I made myself a cup of tea and put a cosy sweater on, ready for a nice, chilled-out evening. The knock at the door made me smile; I knew it was Anna.

"Come in!" I called through, and she entered singing "I wish it could be Christmas everyday", nice and loud.

I giggled at her antics and looked her up and down. She was wearing a fleecy jumper and tight black jeans with boots. She always looked amazing, regardless of what she was wearing or doing. I pointed to the coffee table, where the presents were.

"Ah, thanks, Evie. I'm sorry I can't stay long, but I wanna get there before the traffic gets too busy."

I nodded in understanding. "No worries. I'll be seeing you in a couple of days anyway. I'm so excited about Christmas with you!" I really was. I felt like a kid again.

"It's also your birthday, don't forget," she reminded me.

I just waved it off. "I don't care about my birthday. Twenty-three isn't exactly a landmark. I'm far more interested in Christmas. Will we be putting milk out for Santa?" I asked, blinking innocently.

She laughed and replied, "Yes, and if you're a very good girl, you can have one of his cookies too."

"I'm always good," I said and winked at her. She just shook her head at me. She grabbed the box and headed for the door. I held it open for her.

She placed the box at her feet and turned to say goodbye. She moved her fringe from her eyes, and smiled at me. I felt my legs go weak just looking at her. She was so gorgeous! She was staring back at me, though I didn't have the faintest idea what she was feeling or thinking.

"See you soon," she whispered and moved to hug me, one arm around my neck and the other around my waist. I did the same and we locked together. It was a tight hug, my face in her hair, her cheek against my neck. I could feel her breath on my skin. I realised after a few moments we were not moving. We just stood holding one another. It felt amazing. I was so tempted to run my hands over her body, smooth my thumbs up under her clothes, but I didn't want to ruin the contact. I felt her breath gain pace, and mine did the same. I wanted to move my head back, see her eyes and kiss her. I felt anticipation in my entire being... But neither of us dared move. Was she feeling the same as me? Did she want to kiss me? Did she feel alive, like I did? Did she feel the same heat and contentment in my arms?

We must have been stood that way for at least five minutes, when we released one another. She looked down at the floor. I did the same and shoved my hands in my pockets.

"Well...see ya," she said, bending to collect the box. I nodded and attempted a smile, watching her retreat down the hallway, when all I wanted to do was run after her. I wanted to grab her wrist, turn her around, pin her to the wall and kiss her the way I had been imagining for years. I wanted to cup her face with my hands and tell her how beautiful she was, how much I loved her. Shit. I loved her. I was in love with her.

She was out of my sight now, and I closed my door, leaning my back against it and sliding to the floor, with my hands over my face, tears of joy and fear spring to my eyes.

I was in love with my best friend. Now what?

A Christmas Beginning

Christmas Eve came a little too quickly for me. The days leading up to it had been a whirlwind of emotions—mainly fear—and some very lovely dreams about Anna, with kisses and caresses, and words of love. Although I enjoyed these dreams immensely, I awoke feeling tortured that they may never come true. I decided to keep my new revelation to myself. Telling Anna I was in love with her would only make her feel uncomfortable, ruin our friendship, drive her away, and break my heart. No. Not gonna happen. Nope. I would keep my friend and happiness, thank you very much.

I arrived at her cottage just as it started to snow; it looked so beautiful in the winter. She had lit a fire already, the smoke flowing steadily up from the chimney. I grabbed my bag with my overnight necessities and presents for Anna. I decided to give her the hair clip I bought for her when we were sixteen, and I had bought her some nice perfume and a purple silky scarf. I was dressed kind of smartly. She had asked we make an effort. So, for me, that consisted of black trousers and shoes, a red shirt and my favourite leather jacket. I wore make-up and earrings, but I wasn't as 'girly' as Anna. Still, I hoped she would think I looked nice. I trotted up her small stone path to the door and knocked loudly. I could hear Johnny Mathis singing and smell wonderful aromas floating through the kitchen window.

"It's open!" she shouted.

I walked in, grinning from ear to ear. She had the whole place covered in white twinkle lights and candles. Wreaths and tinsel covered her stairs and banisters. I continued walking and stopped dead at the kitchen. Anna was casually leaning against the counter, stirring a pan on the old-fashioned stove, her hair tucked behind her ear. She was wearing a black dress that was almost painted on and short enough that her glorious legs were on display. Her feet were, of course, bare. When she turned to look at me, I stopped breathing. I actually forgot what lungs were for. The dress was simply stunning, and she wore a long, silver pendant that hung in front of her breasts. Her fair skin was glowing against the lights and candles, her hair swept off to one side and over her left shoulder. She was appraising me too, up and down very slowly. When she reached my face, her eyes sparked with a recognition, a feeling—desire. I dropped my bag and the noise it made shook us both out of whatever had captured us. We giggled, out of nervousness I think, and she moved toward me.

"Happy Birthday, Eve," she said, leaning forward to brush my cheek with her lips. It burnt from the touch and, again, I was breathless. *Who needs to breathe anyway?*

"Thanks," I said. "Can I do anything to help?"

"Yes, actually. Could you set the table?"

I nodded. I knew where everything was, so I set about my task, gathering two plates, glasses, sets of cutlery, a candle for the centre of the table, wine glasses. I paused, smiling, beaming, pretending that we were living together, that this was a usual occurrence—the most beautiful woman alive cooking in the kitchen, while I went about setting our table and thinking of ways to make it special and romantic. I laughed at myself…crazy woman.

"Ya know, they saying laughing at yourself is a sign of insanity," I heard her tease. I looked up to find her leaning against the doorway and smirking.

"Yeah well…many geniuses were dubbed insane. Maybe I'm just freakishly intelligent?" I teased back. Easy banter with Anna was my favourite Christmas present so far. She shook her head at me and walked back to the kitchen.

We had a fantastic dinner of home-made stew and bread. She was a fabulous cook. After, we sat on her sofa—I swear it was the comfiest in the world—in front of the roaring fireplace, just listening to the Christmas carols in the twinkle lights, while snow fell outside. She reached behind the sofa and brought something out, handing it to me. I looked down and gasped. It was the brown envelope she'd given me when we were five, still with stickers and sparkles on, though looking rather crumpled now.

"Where did you get this?" I whispered.

"Your dad gave it to me. He said he found it when you were moving out and he knew it was from me. he said I should try and give it back to you."

"I'm so glad. I thought I'd lost it," I said, smiling at her.

"Why didn't you open it?"

I thought for a moment. That was a toughie.

"Because I wasn't sure if you were real. I was scared if I opened this there would be proof inside that you weren't. And that was a reality I just…didn't particularly want to be a part of. Ya know?"

She nodded. "Open it now."

I turned it over and gently pulled the top away. My hands trembled. I pulled out something colourful, with words scribbled all over. Looking more closely, I saw what it was and laughed. At age five, Anna had drawn me my very own comic book, in which she and I were heroes with special powers, battling my school bullies and then flying off together. The drawings were really very good and she had obviously practised her writing very hard in order to write all the speech and narration. I was stunned. I looked up and saw her grinning happily. She knew I'd love this. I jumped forward and hugged her.

"Thank you, friend," I whispered.

"You're welcome," she answered and patted my shoulder.

I got an idea and ran to my bag in the hallway. Reaching in, I grabbed the hair pin, still in the paper the jeweller had wrapped it in, and ran back into the living room.

"I bought something to give you…that night. That Christmas Eve and just…well…ya know. Anyway…I want you to have it now" I placed it in her lap.

She smiled excitedly and ripped the paper from it, exposing the colours. Her fingers gently swiped over the butterfly. She peered up at me, and there were tears in her eyes.

"Eve, it's beautiful," she whispered. She reached up and placed it in the side of hair that was swept from her face so it was on display. The warm glow of the fire illuminated her hair and made her face shine. She looked amazing.

"Does it look OK?" she asked.

"Beautiful," I said. It came out in an exhaled breath. She blushed and turned away.

I didn't know what to do anymore. I wanted to run away from everything I was feeling, it was too much. Especially one-sided. It was heart-breaking. But I also wanted to lean forward and put my mouth to hers, my hands in her hair and lie her down on this sofa with me on top of her, acting out every dream and fantasy I had ever had.

She stood up in front of me with her hand out. "Dance with me?"

Johnny Mathis was still singing, and to me, he was the embodiment of Christmas. I got up and she brought our bodies together. Not too closely, but still too close for me to be comfortable. We were swaying and humming along with the tune. The snow falling outside, the lights and candles around us. Everything was perfect.

"This has been the best Christmas Eve I've ever had," she murmured in my ear. I shivered. *Stupid body. Control yourself, for God's sake.*

"Me too," I replied. The hand on my back began making slow circles, fingertips brushing against the fabric of my shirt. Didn't she know what this was doing to me? She let her thumb brush against my skin, over and again. I squeezed my eyes shut, taking a deep breath.

"What are you thinking about?" she whispered to me.

I was feeling too much to have any kind of filter right now, so again my mouth took over.

"I'm thinking about…trying to keep my hands still," I said quietly as we continued to move.

"Don't," she urged.

My body responded immediately and took over. My hand travelled up from her waist and down again, over her back. I pulled her closer to me and our fingers brushed. We'd stopped dancing and were completely still, not really looking at one another, our hands mapping what they could. We were both breathing heavily, our hearts racing. She trembled when my hand passed over her hip. When she looked up at me, I almost fainted. It was all there, in her eyes. Desire, passion, fear…love? It was too much, I couldn't feel this much. I thought I was going to explode. I quickly released her and started backing away, but Anna caught me. She grabbed my wrist and pulled me back to her.

"No more running away," she said firmly. Her hands grasped either side of my face, her thumbs caressing my cheeks. I held her wrists and allowed my thumbs to rub over the skin there.

"No more running," I promised.

Her face was so close our lips were almost touching. I didn't want this, not if she didn't feel the same. I retreated again, but only a few inches this time. She sighed in disappointment and protest.

"Anna…I love you. I'm so crazy in love with you I can't think. You are the best, most wonderful person I know, and I want to be with you…forever. Or as long as you'll have me. I always thought there was no way you could be real, because you are so beautiful, and amazing, and perfect, and I couldn't imagine someone like that actually existing, and it terrified me. But now I know for sure you do exist, I never want to let you go…"

I rambled on in hushed tones, until her finger on my lips stopped me. She was smiling and we both had tears in our eyes.

"I love you too," she said, before her mouth replaced her finger. We both moaned as our lips touched and I pulled her in to me. I wanted to soak her in, I wanted her to be a part of me forever. We kissed and kissed, gently at first, savouring the moment, but it quickly burned with a passion that I had been craving for so long and we were frantically seeking each other's mouths. Our tongues collided and we groaned and hissed at each caress as waves of feeling crashed over us. She pulled back, her lipstick smudged, hair a mess and eyes shining bright.

"Merry Christmas, Eve," she said, smiling.

"Merry Christmas Eve," I replied.

She stroked my face and I leaned in to the touch. Her hand travelled down my arm to my hand, and she pulled me toward the bedroom. My legs were shaking, my palms sweating. Every inch of me trembled with anticipation. But this time I didn't ignore it, or fight it. I gave into it and showed her exactly what I was feeling. I allowed my body to take over.

It was amazing and I knew it was the best Christmas present I would ever receive. A best friend, a lover, a life.

And here we are, three years later. I live with Anna in her cottage, and we are so in love that every day is magical. I know that sounds ridiculously soppy and romanticised, but I promise it's the truth. I discovered that magic isn't just an imaginary friend or the Christmas spirit. Magic can be found in love, in living. Anything can be magical. Anna taught me that, and for the rest of my life I look forward to creating our own magic, together and every day.

But you'll have to excuse me now. My wife is heavily pregnant, and the due date is tomorrow: Christmas Eve.

Merry Christmas.

A
MIDNIGHT CLEAR

Debbie McGowan

ACKNOWLEDGEMENTS

Thanks to:
Tracy and Andrea, as always,
for seeing words that aren't here/there,
for your love, support and cake.
And also to Al. You are truly a wonder.

. . .

Nidge…guess this one's for you, flowerest. Do do do.

Friends, you and me.
You brought another friend,
And then there were three.

We started our group,
Our circle of friends,
And like that circle -
There is no beginning or end.

Advent

"The train arriving at platform three is the delayed 22:08 service for Manchester Piccadilly, calling at…"

The announcement diminished into the clear midnight-blue sky, along with the mingled, evaporating breaths of passengers boarding and alighting. Every carriage was crammed full, not a free seat visible through the heat-misted windows. She shuffled forward with her fellow boarders, head down, shoulders pulled in tight, attempting invisibility. If she could just get past the doors, into the warmth. She didn't even need a seat, and would probably crash out if she did sit, if she could only make it inside.

"Excuse me, love."

The deep, coarse voice sounded near her left ear. She closed her eyes and sighed, turning and starting to walk away from the train without even looking to see who had spoken. She didn't need to, as once again the guard shadowed her all the way along the platform, back through the gate and out onto the concourse. She glanced up, her eyelids so heavy, her eyes aching with sleeplessness and the cold. It had never occurred to her before that eyeballs could hurt.

The guard gave her a defeated smile—that same smile he'd offered three times already that evening.

"I'm sorry, love," he said, and he did sound sorry, for what it was worth. "If you do it again I'm going to ring the police."

The thought crossed her mind that it wouldn't be so bad if they did come and take her away to a cell. She could rest and it would be warm. But it was too dangerous.

"And a Merry Christmas to you as well," she muttered in spite, although she was too exhausted to properly follow through with the sentiment. Instead, she adjusted the straps of her rucksack and trudged out of the train station, onto the wide main road, the bitter wind battering her side with such force that the earache was instant. She turned her back to the gust and walked on. Tomorrow was another day, with different staff on different shifts, she knew. She'd been travelling this way for three weeks now—hop on a train and stay on it for as long as she could, get off, throw away the fare evasion notice, wait for another train, hope she didn't get caught before she made it on board, or else it was another night in another doorway, bus shelter, or, if she got lucky, a bin shed. The ones behind restaurants were the best, because then there would be food.

This town was deathly quiet, with not much still open—a fast food place, a pub, an old-fashioned cinema with people streaming out in a warm blast of popcorn-scented air. She slowed a little as she passed, absorbing the heat and the smell. How long since she'd eaten? Not since Blackpool, and that was two days ago, maybe three. She couldn't remember anymore. Her brain didn't seem to want to work, but she kept trying to think, working backwards, retracing the places, the people, all now blurring into one. She stopped and pulled the tattered paper wad from her pocket. *Yes: two days.* Blackpool was where she lost her pencil.

She moved off again carefully, the numbness in her feet now spreading up her legs, a cold, biting numbness, rather than the sort that obliterates all feeling. With her next step, her left knee buckled, and she pushed her foot down, bracing against the pain. She needed to stop walking for a while, but where? Shop doorways had bars across them, and there were no bus shelters. Around the back of the fast food restaurant she could see them, the bins, a man in black and white trousers, dumping steamy rubbish. Three weeks on the street had made her senses keen, and she could smell it from where she stood. Wonderful, unmistakeable combination of tomato, spicy meats, melted cheese and bread dough. Her legs took her there without her conscious control, and she clung to the locked gates, peering into the now dark yard, the sounds of laughter and conversation coming from behind the closed door. She swallowed back the saliva and blinked hard. No point crying. The tears would only freeze on her face and no-one was there to see them, wipe them dry, kiss them away.

Back onto the gusty high street, a gritting lorry indiscriminately spat its load, the coarse salty lumps sand-blasting her legs. A cold one tonight, the women on the train had said, expected to drop to minus four, chance of snow, a white Christmas. There was a time when that phrase would have excited her more than any other. Now it scared her to death, because that might just be how it ended. The prospect squeezed at her empty stomach, so empty it was long past rumbling. Her hunger was an excruciating hollowness that burned right through.

The orange flashing came into focus just after the sound of the car horn registered. She stepped back, peering inside the dark saloon car, the driver shaking his head in despair. She didn't have the energy to apologise, and he didn't care enough to accept. She waited for him to turn out onto the road, looking to see where he had come from. A petrol station. Better than that, a petrol station with an arrow painted on the edge of the front wall, pointing around the side of the building, and a sign: *Customer toilet. Ask for key.* She stayed where she was, watching the driver of the only car on the forecourt, biding her time. He tapped the nozzle, returned it to the pump, and headed inside to pay. She slowly wandered over, waiting near his car until she saw him come out again. She moved off.

"Merry Christmas, Tony," she called to him as he walked past. He stopped and turned back.

"Excuse me?"

She looked at him and faked a laugh. "Oh my God. How embarrassing! I thought you were somebody else. Sorry."

He frowned in puzzlement. "No problem." He got back in his car, and she quickly went inside the shop, straight up to the counter. She smiled at the guy on the till and pointed back at the man who had just left.

"Hi. My dad forgot to ask, but I'm desperate. Can I..." She crossed her legs and nodded meaningfully in the general direction of the toilet.

The guy on the till stared at her for a few seconds while he figured out what she meant. "Oh! Yeah, sure." He climbed off his stool and unhooked a ring the size of a dinner plate from the wall. He passed it over the counter.

"Thanks," she said and scooted away before he noticed that the man and the car were gone.

The customer toilet wasn't much warmer than outside, but it was out of the wind and she could at least sit down for a while. No toilet seat either, so it wasn't even that comfortable, but she honestly didn't care and leaned back, resting against the cistern, fighting the urge to close her eyes. She reached into her pocket and extracted the wad of paper, clumsily unfolding it and running her numbed, reddened fingers along each row of boxes. It didn't have a chocolate behind each door; no reindeer, nor a jolly fat man dressed all in red, but right now, this advent calendar meant more to her than anything else in her possession, and she was so angry to have lost her pencil. She'd even tried stealing one from a newsagent's, and he was really nice about it—gave her a good telling off and a Mars bar, but he wasn't going to let her take the pencil.

She thought back to the beginning—the first of December, sitting on the number 78 bus all the way into the city. She'd remained on it when everyone else got off at the bus station, crouching out of sight until the driver left and went for his break. Later, from the safety of her seat on the daily shopping coach, she had watched him return and scratch his head in confusion, convinced the exit door had been closed when he left. He shrugged and climbed aboard, preparing for his next route, as her coach pulled out of the station and away from her hometown.

She straightened the papers and carefully peeled back the ripped flap marked with the number '1', peering at the tiny likeness of a 78 bus underneath. Her first day of freedom. Under number '2' was the lit-up cottage she had noticed as the coach sped through the hilly countryside of northern England; number '3' concealed a railway bridge decorated with icicles, where she had sheltered that third night. And so on it went, the image behind each door marking her journey from the first to the nineteenth, depictions of those small yet incredible things that had filled her with hope, kept her spirits up.

The best so far was behind number '14', for there was the blanket a wonderful man gave to her as she cowered and shivered in a corner of Liverpool

Lime Street station. She stayed there for three days, being cared for by others on the street. Some people waiting for a taxi gave her their chips and the phone number for a hostel. She thanked them, truly grateful for their kindness, but she couldn't go there. She had to keep moving, keep heading south, and she'd had to ditch the blanket on the seventeenth, still drenched by the heavy overnight rain, too cumbersome to carry and useless anyway now it was wet. It was a terrible loss, marked by the letters 'RIP' behind door number '17'. That day she had cried.

With her self-made advent calendar safely stowed once more, she reached into her bag for the last dregs of cheap brandy from the bottle she'd been given in Blackpool. She lifted it to her flaking lips and tried to sip slowly, closing her eyes, waiting for the sting to subside and the warmth to descend down her throat, into her empty stomach, from where it radiated outwards, flooding up through her chest and neck and down into her legs. Never in her life had she drunk alcohol, but the woman with the trolley full of rubbish told her, through chuckles at the choking and gasping, it would keep her going through the nights ahead. And she'd been right, that woman with the trolley full of rubbish (there was one in every town, she'd discovered), for when there was no food, nowhere to get out of the wind and rain, the brandy, disgusting and bitter as it was, made it all seem to matter so much less. She was going to have to steal some more tomorrow, but for now she'd got just enough to take the edge off the cold December night. She stopped fighting and let her mind drift away.

"Right, you! Out!"

The shout startled her back to reality, accompanied by loud banging from outside.

"Open the door!"

She pulled herself to her feet and staggered, dizzy with the shock of being woken and the lack of food and sleep, shot back the bolt, pulled the door open and blinked.

"I…" She couldn't think what she could say to excuse her actions, or to get him to let her stay. "I've got an upset tummy," she tried. The man shook his head and held out his hand, staring down at the key on its dinner-plate ring. She bent down to retrieve it, but her hands were too cold, and she dropped it again. The man huffed impatiently. On a second attempt, she succeeded. The man snatched the key and stepped aside, waiting for her to put her bag on her back and leave.

"Take your bottle too," he said, then, "dirty alky."

She picked up the empty brandy bottle and slumped past, head down, ashamed. She put the bottle in the bin next to the petrol pump and trudged across the forecourt, aware all the while of the man's eyes following her, the disgust she had seen there still etched into her mind. She thought she'd be used to it by now, but she wasn't. It reminded her too much of what had forced her to do this, to run away.

Back on the street, she wandered on, less fussy in her search for somewhere, anywhere, that could offer just a little shelter from the icy wind whipping painfully around her, snatching at her skin. Zombies' fingers. That's what it felt like. Clawing at her face and raking through her hair. Her imagination pushed her towards panic and she quickened her pace. Of course, she knew it was all in her head, but she was breathing too fast and her heart was racing. She came upon a parade of shops with an awning across the front, and drew to a halt, leaning against the window of a card shop, trying to slow her breathing.

A panic attack. That's what her form teacher had said it was. She just needed to calm down. She put the cuff of her coat over her mouth and breathed the stinky hot air, counting to ten with each breath. It was working, but now the tears came and there was nothing she could do to stop them. She slid down the window and crumpled, knees up, her head resting in her hands, trying to regain control the only way she knew how; with anger, letting it surge up through her body, filling her with hate and rage. *They* had made her into this. It was *their* fault she was freezing to death on the streets, alone, and it was Christmas. *Bloody Christmas.* She could see them all now, huddled in their stupid little prayer group, asking Jesus to forgive her, to heal her. *You must pray too,* they said. *Pray to the Lord our Father, ask for His forgiveness and understanding.*

Strange that such anger could calm so quickly. She nodded to herself and smiled, feeling kind of warm all over now, because that's what rage does. It makes the blood pump, forces the body to fight back, although her head was aching and she was still starving. Nothing to be done about it, she rolled onto her side and curled up as tightly as she could, pulling her knees inside her jumper. The pavement was unbelievably cold and hard against her hip and thigh. She put up with it for as long as she could, and flipped onto her other side.

"Hey. Are you OK?"

She jumped at the suddenness of the question and banged her head against the shop front.

"Fine," she said, staring at the stranger, his features shadowed by the streetlamp behind him. She closed her eyes and put her head down again, hoping he'd take the hint and move on. But he didn't.

"I, err..." he began, then nothing else. She listened, still with eyes shut, to the sound of coins jingling. She opened one eye ever so slightly and watched the man, now with his hand in front of him as he studied the coins on his palm. He put the coins away and reached into his back pocket, advancing very slowly. "Here," he said, waving something at her. *A fiver, maybe?* She couldn't tell. She shuffled into a sitting position. The man crouched in front of her. She stared at the note in his hand.

"I'm not a prozzie," she said.

"Sorry?" He lost his balance and wobbled on his toes.

"A prostitute," she clarified. "I'm not one of them."

"Ah. I get you." The man laughed quietly. "I didn't think you were. I mean…" He paused and sighed. "It's cold, and I thought maybe you could go to the twenty-four-hour McDonald's and, I don't know, hang around the place, munching fries really slowly, or something. Stay out of the cold awhile."

She studied him as best she could in the streetlamp. His features were still mostly in darkness, although she could make out the twinkle of light in his eyes. They seemed kind and honest.

"Really," he said, stretching his arm out so that the money was inches from her face. "Take it."

She took it. He got up and turned away, ready to walk back up the street. She stared at the twenty-pound note in her hand.

"Thanks," she shouted. He looked back at her and she saw his face properly for the first time. He gave her a nod and the briefest of smiles, and then he was gone.

What Child Is This?

They hadn't been in bed that long, but it was the second time the sound of cursing and muttering just outside the bedroom door had awoken him. Josh glanced at the clock: 11:28.

"What's she doing?" he whispered to himself, not that it mattered. George was awake too. He sighed loudly and got out of bed, flinging the bedroom door open.

"What's up?" he asked. His mother was slowly making her way back down the stairs.

"Nothin', love. Can't sleep, that's all."

He nodded once and started to close the door.

"And I've run out of bloody cigs."

He sighed again. "Fine. I'll go to the all-night garage and—"

"Don't be bloody daft. I'll manage till mornin'."

"You might," he said, "but I'm not sure we will."

"Sorry, love." She smiled guiltily.

George went back into the bedroom and grabbed his jeans.

"Do you want me to go?" Josh offered.

"No. It's all right. You're probably still over the limit anyway."

Josh couldn't argue with that. He and Eleanor had been on the 'festive' bourbon for most of the afternoon, reminiscing and getting all emotional, like best friends do when they've had a few too many. However, he wasn't a drinker, and whilst he felt sober now, it didn't necessarily mean he was.

"You keep the bed warm," George said, shoving his bare feet into his shoes. He leaned over and kissed Josh on the forehead. "Won't be long."

The nearest all-night garage was in the town; but for the last remaining autumn leaves fluttering in the cold winter wind, the roads were deserted. George switched on the car stereo, and Nat King Cole's rendition of 'The Christmas Song' filled the peace of the night with a haunting and wondrous promise. The song was coming to the end as he pulled up at the garage, and he waited for it to finish, letting the music flow all around him, filling him with a warm, fuzzy feeling that was still novel to him. He wasn't a warm, fuzzy kind of person, and for most of his life, Christmas had, to put it simply, sucked big time.

The song finished, and George got out of the car, glancing along the street as he walked over to the booth, spotting the outline of what could as easily be a person as a pile of black rubbish sacks outside one of the shops.

"Yes, please?" the man behind the glass window of the booth prompted.

"Err…" George momentarily forgot what he'd come for. "Oh, yeah." His mind was still filled with Christmas lyrics, but he successfully exchanged cash for a packet of cigarettes and wandered across the forecourt, shoving the change in his pocket, chancing a glance along the street again. The black outline had changed shape now, so it had to be a person. Maybe they'd fallen over drunk on the way home from a night out, or collapsed and needed help. He returned to the car and left the garage, turning right instead of left, so he could drive past and investigate.

"Definitely a person," he concluded. He slowed down, parked on the other side of the road a little further on, and walked back, crossing diagonally to get a better idea of the situation before he approached. He stopped on the edge of the kerb and studied the person for a moment or so. They were small in build, their coat and trainers suggesting they were young, and homeless, because they were filthy and he could smell their body odour, even at a distance; a mix of sweat and urine. The person rolled onto their other side, eyes still shut.

"Hey," George said gently. "Are you OK?"

The person in front of him startled and sat up quickly, banging their head back and making the whole shop window judder with the force of the jolt. The girl—he assumed, though she was barely old enough to say with certainty—glared up at him.

"Fine," she snapped. She closed her eyes again. George didn't know what to do. Ask if she needed help? If she needed money?

"I, err…" he began, then nothing else. Maybe he could just offer her some money—enough to buy a sandwich at the garage, although it was cold and she could do with finding somewhere inside. He pulled the change from the cigarettes free of his pocket and examined it. A two-pound coin and a few coppers wasn't going to get her very far, and he felt it would be insulting to offer it. Being homeless didn't make her worthless. He put the money away again. OK, so twenty quid was a bit on the generous side, but that's all he had. He approached and crouched in front of her, trying not to intimidate.

"Here," he said, offering the twenty-pound note. She glared at it and then at him.

"I'm not a prozzie," she snarled.

"Sorry?" Her response surprised him, and it took a few seconds for the meaning to register, at which point he lost his balance and nearly fell backwards. He righted himself and adjusted his position.

"A prostitute," she said. "I'm not one of them."

George laughed to cover his embarrassment. He must have looked really stupid. "I didn't think you were. I mean…" He paused, trying to gather the words to explain his thinking. "It's cold," he said, and it was. If he spent much longer in the same position he'd need her help to get back up again. "I thought maybe you could go to the twenty-four-hour McDonald's and…" He was probably stereotyping, he didn't really know, as it was the first time he'd properly talked to a homeless person, but he imagined they didn't get much opportunity to eat, or else why would there be soup kitchens? "I don't know," he hedged, trying to make the advice sound like it wasn't him telling her how to survive the bitter December night. "Hang around the place, munching fries really slowly, or something? Stay out of the cold awhile."

She was still studying him suspiciously, and he didn't know what else to say to convince her.

"Really," he said, leaning a little closer. "Take it."

She took it finally, and George carefully stood up. It was so cold. How was she even lying on the floor? It was overwhelming him; he turned quickly so he couldn't see her anymore, and stepped off.

"Thanks," she called after him.

He looked back at her and smiled, trying not to notice the desperation, the sadness in her eyes. He gave her a courteous nod and returned to the car, fighting to clear his mind of the image of her face. The engine started up and the heaters blasted him with warm air. He turned them off, the guilt too powerful to appreciate their luxury. The car stereo kicked in; another Christmas song. 'Let It Snow'. It had to be the first year ever he was wishing desperately that it wouldn't.

George arrived back home and gave his mum the cigarettes without a word.

"Ta, love," she said to his retreating back. She watched him all the way up the stairs. "Are you all right, Georgie?"

"Yeah, just tired. Night, Mam."

She heard the bedroom door close behind him. He didn't seem all right to her. She shrugged it off and went out to the back garden to smoke. Now she'd had her painkillers, a quick cig would settle her for the night.

Upstairs, Josh had been fast asleep, but he awoke when George got into bed. He snuggled up to him.

"Brr," he said, shivering for effect. "It's a bit cold out there, is it?"

"Yeah," George confirmed vaguely, his mind very much preoccupied with the homeless girl.

Josh sensed something was bothering him, but it was gone midnight, George was on an early shift, and the alarm was set for five-thirty.

At two in the morning, when Josh's insomnia hit, he quietly slid to the side of the bed, padding silently away to the bathroom, none of which would normally disturb George, but he was already awake. Josh flushed the loo and washed his hands. He returned to the bedroom.

"Do you want a drink?" he asked.

"Yeah, please," George replied miserably.

Josh went down and made two cups of hot chocolate, listening to the radio playing away quietly in the room next to the kitchen. It was for company,

George's mum said, and she'd be out for the count. The kettle boiled and Josh went back upstairs, depositing the cups before he switched on the lamp and climbed back into bed. George looked up at him and attempted a smile.

"What's the matter?" Josh asked.

George wrinkled his nose. "It's a bit silly, really. I saw a homeless girl outside the shops by the garage and I can't stop thinking about her."

"I see."

"It's bloody freezing out there. How do people survive nights like this?"

George shuffled up the bed, and Josh passed him his hot chocolate, watching him all the while. He was completely consumed by his thoughts, which wasn't like him at all.

"Why are you bothered?"

"I don't know. It's not like I've never seen a homeless person before, but..." He shrugged. "It's just so unfair. I mean, here we are, all cosy and tucked up in bed together, in a warm house, and she's out there somewhere on her own in the cold."

"Did you used to bring home stray dogs and cats?"

George smiled. "No, I didn't, actually. Monty's the first dog my mum's had that gets on with other animals, so I couldn't." He sipped at his hot chocolate. "It's stupid, isn't it?"

"No, although it's a bit pointless worrying about it."

"Yeah, I know."

"And it's just a tiny bit soppy."

George turned so he could see Josh's expression. He was holding back a grin. "Soppy," George repeated.

"For you, I mean."

"So it wouldn't be soppy if you got all choked up over a homeless girl freezing to death at Christmas?"

"The Little Match Girl."

George rolled his eyes, knowing what was coming next.

"Her little hands were almost numbed with cold. Oh! A match might afford her a world of comfort..."

"Yeah, OK. I remember it, though not word for word like you do, obviously." It still amazed George that Josh had memorised all the stories of their primary school days. Amazed, and made him adore him a little bit more. "How's that supposed to make me feel better? The little match girl died."

"Hmm. I didn't really think that through, did I?"

"No, you didn't."

"Sorry." Josh sipped his drink thoughtfully. "Maybe you could donate to Crisis or something."

"That's just it. I gave her money and it's not enough."

"It's more than most people do."

George stared into the cup he was nursing. "I'm being silly. Just ignore me."

Josh took hold of George's free hand. "At the risk of sounding like a crazy old romantic, part of the reason I love you is your silliness." George's eyebrow went up. Josh laughed and kissed him, but then said more seriously, "It's not silly to care."

They didn't converse any further, instead finishing their drinks and settling down to try and sleep some more, but George barely managed a wink all night and staggered to the bathroom at five-thirty, utterly exhausted.

The morning at the farm wasn't looking to go any better. One of the Shetland ponies was sick: an old girl with heart problems. Jake the farmer had already called the vet. The cold weather meant both vets were out on emergency calls, and George and Jake took it in turns to sit with the sick pony so she didn't become too distressed. At least it kept George's mind occupied for a few hours. When the vet eventually arrived, he checked the old girl over and changed her medication, advising them that there wasn't much to be done, except to keep her warm and comfortable. George's sense of powerlessness was growing by the second.

By the time he arrived home that afternoon, he was miserable as sin but was trying his best to stay chirpy. They needed to go to Eleanor's to deliver presents, after which he and Josh had planned on heading to a restaurant, as they had an anniversary to celebrate. They dropped George's mum at her friend's flat, from where the two women would later go out to play bingo, and drove to Eleanor's. The house was in full festive uproar, with just-baked gingerbread men cooling on the rack and freshly brewed coffee in the pot. The children were ridiculously excited, and George gave his fullest efforts to playing with them, but the adults picked up on his unusual despondency and kept giving Josh meaningful looks.

After they'd said their goodbyes and were sitting in the car outside, with an hour left before their restaurant booking, Josh turned the blowers on, watching George whilst they waited for the windscreen to clear.

"What do you want to do?" Josh asked.

George shrugged. "What d'you mean? We're going for a meal, aren't we?"

"Do you still want to?"

"Of course I do."

"If you're not in the mood, it's fine."

"We booked it a month ago."

"We can cancel and go another time."

George didn't respond, as he really wasn't in the right frame of mind to enjoy an evening of being waited on and cooked for, even though he'd been looking forward to it—until yesterday. Now it felt wrong.

"OK," Josh said decisively. He wasn't sure what he was about to suggest was a good idea, but he couldn't bear to see George so down. "Do you want to go and look for the girl?"

"How? She's not gonna be where she was last night, is she?"

"She might be, and if she's not, then we can check elsewhere. There are a few places around town where homeless people congregate. Maybe she's found her way to one of those, or even to the hostel."

"And then what? If we do find her?"

"I don't know. That's your call."

George thought about what Josh was suggesting. It was absurd, and he knew he was only saying it to placate him, but he wanted to try. He nodded. "Yeah. Do you mind?"

"Of course I don't, or I wouldn't have suggested it. If we find her, it'll hopefully put your mind at ease, and if we don't, at least you'll know you've done everything you can."

George smiled and took Josh's hand, lifting it to his lips and kissing it gently. "And at the risk of being called soppy again, *that* is why I love you."

Let It Snow

The plan hadn't worked. The train station staff were too vigilant, there were video cameras everywhere, guards who actually communicated with each other—she didn't even get past the ticket barrier! It was looking like she was stuck here, for now. And really, if she thought about it, there were far worse places than this—home, for starters. For as much as it was a roof over her head, and she had a bed and food most of the time, no amount of comfort could compensate for being locked away from the world.

Our child the sinner!
The Devil is within!
Pray for salvation!

Loonies.

She remembered one time, when she was eight, maybe nine years old, the preacher had terrified the congregation with stories of children taken over by evil, committing terrible atrocities against each other. It was progress, he'd told them, that these poor mites were no longer punished for their sins. Now they were to be prayed for, that Jesus might enter their lives once more. Until then, it was the responsibility of all the flock keep them safe. *Keep them safe?* If it hadn't sounded like nonsense to her then, it certainly did now. How was locking someone up keeping them safe? In fact, it put her at far greater risk, because she would have done *anything* to escape, even if it had meant taking her own life.

So, by comparison this *was* heaven. She *was* safe, although she was also dog-tired. The thought made her giggle, with the skinny runt of a stray cat that had curled up on her lap a short time ago now sleeping soundly, stealing her body heat and sharing its own in repayment. Jinja, she'd nicknamed him, because he was like a scrawny ginger ninja, the way he had crept up on her and made himself right at home.

Unfortunately, she now had an extra mouth to feed, although she still had ten pounds left from the twenty the man had given her last night. She'd been planning on getting a bottle of brandy, yet Jinja had somehow made her need for alcohol less desperate. Would he run off while she went to buy food? She really hoped not, and that surprised her. She was choosing the company of a flea-infested mangy kitty over a surefire way of getting through another night on the cold streets of this godforsaken town in the middle of nowhere. And how wonderful it was that *He* had passed it by. She was *safe!*

"OK, Jinj. Gonna go get us some din-dins," she explained, lifting the tiny animal so she could stand. He didn't care as long as he was warm. She took him with her, talking quietly to him all the way to the mini supermarket, and now she faced a further dilemma, because it was a busy road, and he might think she'd abandoned him when she went inside. There were hooks on posts for attaching dog leads—not an option for a cat, especially one with no collar. Instead she opened her coat—loose on her after three weeks of surviving on scraps and wits—and carefully placed him inside. He was quite happy with that and started purring. It felt nice.

The brightness of the lights in the shop hurt her eyes after the darkness of early evening, and it was cold in there, with the air conditioning, the staff all wearing body warmers. She adjusted Jinja's position and wandered up and down the narrow aisles in search of the pet food section. She found it and scanned the shelves, soon realising that she'd have to opt for the more expensive stuff in little plastic pull-ring pots so he could eat straight from the container. She selected a two-pack, and made a beeline for the fridges, on the lookout for pasties, knowing they would be the cheapest and most filling kind of food. As a sensible afterthought, she picked up a bottle of water at the till, paid for it, her Cornish pasty and the cat food, and left.

Or nearly left.

"Right, miss," the man said. He stepped in front to block her exit. "Let's see what you've got there."

She tried not to freak out, shaking her head rapidly. "N-n-nothing," she stammered. His eyebrows rose.

"So you're telling me there's nothing inside your coat?"

"Yes, sir. I mean no, sir." She gulped. Her heart was thumping hard and fast. What if he called the police?

He advanced on her, talking into his radio to request female assistance for a shoplifter search. She backed off.

"Please. I haven't stolen anything, I swear."

"So, show me what's in your coat, and you can be on your way."

"It's a…" She didn't want to tell him, frightened that he'd make her put back the things she'd bought. She knew she shouldn't have brought Jinja into the shop, but how could she explain that to the security guard? Now the female sales assistant was standing next to him and they were both staring at her, waiting for her to open her coat. Hands shaking, she slowly, carefully unzipped the top couple of inches. The cat poked the very tip of his nose out. "He's very poorly," she said, hoping it was a lie, because in the bright shop lights he really didn't look that healthy.

The security guard tutted and shook his head.

"D'you still need me?" the sales assistant asked him.

"No, cheers. I'll handle it from here." He waited for his colleague to leave, continuing to watch the strange girl and her cat for a moment.

"Please let me keep the food," she begged.

"You paid for it, didn't you?" he asked. He'd watched her come through the checkout and knew that she had. She nodded in response. "Then off you go."

She smiled gratefully and fled.

See, this was what *they* didn't understand. They lived in their own little bubble, just them and their friends from church, filling themselves and their children with fear of the cruel, evil world, but she had met so many kind and generous people over the past three weeks. Most of those on the streets would share what they had, even though they had so little themselves. They didn't judge her. They didn't pray for her deliverance from evil, or tell her she was unclean. Even the guard at the train station, who'd had every right to call the police on her, especially when she'd turned up there this morning, just sent her on her way with a threat of what he'd do if she ever set foot in the place again. And then there was the man who had given her money. Maybe it wasn't such a bad thing to be stuck in this town after all.

Back to her alley then, with her pet alley cat, to eat and rest awhile before the cold of night descended entirely. She had no idea how they would stay warm tonight, but they'd get through it together, somehow. She had faith—not the sort that *they* had, but her own variety—belief in herself and the things she could achieve if she set her mind to it. After all, wasn't she here now, more than a hundred miles from home, surviving on her instincts?

Jinja guzzled the food hungrily and she tipped some water into the empty food container. He lapped until it was all gone and sat back to clean his face, while she ate her pasty, ravenous and fighting the urge to wolf it down, chewing each mouthful for as long as she could. It would fill her up that way, and she still had a little over five pounds left, so they could do the same tomorrow. After that, she didn't know yet, but she'd come up with something. Even if she had to steal, she'd make sure Jinja didn't go hungry for as long as he stayed with her.

He was done cleaning now and immediately climbed back onto her lap, though she herself was in need of a pee, which was the easier of the two to deal with. She lifted the cat, wandered a little further along the alley and shuffled down her pants, relieved herself and returned to her seat on the damp, torn pillows. They were starting to freeze, but if she stayed perfectly still it wouldn't be so bad.

To pass the time she started singing to herself: Christmas carols, because she'd never been allowed to listen to pop music. She'd heard it sometimes on her friend's phone at school, but it was banned from the house, along with anything else that might cast its evil influence over her. The school had offered to pay for an internet connection, if money was the problem, explaining that she needed it for her homework. *They* were adamant. No internet, no phones, TVs, video games, radios, books that were not the bible or recommended church publications. Her one friend at school—the only one who refused to mock the way she dressed and the way she looked—would give her an earphone so they could listen to music together. But since September, when they'd started their GCSEs, they'd rarely seen each other outside of form time, because they'd chosen different subjects.

Chosen. Like she'd had any say in the matter: French, so she could communicate with the mission workers overseas, and food technology, because it was the least dangerous of all the subjects. She wanted to choose music, but it was too modern and would poison her mind with its glorification of sex and drugs. She'd have loved to have taken IT, or better still extra science classes. It was absolutely out of the question. A discipline built on lies, *they* said. No child of God would be subjected to that.

"To hell with God," she growled, breaking out of the chorus of 'Hark! The Herald Angels Sing'. The cat got up, kneaded her thighs for a moment, and curled up once more. The temperature was dropping rapidly, her lap now the only part of her that was warm. She tucked her hands underneath the cat and rested back against the fence panel. At least the alley was out of the wind and, apart from Jinja, she'd not seen a living soul in the entire time she'd been there. The street from which the alley ran was less busy now too, and she heard the sound of distant church bells drift on the frost-stilled evening air.

"Quarter to," she said as they finished their three-quarter peal. Quarter to what? It had been dark for what seemed like ages, but she knew the dark hours lasted longest, and not just because of the time of year. The nights were more dangerous—even when she found somewhere to hide away she had to stay alert. But it was so hard in the icy cold! She kept reminding herself that feeling sleepy was a symptom of hypothermia—she'd been told that at Scouts, before *they* decided it was inappropriate for girls and boys of her age to be mixing together. That was the first time her wickedness slammed up against the iron will of her parents, and if they'd known then what she knew now—that the lessons learned in Scouts had ensured her freedom and survival—they'd have never let her go to begin with. Anyway, back to where her thought process was heading; she was feeling very, very sleepy and fighting to stay awake, which had been the same for three weeks now, battling to keep her eyes open until exhaustion got the better of her. What she wouldn't give for a decent night in a warm bed...

"Get out of here!"

The yell came from the other side of the fence panel presently serving as her back rest, and she jumped to her feet in an instant, startling Jinja, who just about landed on all fours and glared at her with his back arched, most unimpressed. Luckily she'd also leapt sideways, so the bucket of water that followed the shout narrowly missed her. Alas, the same was not true of Jinja, and for a moment the pair of them remained completely motionless, she staring in horror at the poor drenched cat, he seemingly in a state of shock. It was only his outline that she could see, but the full extent of his starvation was painfully apparent, as was his shivering.

"Oh, poor boy!" she said, scooping him up from the floor and shoving him inside her coat, not caring that she too would now be soaked to the skin. The shivering was violent, and she didn't know what to do for the best. At the very least, she needed to give him the other tin of cat food and buy some more, but she couldn't go back to the mini supermarket. There was no way they'd tolerate her taking him in there twice.

She hooked her rucksack over one shoulder, gave the fence panel a kick, and made her way back to the road, from there to search for somewhere else she could get cat food. The church bells rang out again: eight o'clock. So much night ahead of them, and for the first time since she left home, she feared for survival, though not her own. She could feel Jinja's little heart hammering away against her chest, and it was so fast! She glanced down the neck of her coat into his wide, pupil-blown eyes. He too seemed afraid, staring deep into her eyes, pleading for her help, and she didn't know how to give it.

She wandered on, past the many shops, most still open for late-night Christmas shopping, the bright glow of the lights dazzling and flaring outwards across her line of sight, like the brightest stars in a deep dark sky. She glanced up; not a real star in sight, obscured by heavy grey cloud, the sort that brings with it...

"Snow!" A young boy came tearing out of the shop to her left, his palms upturned, face beaming with delight. "Look, Mummy! It's snowing!" he said excitedly to the weary-looking woman who followed him out, shoving her change into her purse and not looking at her son or the large flakes of evidence now fluttering down all around them.

The cat wriggled and clawed inside her coat, reminding her that she had released her grip on him. She shuffled him up and glanced inside the glass-fronted shop. A chemist. She wasn't going to get cat food there. She sighed and stepped off, but then stopped again, noticing something else lying amongst the settling snowflakes. A ten-pound note, right where the woman had been standing a moment earlier. She froze, caught in a dilemma. Three weeks on the streets and the only thing she'd tried to steal was a pencil. OK, not paying train fare was technically stealing, but the train would still run whether she paid or not, so it kind of didn't matter. She peered through the white haze along the street, to where the woman was attempting to capture her son's mittened hand, whilst he skipped and danced around in joy, trying to catch the snow. The ten-pound note belonged to that woman. But chemists sold those little heat packs that stay warm for hours, and Jinja was sick.

And in that moment she realised that if God's will really, truly existed, then He had made this happen. He had sent Jinja to her, delivered her to this location and provided her with money to care for the poor sick creature. Even if nothing else was, this must surely be God's work. She picked up the money and went inside the chemist shop, no questions or queries about what was in her coat this time. She bought two packs, each containing three heat pads, and a block of Kendal mint cake, knowing that every penny she possessed would be needed to give Jinja the best chance.

It had been less than five minutes that she had spent inside the chemist and the snow had already completely covered the pavements, cars now slowing as their drivers braved the suddenly treacherous conditions. She continued on along the street, coming up on a shopping mall that spilled so many beautiful, rich smells out into the strangely dry night air. Perfumes and soap, chocolate and coffee—such a wonderful mix that she couldn't help but be drawn to it, the heat of the mall flooding over her frigid body and making her hands tingle with pins and needles, as she wandered slowly through the avenue of shops, gazing up at the bright, festive displays on either side. She couldn't stay in there forever, not even for the night, but she was going to drag out her visit for as long as she could.

The escalator to the floor above was coming up in front of her now, a vast signpost directing shoppers to the locations of different shops and facilities. Her lips moved as she read through the list. First floor: the food court and a few names of shops. She scanned down the sign to the next heading. Second floor: toilets and baby changing...

"Toilets," she said out loud. She had an idea. Up the escalator she went, her stomach clenching in response to the aroma of fries and burgers, noodles and chicken, up again to the second floor and to the toilets, grateful that they were empty. She carefully unzipped her coat, lifting the still damp cat from inside, and put her hand under the drier to make sure it was warm. It was, but it was also a modern, powerful drier, and Jinja was too fragile, not that she imagined any cat would be particularly happy to get hit with eighty-mile-an-hour hot air.

She positioned her palm at an angle, deflecting the air towards the cat. He scrambled up onto her shoulder, and she bent her knees slightly, bracing herself against the wall. Jinja started to calm down, seeming to understand that she was doing it for his own good. A woman came into the toilets and glanced at her, using the mirror to look again as she stepped inside a cubicle, her mouth dropping open when she saw the cat and realised what was going on. Another woman arrived and stopped in the doorway.

"Good God above!" the woman said loudly, putting her hand over her nose and mouth.

"What the hell is that stink?" asked someone behind her. Both of them sneered in disgust, turned and left again.

She could've died of embarrassment. She knew it was her and Jinja that they could smell. She hadn't had a wash since November.

The first woman now emerged from the cubicle and went to the washbasin, noticeably breathing through her mouth. She turned and smiled, nodding at Jinja. "Cute cat."

"He got wet, and I couldn't think what else to do." She choked on the last few words and stifled a sob. "I'm sorry it smells so bad."

"Aww, it's OK," the woman said kindly, though she kept her distance. "Don't you worry. He's lucky he's got you taking care of him, hey?"

She nodded tearfully. "I think he's sick too."

The woman peered at Jinja, her brow creasing in concern. "Yeah. I think you're right about that, hun. It might be a good idea to take him to the vet."

She sniffed back the snotty tears. The woman had finished washing her hands and there was only one drier.

"Sorry," she said, backing away. "We'll go now." She put Jinja back inside her coat and picked up her rucksack.

"He's got lovely fur," the woman said with a grin. "Beautiful colour, although I might be a bit biased."

She eyed the woman's long red hair and found herself grinning back. The woman put her hands under the drier, the air blowing her hair so that it rose and fell, like an ocean tide on a shoreline. *Like the Red Sea*, she thought, except the Red Sea wasn't really red. She knew that. She also knew it was time to go. She zipped up her coat and turned to leave. "Merry Christmas," she said.

"And to you," the woman called after her. "Look after each other."

"We will."

I Saw Three Ships

Josh flicked the windscreen wipers back to their intermittent setting. "It's easing off now," he said, his intention being to reassure George, who hadn't spoken a word since it started snowing. "It might stop completely before long. You never know."

Still no response, Josh turned his attention back to the traffic lights as they switched through amber to green. He set off again in the slow crawl of traffic through the town centre, to the next set of red lights. It was fascinating to watch the young and able-bodied pedestrians taking such delight in the snow, contrasted with others less mobile, struggling to stay upright. Like ice skating. He wasn't too bad at it, surprisingly, as physical activity wasn't his forté, but mental discipline can be a very useful tool for convincing yourself that staying on your feet is easier than falling over, and the less attention he paid to what he was doing the more fleet of foot he became. He was tempted to wind down his window and pass the tip on to the poor woman skidding across the road in front, to great comic effect. He giggled and kept his advice to himself.

The lights had already changed, but he waited for the woman to safely reach the other side before he set off again, occasionally glancing across at George, unseen, for George was frantically scouring the pavements on one side of the road and then the other. It was their fifth time along the high street, and they had toured every other route running from it, interspersed with visits to the places their friend in the local police had suggested. He didn't say as much, but Josh could tell by his tone that he thought they were quite mad. Nonetheless, he advised them to try the squats in the tower block, mostly inhabited by addicts, so if the girl was a user she may have found her way there. Otherwise there was a disused car lot next to the railway arches and a few doorways in town centre back streets that the night patrol cleared every couple of hours. They'd tried all of those places, other than the tower block squats, with no success.

"We're not gonna find her," George said resignedly.

"Do you want to try the hostel again?"

"There's no point. She could be anywhere by now. We should just go home."

"Is that what you want to do?"

"No, but—"

"Then we'll keep looking for a little longer," Josh said.

George rested his chin on his hand and sighed.

"OK. How about this?" Josh suggested. "Let's go to the milk bar for a hot chocolate and wait for the shops to shut. If she's a runaway, she might be keeping out of sight." He didn't get an answer, but chose to interpret George's noncommittal shrug as consent, and pulled into the next available parking space. It wasn't far from Milky's milk bar; that end of the high street was away from the main drag of shops and much quieter. However, the same could not be said of Milky's itself, with just a couple of stools available at the high bar across the front window—perfectly suited to their surveillance needs.

"What do you fancy?" Josh asked. Even in his current worried state, George managed a cheeky grin at the question. Josh shook his head in mock dismay.

George scanned the menu board. "Hot peach melba milkshake," he said decisively and then scanned it some more. "Or blueberry pie and custard." He frowned. "Or—"

"Why don't we get a peach melba *and* a blueberry pie and share?"

"But then there's the banoffee hot chocolate. That's what I had last time, and it was awesome. Agh!" George was useless at these sorts of decisions. The big important stuff he could handle. Picking something from a menu? Not a chance!

"Shall I choose?" Josh suggested.

"Yeah."

"OK. Go and sit."

George did as he was told, leaving Josh to order the peach melba and blueberry pie and custard hot milkshakes, which were delivered a few minutes later in tall heavy sundae glasses with short stems and wide bases, like those from the seaside fish and chip restaurants of days gone by.

"They're hot," the girl warned, carefully setting them down.

"Thanks," Josh said, frowning as he watched her retreat. "I'm not sure that's appropriate."

"What's that?" George asked.

"Calling them maids."

"Calling who maids?"

"The staff. Their aprons have their names and 'Milky's Maid' embroidered on them. Look." He nodded in the direction of the other girl now heading over to a table behind them, her apron pocket emblazoned with red lettering declaring that she was Penny the Milky's Maid. "I wonder what they call the male staff?" Josh pondered. "Valets? Butlers?"

"Maybe they're maids too," George contended. Josh looked to see if he was serious and saw his eyes twinkling. He was perking up at last.

"I bet you'd like that," Josh teased. "A male maid in a frilly apron, waving his feather duster at you."

"Damn! How did you guess? It was meant to be a surprise."

"You'd best not have bought me a feather duster for Christmas! Or an apron."

"Oh yeah?" George leaned across, closing in on Josh so that their faces were inches apart. "What you gonna do about it?" he challenged, staring straight into Josh's eyes.

"Make you wear it," Josh said, staring right back.

"Uh huh?" George moved closer still.

"Uh huh," Josh repeated. He was tingling all over, from the sensation of George's breath against his face, the scent of his aftershave, those wonderful green eyes. He shivered, and George laughed and then kissed him. Josh blushed. "Must be the hot milkshakes," he justified, waving his hand in front of his face.

"Yeah. That'll be it." George picked up the closest of the untouched drinks and sipped, letting out a groan of pleasure as the thick, warm, creamy peach registered on his taste buds. "Oh my word. You learn to make this and I will gladly go butt-naked in a frilly apron for you."

Josh slid off his stool as if he was about to head for the counter and ask for the recipe. With his talent for mind-hacking, he'd probably wheedle it out of them too. However, he didn't get that far, as the door to the milk bar opened and a woman staggered in, a few strands of long hair blown across her face, the rest covered in snow. She shifted the bags from her right hand to her left and swept her hair back.

"Man alive!" she said breathlessly. "It's like Siberia out there."

That brought an abrupt end to George's recovery.

"Hey, Shaunna. Been shopping?" Josh asked.

"Yeah. Last minute bits and pieces. The mall is chaos, so I thought I'd stop off for a hot choc on the way home. How about you two? You been shopping?"

"No. We were just out, erm, driving," Josh said cagily, then added, "It wasn't snowing when we set off."

Shaunna accepted his explanation and left her bags with them whilst she went to order her drink.

Josh glanced at George. "Are you OK?"

George nodded. He patted his pocket for his phone; it wasn't there. "What time is it?" he asked. Josh swivelled on his stool and checked the clock.

"Ten past nine."

George frowned and turned to see where the clock was, as he hadn't noticed there was one. He shook his head in despair at himself; the clock was easily four feet in diameter and took up a third of the back wall. "Right. Enough," he said, determined to snap out of it. Shaunna returned with her drink and hopped up onto the next stool along.

"Either we're special, or not to be trusted with hot drinks," Josh remarked. "They brought ours over."

"Ah, yeah. They usually do, but Amy saw me come in and made mine while we were gabbing."

Josh laughed. "You come here often?" he asked, tongue-in-cheek.

"Hmm. Far too often," Shaunna confirmed wryly. She settled on her stool and sipped at her banoffee hot chocolate, watching a group of young people arrive, all chattering teeth and snow-flecked coats. One of the girls pulled off her hat and loosened her hair with her fingers, the bangles on her wrist jangling together musically. "Ooh," Shaunna said, struck by a thought. "Can you pass me that bag? I want to show you what I've bought Iris."

Josh did as requested.

"You bought my mum a present?" George asked.

"Yeah," she confirmed.

George was about to ask why, but as he watched her rummaging through her purchases, her face breaking into a smile when she found it, he realised it didn't matter. Shaunna handed the tiny box to Josh. He opened it and took a moment to admire the object within.

"That's perfect," he said, passing it across to George, who tipped it this way and that, frowning in puzzlement.

"What is it?"

"It's a Westie," Shaunna explained.

"Yeah. I can see that, but what do you do with it?"

"It's a charm, George," Josh told him, like it was the most obvious thing in the world. George still looked confused. "For the bracelet we bought?"

"Ah!" He nodded. "Cool. She'll really like that, whatever she says."

"Why," Shaunna asked cautiously. "What will she say?"

Josh and George both quickly picked up their drinks.

"She's gonna swear at me, isn't she?"

"Erm, she might," Josh said.

"Oh, well." She returned the box to her bag. "At least I can prepare myself. They had some amazing charms in the shop. I'd quite like a bracelet myself."

"Maybe you could ask Santa next year," Josh suggested.

"I think I might just do that." She checked the time and picked up her glass. "I'd better get a move on or I'll miss the bus."

"Do you want a lift?"

"No, it's fine. Come to think of it, weren't you supposed to be out for a meal tonight?"

"Something came up. Anyway, don't deflect, Hennessy. We can drop you off on the way. It's no problem, really."

Shaunna thought for a moment and nodded. "OK. Thanks. But can you drop me at Adele's rather than home?"

"Sure."

With that settled, they chatted about Christmas whilst they finished their drinks, and left soon after. It was still snowing, the ground now covered in a soft, two-inch-thick white blanket. The high street was completely deserted, with no signs of homeless girls in doorways and very few cars still out on the roads. In fact, they saw more gritters than they did cars. When they reached Adele and Dan's apartment, Josh observed the darkened windows; George was too consumed by worry to notice anything at all. Shaunna reached forward and kissed George's cheek.

"Cheer up. It's Christmas," she said. He offered a smile that told her he didn't want to talk about it.

Josh got out and pulled his seat forward, taking the bags from Shaunna so she could climb through from the back. She gave him a hug.

"Thanks for the lift."

"No problem," he said, leaning in closer to reciprocate the hug as best he could whilst still holding her shopping. He lowered his voice so George didn't hear. "Careful on those steps. You know? The ones up to Adele and Dan's *ground* floor flat. They might be a bit slippery."

Shaunna pulled away and stared at him. He winked. She let out a breathy laugh of disbelief. "So much for it being a secret. Sometimes I hate having psychologists for friends."

Josh gave her a cheeky smile. "Could be worse."

"Yeah. It could." She paused a moment longer, but decided not to say what she was thinking. She hugged him again and took her bags from him. "See you Christmas Eve, which is…the day after tomorrow!"

"It surely is. About one o'clock?"

"Perfect. Night." Shaunna waved a bag-laden arm and was on her way.

"Good night," Josh called after her. He got back in the car and waited until she was safely inside the building, before he carefully pulled away, squinting through the lamp-lit snow all the way to the bingo hall to pick up his mother-in-law, and heaving a tremendous sigh of relief when they arrived home, safe and sound.

Zat You Santa Claus?

First light dawned early, reflecting its deep dusky pink off the snow-covered ground outside the railway arch. She could smell bacon and squeezed her sides in an attempt to push away the hunger tearing through her in a furious storm. And she needed the toilet—the sort that she couldn't just do in a darkened corner. If she waited, the urge would pass eventually. She shuffled sideways and bent her stiff knees up, curling around Jinja and tenting him under the fleece she had bought in a discount shop in the mall last night. It had taken nearly all of the money, leaving her with about eighty pence in change, but with the help of the heat pads and each other's company, they had both stayed warm overnight.

She made it through the stomach cramps and drifted off again, glad of Jinja's company and the daylight blossoming around them. It made her feel safer, and she napped fitfully, trying to ignore the truth that she knew in her heart, until she could do so no longer. Jinja was sick and she couldn't look after him. Even if she knew where to find a vet, she had no money to pay for treatment. She couldn't even feed him, or herself. As if sensing her sorrow, Jinja staggered to his feet and moved closer, snuggling up against her chest. She stroked his head and swallowed hard, the escaped tears forming tiny beads on his fur. He shuddered as he repositioned himself, training his head gently against her hand and attempting a purr.

She closed her eyes, trying to push away the thought of what lay ahead. No money, no food, no water. There were two heat pads left, which might get him through tonight, but he was so weak. If he didn't eat soon, he would die, and there was nothing she could do to help him. She should never have offered him food to begin with. After all, cats could look after themselves, couldn't they? They just went wherever they could get a free meal. She should've walked away from the alley, left him to find his way home, because he must live somewhere. She stood up and picked up the damp fleece, folding it into a clumsy square and stuffing it into her rucksack. Yes, return him to the alley, so he could go home. That's what she must do.

"Come on, Jinj," she said. She lifted the sleepy animal and cradled him in her arms but kept him outside of her coat. He needed to become accustomed to the cold again. Stepping out of the dark archway, the snow rose up over her trainers, but she barely noticed, and she set off, back towards the town centre.

The streets were strangely quiet, with cars and buses silently trundling by, their engines hushed by the white coating on the pavements and buildings. But for the tyre tracks, the roads were white too. The shops were busy, their festive lights sparkling all around her, and in another time or place it would have been magical. She passed a coffee shop and stared longingly at the counter display; a parade of gingerbread men standing sentry around a pyramid of mince pies. She hated mince pies, but right at that moment would gladly have scoffed the lot. A man with a takeaway cup exited as she passed the doors and slammed right into her.

"Watch it!" he shouted, and it was true that she hadn't been looking where she was going, but neither had he.

"I'm sorry," she mumbled and continued on her way, nearing the shops between which the alley ran. She felt her stomach lurch and her throat tighten, but she had no other choice. That's where Jinja belonged. From there he would find his way home, back to his real owners.

Across the road was a man in a Santa suit, and she watched him struggling to secure his beard. It was a distraction, to keep her mind off her most dreadful mission. With the beard now in place, Santa pulled on his hat and stuffed a cigarette in his mouth. She was horrified. She was long past believing these men were the real Santa Claus, but they could at least act the part. Now a man on a push bike had drawn up alongside fake Santa.

"Alright?" he said.

"Yeah," Santa confirmed, exhaling a stream of blue smoke. "You at The Bell tonight?"

"I can't, mate. Got the kids."

"Kids," Santa repeated, shaking his head, his beard following the action half a second later. "They're a bloody nuisance."

Definitely not a nice Santa, she thought. This man, with his charity collection tin, was going to take money from children, and they would be so excited to think that they were helping *him* do good work. It was wrong, and it made her angry, because there was no-one there to help. The people at church went on and on about all the good work they did, and they were liars too, who judged and hated and prayed for forgiveness and deliverance from evil. *They* were the evil ones, not her. And right at that moment that's what she needed. A *real* Santa Claus to whisk her and Jinja away, take them to be with him and Mrs. Claus and Rudolph in Lapland, or the North Pole, or wherever it was, where they could live happily ever after. But there was no Santa Claus—just a smoking, swearing man who hated children.

She stopped walking but remained facing forward, her destination now to her left. It was time. She turned, reluctant, desperate, and slowly squelched her way through the untouched snow, focusing on the raised bump about halfway along the alley: the pillows on which she had sat yesterday, when Jinja first came to her. She looked down at him, relaxed in her arms, his front legs hanging either side of her hand, his heartbeat pulsing against her palm. She gasped at the cold air, the tears flowing like a waterfall and stinging her cheeks as she kept on pushing forwards, towards the bump in the snow. She reached it and stopped, blinking hard to clear her eyes, knelt down and gently set Jinja on the pillows, like a tiny feline prince on a glistening crystal throne.

"Time for you to go home now, Jinj," she said, each word catching in her throat as she choked on her sobs. "Thank you for being my friend. Get well soon."

The tiny orange cat stared up at her with those big green eyes, so full of trust. Because he *had* trusted her, relied on her to make him better, and she was leaving him here to die. She was no better than fake Santa Claus, or the people from church. Or *them*. She wiped her nose on her sleeve and turned away, her cries making her whole body convulse as she trudged back up the alley, stepping in her own footprints, forcing herself towards the street.

"Mow," came the little cry from behind, but she could not look back. She *must not* look back. "Mow."

"No! Go home!" She walked faster, staring straight ahead, training her ears to the sound of carol singing floating from a nearby window: 'It Came Upon A Midnight Clear'. She knew it well, every word.

O ye beneath life's crushing load,
Whose forms are bending low,
Who toil along the climbing way
With painful steps and slow...

She stopped walking, watching a jet of steam spewing from the back of the shop, imagining it to be the breath of angels. She was almost at the road now, and started to sing along.

Look now, for glad and golden hours
Come swiftly on the wing;
Oh rest beside the weary road
And hear the angels sing.

"Mow."

The gentle pressure against her calf was impossible to ignore, and she looked down, meeting Jinja's questioning gaze.

"Why didn't you go home?" she asked, no longer sure if she was directing the question at the cat or herself. She bent down and gently lifted him to her chest, where he immediately climbed inside her coat and started purring. She wrapped her arms tight around him, and in that moment she realised that he was home, for she was all he had.

She set off once more along the high street, crowded with people jostling against each other, although the shopping mall clock told her it was only 11:38 a.m. She glared at fake Santa as she passed him by, disgusted by the sound of his jolly, "Ho ho ho! Merry Christmas. Thank you. Merry Christmas," repeated over and again to children stretched on tiptoes so they could feed coins into the collection box jingling in his hand. It was probably a pointless charity anyway, more Christian do-gooders trying to deliver sinners from evil. She squinted to read the label on the red plastic container, some of the words covered by his gloved fingers, but enough visible for her to work out the rest. She crossed the road in a daze and approached fake Santa.

"Excuse me," she said politely, even though she wasn't feeling very polite at all. She studied his ID badge to make sure she'd read the collection box correctly. "Can you tell me where New Lane Animal Shelter is?"

"In New Lane, love, obviously."

"And where's that? Is it nearby?"

"About ten minutes' drive away."

She nodded as she took in the information. "Would I be able to get a bus there?"

"Yeah," fake Santa said vaguely, holding out the collection box for another child. "Merry Christmas, ho ho ho," he boomed loudly and then turned back to her. "The 4A from the bus station."

She thanked him and moved off again, fake Santa's 'ho ho ho's fading away behind her. She knew where the bus station was, because she'd been kicked out of there last night, before she found the railway arches. She arrived and slowly traversed the circle of bus stops, reading the timetables in search of the one for the 4A. She found it and examined the route; no mention of New Lane. She continued to the next stop, and the next one, and the next, completing the circuit.

"Which bus are you after?" a voice asked. She turned to find two older women, all wrapped up in hats and scarves, their eyes looking over her filthy coat and jeans, not even trying to conceal their disgust.

"The one to New Lane," she said.

"4A. That stop over there." The woman pointed to the one she had already visited.

"But it doesn't say New Lane on the route."

"No, love. You need to get off by The Red Lion and walk up a bit further. New Lane's on the left."

"Thanks," she said.

The two women plodded away, muttering quietly to each other. She could hear them and it was about her, but she was past embarrassment, desperate to get Jinja to the animal shelter. They would be able to look after him and find him a nice home. She was sure of it.

The bus stop was completely in the shade, and it was tough waiting out the forty minutes until the next bus arrived. She climbed on board and smiled at the driver.

"To The Red Lion, please," she said.

He poked a button on the ticket machine. "One twenty, love."

Her heart sank. The ticket was now hanging out of the side of the machine, and the driver was frowning at her impatiently.

"I'm sorry," she said, "but I only have eighty pence and I need to take this cat to the animal shelter." She slowly turned away, preparing to get off the bus, hoping but not thinking for one minute that he was going to let her stay on.

He sighed and pushed the ticket into her hand. "Go on," he said.

"Oh. Thank you!" she gushed, feeling the tears well again. She sat on the nearest seat and peered inside her coat to check Jinja was all right. He was fast asleep. She turned her attention to the outside world. Ten minutes, fake Santa had said, so she had a while to wait yet, but she didn't want to miss her stop. They left the town centre, and she felt herself starting to relax. The bus was warm, the motion comforting and hypnotic. She drifted off to sleep.

"Love?"

She fought to get her eyes open again.

"You wanted the animal rescue, yeah?" the driver asked.

"Oh. Yes. Thanks." She hurried to her feet, dizzy and disoriented, and got off the bus, the blast of cold air instantly bringing her to her senses. The doors swooshed closed; she turned to watch the bus depart and then looked around her. A pub and a few houses, behind which were fields stretching back for miles, all covered in snow. Jinja fidgeted inside her coat.

"Nearly there now," she told him, setting off in the direction the bus had just taken, a left turn visible up ahead, the 'New Lane' road sign soon coming into view. "Nearly there," she repeated, yet the words brought no solace. She already loved Jinja and didn't want to leave him, even though it was for the best. She knew that, but it didn't stop the sense of loss from breaking her heart now, as she turned into New Lane and saw the animal shelter, each step making it harder to take another. She unzipped the top of her coat and planted a kiss on Jinja's head. He poked his nose over the fastening and gazed up at her.

She stopped outside the gates, trying to work out which of the many signs she needed to read first.

New Lane Animal Shelter

Open daily 11–4

We are now closed for Christmas
We reopen on January 2nd

Do NOT leave animals here!

For emergencies, please call...

She sank to her knees.

"Nooooo," she yelled. "No! No! No!" She banged her fists on the gate, but there was no-one nearby to hear her cries; no-one to care.

Almost no-one.

. . .

"It's not like you to lose your appetite," Sophie said. She scooped the last of the gravy-coated sprouts up onto her fork and into her mouth, and sat back, totally stuffed. George pushed his plate away, unsure whether he felt more guilty about eating the food or wasting it. Either way, his plate was still three-quarters full.

"I should've just done some extra hours at the farm," he said.

"You'd rather do overtime than have lunch with me? Thanks a lot!" Sophie joked. George attempted a smile.

"Sorry, Soph. I'm not feeling very festive."

"Get another of those ales down you and you'll be fine." She got up to go to the bar. "What shall we have this time? Rudolph's Ruin?"

"Yeah, go on then."

George watched Sophie order their drinks and chat with Bob the landlord. They were in their local pub, just a few minutes' walk from the terrace where he and Josh lived, next door but one to Sophie's partner, Sean. A year after moving in, George and Josh were finally getting around to all the jobs that needed doing, which was why he was in the pub, and Sophie was keeping him company. It was a bit early in the day for beer, but there was no way he could stay at home with the windows half in and half out.

It wasn't the glazier's fault; two weeks ago, when he was scheduled to fit their new double glazing, he'd come down with flu. But he'd promised they'd be done before Christmas, which was why he was doing them now, on the twenty-third of December, in the snow. Josh, likewise, was on a pre-Christmas deadline to submit his latest journal article, and was not impressed. So, with the university closed until the new year, George had agreed to remain in the vicinity 'in case of emergency', whilst Josh went to Shaunna's to get some work done. Or not, as the case may be, as now he was calling George's phone. George pressed 'answer'.

"Hi, you."

He got nothing in return and moved his phone away to check the screen. No signal. He went outside, wondering how the people who took part in The Red Lion Quiz actually managed to cheat.

"Hello?" he tried again, pulling his open shirt around him and shivering. His jacket was on the back of the chair in the pub.

"Hey. Are you OK?" Josh asked, his voice broken by the bad line.

"Yeah. Freezing my extremities off."

"Are you at home?"

"Nope. I'm standing outside the pub. No signal."

"Ah. I see."

"You on your own?"

"Apart from Casper the Crazy. Kris bought him a squeaky toy and…"

Josh paused so that George could hear the manic squeaking in the background. He started laughing.

"Yes," Josh continued, "not so much of the 'somewhere quiet and conducive to work' happening. I'm so glad we don't have a Labrador." Josh's voice became muffled for a second as he said, "Ew, thanks, Casper," followed by a distant thud and the sound of dog's feet scurrying away. Josh spoke into the phone again. "Have you been back to the house?"

"Not yet," George said. "The glazier reckoned he'd be done before it went dark, though."

"Hmm. A likely story. Oh, well. I'll let you go and get warm."

"OK. I'll give you a call when it's safe to come home."

"Thanks. Love you."

"Love you too." George hung up and put his phone in his pocket, rubbing his hands together as he turned to go back inside. But then something caught his eye, and he stopped, as if he had indeed spent long enough standing there to be frozen to the spot. He watched the slight figure shuffling slowly along the pavement on the other side of the road, arms clasped beneath what looked like a pregnancy bump, face downturned.

"Hey!" he called out. She didn't appear to have heard him. For a second, he considered going back inside to get his coat, but she might have gone by then, not that there was anywhere to go, although he'd been thinking about her for two days straight and could well have imagined her. There was only one way to find out. He walked as quickly as he dared across the slushy road, his feet sliding dangerously as he stepped up onto the pavement opposite. The part-melted snow was starting to re-freeze.

"Hey!" he shouted again, now just a few feet behind her. Other than walking faster, she gave no other indication that she was aware of his presence. He too increased his speed, and had almost caught up with her, when he lost his footing and skidded forwards, landing hard on his back. "Ow," he said. Now she reacted. She stopped, turned and slowly dropped her gaze to the floor. He grinned with embarrassment and struggled to his feet.

"Hello," he said. "Again."

"Hello," she replied.

"It was you, in town the other night, wasn't it?"

She nodded.

"I thought so. I didn't notice that you were, err…" He frowned. "That must be hard, being on the streets and…"

She was studying his face intently.

"I tried to find you," he said, but then realised it made him sound like a predator. "Yesterday. I wanted…I mean, I needed to make sure you were—"

"I told you," she said, cutting him off. "I'm not a prozzie."

George shivered. He was *bloody freezing.* "I know. That's not why…I, err…I went out. I was…" He rubbed his arms and breathed out a huge misty breath, trying to rally the words. She was still watching him, staring deep into his eyes.

"Have you got a speech impediment?" she asked. George was taken aback by the abruptness of the question.

"Um, sort of. When I get worked up, I…" He stopped and shrugged.

"You can't get the words out?"

Now it was he who nodded.

"Worked up? Aroused, you mean?"

"No!" George banged his hands against his sides in frustration. She was a clever girl; streetwise. Maybe he'd got her all wrong. He took another deep, juddery breath in.

"You're cold," she said.

"Yeah. Coat." He waved in the direction of the pub.

"You'd best go back there then."

He shook his head and stayed where he was. She couldn't understand why he wasn't just going away, and she had to be working on some basic survival instinct that was backfiring horribly, because she'd exhausted all of her options. It was bad enough being stuck in that little town with no money. Now she was stranded in a desolate village with a sick cat, and she really wanted—no, *needed*—this man's help, but her brain seemed hellbent on self-destruction. In fact, the only thing keeping her from walking away now was her promise to the woman in the shopping mall toilets—the one with hair like the Red Sea.

Look after each other.

We will.

"Do you know anything about animals?" she asked.

This time her question had the opposite effect, seemingly liberating his words. He laughed lightly. "A little. Why?"

She unzipped her coat and looked at him meaningfully. He took a step closer. She tensed up.

"I promise I won't hurt you," he said. He waited, and she came to him, shifting Jinja upwards with her arms.

"He's sick," she said.

George leaned over and peered inside the girl's coat at the listless young cat. "Yeah. He is. Come to the pub with me."

Her eyes widened in fear, and she backed off. "How do I know you're not trying to lure me into some paedophile ring?"

George shrugged. "You don't, I guess. But if I was, I'd be the one showing *you* baby animals."

She narrowed her eyes at him for a moment. He was grinning at her.

"I'm in the pub with my friend, and there are other people in there too."

"They might all be in on it. Or maybe you just want me for yourself."

"OK. Would it help if I tell you that you're, um, not my type?"

"You might just be saying that."

George was so cold now he was beyond shivering and getting a little impatient.

"Right. Listen. My name is George. I work at Farmer Jake's, which is why I know a bit about animals, although mostly horses and ponies. I live with Josh, just up the road. After I saw you the other night, I couldn't sleep, worrying about you out in the cold, and dragged him around town for three hours, searching for you. I've just left a roast dinner, because I felt guilty eating it, because of you. I've been drinking and Josh has got the car, but if you come with me, I'll call him and get him to take us to the vet."

"But I've got no money."

"I'll pay."

"Why?"

"Because...because it's Christmas."

"And you're a nice person?"

"I try to be."

"Look, George, if that's actually your name..."

"It is, honestly."

"I really want to trust you, but...I'm sorry."

"Don't apologise. You don't know me."

He was glad she was being cautious, but it was so incredibly cold and the cat was so sick that he needed to find a way to help that didn't put her in any more vulnerable a situation than she was already. He had an idea.

"Tell you what," he said. He reached into his pocket for his phone and held it out to her. "Have this, and I'll use my friend's phone to call Josh. That way if you feel even slightly in danger, you can ring the police, or Childline, or whatever."

"But you don't know me either. I might run off with your phone."

"I'll take my chances." He put the phone in her hand. "So what d'you reckon?"

She thought for a moment longer and nodded.

"Cool." He smiled, relieved they'd worked something out. He crossed the road, heading back for the pub, and she followed. "What's your name?" he asked.

"Libby. And this is Jinja."

"Nice to meet you both."

"Did you say something about roast dinner?"

"Yeah." He opened the pub door, taking a moment to delight in the wave of heat that washed over them. He indicated to where Sophie was sitting, two full pints on the otherwise empty table in front of her. She opened her mouth to say something but then closed it again when she saw that George was not alone.

"Go sit," he told Libby. She stayed right where she was. He tutted and went to the bar. "Bob. How quickly can you put together one of those roast dinners, and could we have it to go?"

"You didn't eat the last one!"

"Err, yeah." His stomach rumbled at the reminder. He turned and gave Libby a wink. "Best make that two."

Not So Bleak Mid Winter

"Oh, this is very serious." The vet shook his head slowly. "Very serious." He sucked his teeth, the air squeaking like a creaky door as it passed through his narrowed lips. He shook his head again. George stifled a sigh. Trevor—the vet—was a brilliant, kind man whose people skills were not the best, and he did 'sunshine and showers' like a desert monsoon. Today was evidently one of Trevor's rainy days, and George hoped Libby was up to hearing the worst case scenario for Jinja's prognosis. However, he was worrying over nothing, as she was quickly proving to be as straight-talking as the vet.

"Is he going to die?" she asked.

Trevor shrugged. He never answered questions like that directly, because 'I don't know' is not what you want to hear from a medical professional. Instead he said, "I'm going to put Jinja on a drip. He's very dehydrated, and hypoglycaemic. It could well be from malnutrition and exposure, but we'll sedate him and run some blood tests to make sure it's nothing more sinister. However, there might be something else causing it, like liver disease, which is why I want to run some tests. If they show abnormalities, I'll need to perform a liver biopsy to know for sure."

Trevor stopped talking and glanced up from Jinja, offering Libby what was meant to be a reassuring smile but was more of a grimace. She was taking it all in and thinking.

"I'll get the consent forms printed for you to sign," Trevor said, temporarily leaving them alone in the consulting room.

Libby was gently holding Jinja, although he was in no state to try and escape. She stroked his head with her fingertip and kept her eyes on him as she spoke to George. "Would you pay to have him put to sleep?"

"It might not come to that."

"No. I mean now. Would you pay for it now?"

George moved around the side of the examination table so he could see her face. "I don't understand. It's probably just malnutrition, like the vet said."

"But it's going to cost so much money. The drip and the tests and the biopsy…" Libby glanced up at George. "Vets are expensive, aren't they?"

"Well, yeah, but—"

"So putting him to sleep would be the best thing to do." She closed her eyes and continued stroking Jinja's head, trying not to think about it.

"No," George said firmly. He waited for her to open her eyes again and held her gaze. "No," he repeated, a hint of anger seeping into his voice. "We've got to give him the best chance."

"I can't look after him."

"You've done a pretty decent job of it so far."

"I was taking him to the animal shelter."

"To abandon him, or because you wanted him to be cared for?"

Libby was fighting the urge to cry. She'd been doing that all of her life—never show *them* weakness—but it had never been this difficult before. George was watching her, and she turned her face away so he couldn't see.

"How did you get to New Lane?" he asked.

"Bus," she answered, relaxing a little. She thought he'd changed the subject.

"And how will you get back?"

She shrugged. "Walk?"

"So you're not gonna get the bus back?"

"I've got no money left."

"You spent twenty pounds in two days?" George deliberately made it sound like an accusation, because he had an inkling he knew the truth, but he wanted her to admit it.

"Yes, I spent twenty pounds in two days!"

"Are you a junkie?"

"Do I look like a junkie?"

"No, but it's quite a lot of money when you've got no bills to pay and only yourself to feed. Did you spend it on clothes?"

Libby laughed incredulously, using her free hand to gesture at her filthy attire.

"Booze?"

That question wiped the look of indignation from her face, replacing it with a troubled frown.

"No. I was going to," she admitted quietly. "But then Jinja came and he needed food, and he was shivering and I knew he was sick, so I…" She thought about the ten pounds she'd picked up, seeing in her mind the woman walking up ahead in the snowy street, holding her little boy's hand. "It could've been for his Christmas present," she said, her thoughts escaping out loud.

George was about to ask what she meant, but he could hear the vet on his way back to them. "I'll pay for whatever Jinja needs, and we'll discuss the rest later," he said quickly.

One look at his face told her there was no point arguing.

"Right then," Trevor said, placing the forms on the table. "This one's for the blood tests and consent for the biopsy if it's needed. Is he your cat, miss?"

Libby nodded.

"Then we'll need your details before you leave. This time of year people bring in animals and don't come back for them."

"But I—" Libby began.

"I'm taking responsibility, Trevor," George interjected. Trevor treated the animals at Farmer Jake's and was also George's dog's vet. He passed the forms to George to sign.

"If you phone after five, we should have some of the results by then."

"OK. Thanks." George put his signature on the various pieces of paper, and the veterinary nurse took them from him. Trevor picked Jinja up and chatted quietly to him as he carried him away, explaining where he was taking him and what they were going to do. Libby listened on and smiled.

"He's weird," she said.

George laughed. "Yeah, he is, but he's an amazing vet. Come on. Let's go."

They returned to the waiting room, where Josh was sitting, reading a leaflet entitled *Caring For Your Guinea Pig*. George tilted his head and read the cover.

"Is there something you're not telling me?" he asked.

Josh closed the leaflet and put it back on the stand. "I was passing the time. I've read them all now."

George glanced at Libby. "So's he," he said. She giggled.

"I'm what?" Josh asked.

"Weird."

Josh had nothing to say to that and headed for the door with George. Libby stayed where she was.

"I'm going to wait here," she explained.

"They close soon."

"D'you think they'll let me stay?"

"Probably not."

She sighed and reluctantly followed them out to the car. Josh unlocked it, and she opened the boot to get her rucksack.

"I know it's cheeky to ask, when you're paying for Jinja's tests and stuff, but can you lend me one pound twenty, please? I'll find a way to pay you back."

George frowned at her. "What d'you want it for?"

"Bus fare. I'm not going to abandon Jinja, I promise. I'll stay around the railway arches so you know where to find me."

"No, you won't," George said.

Josh was already in the car with the door open. He was listening to their conversation and rubbing his hands together to try and stay warm. "Can you two do this in the car?" he asked. Neither of them seemed to have heard him. He huffed and slammed the door, cranked the blowers up to full and sat on his hands, jiggling his legs. George's door was still open and the dashboard thermometer displayed minus two. It was going to be a bitterly cold night.

Now Libby was trying to explain to George that she had no money to phone the vet, and George was trying to tell her she wasn't going back into town, but he was struggling to speak, and she was using it to her advantage, interrupting him before he could say what he needed to. After a few minutes of listening to them arguing, Josh exhaled loudly and got out of the car again.

"Libby. You're not getting the bus back to town, because you're not going back to town. You're coming to our house, to have a shower, wash your clothes, get warmed up and have something to eat."

"No I'm not!" she protested angrily.

"If you don't, I'm calling the police."

"I'm seventeen."

Josh looked her over and blinked slowly to make it clear he didn't believe her, although whether she agreed to go with them or not, there was a very real possibility that they would need to contact the authorities at some point, because she looked to be fourteen or fifteen at most. For now, the threat was enough to secure her compliance, and she threw her rucksack back into the boot, stormed around to the side of the car and got in. George pushed the seat back and got in too. Josh reversed out onto the road, locking eyes with Libby momentarily in the rear-view mirror. She was scowling at him, and he smiled, amused and completely undaunted by her stubbornness, for he was well versed in these matters; living with George and Iris guaranteed it.

They travelled in silence and pulled up outside the terrace. Libby glanced out of the window. "Have you got a bath?" she asked.

"Yeah," George confirmed. The glazier was currently adjusting the hinges of their new front door. "Not sure if we've got a bathroom window, though."

He needn't have worried, as the door was the very last thing to go in, and the glazier's assistant was in the process of clearing up the debris of brick dust and PVC off-cuts in the living room.

Josh went to investigate, leaving the keys with George. He and Libby hadn't moved to get out, and Josh assumed they needed to talk without him there. He'd had a feeling it would come to this, when they were out searching for her the previous evening, and his agreement to help was essentially his consent to putting her up for a short while. He was perfectly fine with it, although he was also worried about her being a minor and the legal implications of taking her in. Depending on what happened over the next few hours, he would most likely be having a hypothetical discussion or two with Children's Services.

George and Libby watched from the car while Josh engaged in a brief conversation with the glazier at the front door before going inside the house to inspect the windows.

"Will he ring the police?" Libby asked.

George nodded. "Probably." He heard a sharp intake of breath behind him and turned so he could see her. "He'll give you a chance to escape first."

"And time to have a bath?"

George smiled. "Yeah. I would think so."

"I stink, don't I?"

"You don't smell too great, if I'm honest."

Libby wrinkled up her nose in disgust at herself. George was still watching her, and she felt very self-conscious. She looked away, keeping her eyes trained on the glazier repeatedly opening and closing the front door. On the last occasion of him doing this, Josh appeared in the doorway, and the two men shook hands.

"I think it's safe to go in," George said.

"OK," Libby agreed nervously. She waited for George to get out of the car. He took her rucksack from the boot and carried it for her.

"I should've asked before now. Are you OK with dogs?"

"I think so. I don't know. I've seen a few strays on the streets, but I've never really been near them before. Is it a big dog?"

"Yeah. Blue's a German shepherd, but my mum's got a Westie called Monty. He's only small."

"You live with your mum?"

"She's staying with us at the moment. I should maybe warn you about her too. She swears a lot."

"That's OK. I hear lots of swear words at sch…" Libby stopped as soon as she realised her mistake.

"I didn't quite catch that," George said and stepped inside the house, beckoning to Libby to do the same. She followed cautiously, feeling a little disoriented and unsure what to do.

"Would you like a drink?" George asked. Libby blinked at him, her expression one of bewilderment. "What's wrong?"

"Everything sounds strange," she said. After three weeks of living outside, the noise was muffled and quiet, and it felt like her ears were blocked.

"Acoustics," Josh said, emerging from the kitchen and passing them straight by. "I'll go and get the dogs." He left again. Libby stared at the closed door.

"I'm going to make some hot chocolate," George prompted. "Do you want one?"

"Hot chocolate?"

"Yeah. You know the stuff? Milky hot drink with chocolate in it." George was being facetious, but Libby's nodded response was vague and far from enthusiastic. "You can have something else, if you want. What do you like?"

"I think I like hot chocolate," she said carefully.

"Haven't you had it before?"

"Of course I have!" She was telling the truth, as she'd had it at Scouts, but that was so long ago she couldn't remember what it tasted like.

"So do you want one?" George asked again.

"Err, yes, please." This house was nothing like her house, and even though she was a little panicked by the new situation, it felt good being here. It was warm and filled with lovely smells—the Christmas tree, and coffee, and food. More than that, it felt safe. *She* felt safe.

"OK. How about this?" George said, breaking her out of the spell the place had put on her. "I'll get the kettle on, then show you where the bathroom is. You can take your hot chocolate with you and have a nice, long soak."

Libby looked at him in amazement. "I can't do that," she said.

"Why not?"

"I'll get cold."

"I'll turn the heating up."

"No. I mean sitting in the water for that long."

George filled the kettle. "It always makes me too hot."

"You just have a bath to get clean."

"Not always. Sometimes you have one because it helps you relax."

"Sitting in two inches of cold water is definitely not relaxing."

George was starting to get some sense of why Libby was living on the streets.

"Come on," he said, "I'll run the bath for you." He went upstairs, and she followed in a daze, stopping at the top of the stairs. She peered through the open door to Josh's study and looked at the other two doors.

"Where does your mum sleep?"

"Downstairs, in the little room next to the kitchen."

"And where do you sleep?"

George indicated to the closed door to Libby's right. "In there."

"And where does Josh sleep?"

"In there," he repeated, pointing at their bedroom door again.

Libby frowned. "You're homosexuals."

"Err, yeah."

"Homosexuals are evil," she said in a sinister tone.

George felt a rising tide of dread surge through him.

"They're to be prayed for," she continued in that same disembodied voice, like someone else was speaking through her. She made eye contact with him and smiled. "I don't think that, but that's what I've been told all of my life."

"Oh," George uttered, trying to keep in the enormous sigh of relief that wanted out. He regrouped his senses. "This is the bathroom," he said, opening the door and showing her. He went inside and started running the bath. "Are you allergic to anything?"

"No, I don't think so."

"OK. I thought I'd better check before I put any bubble bath in."

At that Libby's face broke into a huge grin. "Bubble bath? I've never had bubble bath."

"Have you only got a shower at home?"

"No. Just a bath."

Each snippet about Libby's life that passed through her lips made George feel a little bit more sick, and he was quite sure what she'd let slip so far was only what she believed was normal.

"You'll have to borrow my bathrobe for now, but I'll give Sophie a call and ask her to lend you some clothes." He stepped past her and opened the bedroom door just wide enough to get through the gap.

"Can I see your room?" Libby asked.

"I'd rather you didn't, if that's all right," George replied apologetically. He didn't care one way or the other, but it probably wasn't wise to be in a bedroom with someone he was fairly certain was under the age of sixteen. The other reason was that Josh didn't share his space well and liked his privacy. It was remarkable he'd agreed to as much as her coming here.

"OK," she said brightly. George reached around the door and grabbed his bathrobe.

"If you pass your clothes out to me, I'll get them in the wash for you." He held out the bathrobe to her, waiting for her to take it. Instead she stared at it, her face fixed in her previous expression, her only movement a very slight shaking of her head.

"Libby?"

"I…" She shook her head a little more vigorously. "I can't. No."

In the bathroom the water level was rising, and he needed to get past to turn the taps off, but whatever he'd just said had frightened her.

"What can't you do, Libby?" he asked gently.

"Clothes."

"OK. Do you want to wait till Sophie brings some round?"

"No…not…not my underwear."

George heard the trickling sound of water sneaking down the overflow, but to get to the bathroom he would need to squeeze past her on the landing. He was at a complete loss, and still they remained, standing face-to-face on the narrow strip between the bedroom and the bathroom, trapped in an emotional impasse.

"George?" Josh's voice called from downstairs. "The overflow pipe's running like Niagara Falls out there."

That prompted Libby into action. She scurried to the bathroom and turned off the taps. George stayed where he was, not wanting to invade her space any more than he already had.

"I could've just said excuse me," he muttered under his breath. Now his brain had re-engaged, he had a possible solution to suggest, although how she'd take it he didn't care to predict. She emerged from the bathroom in a cloud of steam, once again grinning from ear-to-ear.

"The water's so deep! Can I keep it like that? Please?"

George smiled. "Of course you can. Listen, what do you think of this? I'll ask Sophie to bring the clothes, you can tell her what size you need in underwear and keep your own on for now."

"But it's dirty."

"That's true," George agreed. "At uni, we used to wash our underwear in the bath and hang it out the window to dry."

"I suppose I could do that," she said doubtfully, but then nodded, eager to get to her bath. "I'll do that."

"In this weather? It'd freeze!"

She deflated instantly.

"You could put it on the radiator in the bathroom."

She liked that idea even more.

"OK. Wash your underwear first and give it a good wring out until there's no more drips. That way it'll dry quicker."

She rolled her eyes. "I do know how to hand-wash clothes."

"Sorry. I'm gonna go make the hot chocolate. I'll be back up in a couple of minutes. Is that OK?"

She nodded and disappeared into the bathroom. George exhaled slowly. That had to be one of the most stressful dialogues he'd ever engaged in, and he wasn't short on experience in that regard. He returned downstairs, where Josh was already preparing the two cups of hot chocolate, his own cappuccino in progress.

"Thanks," George said, coming up behind and wrapping his arms around him. Josh turned within the embrace and kissed him gently.

"Are you coping?" he asked.

"Yeah. Are you?"

"I am, actually. How is she?"

George closed his eyes and took a deep breath. "I think she's been abused," he whispered.

"Ah."

"She didn't want to part with her underwear. We figured it out in the end, but that poor kid has had a rough time. I can't even begin to imagine what you go through that makes you run away from home in the middle of winter." George withdrew and picked up one of the cups. "I'll take this up to her, then you can tell me what Sean had to say."

Josh laughed quietly. "You know me far too well."

"Yeah, and I'm OK with you telling him. I trust Sean, but this puts both of you in a tricky situation."

"Yes, you could say that. Anyway, shoo." Josh flicked his hand to send George on his way.

Outside the bathroom was a small pile of clothes, folded neatly and balanced on top of white and pink training shoes. George tapped lightly on the door.

"Room service," he called. The door opened a couple of inches, and Libby peered through the gap. She reached an arm out and took the cup.

"Thank you," she said, her voice cracking with tearful gratitude.

"It's your reward," George said, "for saving Jinja. Have a nice bath."

She managed a smile and closed the door again. George picked up the little pile of clothes and took it downstairs, straight to the washing machine. The smell was appalling, but he barely noticed, for everything was absolutely soaking wet. A lump rose in his throat and he bustled past Josh, trying to disguise it. Josh waited until the washing machine started up and grabbed George's hand, pulling him close.

"Don't," George warned, but it came too late. Josh had already reeled him in and was holding him tightly. He cried silently on Josh's shoulder, trying to contain it so Libby wouldn't hear, whilst Josh rubbed his back, shushing and comforting him. Eventually, when he'd pulled himself together a little, he asked, "Was Soph at Sean's?"

"She was," Josh confirmed. "Why?"

"Libby needs clothes and underwear."

"Do you want me to go?"

"Yeah, if you wouldn't mind." He stepped away and wiped his eyes, looking around him, frowning as it dawned on him how quiet it was. "Did you leave the dogs next door but one?"

"No. They're in the living room. I think Sphinx has worn them out." Sphinx was Sean's cat—a cantankerous old Persian-Siamese moggy who did just as he pleased. In fact, he was so bossy that it was more accurate to say that Sean was Sphinx's human.

"I hope Jinja is less of a handful than Sphinxy."

"If he survives," Josh said ruefully. "Do you think he will?"

George shrugged. "I hope so."

. . .

It was almost two hours later and coming up to half past five before Libby made it out of the bathroom, now dressed in a new, clean outfit—not a borrowed one, but clothes Sophie had bought for her, along with a new set of underwear, trainers and socks. The grease and grime that had turned her hair a dull grey-brown was gone, revealing shiny chestnut brown. Libby tugged at it, feeling very shy and exposed in the presence of all of these people. Somehow, having the undivided attention of four adults in close proximity felt less private than her nights in bus shelters and shop doorways, with the world passing her by, because most people tried not to notice her at all.

"I'll go and make drinks," Sophie suggested and left the room.

"Good idea," Josh said. "Sean, come and have a look at this, erm, data for me, will you?"

Sean followed Josh from the room, upstairs to the study. Josh and Sean were both psychologists and worked together, but the data was purely a ruse, to give Libby some space, and also to see what else Sean had been able to find out.

Libby remained in the doorway, her eyes trained on the two sleeping dogs lying in front of the fire.

"They're very well-behaved," she said.

"Yeah. Most of the time," George agreed. "It's OK, you know. You can come in."

She edged into the room and perched on the sofa. George was sitting in the chair.

"I called the vet," he said, in part as a distraction, but also because he sensed she didn't dare to ask in case the news was bad. She looked at him hopefully, and he smiled. "Jinja is going to be fine. They're keeping him on a drip until tomorrow, and then we can go and get him."

Libby sagged in relief. Sophie returned with two cups and placed one on the coffee table. Libby peered over the rim and frowned in puzzlement.

"It's Christmas," Sophie said, to explain the presence of the whipped cream and mini marshmallows floating on top of the hot chocolate. Libby picked up the cup and sipped carefully.

"Mmm. Yummy!" She took another sip and sighed loudly in pleasure.

Sophie looked at George and shook her head, for what Libby had done was so like the way George expressed his enjoyment for food and drink it was uncanny.

Josh and Sean now returned downstairs, and Josh used his eyes to signal to George that he wanted to talk to him in private. They went to the kitchen and closed the door.

"Sean's had a chat with the emergency social worker. She said there's no Libby on the local authority missing children list, so I asked Aitch to check the police database, and he couldn't find anything either."

"What does that mean?"

"Either she's given us a false name, or her parents haven't reported her missing. The social worker said she'd sort out an emergency placement for tonight, and—"

"No."

"George."

"No! She can stay here."

"We'd need to be approved foster carers for that to happen."

"And she's going to be safer in a children's home with staff who want to be at home with their own families than here with us?"

"I know it makes no sense, but—"

"We've both been police-checked to work with children."

"But we'd need to complete the training and assessment of our suitability. If her parents aren't happy—"

"Screw her parents! She's run away from home for a reason."

Josh ran his hand through his hair. George was getting angry, and Josh was essentially playing devil's advocate, because he agreed with everything George was saying.

"If she's been abused…" George started.

"You don't know that."

"But if she has, then they won't make her go back home, will they?"

"No, but they will try and place her in her local authority."

The kitchen door opened, and Sophie peered around the edge. "We've had something of a development," she said.

George's eyes widened in worry.

"It's OK," she assured him. "Libby's very upset and she wants you."

"What happened?"

"Sean asked her why she ran away, and after she'd finished accusing him of trying to make her go home, she told him she'd been trying to escape for four years, but this was the first time they forgot to lock the door. Her parents have kept her imprisoned since she reached puberty."

I'll Be Home…

Iris waddled back in from her smoke in the garden, puffing and panting like an old steam train.

"It's as bloody cold as it looks," she told Josh, who was washing up and staring out of the new kitchen window, so clean it was effectively invisible. The snow was still there, now encrusted with ice and glistening beautifully in the pale-yellow winter sun, but making him glad he didn't need to drive anywhere for the foreseeable future—apart from a quick trip down the road to the vet, of course, which they would make once George was home from work. He'd set off for the farm at 5:30 a.m., and they were on short shifts today, so he'd be home just after midday—in about ten minutes.

"You reckon she's all right?" Iris asked. They'd not heard a peep from Libby all morning.

"I hope so. Do you think I should go and check on her?"

"Hmm. Mebbe it'd be better if I do it, love."

Josh conceded without argument; his experience with teenagers was minimal and mostly from a professional standpoint, whereas Iris had brought up George on her own, and a mighty fine job she'd made of it too, in Josh's opinion, although he was probably a little bit biased. Nonetheless, she knew what she was doing, so he stayed where he was, watching and learning.

Iris approached the closed living room door and knocked.

"Hello?" a little voice came from inside.

"Are you all right, love?" Iris called.

"Yes, thanks."

"D'you fancy some brekkie, or owt?"

"Err…" came the confused response from the other side of the door.

Josh tutted. "Try it in English, Iris."

She glared at him in disdain for mocking her Mancunian accent, although it was always done in fun. She turned back to the door, and in highly exaggerated received pronunciation, said, "Would you care for a spot of breakfast cereal, or perhaps a round of toast?" She sounded like someone impersonating the queen—badly. Josh snorted with laughter. Iris ignored him.

"Oh!" Libby replied. "Yes, please. Can I have some toast, please?"

"With jam?"

"Yes, please!" came the delighted response.

"Right you are, love," Iris said and headed back for the kitchen. "The young lady would like a rind of toast with preserve," she told Josh. He continued giggling for a moment longer, but was immediately silenced by Libby's next words.

"Can I come out now, please? I need to use the bathroom."

Josh screwed his eyes tight shut, his face contorting as if he were physically in pain. "Of course you can, Libby." He went and opened the door for her. "You can come and go as you please."

She smiled at him guiltily and darted upstairs. Josh returned to the kitchen.

"Over my dead body is that child going back to her parents," he muttered. Iris patted him on the arm.

"They'll be linin' up the corpses, love. Don't you worry."

Every adult who had come into contact with Libby since George brought her home felt exactly the same. They were no closer to figuring out where she lived, and she had stuck to her age cover story when questioned by the social worker the previous evening. Thus, for now they were winging it, on the basis that they only needed to do what was 'reasonable' to protect her welfare, until such time as Children's Services could investigate further. Making it clear to Libby that she could leave any time she liked was vital, not just to protect her, but also to cover themselves, particularly in the event that her parents did come forward.

Josh's job afforded him a somewhat rigid adherence to rules—so long as he felt they were justified—never mind that the way they were playing the system was what put children like Libby at risk of abduction. But he couldn't bear the thought of her spending Christmas in a local authority children's home any more than George could. The social worker had agreed Libby could stay until after the holidays, when they'd meet with Children's Services in order for her case to be properly assessed and a placement arranged with registered foster carers. She understood what was going to happen and seemed happy with the arrangements. In fact, happy was rather understating it, as was evidenced by her huge, radiant smile as she came into the kitchen.

"Good morning," Josh greeted her.

"Good morning," she replied, although it was five minutes past twelve. "I just brushed my teeth," she announced excitedly.

"Aye, fu—bloomin' 'eck," Iris chuckled. She was doing her best not to swear in front of Libby, although it wasn't easy breaking the habit of a lifetime. "All the small things, eh?" she said and trundled off to the living room to tidy away the duvet and pillows. "Oh!" she said, looking through the doorway at the neat pile of bedding on the arm of the sofa.

"I didn't know where to put my stuff," Libby explained. She tried to make it sound matter-of-fact, but Josh noticed her flinch as he turned to pass her the plate of toast he'd made.

"It's OK. We can take it upstairs in a little while. Eat your toast before it gets cold."

She tore off a corner with her teeth and chewed, the pleasure instantly registering on her face. Josh smiled, relieved to have got past their earlier misunderstanding.

"I'm quite happy to get a drink for you, but feel free to come and help yourself whenever you need one, OK?"

She nodded because her mouth was too full of toast to reply.

"And George will be back any second, so we can go and pick Jinja up from the vet."

She tried to chew faster so she could speak. Josh watched her, moving his head in time with her chomping. She swallowed hard. "When I get a new home, will I be able to take Jinja with me?"

"I don't know, Libby, but there are probably foster parents who would be OK with cats. Ah! Cats!" He'd just realised something that hadn't occurred to him before. He'd arranged with Shaunna that she and Kris would come over at one o'clock, and Kris was allergic to cats. In the past, his reaction had been anaphylactic, but he'd had desensitisation treatment, so it was nowhere near as severe as it used to be. However, at the very least Josh was going to have to warn him beforehand, and maybe even suggest cancelling their planned afternoon of sherry and mince pies.

"Do you think you can cope with visitors, Libby?" Josh asked.

She nodded enthusiastically. "Sophie and Sean?"

"No. Shaunna and Kris. They're good friends of ours. We all went to high school together."

"Won't they mind me being here?"

"Of course they won't mind. They've got a daughter, so they're used to having young people around."

"What's their daughter's name?"

"Krissi."

"Krissi," Libby repeated, trying to commit it all to memory—for what purpose, she didn't know. "Is Krissi my age?"

"No, she's all grown up. Even so, I think they'll be really pleased to meet you."

"OK," she agreed unconvincingly.

"Are you sure? I can cancel, or rearrange it for another time."

"No. Don't do that. You've been so nice to me, and I know you don't really want me to stay."

"Why do you think that?"

"I just get a feeling."

Josh sent a text message to Shaunna, to inform her of the situation, and then turned his attention to Libby, subtly studying her whilst she finished her toast. She was right; he didn't want her to stay long-term, for lots of reasons that he couldn't even begin to explain to her. He was usually good at hiding his feelings, and a little concerned that she'd picked up on them, but he also had great integrity, so he offered her the most honest reassurance he could.

"I do want you to stay for Christmas, though."

Libby smiled. "Thanks. I want to stay too."

"Good," Josh said, and he meant it. His phone vibrated; Shaunna and Kris were still coming over.

"I've only got one friend at sch—sixth form," Libby said. "She lets me watch TV and films on her phone."

Josh put his phone away and re-established eye contact so that she knew he was listening. She hadn't talked about her life at all, other than what she'd told Sean, and Josh didn't want to push her or plant ideas in her head.

"We don't have a TV at home," she continued, "or a radio, or video games, or books, or the internet, because the church says it's only there to tempt us into evil. My friend's mum told her off for using all her internet allowance, so my form teacher lets me go on YouTube at lunchtimes, even though *they* told the school I wasn't allowed to use the internet. My form teacher said she would rather get sacked than do what *they* tell her to. And she said video games can be educational."

"That's true, they can, although they can also be very dangerous."

"Have you got video games?"

"Yes."

"Are yours dangerous?"

Josh laughed. "No. They're just cartoon racing games and adventures."

"Can we play them later, please?"

Josh thought for a moment and nodded. "That sounds like a perfect way to spend Christmas Eve to me."

The front door opened, and George came in, followed by Blue, who looked very sorry for himself. He didn't like the snow. He waited in the hallway to have his paws checked for compacted ice, after which he padded off into the lounge to laze in front of the fire. George came through to the kitchen and put his cold hands on Josh's cheeks.

"George!" Josh shrieked and pushed him away. "You stink!"

Libby held her nose. "Pooey! I hope I didn't smell that bad yesterday."

George just grinned, left his wellies by the back door, and went up to shower. When he returned, he was dressed in a thick red and white checked shirt worn open over a white t-shirt, with jeans and boots. Josh eyed him up and down.

"Who needs frilly aprons?" he remarked with an appreciative smile. George raised an eyebrow.

"You look like a cowboy," Libby observed.

"Funny you should say that, Lib."

"Why?"

"I used to be one."

"What? A real cowboy?"

"Yep. On a cattle ranch in the good ole U-S-of-A."

"Wow! That's so cool!"

Josh leaned in and whispered in Libby's ear, "Except he's frightened of cows." Libby giggled.

"Yeah. I wasn't a very good cowboy, huh?" George admitted. "But I'm not frightened of cats, especially little ginger cats who are waiting to come home."

Libby was at the front door before he reached the end of the sentence.

"I guess we're off to the vets," Josh said.

George nodded. "I guess so."

So that was where they went.

Jinja was still quiet, but he was looking a million times better. His coat had picked up a bit of a sheen, and his eyes were sparkling and alert. He got up and started meowing as soon as he heard Libby's voice, and she was so excited to see him that she scooped him up right away and kissed his head repeatedly. He didn't seem to mind one bit.

With the reunion successfully completed, they bought a litter tray and carry-box from the vet, setting it down on the floor when they arrived home, to give Blue and Monty a chance to have a sniff without frightening Jinja, and vice versa. Blue was used to Sphinx, who could be quite spiteful, so he gave Jinja a very wide berth, and went to lie by the fire again. Monty followed the cat all around the room, until Jinja jumped up onto Libby's lap to get out of his way. Disgruntled, Monty trotted off towards the kitchen and scratched at the back door. Iris let him out on her way in.

"We'll have to try and keep the cat inside for the time being," George said, "but I think they're all going to get along just fine."

As he finished speaking, there was a knock at the front door, followed by it slowly opening, letting in a gust of icy air, and then a tuneless chorus of 'We Wish You A Merry Christmas'. Libby turned and watched, enthralled as first a bottle of sherry came into view, then a pair of flashing antlers, then another pair, and finally two heads peered around the door, big grins on both faces. George tutted.

"That's Shaunna and Kris," he explained to Libby, but the explanation went unheard, for Shaunna and Libby were now staring at each other in wonder.

"Red Sea lady!" Libby gasped.

"Hello," Shaunna uttered, otherwise lost for words.

Libby set Jinja down on the sofa and ran to Shaunna, throwing her arms around her. Shaunna was completely taken aback, but reciprocated nonetheless. Everyone else watched the scene before them with matching mouth-open expressions of astonishment.

"By any chance, is this the girl you were talking about?" Kris asked.

"It certainly is," Shaunna confirmed. "And look at you!" She glanced past Libby to Jinja, who was sitting and watching his mistress in pure adoration. Shaunna slowly stepped back, gently holding Libby's arms as she spoke to her. "How did you end up here?"

"George," Libby gushed. "What you said about looking after each other? I promised that we would, and then I left Jinja, but he wouldn't leave me. Then I tried to take him to the animal shelter, but it was closed. If George hadn't helped us, I couldn't have looked after Jinja and he couldn't have looked after me. George saved our lives."

"I wouldn't go quite that far," George protested bashfully.

"It's true," Libby argued. "If we'd still been on the street now, we'd have died of hypothermia."

Kris and Shaunna looked at each other and nodded in agreement.

"It's going to be minus ten tonight," Kris said, trying and failing to stifle a sneeze.

"Just as well we've got all this sherry to warm us up then," Shaunna said, passing over the enormous bottle to Josh.

"Can I have a little glass too, please?" Libby asked.

George shook his head. "You're not old enough to drink."

"Children are allowed to drink alcohol at home with their parents."

"And would you be allowed to at home?"

"No, but I wouldn't be allowed to talk to homosexuals either."

Shaunna started laughing, amused by Libby's bluntness. Kris sneezed again.

"Are you really OK with the cat?" Josh asked. Kris waved his arm to dismiss Josh's concern and then sneezed again, and again.

"I'll be fine," he lied, because he was starting to get a bit wheezy.

Libby felt terribly guilty. "I'll go and sit upstairs with Jinja," she offered.

"No. It's OK," Kris assured her. "It'll settle down in a—" another sneeze "—minute." Now his eyes were streaming too.

"If I can borrow a pencil, I'll stay in the study and draw. I don't mind."

"Are you sure, Libby?" George asked. She nodded to confirm it and picked Jinja up. George shrugged. "Come on then. Let's get you a pencil and some paper."

"It's OK. I only need a pencil. I have something I have to finish today."

She followed George from the room, upstairs to the study, where he gave her his full set of pencils, running from a 6B through HB to 6H.

"If you get fed up and fancy reading a book, they're all up there," he said, pointing at the loft hatch. "The remote control for the stairs is on the desk."

"Thank you."

"You'll be OK?"

"Yes."

"Positive?"

"Yes!"

"OK. We're just downstairs if you need us."

"I know."

"I'll see you after then." George stepped towards the door. "Or if you need a *non-alcoholic* drink or…"

She sighed loudly. George relented and returned to the living room, where Kris and Shaunna were now sitting on the sofa, waiting for him, and all of a sudden they looked very serious. His stomach flipped in expectation of bad news, and he sat on the floor next to Blue, his gaze flitting between his two friends. Shaunna smiled and took Kris's hand.

"We need to tell you something, George, but first we want to ask you a favour."

"Um, OK."

"We've already cleared it with Josh."

George looked to Josh to see if that was true, not that he doubted Shaunna. Josh nodded.

"The more the merrier by this point," Josh said. George didn't understand. He shrugged at Shaunna in query.

"Would you mind looking after Casper for us for a few days?"

"Ah!" Now he realised what Josh had meant. With his mum staying, as well as Libby, Monty, Blue, Jinja, plus Casper the crazy Labrador, it was going to be a very full little house. "Are you going away?" he asked.

"Yep."

"Cool. Anywhere nice?"

"I'm going to Manchester," Kris said, lowering his voice just enough for it to sound like he'd done it so Iris wouldn't hear yet still loud enough that she did. "So not that nice really." George laughed.

"I heard that!" Iris shouted on her way up to the bathroom. Kris smiled sweetly, and she glowered in response.

"So where are *you* going?" George asked Shaunna.

"I don't know yet."

"OK." He was getting very confused by it all. They said they had something to tell him, but none of what they'd said so far was especially surprising. They'd separated a long time ago, so there was nothing wrong with them spending Christmas apart, even if they did still share a house.

"There's more," Shaunna said. George met her gaze. "We're getting divorced."

"Right?"

"In case we want to remarry."

"Oh." George didn't know what to say. He wanted to ask them what had changed, because there must be something, and he could see that they wanted him to ask, but could he find the words? "So, err…" he began, stopped, frowned, took another breath. "Is it…what I mean is…ah, crap." He ran his hand over his head, frustrated.

All of a sudden there was a flurry of movement, like a whirlwind whooshing down the stairs and into the room. Libby went straight over to George and knelt in front of him. If he'd had the power of speech, he would probably have shouted at her to get out of the way, but she waited where she was, staring into his eyes until his gaze locked with hers. She reached behind his head and fiddled about, slowly bringing her hands around each side, miming holding something in front of his face and folding it up.

"Mental gag removed," she said.

"Libby! I'm trying to have a serious conversation!"

"Yep." She grinned.

"Are you done with me?"

"I think so. I was just wondering, though. What were you trying to tell me when you saw me in the road yesterday?"

"That I thought you were pregnant, but it was only Jinja inside your coat."

"Oh!" Libby giggled. "In that case, yes. I'm done with you." She gave him a hug. "Merry Christmas, cowboy." She got up and left the room, all eyes on her.

"What was that about?" Kris asked.

"I've no idea," George said.

Josh smiled. "I have."

A Midnight Clear

Libby stayed upstairs in Josh's study for the duration of Shaunna and Kris's visit. After four years of only seeing other people at school and church, she was well used to her own company, but closing the door had made her panic, so she'd kept it open, concentrating on finishing her advent calendar and trying not to listen to the conversation taking place downstairs. It was very emotional with lots of tears and occasional shouting, yet she didn't feel in the least bit threatened. The three weeks of living on the streets, hopping trains and buses from place to place, had almost felt like a holiday, no longer hidden away in a bare room but for the bed, and the pencils and paper stolen from school, concealed inside her clothes so she could sneak past *them*. Now she was here, in this little room, in a tiny house, in a village that to her was in the middle of nowhere, doing what she had always done to get through the hours alone, except she wasn't alone anymore. She had Jinja.

Maybe *they* weren't completely wrong, though. Maybe God does show you the right path if you choose to see it. She'd hated that guard at the time, but if he'd let her on the train, if the man in the garage had turned a blind eye to her sleeping in the toilet, if that water hadn't soaked Jinja in the alley, they wouldn't be here now, in this house with these people—the sort of people her church would condemn to eternal hell and damnation for their evil ways. But they weren't evil. They were wonderful and kind.

The sound of movement downstairs brought her out of her daydreaming, the voices louder now as they were coming from the hall. Shaunna and Kris were going, and she wanted to say goodbye to them. She most likely wouldn't see them again.

"Stay," she said to Jinja, who was curled up cosily on Josh's spinny chair and had no intention of going anywhere. Libby quickly ran down, pausing a couple of stairs from the bottom to watch the adults saying their goodbyes. Shaunna looked up at her and smiled.

"Merry Christmas, Libby," she said. Libby stepped down and gave Shaunna another hug.

"Merry Christmas," she replied. She turned to Kris. "And to you, Mr. Sneezy."

Kris took off his light-up antlers and gently placed them on her head. She peered up, trying to see them. "They suit you," he said.

"Yeah, but you've got the red nose to go with them." She gave him a cheeky grin. Kris rubbed his nose, and she shook her head to tell him it had made no difference. He made a sad face and followed Shaunna outside, both of them waving as they set off down the icy path towards their taxi. Josh closed the door and pulled his sleeves down over his hands; it wasn't for effect.

"OK, so Krissi's going to drop Casper off after work, which gives us about three hours to play video games. What do you think, Libby?"

She nodded. "Yes, but I want to give you my present first." She ran back upstairs, returning a moment later with Jinja in one hand and the grey, crumpled paper in the other, which she passed to George. The two sheets were stuck together around the edges and folded in half, with a pencil outline of a star on the front.

"I used your glue," Libby confessed to Josh. "I hope you don't mind. It was on your desk, and I wanted it to be a surprise." She blinked up at him nervously.

"That's fine," he assured her with a smile. He watched George open the handmade card, revealing the twenty-four numbered doors: carefully torn squares in the top sheet of paper, underneath each a tiny pencil drawing.

"These are the best things that happened to me since I left home," Libby explained.

George nodded in understanding, noting the sketch of a Christmas tree at the bottom of the page, in front of it a road sign for Trafalgar Square. "You know the streets aren't paved with gold, don't you?" he joked, mostly to cover how overwhelmed he was.

"Yeah, I know. I needed to have somewhere to aim for, but I don't want to go to London anymore."

"I'm glad about that," George said. He wanted her to stay close enough for him to keep an eye on her and make sure she was being well cared for. He carefully opened the doors in order, taking in the images of buses, cottages, doorways and bridges, all sketched with great care but a little smudged by the friction of their journey. "Who died?" he asked when he got to number seventeen.

"My blanket. A man in Liverpool gave it to me, and it got wet."

George continued on through doors eighteen and nineteen, the latter depicting a tiny Blackpool Tower.

"That was the day I lost my pencil."

Now the pictures became slightly more elaborate, with shading and much cleaner edges. Under number twenty was a tiny caricature of a person pushing a shopping trolley, the wire mesh carefully pencilled in with the delicate strokes of a hard pencil.

"There's people like her everywhere," Libby said, "but she was kind of nice, sharing her brandy with me. It made me feel all warm inside."

"It's very bad for you," George scolded lightly.

"So are McDonald's fries," Libby remarked dryly, as a carton of those was what he found under door twenty-one, resting on top of a twenty-pound note.

"I wanted to put your face on there instead of the queen's, but I'm not that good at drawing," she explained.

"These are awesome, Libby," George said earnestly.

"And he should know," Josh added. He indicated to the sketch of a horse on the wall next to where they were standing. Libby moved closer and examined it.

"Wow!" she said. "Will you teach me how to draw like that? Please?"

She didn't get an answer, as George had moved on, through door twenty-two—the day Libby and Jinja found each other, with its tiny cartoon cat sitting within a heart—to door twenty-three. The day George finally caught up with her, opposite The Red Lion pub, a moment captured by a slightly out of proportion miniature cowboy on a horse, and underneath it the words, 'The Real Santa'. George gulped back the tears and bravely pushed on to the last door, behind it a simple line drawing of a house with smoke coming from the chimney, a snowman standing outside and the letters 'PTO' scribbled in the corner. George followed the instruction and flipped over to the back of the makeshift card.

To our very own Santa and Mr. Claus.
Thank you for giving us a home for Christmas.
Love from Libby and Jinja
xxx

George started to cry and put his arms around Libby, too choked to tell her how much he liked the present. She was about to apologise for upsetting him, when a voice piped up from the kitchen, "Is he bein' a soft shite again?"

"I'm afraid so," Josh replied, although he was struggling a little himself. Iris waddled down the hallway and tutted at George.

"Don't worry, love," she said to Libby, "he's always been a bit of a crybaby." Iris gave Libby a wink and went into the living room, setting herself down at the far end of the sofa. "Did someone say they was makin' a brew?"

"I will," George said, wiping his eyes on his sleeve. "Thank you so much for this, Libby. It's beautiful."

"Do you like it, really?"

"I love it." He took it and placed it in the centre of the mantelpiece, stepping back to admire it. Iris coughed into her hand to get his attention. "Yeah, all right, Mam. I'll do it now." He turned to Josh and Libby. "And you two can set up that video game."

. . .

Josh lay in bed, listening to the pat-pat of gentle footfalls overhead. It was almost midnight, and they'd gone to bed a couple of hours ago, exhausted by a day of emotionally charged interchanges, but excited because it was Christmas

Eve, with that most magical night about to begin. He spent a moment indulging in childish fantasy, of Santa and his sleigh, parked on their rooftop, the sounds above him the hooves of reindeer, pawing impatiently, eager to push on with their mission of delivering gifts to children all around the world. It dawned on him how many children like Libby would be out there alone tonight, with no dreams of Santa Claus, or presents under Christmas trees, desperately trying to survive and make it through to daylight.

Josh did not know what it was like to do without. He had always shared what he did have with his friends, but he'd never felt compelled to give to charity; to offer help, unconditionally, to a stranger in need. He'd been happy to leave that kind of thing to George, who had brought about something of a Christmas miracle, and was presently lying beside him in a deep, unstirring sleep. Josh carefully slid out from under the duvet and put on his dressing gown.

The loft stairs were extended, the light shining down from the hatch above casting a tungsten glow over his otherwise dark study. He remained quite still, listening to the gentle swoosh of pages being turned, and then began to climb the steps to the space above and his 'library'. Libby was sitting, cross-legged, on the rug between the bookshelves, an open book resting in her hands. She saw him and gasped, quickly closing the book. The look she gave him was one of pure terror.

"I'm so sorry," she said. "I should've asked, but I didn't want to wake you, and George said there were books up here. I just wanted to have a look. I'm sorry."

Josh stepped up into the loft. "What are you reading?" he asked. She held up the book for him to see. It was a hardcover volume, bearing the title *Classic Christmas Stories*.

"It was sticking out from the other books," she explained.

"Ah. That's because I was reading it the other day."

"There's a bookmark," she said, turning to where a red tasselled strip of card marked the beginning of the story of 'The Little Match Girl'. "I started to read it, but it's hard to understand."

"Would you like me to read it to you?"

"Oh, it's OK. We should both be asleep, or else Santa won't come." She gave Josh a carefree smile, and he sensed the hope it concealed. He smiled back and went to sit next to her.

"Does your church believe in Santa Claus?" he asked.

"No. We do celebrate Christmas, though, but it's all prayers and being thankful for the birth of Jesus and remembering how lost we all are without him."

"Sounds fun," Josh remarked, trying to sound neither sarcastic nor judgemental, although he was being both.

"It's not *my* church, so you can say what you like," Libby told him sternly.

Josh took a deep breath to once again quell the anger he felt for how her parents' religious beliefs had led to Libby's incarceration. Whether it was the teaching of their church or not, they had tried their damned hardest to destroy this little girl; it was her own resilience that meant they had not succeeded. "I'd best not say anything," he said. "But I wanted to ask you something else."

"What's that?"

"Mental gag removed?"

She tutted. "It's so obvious!"

"Is it?"

"Yes! George gets all tangled up, thinking he can't speak, but he can. He's just convinced himself he can't, that's all."

"He's got a condition that causes it."

"So? It worked, didn't it?"

"Yes," Josh admitted. "Yes, it did."

"Do you think I'd be good at this stuff?" She glanced up at the bookshelves, bowing under their load of hundreds of psychology books.

"You're already good at it, but maybe you could read a few and see."

"I won't be here long enough."

Her statement made Josh feel uneasy, and he focused on the open book in her hands to avoid looking at her.

"Does it have a happy ending?" she asked. "The Little Match Girl?"

"Sort of. She goes to heaven to be with her grandmother."

"Do you believe in heaven?"

"No."

"So why were you reading it? The happy ending only works if you believe in heaven."

She was staring at him so intently, searching his face for understanding. He met her gaze.

"I was reminding myself of the story, so I could make the right decision."

"About me?"

"Yes. About you."

"I thought you wanted me to leave."

"I don't want you to end up like the little match girl."

Libby sighed. She didn't want to think about leaving, not yet. She shuffled closer to Josh and set the book down in his lap, leaning in so she could still see the delicate watercolour illustrations, her head resting against his shoulder. Instinctively, he put a protective arm around her and kissed the top of her head.

"It's Christmas Day," he whispered.

"I know," she replied, also in a whisper. "Yes, please. I would like you to read it to me."

"OK." He repositioned the book so he could see it better and was about to start, when she covered the page with her hand and peered up at him.

"But only if it has a happy ending," she said.

He continued to look into her eyes a little longer, and then smiled. He began to read.

"Most terribly cold it was; it snowed, and was nearly quite dark…"

THE END

THE LITTLE MATCH GIRL

BY
HANS CHRISTIAN ANDERSEN

Most terribly cold it was; it snowed, and was nearly quite dark, and evening–the last evening of the year. In this cold and darkness there went along the street a poor little girl, bareheaded, and with naked feet. When she left home she had slippers on, it is true; but what was the good of that? They were very large slippers, which her mother had hitherto worn; so large were they; and the poor little thing lost them as she scuffled away across the street, because of two carriages that rolled by dreadfully fast.

One slipper was nowhere to be found; the other had been laid hold of by an urchin, and off he ran with it; he thought it would do capitally for a cradle when he some day or other should have children himself. So the little maiden walked on with her tiny naked feet, that were quite red and blue from cold. She carried a quantity of matches in an old apron, and she held a bundle of them in her hand. Nobody had bought anything off her the whole livelong day; no one had given her a single farthing.

She crept along trembling with cold and hunger–a very picture of sorrow, the poor little thing!

The flakes of snow covered her long fair hair, which fell in beautiful curls around her neck; but of that, of course, she never once now thought. From all the windows the candles were gleaming, and it smelt so deliciously of roast goose, for you know it was New Year's Eve; yes, of that she thought.

In a corner formed by two houses, of which one advanced more than the other, she seated herself down and cowered together. Her little feet she had drawn close up to her, but she grew colder and colder, and to go home she did not venture, for she had not sold any matches and could not bring a farthing of money: from her father she would certainly get blows, and at home it was cold too, for above her she had only the roof, through which the wind whistled, even though the largest cracks were stopped up with straw and rags.

Her little hands were almost numbed with cold. Oh! a match might afford her a world of comfort, if she only dared take a single one out of the bundle, draw it against the wall, and warm her fingers by it. She drew one out. "Rischt!" how it blazed, how it burnt! It was a warm, bright flame, like a candle, as she held her hands over it: it was a wonderful light. It seemed really to the little maiden as though she were sitting before a large iron stove, with burnished brass feet and a brass ornament at top. The fire burned with such blessed influence; it warmed so delightfully. The little girl had already stretched out her feet to warm them too; but—the small flame went out, the stove vanished: she had only the remains of the burnt-out match in her hand.

She rubbed another against the wall: it burned brightly, and where the light fell on the wall, there the wall became transparent like a veil, so that she could see into the room. On the table was spread a snow-white tablecloth; upon it was a splendid porcelain service, and the roast goose was steaming famously with its stuffing of apple and dried plums. And what was still more capital to behold was, the goose hopped down from the dish, reeled about on the floor with knife and fork in its breast, till it came up to the poor little girl; when—the match went out and nothing but the thick, cold, damp wall was left behind. She lighted another match. Now there she was sitting under the most magnificent Christmas tree: it was still larger, and more decorated than the one which she had seen through the glass door in the rich merchant's house.

Thousands of lights were burning on the green branches, and gaily-coloured pictures, such as she had seen in the shop-windows, looked down upon her. The little maiden stretched out her hands towards them when—the match went out. The lights of the Christmas tree rose higher and higher, she saw them now as stars in heaven; one fell down and formed a long trail of fire.

"Someone is just dead!" said the little girl; for her old grandmother, the only person who had loved her, and who was now no more, had told her, that when a star falls, a soul ascends to God.

She drew another match against the wall: it was again light, and in the lustre there stood the old grandmother, so bright and radiant, so mild, and with such an expression of love.

"Grandmother!" cried the little one. "Oh, take me with you! You go away when the match burns out; you vanish like the warm stove, like the delicious roast goose, and like the magnificent Christmas tree!" And she rubbed the whole bundle of matches quickly against the wall, for she wanted to be quite sure of keeping her grandmother near her. And the matches gave such a brilliant light that it was brighter than at noon-day: never formerly had the grandmother been so beautiful and so tall. She took the little maiden, on her arm, and both flew in brightness and in joy so high, so very high, and then above was neither cold, nor hunger, nor anxiety—they were with God.

But in the corner, at the cold hour of dawn, sat the poor girl, with rosy cheeks and with a smiling mouth, leaning against the wall—frozen to death on the last evening of the old year. Stiff and stark sat the child there with her matches, of which one bundle had been burnt. "She wanted to warm herself," people said. No one had the slightest suspicion of what beautiful things she had seen; no one even dreamed of the splendour in which, with her grandmother she had entered on the joys of a new year.

The End

FROM ALL OF US TO ALL OF YOU

Ofelia Gränd

ACKNOWLEDGEMENTS

I want to thank everyone that's been involved in getting this story published. I'm especially grateful to Jonathan Penn, the awesome author, Charlotte Neumann, the awesome teacher, and of course my dearly loved husband for being supportive even though he thinks I'm crazy.

12th of December

"You can close up and head home now."

I looked up from the tiny screen on the cash register and smiled over at Monica. She always made sure to let me off a few minutes early when we were the only two left working. I was just a common cashier, whereas she was far more important; she was in charge of the lottery ticket scanner, for crying out loud!

Monica was awesome. She'd been working in this crappy store for more than forty years, and she still smiled every day. Her nails were perfectly manicured, and her hairdo—though the color was now gray instead of the screaming red it'd been when I was a child—was impeccable.

"Thank you," I said, and started to log off.

"Not to worry, dear. I know you young men probably have some shenanigans scheduled for tomorrow."

Me? Young? I scoffed. I was twenty-four, not some teenager out partying in the middle of the week just because it was the Saint Lucia Day celebrations. This year the thirteenth happened to be on a Saturday. The kids got lucky, I suppose. Or not. Half the fun, as I remembered it, was that the cool kids could show up hung-over in school the next day.

Lucia is one of the few saints celebrated in Sweden. Apart from it bringing people to church, there isn't much religion to it, though. I guess the church picked the day to coincide with the winter solstice; that way they could merge the religion into an already existing heathen holiday.

"Actually, I do. I'll be setting my alarm extra early since I'm going to Saint Lawrence Church to see Annie, my niece, as Lucia with *real* candles in her hair. I've even heard a rumor that she'll be reading a poem."

"Oh, that's not shenanigans, that's tradition."

It was. The Lucia tradition was one of the few things I truly liked about December. Advent Sunday was nice, with its lit candles, and blossoming hyacinths, but it was also a reminder that Christmas was approaching. Not that Lucia wasn't a reminder. God, only eleven days left!

"But is there a Lucia procession on a Saturday? I didn't think the schools were allowed to demand the children's attendance on the weekend."

"No, the schools are celebrating today, but she's in the church choir."

"Oh, how lovely!"

"You should come," I said, not knowing why I was inviting her. She was my favorite colleague by far, but it wasn't as if we had that kind of relationship. She mothered me here at work, but that, I'd always assumed, was more out of pity than actual fondness. I couldn't say that she knew my mom—because no one did—but she knew *of* her, and if you knew of her, then you knew about my dad, too.

"I would love to, dear. At what time?"

I stared, open-mouthed, at her for a second or two. "You would?"

"Yes, I haven't been to a Lucia procession since Hannes was in school. He made such a cute star boy, with his shining blue eyes and blond curls." Her gaze turned dreamy. "He always keeps it short nowadays," she said with a disapproving frown. "Strange, isn't it? Some of us do everything in our power just to get a few waves, but when someone is blessed with corkscrew curls, they practically shave it off!"

"We always want what we can't have, I guess... The procession starts at eight thirty."

"That's lovely, dear. I'll be there. Are you bringing anyone?"

"To church?" I spluttered. I didn't have anyone to bring. I wanted to have someone, but who would I invite to take part in my lousy life? It wasn't as if I had anything to offer.

A little twinkle lit her eyes as she said, "Not a special someone you'd want to sit next to on the church bench, watching the children sing in their white gowns, praying no handmaidens will hold their candle too close to their mouth, and pass out due to lack of oxygen?"

I burst out laughing. "No, no one that special."

"Good, good." She looked at me with loving eyes, and I was a little shocked by seeing that. Maybe our relationship wasn't completely built on pity. Then she mumbled, almost inaudibly, "I'll see if I can guilt Hannes into coming."

I stared at her. *What did she just say?*

"Off you go, sweetheart. I'll see you in the morning. Will your mother be there?"

I nodded. She didn't ask about my father, probably knew that the likelihood of seeing him there was very slim, even though it was his grandchild performing.

"See you tomorrow," I muttered, still not really grasping what she'd said about bringing her son, or rather guilting him into coming. She knew I was gay, everyone did. She could hardly mean to set me up on a blind date, could she? I'd never thought Monica was that kind of person, and she'd never told me her son was gay. I thought that, maybe, sort of, that was something she would have told me if he was, since we had discussed me being gay plenty. It wasn't like she'd lacked opportunity to tell me if her son was too. Maybe she hadn't wanted me to know.

I remembered that she had been raging mad when one of the summer workers had said something behind my back about me being gay. The owners had tried to hush it down—not the fact that I was gay, as there was no hushing that down—but that there was a problem with it. There wasn't a problem, not really, just one kid who didn't want to work alone with me, because he thought I would jump his bones. Monica had been furious on my behalf. The kid had said something along the lines of him being uncomfortable knowing that I might be turned on by him. Monica had told him that *she* felt uncomfortable knowing that he might be turned on by her. The kid, of course, had tried to tell her nicely that that wasn't the case. Monica was older than his mother, he wasn't going to get turned on by her. Monica had then told him, and not so nicely by all accounts, that it wasn't the case in his situation either. She assured him that I didn't go for snotty-nosed kids—and I didn't, she had that right—but that didn't stop people from talking. Being the gay son of a locally famous drunk kind of invited gossip. Monica hated gossip, and had always been protective of me. But, as I mentioned before, I'd interpreted it as a sign of pity, nothing more. Maybe she was being protective because her son also was gay, and it pissed her off when people blathered about it.

13th of December

Why were church benches always so damn uncomfortable? I hadn't been sitting for more than fifteen minutes, and already my ass was sore. Caroline and her husband, Martin, sat in the front row. The first three were reserved for parents; uncles had to make do with the fourth, or even further back. I had arrived early, and sat firmly by the aisle on the fourth. No one was going to block my view of Annie walking down the aisle in her white full-length gown, with a red silk ribbon at her waist, and a crown of candles on her head. My little girl was Lucia, she and about ten other six-year-olds, but that didn't matter. Annie would soon grace that candlelit aisle, at the head of the procession, singing *Santa Lucia*.

I was breathless with anticipation.

"Good morning, sweetheart."

I looked up to see Monica standing next to me. She was alone, and I almost sighed in relief. I was a little curious about her son, but I didn't want to be on a blind date in church. I didn't want to be on a blind date at all.

"Hi," I said, indicating that she should sit next to me, away from the aisle of course.

She smiled. "Isn't your mother coming?"

"Oh, yeah. But, she'll sit in the back."

"You sure? I wouldn't want to take her seat."

People assumed that just because my dad was a drunk, I would hold my mother's hand wherever we went. It pissed me off that I usually proved them right, but I was working on that. I was close to my mother, unfortunately more out of guilt than anything else. I'd done my therapy-time; I knew about her co-dependency and, by extension, mine. That, if anything, made me furious. Why couldn't she just kick the bastard out? It wasn't as if she loved him. Then again, just because I'd done my therapy-time, and had all the nice words to describe how our family worked, that didn't mean I'd recovered.

"You're not. If she wanted to be in the front, she would've been here by now."

I patted the seat next to me, angry that my mother wouldn't come sit in the front. Normally she would guilt me into sitting in the back with her, but this was too important to me. And I did it a little out of spite. There was no denying I would've been far more comfortable in the back, but this was Annie. If sitting out here where everyone could see was what I had to do to be able to hear her read her poem, then I would. I tried not to think about the other people in church, and what they would think when they saw me. I knew they judged my mother, and pitied me, hell they would even pity Annie, and normally I would hide in the back. But, not today!

Monica actually made it better. Now they wouldn't think *that poor deserted boy*. Now they would think, *Oh, how nice of her to sit next to him*. Okay, maybe that wasn't better, but still, they wouldn't think I was alone. People thought that just because you stuck to yourself, you were lonely. I wouldn't call myself lonely. Okay, I was pretty lonely, but I chose to be. Better to be lonely, than have to explain the whole thing.

One failed stint at the university had taught me everything I needed to know about myself. I'd gotten free therapy through school, but even though my therapist had made some good points, what I'd really learned was that I couldn't handle the real world. I couldn't cope with the pressure of having to accomplish something, be someone. So, I'd moved back home to our small southwestern town, and gotten a job as a cashier at the smallest food market that wasn't a neighborhood corner store. I'd been a cashier there for four years now.

"Natten går tunga fjät..." Oh, here they came. Monica, grumbled something next to me, before turning her attention to the children striding down the aisle. I almost became a little teary-eyed. They were adorable, all of them, and Annie was beautiful. She was concentrating really hard on holding her head straight and her hands palm to palm, while singing along in the *Santa Lucia* song.

The dark church instantly became brighter when the children took their place in front of the altar. After a few songs, four of the Lucias took a step forward. One by one they each lit one of the four tapers in the large candelabra, and then read a verse.

I saw Annie's hand shake when she held the match to the wick, but she read her poem flawlessly. It was nerve-racking to read a verse in front of this many people, and she didn't even stutter. I was so proud.

When the four candles were lit, and the girls had returned to their places among the others, they sang a few more songs before the procession took its leave. First the Lucias, then the handmaidens, then the star boys, and last the gingerbread men, and the brownies.

There was applause, of course. What parent wouldn't applaud their child after such a performance?

"Lucia bread and glögg in the parish house?" I asked Monica with a smile.

"Yes, of course," she answered, almost as excited as I was.

. . .

"I'm sorry, Mom."

I didn't recognize the voice. I looked up from my Lucia cat, an S-shaped saffron bun which, to my disappointment, had been made without the saffron, and saw who had spoken the apology: a strapping man about my age. There

122

was no doubt he was Monica's son, the resemblance was striking. When she'd said that he had shining eyes, I'd thought she meant that they had been shining when he walked in the Lucia procession as a child. Now, I understood that she meant the way they sparkled.

Monica looked affronted. "Of course you are."

"Really, I am. I...eh...the car wouldn't start, so I had to walk. But I saw the procession from the back."

Monica glared at him, and I once again got the feeling that this was more like a blind date than a simple get-together. The way her son wouldn't look at me told me that he felt a little uncomfortable too.

"Well, dear," she said, turning to me, "this is my son Hannes. Hannes, this is Simon." We shook hands like good little gentlemen and added a polite nod. "Good, now you two talk, while I go and get us some more glögg."

"Eh—" I began as she walked away.

"I'm sorry," he blurted out. "She means well, she really does, but...you know."

"Yeah, I'm not your type."

"What?" Hannes looked alarmed.

"The blind-date thing, I'm not what you're looking for."

"Blind date?"

I pointed discreetly back and forth between us. "It's okay, no hard feelings. It wasn't like I asked her to set us up," I said with a smile, even though it hurt a little to see him *that* taken aback by the thought of dating me.

"I'm not...she didn't...it's not...I'm not gay! It's not a date...She just wants me to make some friends. Last week she arranged for me to help a young lady change over to snow tires in hopes of us getting along."

Shit! I wished the ground would open and swallow me whole. I tried to pretend I hadn't misinterpreted this whole situation. "Helen? Yeah, I heard that. It's her first car, and she hadn't understood that she had to change tires before the first of December. Quite a drama outburst when she realized she'd been driving illegally," I said, with what I hoped to be a casual smile.

"You know her?"

I made a so-so gesture. "We work together."

"Of course," he said, and then started to look around the parish house. I tried to think of something to say to break the growing tension, but felt that I'd already said more than enough. I wondered what he thought of me for assuming his mother had tried to set us up.

"So, err..." What the hell should I say?

"I hope you wanted both raisins and almonds, because we got it before I could stop the woman serving it," Monica said happily, as she handed us each a small paper cup of glögg.

123

"Sure," I said, even though I preferred mine without the chopped almonds. At least it was the non-alcoholic kind, which I preferred. I hardly ever drank. If it was more awkward to decline than to accept, I would have a glass of white wine, but apart from that I avoided alcohol. I sipped on the hot beverage, and gazed through the crowd to see if I could locate my mother.

I saw her talking to Caroline and Annie. Annie was still in her Lucia gown, and when I caught her gaze I waved.

"I, err…I'll head over there," I said, and nodded toward my family. "But it was nice meeting you," I said to Hannes. I gave Monica a strained smile before getting to my feet.

"Hold on a minute, dear. I was going to ask you if…" I looked at Hannes in time to see him roll his eyes, "…you could help me and Hannes move his stuff into his new apartment?"

"We don't need that, Mom." Hannes interrupted before I could answer. I got the distinct feeling that he really didn't want to see me again. *Not much of a date*, my inner voice mocked. Maybe I would've wanted to avoid me too, if I was in his position. How many people assumed that they were being set up on blind dates at eight thirty in the morning, in church, during a group of six-year-olds' performance, anyway?

God, he wasn't even gay, and here I'd told him that it was okay if he didn't want to date me. He didn't, and it was okay, damn it! Why was I still stuck on this? Probably because he was cute, hot even, but mostly cute. Hell, it wasn't like I didn't make a fool out of myself on a regular basis. I just had to do what I always did—swallow my pride, pretend that nothing awkward had taken place, and the next time I saw him, treat him politely, but impersonally, like a customer.

"Don't be like that," Monica told him. "It'll be much quicker if we have some help. What do you say, Simon? If you help us move, I'll treat you boys to dinner."

I looked at Hannes again, but he wasn't looking in my direction. I didn't want to intrude, but I didn't want to disappoint Monica either. "Err, when do you need me?"

"Yay." Monica clapped her perfectly manicured hands in a girly fashion. "I know you have the weekend off, but tomorrow?"

I didn't have any plans, I never did. When I didn't work, I spent my time either confined in my apartment, wandering around town, or in my childhood home with my mother.

"Sure."

"Great! Around nine? At my place? You know where I live, right?"

"Yes," I said. "See you then." I gave a twitchy wave before heading over to my family.

14th of December

I groaned when the alarm woke me up. *Stupid day!* I jammed the snooze button. *Stupid month!* Yesterday, right when we'd been about to leave the parish house, Caroline had dropped the bomb—she wouldn't be coming for Christmas. They'd decided to celebrate the holiday in Gothenburg with Martin's parents this year.

I'd wanted to strangle her right there. How could she do that to me! Not only had she ripped apart our tradition, she'd killed what little holiday cheer we could get by taking Annie away from us—selfish thinking, I know—but, as if that wasn't enough, she'd held off on telling Mom until there were only eleven short days left.

Mom had instantly reverted into her shell—something she only ever did when Dad was saying nasty things—and left. I'd stayed a few more minutes just to glare at my sister. She knew perfectly well what she'd done, and that was precisely why she'd waited to tell us until we were in a public place. Mom wouldn't do her guilt-tripping thing in public, and I wouldn't be snarky, because we didn't do things like that when someone outside of the family could see. Caroline knew the rules.

The result of this whole thing was that I'd promised Mom to come stay during Christmas. Like, stay over night. I'd promised her to come on the twenty-third, help her prepare the baked Christmas ham, and decorate the tree. Then I would sleep in my old room, and we would have Christmas breakfast together.

The mere thought of it made me want to throw up. Why didn't I grow a backbone, and let Mom deal with the situation she'd put herself in? I didn't want to spend Christmas with my parents. I didn't want to see Dad pass out during *From All of Us to All of You.* Hell, some years he didn't even last until three p.m. Mom could sit there, stiff as a board, and watch Donald Duck and the others by herself.

She could have left him years ago if she'd wanted to. But, no, she stayed, and sat there on the sidelines while he drank their lives away. It wasn't as if she couldn't manage on her own, and we would help her—both Caroline and I—if she needed us. Heck, I understood why Caroline didn't want to bring Annie over. Who wants their daughter to see granddaddy pissed as a newt on Christmas Eve? Our Christmases definitely would not fit in an Ingmar Bergman movie, nor would they in any of Astrid Lindgren's fairy tales. My upbringing was far more kitchen sink realism than that.

The alarm sounded again, and I dragged myself out of bed. Why had I agreed to help Monica move her son's stuff today? Because he was cute, and I didn't know how to say, "No". He was also not gay, something I had to keep reminding myself.

I made a cup of coffee, forewent the shower—since I assumed I would be sweating soon—put on a pair of jeans and a T-shirt, grabbed a jacket, and headed for Monica's house. I brought my car in case we needed some more space for loading stuff.

When I got there, Hannes was standing in the driveway, looking nervous. Why was he nervous? Did I really make him that uncomfortable? I parked the car and stepped outside.

"Hi," I said with faked cheerfulness.

"Morning," he grumbled.

God, his voice made me shiver. Had it been that raspy yesterday?

"You don't have to help, if you don't want to," he said. "She'll understand."

"Oh, it's okay. I'm here now, might as well be of use."

He smiled. A smile that warmed my insides. "You always were kind."

"Huh?"

"Back in school. You were one of those kids that stuck to yourself, but you were always friendly and helpful if someone needed a hand with something."

"You noticed me in school?" Damn, I wish I'd noticed him in school. We couldn't have been in the same year, I would have known—if not him, then at least of him. So he was probably a year or two older than me, or younger. I looked at him, could he be younger? No, probably older. He had a sort of authority about him that made me assume he was older.

"Yeah, I always did notice you." He smiled for a moment, but his features gradually morphed into a bemused frown. Then, he glared.

"Simon, dear! How good of you to make it." Monica sounded happy, as always. "We've rented a trailer, but I'm not sure if I'm able to drive it, and Hannes doesn't like to drive with one. Do you know how to drive with a trailer?"

"Sure," I said. I'd driven with a trailer several times without any problems.

When Monica and I came back from the gas station with the rented trailer hitched to her car, Hannes had already carried some boxes out to the lawn.

"He doesn't have much," Monica told me. "And really, it wouldn't be a bother to have him living with me, since I'm alone in that big house, but I don't think it's good for a twenty-six-year-old to be living with his mother, do you?"

Ah, so older, then. I shuddered at the thought of living with my mother. "No, I guess not."

"He's a good man, just needs to find his way, and someone to share his life with." There it was again, that little gleam in her eye that made me think she was matchmaking. I had to be imagining since Hannes had clearly stated that he wasn't gay.

"Doesn't he have a girlfriend?" I asked, more to break my line of thought than from any real interest.

"Hmpft, he's had plenty. All of them lasting about a week. No, he doesn't need another girlfriend, he needs the one."

"The one?"

"One of the ones, whatever." She waved in a dismissive gesture. "Someone special. Someone more like you." *Like me?* I wanted to shout. What the hell did she mean? "No one is special to him, and he needs someone to care for, otherwise he'll just keep on drifting. Working way too much, and not caring for anything that's important."

"I'm sure you're special to him." I said, winked, and squeezed her arm affectionately, before jumping out of the car. This was one strange day, and I had no idea how to handle it.

. . .

The move was well organized. All the boxes were neatly packed and labeled, and the furniture was disassembled with all the associated screws and nuts taped onto each piece. The only thing that caused any problem was the sofa. No matter how we turned it, we couldn't make it fit in the trailer with the other stuff.

"We'll have to come back for it later," I said, wiping the sweat from my forehead.

"I guess," Hannes said, and started to close up the trailer.

"So, where are we going?"

"Oh, he'll be living about a block away from you," Monica chimed in.

"Err, okay." I climbed into the driver's seat without looking at Hannes. Why hadn't either one of them mentioned that before? Well, of course Hannes hadn't mentioned it. He probably didn't know where I lived, and he hadn't said more than ten words in total since that scowl he'd given me. He'd chatted a little with Monica, but to me he'd just grunted a few directions.

We drove in silence—no shocker there—Hannes only pointed out when I should turn to get to the right house. The atmosphere was awkward, and I was finding it difficult to ignore that I'd made a fool of myself. All I could think of was Hannes' horrified expression the day before, when he realized I thought we were on a date.

I couldn't understand why Monica was in such a good mood. Why on earth was she twittering like a bird in the backseat? Didn't she realize that this was a very embarrassing day?

My muscles were sore, and I knew I would be stiff in the morning, but I didn't let that slow me down. As soon as the car was parked, I was on my feet, ready to carry those boxes once again. I wanted this move to be over, and I wanted to go back to my place, have a shower, and veg out on the sofa. There, I could forget about Hannes' shining eyes and cute butt. I wouldn't have to see his muscles strain when he lifted a heavy box, or the way they moved beneath his skin when he tried to angle the sofa to make it fit in the trailer.

I rushed up the stairs with a box marked "Kitchen," and didn't stop until I put it down on the kitchen floor. At home I could take a long hot shower and forget that he'd had plenty of girlfriends. That thought made me perk up a little. To get into the shower and let Hannes guest star in my fantasies would be really nice.

No matter how hard I tried, I couldn't help myself from glancing in Hannes' direction every time I passed him on the stairs, or put a box down when he was in the apartment. His hair, short as it was, got disheveled when he started to sweat again, almost as if the curls wanted to make an appearance. He caught me looking, and for a moment I thought he was looking at me too, but then he glared, and stomped out to the staircase.

I watched him go. Had he been checking me out? I was almost certain that he had. Maybe I could…No that was just stupid thinking. Even if it looked as if he might be interested, he'd told me that he wasn't.

"You ready to head back for the sofa?"

I jumped an inch, or five, and whirled around to find Hannes watching me. "Yeah, sure," I said, trying hard not to blush. What had I been thinking? Letting my imagination wander like that in the middle of his apartment, which wasn't any bigger than mine, I might add.

"Mom will stay and unpack a little," he explained, glowering at me. I wondered if I'd done something to annoy him. Surely he couldn't know what I'd been thinking?

"Okay," I said.

In the hallway I accidentally brushed up against him, and he quickly stumbled away from me. I tried not to be hurt, but really, did he think I had something that was contagious?

I didn't say a thing during the entire ride back to Monica's, and neither did he. He was always talking to her, so I didn't understand why he couldn't say a few simple words to me. Earlier I'd decided not to say anything about it, but this was bordering on ridiculous—two grown men who couldn't speak when left alone.

"Have I offended you?"

"No, why?" He didn't look at me when he answered.

I sighed. "You can't even stand to look at me when you talk to me, which hasn't been very often, by the way."

He turned toward me, and smiled. I felt a burning need unfurl in the pit of my stomach. Damn, he was beautiful, but why did he smile?

"What do you want me to say? I'm sorry my mom hounded you into moving my stuff on your day off?"

"She didn't."

"Right, you just offer your services to anyone needing a hand. Like you didn't have anything better to do on a day like this." I didn't, but I wasn't about to tell him that.

The sofa fit easily in the empty trailer, and though my arms cramped on our way up the stairs, we managed to get it into Hannes' apartment in one piece.

"Great," Monica said, beaming. "So where do you boys want to go eat?"

Oh, this is my cue to get out of here. "I'll have to take a rain check on that, sorry."

"Oh, no, Simon. Don't run away now."

"Let him go, Mom. We've badgered him enough for one day." Hannes actually smiled at me again. Monica pouted, but he ignored her. "Thank you for your help."

"You're welcome," I mumbled, not sure what to make of his sudden friendliness. He was probably just happy to see me go, I thought to myself.

"How about dinner on Wednesday?" Monica asked.

"Mom, leave him be."

"No, it's common courtesy to feed someone when they've dedicated a day to carrying your stuff."

"Of course," Hannes answered. "How about you coming over for pizza, in a couple of days, when I've gotten a few things unpacked?"

"Err…okay?" Now, I was really confused. Did he want to spend time alone with me, or did he plan to blow me off?

"Great, thanks again!" He turned and walked toward the kitchen. What a strange man.

16th of December

I was back at work. I'd worked yesterday too, but there seemed to be a significant difference between yesterday and today. Yesterday, I'd only had one customer who wished me a Merry Christmas. Today, there'd already been five, and I'd only been here three hours. My stomach knotted. I hated the holidays.

This year, I hadn't even been lucky enough to get scheduled to work on Christmas Eve. I would be working on the twenty-third, as well as the twenty-fifth. Had I known that Caroline would celebrate Christmas in Gothenburg instead of Falkenberg, I would've tried a little harder to find someone who wanted to change shifts. No one wanted to work on Christmas Eve, so it wouldn't have been hard. But I hadn't, since I thought I would spend the day with Annie, and now I'd promised Mom. *Damn holidays!*

"What's gotten you all worked up?"

"Huh?" I looked up to see Hannes standing there with a six-pack of beer in his hand. He put it on the conveyor belt, waited for me to ring it up, and let it continue down the belt on the other side of the cash register, before looking up at me, again. "Slow day?"

"Nah, it's picking up."

"Holidays, ha?"

"Yup."

"So, you free tonight?"

"Err, yeah." Another customer came and started loading her groceries onto the belt.

"Want to come over, have something to eat?"

The cash register beeped as I worked. "Sure, what time?"

"Seven?"

I nodded.

"We'll order in, that okay?"

"Great."

"Good, see you then." He walked away after waving to Monica, who was working at the customer service checkout, as usual. She was the one who understood the postal and lottery systems best and always ended up behind that counter, no matter where she started her workday.

· · ·

I was nervous. Why the hell was I nervous? It was pizza, or whatever, as payment for carrying boxes on my day off. Nothing to fret about. Except, I always felt insecure when I was supposed to meet someone. The pressure of keeping conversation going, and not appearing too strange, felt like a burden—especially since everyone already knew how strange I was. If they didn't think of me as strange, they at least felt sorry for me.

I rang the doorbell, and waited for Hannes to come open the door. When he did I stood gaping. He was naked! Well, not naked. He had a towel wrapped around his waist, but he was dripping wet, and there were water droplets caught in his eyelashes.

"Sorry, I'm running late. Have a seat," he said, indicating the sofa. "I'll be right out."

I took off my shoes in the hallway, and went to sit on the sofa. Why had he opened the door clad in a towel? That wasn't fair. He had to know what he was doing to me. Or maybe he didn't; of course he didn't. He didn't think I would be lusting after him once he'd told me he wasn't interested. I was so damn stupid.

"So, what would you like? Pizza? Thai? I think I have the menu to that new Indian place down by the old train station, but I haven't tried it, have you?"

I shook my head. Hannes in sweats and a tee shirt was just as beautiful as Hannes in a towel, but now, at least, I could look at him without wanting to rip anything off of him. Or not really, but I told myself that I didn't want to rip anything off him.

"Pizza works for me." And it was the cheapest.

"Okay, pizza it is! What do you want on it?"

"Uh, just ham."

Hannes frowned. "Just ham?"

"Yeah, and pineapple."

"Okay..." Hannes took his phone, and went to the kitchen to place the order.

"It'll be fifteen minutes," he told me when he got back to the living room, or the only room really. "You want to watch a movie?"

"Sure."

He started to rummage around in a box that he'd placed next to the TV, and dug up some DVDs. "Sorry, I don't have much. Mostly Tim Burton, actually."

"That's fine." I knew nothing about movies, or who Tim Burton was.

"Sweeny Todd?"

"Absolutely," I answered, without knowing what I'd said yes to.

We ate our pizza and watched the movie. A musical—and he'd told me he wasn't gay, seriously? Though, I must say that I enjoyed it. I'd always steered clear of musicals because of Dad's hatred for them. Mom and I had watched a few, after he'd passed out some nights. She'd had this list of must-sees, movies she thought everyone should be familiar with, and some of them had been musicals. I couldn't really remember which I'd seen, but at least she'd tried to educate me.

The further the movie progressed, the more comfortable we made ourselves on the sofa. Hannes chatted along, and pointed out things in the movie that he liked, what was typical Burton, and so on. More than once, our arms brushed, and this time he didn't jerk away. I even tested it by intentionally touching him. He didn't invite, or act on it, but he didn't pull away either.

When the movie ended, I didn't feel that I had a reason to stay any longer. So, I sat up straight, and told him that I should head on home. As he followed me to the hallway, I thought I caught him checking out my ass, but that was probably a delusion on my part.

"Thanks," I said as I put on my shoes, "That was great."

"Yeah? If you'd like to, we could watch another Burton some other day."

"I'd love to."

I stood up and he took a step toward me, opened his mouth a little, and licked his lips. I nearly groaned. God, he was pretty! I almost thought he was going to kiss me. He was so close, his mouth opened, lips glistening. I leaned toward him a little, not obviously so, but definitely making it easier for him if he decided he wanted to kiss me. He leaned in a little too, and I was just about to close to my eyes, when he cleared his throat.

"So, you probably don't think Helena Bonham Carter is hot? I mean, if you're gay, you don't think she's hot, do you?" I stared at him. "I think she's hot. She's married to Tim Burton, did you know?"

I shook my head, and reached for the door handle. God, I was stupid! I had to get out of there. Hell, he probably thought I was insane, but I just couldn't stand the mixed signals any longer. The worst part was that there probably weren't any mixed signals at all. My brain had a mind of its own. *God!*

19th of December

Two days had passed since the disaster in Hannes' hallway; only four anxiety-free days to go. That was a lie, of course. People were already getting into their holiday cheer, which in turn spiked my anxiety. I hated holiday cheer, but I tried to be polite about it. Every time someone would wish me a Merry Christmas, I would shudder, but smile, and wish them one in return.

I really didn't understand why we put ourselves through it. All these expectations only led to disappointments. Everyone was stressed; parents were stressed, old people were stressed, even the children were stressed. There was so much pressure everywhere, traditions to follow, hopes and wishes to be fulfilled—no wonder alcoholics opted for staying drunk, or passed out, during the festivities. The twenty-fourth of December was the worst day of the entire year, not that I looked forward to New Year's Eve, Easter Eve, Midsummer Eve, or any other Eve, but Christmas Eve? I wished I could wipe that date out completely.

"Hi, there."

What is he doing here? It surprised me to see Hannes choosing my line. We had three other checkouts open. Not to mention that there were other grocery stores closer to where we lived. He could easily have avoided me if he'd wanted to, so what was he doing here?

"Hi."

"You okay?"

"Splendid," I muttered, with as much sarcasm I could muster.

"Seen any cute guys?" He wiggled his eyebrows.

"Just the one," I heard myself say before I could bite my tongue. He didn't seem to think I meant him, though.

"If I had your job, I would be flirting every day."

"Good for you," I mumbled under my breath. I didn't know why I felt surly. It wasn't as if he hadn't told me from the beginning that he wasn't interested, it was just that my stupid little brain didn't get the memo. When he said he'd be flirting every day, I wanted to strangle those girls, or him—or, really, both!

"Err…are you free tonight? You want to come over?"

"I'm free, but I don't know…" Didn't he know I was humiliated? I'd been sure he was about to kiss me, leaned in for God's sake, but instead of kissing me he'd started talking about some woman.

"Come over! We could watch *Big Fish* or *Alice in Wonderland*." Did he look hopeful? I thought he looked hopeful, which, of course, had to be utter nonsense. Maybe he was playing me, wanting to see if he could get the stupid son of a drunk to fall in love with him. Why would he do that, though? That was just dumb! When did I become this dumb?

"I don't know…" I wanted to, and that was what bothered me the most, that I really wanted to. It was nice to spend time with someone, even if he was going to talk about women he found hot.

"Come on, I'll cook."

"Can you cook? Because I don't like yucky food," I jested.

He smiled as if I'd just said the greatest thing. "I do know how to cook. If you tell me what you like, I'll make it for you."

My mind went blank. What did I like that was cheap? Pasta, I liked pasta. That was good, right? Or did it seem childish to say that you liked pasta?

"Erm…ah, I like just about anything, really."

Hannes frowned, in that same way he had when I'd said that I just wanted ham on my pizza. "So, say something. Anything you like."

"Pasta?"

"Sure, I can do pasta… You like crayfish?"

"Yes." God, I hoped he didn't plan on making me anything expensive.

"Saffron?"

I nodded. I loved saffron, in buns, pancakes, and with seafood, but it was expensive as hell. Mom had always saved and scraped for us to be able to have the same things as everyone else during Christmas. Saffron, though it might seem like a small expense in the scheme of things, was more often than not left off of the shopping list. Dad's whiskey had to be prioritized.

"Good," he said with a smile. "Seven o'clock work for you again?"

"Yeah," I croaked.

. . .

I stood outside Hannes' door, wondering what the hell I was doing. Pining after straight men had never been something I'd wasted time on, at least not since I became old enough to realize that straight men would never change their minds about wanting me. Feeding this infatuation would give me nothing more than a broken heart. I knew that, but that didn't stop the little flutter I felt in my belly when I raised my hand to ring the doorbell.

Hannes practically threw the door open. "Hi! Come on in. The food's almost ready." He was talking rapidly as he walked back toward the kitchen, looking a little nervous. "I made tagliatelle with shrimp, mussels, crayfish, saffron, and cream sauce." He made a gesture indicating that it was something he'd just thrown together in a twinkle, even though I could see that he'd made quite an effort. The mussels were fresh, their shells had opened in the pot, and he had peeled the shrimp himself, no pre-peeled frozen crap. I had thought I couldn't get more confused, but…Why did he go to all this effort? For me?

The kitchen table had been set with care, including wine glasses and candles. I stared at it. This felt like a date. Like I was being wooed, and I wasn't. He'd told me he liked girls, not guys. He wasn't gay, so what on Earth was I doing here?

"Have a seat, it's just about done."

I sat down, still not sure if I really should.

"Wine?"

"I, eh..." Oh, screw it, I could use a glass of wine. "Sure, thank you."

He poured me a glass, then served the pasta, with a salad, and some garlic bread. I ate in reverence. It was delicious, and I wanted to cherish it since it was probably the only time he would cook like this for me. I shouldn't let him cook again, it wasn't good for my mental health. The voices in my head were arguing it out, one telling me this was a date, one saying Hannes was just being friendly, and yet another telling me I didn't deserve this, and even if he'd been gay there was no way he would want me.

Dinner for two, with white wine and candlelight, that wasn't a date: that was what this was. I had to get that into my thick head. The sultry music playing in the background wasn't there to be romantic, it was simply something he'd been listening to while cooking. Preparing food, for what had to be hours, was something you could do for a friend, right? Candles, wine, and romantic music, that could be a dude's night in, couldn't it?

"So... How was your day?" Hannes asked after a while.

"Okay, nothing unusual. You know, just people shopping."

He smiled and watched me eat. "Yeah? No funny episodes to share?"

I had to ponder that. Had anything funny happened today? Sometimes I got a little blind this time of year, a little self-centered, and had to be reminded that there was a world outside my silent monologues. But, no, I couldn't think of anything special. Mrs. Johansson had forgotten her wallet, again. One-eyed Krister had tried to buy one match, again, even though he knew he had to at least buy one box. He got to buy them one box at a time, because Monica was nice enough to break a package every now and then. That way he didn't have to buy ten boxes; he could just buy the one. It wasn't easy being a drunk at the end of the month, though I would argue that the nineteenth was still fairly in the middle. Monica felt sorry for them when they were in desperate need of a smoke and had drunk all their money away. She was a far nicer person than me—at least when it came to the drunks.

"No, sorry. You?"

"Nah, I'm not starting my new position until January, so I have about two more weeks off."

"Oh." I didn't know that. "Where will you be working?"

"I'm a police sergeant."

I sat up straight in my chair. "You're a what!" Jeez! Had I ever done anything illegal?

Hannes laughed. "See, that's why I didn't tell you. You look like you're about to bolt."

I felt as if I was about to bolt. I was in a police officer's home. Having dinner, chatting, as if he was normal people. *Oh my God, I'd been driving with him in the car. What if I'd run a red light, or something.* Not that I ever had, but it wouldn't surprise me if I had done it when he was in the car.

"Relax, Simon. I'm not gonna put you in cuffs…unless you want me to." He winked, and I spluttered wine all over my plate before, of course, choking on some. What the hell? Hannes got a little worried when I couldn't seem to stop coughing, and asked me if there was anything I wanted him to do. Luckily, I couldn't respond verbally, or I would probably have asked him to cuff me, so I just shook my head.

"You…err," I croaked, "you've just moved back to town?"

"You thought I'd been living with my mother until now." He looked horrified, and I wheezed out a laugh.

"I don't know, she hardly ever talks about you."

"She doesn't?" He looked surprised. "I thought I was the only thing she talked about."

"Really?" I had to think about when Monica did talk about Hannes, but couldn't really come up with any particular occasions. I mean, I'd known she had a son, but she'd never mentioned his work, or where he lived, or anything really. "No, she doesn't talk about you very often, not to me at least." She was far too busy mothering me to talk about her real son.

"Huh," Hannes seemed thoughtful. "That's strange."

I shrugged. "Where did you live before?"

"Gothenburg. But I got tired of the big city, gang violence, and all the crap that just doesn't happen around here. So when a position opened up, I applied, and I got it. Mom's pleased, of course, though she worries that I'll be lonely."

I nodded my reply, remembering the blind date that in reality was a playdate. My first. No parent before Monica had wanted their child to play with me.

. . .

After dinner we put on a movie, and relaxed on the sofa. It was another Tim Burton. Some strange tale about a man who caught a fish in a river with a wedding ring, but I couldn't really concentrate. I'm sure it was beautiful, or funny, or thoughtful, but I couldn't take it in. My mind was preoccupied with trying to solve the date puzzle, or rather the non-date puzzle.

I felt as if I'd been wined and dined, and the comment about the cuffs didn't help my poor little brain along, at all. Why did he cook for me, and not just cook—he made me feel cherished. His arm kept touching mine, ever so lightly, but frequently enough for me to suspect it wasn't a coincidence. Or was it? Maybe he was so caught up in the movie, that he didn't notice how often he was touching me. I moved away, just an inch or two. He looked at me, a little confused, hurt almost.

"You okay?"

"Sure, I was just err…heading for the bathroom."

"Oh, you want me to pause?"

"No, it's alright. I'll be quick."

In the bathroom I stopped in front of the mirror, and tried to slow my breathing. What was I doing here? Really, I was swooning over a straight man…and why? Because he was hot, sure, but that wasn't really it. I mean, the world is full of hot men, and I don't go around pining after all of them. He had me so confused, I was at my wit's end. At one moment he was touching me, saying things no straight man ever should, even had me thinking he was about to kiss me, and in the next he'd be talking about women.

I splashed some water on my face, before I stared deeply into my own eyes in the mirror, and muttered, "Go home, Simon. Tell him you have to get up early tomorrow, that you're tired. And then, next time he asks you to come over, you say no. No! Can you do that?"

"Are you alright in there?" Hannes shouted from the other side of the door.

Great. "Yeah, I'll be out in minute!" God, how embarrassing.

"Are you sure?"

"Yes!" *Damn it!* But, of course, I didn't say the last part.

"Okay." I heard him go back to the living room, waited a minute or two before I unlocked the door, and stepped out.

I stopped in front of the sofa. He'd paused the movie and was looking expectantly at me. "I think I'll head home. I'm feeling a little tired."

"Are you sure? You're not ill, are you?"

"No, no, just tired."

I went toward the hallway to put on my shoes and my jacket. "I'll be fine as soon as I get some sleep."

"You sure? If you're not feeling well, you give me a call, you hear?" I nodded, and he stepped in close. He raised his hand to rearrange a lock of hair on my forehead. "I like your hair," he mumbled as he put the lock behind my ear.

I looked at him, dumbfounded. Really, what was he doing? "Erm, thank you for tonight. The food was delicious."

"Oh, my pleasure! I would love to do it again sometime."

I nodded, and turned to the door. Seems like it didn't help practicing saying "no" in the mirror. My therapist was wrong about that, that's for sure.

23rd of December

I was about to have an ulcer. If anyone else said "Merry Christmas," I would strangle them. Right there on the spot! I had about thirty minutes left till the end of my shift, but I wouldn't be any freer once I got out of here. It would be many, many hours before I would be able to breathe again. Okay, maybe twenty-four—nah, that was being optimistic. More like thirty.

After this, I would go home, have a quick shower, pack an overnight bag, and head over to my parents' house. Seriously, there was nothing merry about that. And, as if that wasn't enough, Hannes kept texting me. Yesterday, he'd even come here. I'd been on my way to the lunchroom for my late break, when I'd seen him. It looked like he was searching for me by the checkouts, but I wasn't sure. Later, of course, he'd been texting me, again.

I didn't know how to interpret the texts. They were short, often funny, sometimes a little sweet, and those were the ones that threw me. Jokes I understood, but an *I was thinking of you…* was a whole other thing.

"Daydreaming again?"

I startled. Really, how can you be startled by someone's voice when you're constantly surrounded by people? "I guess."

Hannes smiled. "What were you dreaming of?"

"A Christmas far, far away where no one would hear me scream."

His smile dimmed. "You don't like Christmas?"

"Crappiest holiday, if you ask me."

"Oh. Why?"

"Because I have to spend it with my parents." I was trying to joke, but I could see it had the complete opposite effect on him. Instead of taking that as something funny, he seemed to recall something about my parents, and you didn't have to be a brain surgeon to know what it was. As if on cue, the pity came.

"But…do you have to celebrate with them?"

I felt a lump in my throat. I knew I didn't have to. My therapist had tried very hard to teach me how to put myself first. She'd talked about how children of addicts always stayed loyal to their parents, no matter what, but that I didn't have to. She'd said I needed to break my patterns. It wasn't my responsibility to take care of them, and my mother was old enough to make her own decisions. No use in hurting myself when there was nothing I could do to make the situation better for anyone.

"Yeah, I kind of do. My sister won't be there this year, and if I don't show they'll be all alone."

"Oh, okay. Why don't you come over to my place tonight, and we'll celebrate a little together, just the two of us?"

"Err, no. I'm going straight over there. Decorating the tree, making the toffee, and of course the dreaded dipping in the pot." I hated dipping in the pot. It was utterly disgusting if you asked me. To dip bread into the stock from the Christmas ham, and then eat it. "I swear, I'll go vegetarian till next year."

Hannes laughed. "Then it'll only be cabbage, toffee, and root beer for you."

"I can live with that."

The next customer in line made a disapproving sound when Hannes didn't go to the end of conveyor belt after he'd paid. He just stood by the till and watched me ring up the woman's items, rocking back and forth on his heels. Several times it looked like he was about to say something, but as soon as he opened his mouth he shut it again. By the time the last of the woman's things was on the belt he started to move away to let her pay.

"Give me a call if it gets to be too much for you, and we'll go for a walk or something. We can even bring your mother, if you want."

"Oh, ah, no. I don't think that would work. I'll text you, okay?"

"And I'll text you," he said, and went to put his things into a plastic bag. Though, he hardly needed a plastic bag for a package of coffee and a chocolate bar. It was like he'd gone shopping, all the way across town, on the twenty-third just for the fun of it. I watched him go, and wondered, once again, what I was doing with this man.

"When are people gonna stop flirting with you," the woman who had been in line behind Hannes grumbled. "It would be much quicker for the rest of us if the people who came here, came for the shopping instead of a chance to talk to you." I stared at her. What the hell was she talking about? Holiday stress must have made her delusional.

24th of December

I woke early, and the first thing I wished was for the day to be over. I think many say they dislike Christmas without really meaning it. But I despise it, I really do. It's supposed to be this happy holiday where families get together, children get their wishes fulfilled, and everyone is watching *From All of Us to All of You* at three p.m. on channel one. That is how Christmas is supposed to be celebrated.

It wasn't that we didn't do all of that. Though, as far as I could remember, the kids in our house didn't get their wishes fulfilled, but other than that we did all the holiday BS. God, I did not want to have to live through this one more year. The knot in my stomach that had been forming there since yesterday— who was I kidding, it had been growing since Advent Sunday—was, if possible, even bigger today.

Instead of Christmas miracles we had a lot of tension, instead of happy laughter we had silence, instead of children playing we had a drunkard snoring. Santa hadn't visited our house since I was six. For Santa to come, Dad would have to be awake, and that was something I hadn't experienced in many, many years. It wasn't Christmas without whiskey fumes. I'd actually been sixteen before I realized that the smell of whiskey wasn't what other people associated with Christmas.

I'd been at a summer party with some of my classmates, and thought it strange that someone would have such a Christmassy smell to their home in the middle of August. Turned out that it was the whiskey they were drinking. Blessedly, I hadn't opened my mouth to ask about it. I'd been about to, I won't deny that, but since no one else seemed puzzled by it, I'd kept quiet just long enough to figure it out by myself. If Dad hadn't always been short of money, I probably would have known that whiskey wasn't a Christmas thing, but since he only could afford to drink it at Christmas, how was I to know?

Thing is, when growing up with a drunk, you get to see plenty of drinking, but you don't learn the social customs around it. I didn't grow up completely isolated from other people. I had an aunt I adored, and a granny who still had her wits about her. But we couldn't invite them over on holidays. They would have seen the state of our family if we had, and if there was one thing my mother knew how to do, it was to keep the ugliness hidden.

Everyone in town knew what was going on inside the walls of our house, but we tried very hard not to let it show. My father wasn't a particularly bad man. He had a sharp tongue, but he'd never hit us, or anything like that. He was just a drinker, a boozer, an alcoholic. And we'd been taught at a very young age to tiptoe around him. We kids didn't know much, but we knew how to be quiet.

This year, I feared it would be even worse than it normally was. Without Caroline and her family here, Mom wouldn't even have to keep up the façade. Every year, she strived to make us look like a normal family. We had all the right decorations, every inch of the house was scrubbed clean, she spent days baking rosettes, gingerbread biscuits, and almond cookies. As always, there were Christmas cloths on every table, all the curtains were Christmassy, the ham was cooked, the meatballs fried, the cabbage prepared, and the pickled herring purchased. All that was left to do was to boil a few eggs, and then Christmas dinner would be served. Mom had done all of that. I'd helped a little yesterday by making the toffee. I did that every year; it was sort of my thing. But why we had done it at all, I didn't know.

I dreaded going downstairs, and that was the only reason I was still in bed. Dad had passed out on the sofa before nine p.m. yesterday. Nine p.m. was quite early—even by his standards—which, more likely than not, meant that he would already be up.

Christmas Eve meant whiskey, something he'd been looking forward to the entire year, so I was pretty sure he'd already started. I should go downstairs, though. By now, he'd be happy. We would be able to have a nice ham sandwich, and a root beer together, before things went south.

I heard Mom go downstairs, and I heaved a sigh before flipping back the cover. Christmas was here. There would be all kinds of televised nostalgia, pictures from the royal family, and other nonsense. All that was left for me to do was to put on my fake smile, and live through it.

My phone beeped as I stood balancing with one foot in a sock. A little surprised, I reached for it, and saw an incoming text from Hannes.

Good morning! I'm free to play superhero if you want to be rescued.

I couldn't help but smile. Not that I knew what I was smiling about. It was Christmas, after all. Still, Hannes had offered to come rescue me.

. . .

In the middle of *From All of Us to All of You* my phone beeped again. Dad was snoring loudly on the sofa, spreading the fumes of alcohol farther into the house with each breath. Mom sat wedged stiffly into the corner on the opposite end from Dad, her fake smile in place, but her eyes dull. To get a text at this time was about the greatest gift I could wish for, one little beep to lure my thoughts away from this sad display of a broken family *celebrating* Christmas.

I whisked the phone out of my pocket at the same moment that Ferdinand the Bull ran into the arena to smell the bouquet of flowers a woman in the audience had thrown in.

The text was from Hannes. I smiled as I touched the little envelope on the display.

Come outside. I want to give you something.

I kept on smiling, peeked out the window, and saw him standing by the mailbox.

"What are you doing?" Mom whispered, as if anything other than a freight train running through the living room would wake Dad up.

"I'm just gonna go outside for a moment."

"In the middle of *From All of Us to All of You?*" Mom hissed, outraged.

"Yes, right in the middle of *From All of Us to All of You*. It's not like Annie is here. We don't have to watch it! We've seen it, like, a thousand times. We know the lines by heart, both you and I."

"It's tradition."

"Yes, Mom. This—" I waved at Dad's snoring form "—is tradition. No wonder Caroline took Annie away from us. If I ever have children I sure as hell won't be bringing them here!" Mom started crying, silently of course, and I felt like a piece of crap. I didn't want to make her cry, I really didn't, but she had to see how we were living.

"I'm sorry, Mom. I'll just be a minute. I'll be back before *Pluto's Christmas Tree* is over."

She sniveled, but nodded, as I headed to the hallway. I stepped into a pair of Dad's slippers, and opened the door. The afternoon was chilly, but not cold. We didn't get a white Christmas this year, not that I cared, I wanted my Christmases to be wet, grey, and depressing—it was tradition.

"Sorry to bother you in the middle of *From All of Us*," Hannes said, and grinned. His nose was a little red from the cold, and I wondered just how long he'd been out here.

"Nah, it's cool. Not as if I haven't seen it twenty-four times already."

"Oh, only twenty-four? We had it on VHS when I was a kid. I swear I've seen it a thousand times."

"Feels like I've seen it a thousand times."

"Yeah, but it's tradition. If I ever have children I'm gonna pin them to the sofa every year, until they understand that it isn't Christmas without it."

I smiled. "I'm pretty sure that's illegal, officer."

He shrugged, and started to look a little tense. I couldn't spot any wrapped gift anywhere, and got curious. "So...what did you want to give me?"

145

I couldn't help but chuckle, when he started to rock back and forth on his feet. Something really had him nervous.

"It's just, I just…" He leaned in, and very lightly pressed his lips against mine. I smelled his cologne as I drew in a trembling breath. It was more of a lip caress than a kiss. He didn't really kiss me, he just kept his lips, lingering, on mine. I didn't know if I should move or stand still. Should I kiss him? I wanted to kiss him. I really did, but this was nice, too. Very nice. Nicer than I'd ever thought I would experience on a Christmas Eve.

When he retreated, I grabbed his arm to stop him from going too far away. "But, you're not gay," I said.

"Yeah, well. Strange that, because I can't think of anything I'd rather do than kiss you." He rubbed the pad of his thumb over my lower lip. "I don't know what I am, Simon. I've never wanted to kiss any man but you. You, I can't seem to get out of my mind, but you're the only one. I want you, and I can't really explain it." He looked downright scared.

"You want to kiss me?"

"I do," he said with a faint smile. "I've always wanted to, even back in school when you were nothing more than a scrawny kid."

I felt his breath warm my skin before his lips touched mine again. This time he didn't linger. His fingers stroked my chin, as he angled my head ever so slightly, and begged for entrance with his tongue. I moaned as I opened for him, let myself go boneless, and felt, more than heard, his answering moan. We stood like that for a long time. My fingers gripping his jacket, and him holding me close while we explored each other's mouths in a slow, soft kiss.

I broke free, and mumbled, "Good," before gently brushing with my lips over the light stubble on his cheek.

"Yeah, good," he said, with longing in his voice. "Inside with you." He swatted my butt. "I'll give you a call tonight, okay?"

"Okay. I'll be back at my place after dinner."

"I'll come over later then, if that's okay?"

"Okay."

"Oh, and Simon?"

"Yeah?" I asked, a little afraid that he would say something about the kiss that would ruin my newfound and unexpected holiday cheer.

"Merry Christmas."

Never had I thought those words would make me smile, but they did. I blew him a kiss, before I ran up the stairs, and hurried inside so I could watch the end of the movie with my mother.

The End.

HOMME FOR THE HOLIDAYS

Jonathan Penn

ACKNOWLEDGEMENTS:

Boundless Gratitude
for the constant and unerring benefaction of
Al, Deb, Joanne, Kaje, Margitta, Ofelia,
and Tami (or Pati, as she's known to some).

Special thanks to Guillaume Loup,
who helped Cade bone up on his conversational French.

Mid pleasures and palaces though we may roam,
Be it ever so humble, there's no place like home.

—John Howard Payne, (1791-1852)

Return

Screech! Screech! Screech! Screech!

Cade Bishop's eyes flew open as his hand flew to the alarm clock, stopping the infernal racket. He lay still and quiet for a while, studying the ceiling. He'd been dreaming about the night four years ago that changed his life forever. For more than a year after the attack, the nightmares had been violent, terrifying, and regular as clockwork. They'd faded over time, to the point where that gruesome experience rarely invaded his sleep. This one hadn't been a nightmare, but it hadn't been pleasant either. His heart rate slowed as indecipherable wisps of the dream faded from memory, and he gladly let them go.

The sound of a nearby breath caught his attention, and he smiled. Now *that* was pleasant. He freed his other hand from the sheets and rolled over to plant a tender kiss on an exposed shoulder. "Alan?" He got a gravelly groan in response. He gave the shoulder a gentle bite. "Alan. Time to get up."

"Hrgh!" Alan rolled onto his back and crossed his forearms over his eyes. "Is this one of your little jokes?"

"Not a joke. Come on, we've got to get moving."

"Mmmm." Alan rolled back onto his side and pulled a pillow over his head.

"Alan!" Cade climbed out of bed, came around the other side, and ripped back the covers. "Hey, this wasn't my idea." He took Alan's hand and tugged hard enough to shift him to the edge of the mattress.

"Alright. Alright!" Alan sat up and blinked, then squinted. "You know, the day I left the service, I swore I'd never get up at oh-dark-thirty again. But for you—" A ferocious yawn ripped through him, stretching his mouth and his arms wide. When it released him, he looked up at Cade and sighed in resignation.

Cade pursed his lips, then blew a flirty kiss at Alan. "I'm going to take a minute to freshen up. Can I trust you to get dressed while I'm gone? Everything's laid out."

"Yes, Dear," Alan singsonged as he swung his legs over the side and stood up.

Cade stepped toward the bathroom, keeping an eye on Alan as he went—suspicious that he would slip into bed again the moment his back was turned. He brushed his teeth and splashed cold water on his face before returning to the bedroom. Alan was gone, and so were his clothes, so he took that as a good sign. He dressed, then emerged into the great room, and found Alan in the entryway, wrapped in his parka, the hood pulled low over his face. He was leaning his head and one shoulder against the front door, gently rocking back and forth.

"Oh, Alan. You look pitiful."

"Please pity me!" Alan turned a woeful pout on Cade. "Why am I up when the sun isn't?"

"May I remind you again, sir," Cade said, with playful formality, "this was your idea? We are leaving at this insane hour so we have time for you to treat me to a Buildwell House Christmas before we go to my folks' place for dinner."

"Oh yeah. That." Alan groaned. "I guess I did this to myself." He groaned again.

"Let's just bite the bullet and do this, shall we? Or, whatever it is you big, strong Marine types say?"

Alan snapped to attention, gave a crisp salute, and roared out, "Oorah!"

"Yeah. Hooray, or whatever…"

Alan smirked and shook his head.

Cade couldn't help the grin that stole across his lips. Alan was so adorable when he was sleepy. Cade took his jacket from its peg and slipped into it, then picked up their bags from where he'd placed them by the door the previous night. He handed one to Alan. "Let's go, okay?"

He took Alan's hand as they walked down the two flights of stairs and out to the parking lot. He pressed the button on his key fob to pop the trunk open as they approached the black Mercedes. They threw their bags in and he slammed it shut, moving quickly to get out of the icy morning air.

He climbed into the driver's seat and, as he buckled up, he looked over at Alan, slumped in the passenger seat. "You did put the gifts in the trunk last night, right?"

Alan's head shot up and his eyes went wide. "I thought *you* were putting the gifts in the trunk!"

Cade shook his head.

"Jeez! Wouldn't that have been perfect—showing up at your parents' house without gifts!"

Cade wasn't about to sweat the small stuff; he was far too excited over the prospect of the day ahead. "No worries. I'll get some heat going, then I'll be right back." He cranked the engine and turned on the heater, then got out and ran back into the building. When he returned, he found Alan sound asleep. He'd taken off his parka and reclined the seat. He was drawing deep breaths through his nose, and each time he exhaled his lips made a little puffing sound. Alan was so dear! Cade swallowed hard around the lump forming in his throat. Lately, he'd been noticing more and more moments like this, where something so simple would stop him in his tracks and make him realize how lucky he was.

He settled himself and closed the door quietly, backed the car out of the parking space, and turned it toward a future he'd been waiting months to see unfold.

. . .

Maintaining his grip at ten and two, Cade pushed hard against the wheel, pressing his shoulders back into the leather seat. He yawned. There was still no hint of the rising sun in his rearview mirror, and the air outside the plush compartment hovered just above freezing. Worse yet, he'd committed the sacrilege of skipping coffee in their rush to leave Durham before six a.m. And yet, the truth was…he felt good. He couldn't remember the last time he'd felt so good. He took his eyes from the road and turned to glance at the slumbering form of Alan Troxler—the man who'd made such a sudden and unexpected entrance into his life less than a year ago. The man who now made it possible to be happy in the cold and dark at Oh-God o'clock.

Though technically it was Christmas Eve, their early start meant traffic was almost non-existent. He'd passed one car ten minutes ago, filled with small children cavorting about in bright red Santa hats. Earlier, there'd been a minivan with one of those fake reindeer behinds sticking out of its grill, as if the poor thing had crashed. He knew there was no accounting for taste, but there were times he was certain there should be.

Looking ahead and behind, he saw no hint of headlights or taillights. It made him feel a little lonely, which was silly; if he wanted to, he could reach over and touch his boyfriend. In fact, he did want to, but he wasn't about to disturb Alan's nap. They had a big day planned, and he wanted his man well-rested.

The dim light from beneath the console drew Cade's attention to a pair of big, bare feet, and he decided it wouldn't jeopardize their safety too terribly if he was to take a surreptitious inventory. He looked for traffic, then back at the floorboard. A few tantalizing leg hairs peeped out from under the hem of Alan's jeans. Sadly not the tight ones for a three-hour car ride, but even this loose pair clung to Alan's massive thighs.

He checked out the windshield again, then gazed back at Alan, scanning from thigh to waist to chest. The tee shirt was tight enough to reveal well-developed pecs. His mind replayed the sensation of combing his fingers through the silky thatch of black hair that covered Alan's chest. When they'd first met, there'd been a nearly-bare patch down the center revealing surgical scars from his war wounds. Now that the hair had grown back the scars weren't visible, but Cade still liked tracing his fingertips over their nubby texture. Alan said they didn't hurt, and it was a good reminder to Cade of just how precious—and tenuous—life really was.

151

After one more check for traffic, he focused on Alan's ear. Those ears were Alan's weak spots. Cade giggled, remembering the sounds that came out of this big bear of a man when his ear was being nibbled.

He followed the curve of Alan's cheek to his eyes. Long black lashes curled away from lids which now obscured the most beautiful eyes he'd ever seen. They were black—black as midnight. Cade easily became lost when he looked into them.

A quick correction with the wheel kept the car from drifting as badly as his thoughts. But he couldn't resist one more look at Alan's face. He grinned. It was surprising how quickly that face had come to feel like home. They'd met last April, only eight months ago, but sometimes when he looked at that face…it felt as if they'd known each other for lifetimes. There was just something about Alan, something so open and warm, that Cade always felt at ease when he was with him. He returned his full attention to the road ahead and resolved to keep his focus on driving, but it was sweet to realize even a boring task like this was better with Alan beside him.

He adjusted the cruise control to a more reasonable speed as they approached Winston-Salem. Then, he switched it off and slowed even more as they got close to downtown. This part of the I-40 had been built before the people in charge of such things had figured out it was better to have freeways go around cities, rather than through them. As such, it wove its way through the center of the town in a series of sharp curves. Whether it was the change in speed, or the centrifugal force from the curves, it woke Alan.

"Mmm. Winston?"

"Yup."

"I must have slept an hour?"

"More like an hour and a half. You were out like a light before we even hit the road."

"Good. I feel a little better. I am so not a morning person."

"Since you're awake…Winston reminds me…Mom used to bring me down here every December to see *The Nutcracker* at the School of the Arts. It's an amazing production! The choreography and sets and costumes are all copied from the Ballet Russe de Monte Carlo."

"Ah, yes." Alan gave a knowing nod. "I see."

Cade rolled his eyes. "The sun's just now coming up. Don't you think it's a little early in the day for you to start humoring me?" He turned a dour face to Alan, then broke into a grin.

"Cade, you know I don't know anything about ballet."

"I was thinking, maybe next year we could come and see it together."

Alan's face tightened.

"Oh, c'mon! You said you don't know anything about it, so that means you don't know if you'd like it or not."

152

"Fair enough. I'll make a deal with you, then. You come with me to a Bulls game next summer, and I'll go with you to the ballet next winter."

"Bulls. Baseball?"

"Yes." The determined look in Alan's eyes told Cade that resistance was futile.

He swallowed hard, then forced a smile. "Okay. It's a deal. I mean, you love baseball. It's important to you, and that makes it important to me."

Alan leaned close and lowered his voice. "You know what?"

"What?"

"If you don't know anything about it, you don't know if you'd like it or not."

Cade chuckled. "There's me—hoist with my own petard!"

Alan laughed.

"I just know you'll love *Nutcracker*. We haven't gone the last few years, but it's a real tradition with us. Kind of like your family's tradition with the Buildwell House."

"Yeah. It's been twelve years since I've been there."

"So, I was thinking, maybe next year we could combine them—a night in Winston for the ballet and then on to Asheville to tour the house?" Hearing his words as they came out, it struck him that he was making long-term plans for being with Alan. That was new. The warm, fuzzy feeling it gave him was new as well.

"Sounds good."

The city receded behind them, and the view from the car returned to monotonous seas of pine trees on either side, broken only by the occasional exit ramp.

"You must be hungry." Cade took his eyes off the road for a moment to glance over at Alan.

"I could eat a horse."

"Hmm." Cade furrowed his brow. "A few exits up, just before Statesville, there's a great little diner. Marilyn and I used to stop there on our trips to Winston. I don't think they serve horse, but I'm pretty sure you can get any other kind of meat you want."

"How're we doing for time?"

"We're good. We can eat and still make it to Buildwell by ten."

"Great!" Alan rubbed his hands vigorously. "Meat Time!" He bent over, retrieved his sneakers from the floorboard, and began slipping them on.

A short while later, Cade exited the freeway and made a few turns, pulling up in front of a classic chrome and glass diner that looked like it had been teleported in from the 1950s. There were only a few cars in the gravel parking lot, and Cade pulled to a stop near the door. The air was icy, but they didn't bother with jackets—sprinting the few yards to get into the warmth.

The inside of the diner looked as rustic as the outside, and it smelled a little rustic too—like decaying wood and Pine-Sol. There was a long stainless steel counter with stools bolted to the front of it. Lining the windows were booths of lackluster chrome and faded red vinyl. As they slid into a booth, the sagging seats let out a groan of protest and the ancient upholstery crackled. Fastened to the far end of the table, nestled between a napkin dispenser and a rack that held menus and condiments, there was one of those miniature individual juke box thingies. This one had a dilapidated look about it and, judging by the songs listed on the card behind the glass, had probably been out of service for about as long as the typewriter that had produced the card.

Alan took a menu and started looking it over. Cade was about to do the same when movement caught his eye. He turned to observe a slender young man in an apron swishing toward an older heavy-set man in a plaid flannel shirt who was seated at the far end of the counter. The waiter warmed the man's coffee and then swished over to their booth.

"Coffee, gentlemen?" He pursed his lips as he offered the pot.

They both turned their cups over on the saucers—the universal sign for "Yes, please."

The waiter cocked out his left elbow, placed his hand on his hip, and gave Cade a condescending smile as he filled his cup. When he turned and started filling Alan's, Alan looked up from the menu. Even from his angle, Cade could see the young man making goo-goo eyes.

"Hi, I'm Jamie. Are you ready to order?" he asked, completely ignoring Cade—or possibly pretending he didn't exist.

"Hi, Jamie. I'm Alan, and I'll have two eggs, over easy, with bacon and sausage."

"Patties or links?"

"Oh." For a moment, Alan looked torn. "Can I have both?"

"You can have anything your little heart desires, Alan."

Cade watched the boy flirt. He felt his cheeks and his ears getting hot. He cleared his throat. Loudly. "Cade here! I'll have the French toast. Please!"

Jamie continued to face Alan, but turned his head and said over his shoulder, "Of course you will, dear." He gave Cade a weak smile, then a wink, and then swished away.

There was a twinkle in Alan's eye. "You're jealous!"

"Don't be ridiculous! Of what? Him? He's a boy with a coffee pot. Why would I be jealous?" But he could still feel the heat on his face, and he needed to splash some cold water on it. "If you'll excuse me, I need to use the restroom." He scooted out of the booth and then paused, looking down at Alan. "Do you think you'll be alright out here on your own?" He raised an eyebrow and tipped his head in the direction of the waiter's exit.

Alan laughed. "Go ahead, Cade. I think I can keep it in my pants long enough for you to pee."

After standing briefly at the urinal, and for a much longer time at the sink, Cade came out of the men's room to see Jamie leaning against his side of the booth, fiddling with the strings on his apron and chatting with Alan. As he approached, the young man looked up, startled, and beat a hasty retreat to the kitchen.

Cade slid back into the booth, scrutinizing the amused expression on Alan's face. "What were you two talking about?" he asked as he pulled out far more napkins than necessary from the dispenser and tucked into his French toast.

"He asked for my phone number."

Cade did his best to keep his eyebrows under control. "What did you say?"

Alan's smile was warm and reassuring. "I told him that the guy in the restroom was my boyfriend, and that he might look kinda puny, but it wouldn't be smart to get him riled up."

Cade tried to snort but couldn't because he'd just taken a bite.

The smile faded from Alan's lips. "I don't know why he'd be interested in me, anyway."

Cade swallowed. Alan amazed him sometimes. He leaned in and lowered his voice. "You really don't, do you?"

Alan shook his head.

Cade leaned closer and whispered, "It's because…" He looked left, then right, then back at Alan. "You're a total hottie!"

Alan laughed and rolled his eyes, but his expression became serious, and he lowered his voice, almost matching Cade's whisper. "I think it's really nice that you're jealous."

Cade drew a breath for another denial, but thought better of it. He sighed. "A few minutes ago, it sounded like some kind of accusation. But you're right. It's weird, though. I don't think I've ever reacted like that before."

"Well, you can count on the same reaction from me when somebody hits on you," Alan said, leaning back in the booth.

Cade watched as Jamie warmed the old man's coffee again. He turned back to Alan. "I can't imagine what it would be like growing up gay in a tiny town like this. Durham and Chapel Hill are cool, and they call Carrboro the Paris of the Piedmont, but out here? Yeesh! People in these parts elect conservatives to Congress. And not just any conservatives—we're talking way-right, wacko uber-conservatives!" In the past, Alan had seemed to enjoy discussing politics, but the look on his face right now said he was a million miles away. "What's up, Alan?"

"I guess I'm just nervous about meeting your folks. I should have come with you last summer, but I'd just started my job, and now it seems like the longer I've put it off, the worse it's gotten."

155

"Alan! You've got nothing to be nervous about. They're really excited to meet you, and you already know they're fine with me being gay."

"I believe you about the gay thing not being a problem, but…"

"But what?" Silence. "Come on, Alan, what is it?"

"What if…I mean, there's no way I can measure up to their hopes for their only child. They probably expect you to pair up with somebody rich and famous, or, at least rich. I have next to nothing."

Cade leaned across the table. "You have everything that matters." He rested his hand on top of Alan's. "Everything that matters to me, anyway."

A swishing sound heralded the return of Jamie, and Cade was astounded when Alan quickly withdrew his hand and leaned back from the table. The waiter tore a slip of paper from his pad. As he began to extend it toward Alan, Cade snatched it from his fingers. "I've got this." He saw the objection begin to form on Alan's lips, and avoided it by rising from the booth and walking over to the cash register with Jamie at his heels.

When he'd finished paying, he turned to find Alan waiting by the door. As they dashed through the cold, Cade pressed the button to unlock the doors.

"Want me to drive the rest of the way? You could catch a few Zs."

"That would be great!" Cade tossed the keys and slipped into the back seat. While Alan was fastening and adjusting his seat belt, Cade leaned forward and crossed his arms, resting his elbows on the backs of the bucket seats and his chin on his hands.

"It's no big deal, or anything, but, why'd you pull your hand away in there? It's not like Jamie would have been shocked."

"Hmph." Alan adjusted his seat belt again. "Just a reflex, I guess." He turned and looked Cade in the eye. "Twelve years of hiding it in the service, and two years in high school before that."

Cade nodded, satisfied with the explanation and relieved there was nothing more serious going on. He failed to suppress a yawn. "I hate mornings! Being up at stupid o'clock has finished me."

Alan gave him a smooch on the forehead. "So get some shut-eye, sleepyhead."

Cade stretched out across the creamy leather bench seat. He used to hate this car for being too big. Right now, he had no complaints.

"It's 40-West all the way, right?"

"Right. Why don't you wake me when we get close to Asheville, and I'll guide you in."

"Enjoy your nap, Cade."

Reminiscence

Alan had felt anxious about meeting Marilyn and Llewellyn Bishop ever since Cade had first suggested they spend Christmas with his parents. Now, as the miles ticked west, and he got closer and closer to Asheville, his gut was churning. As soon as one awful scene finished playing out in his head, another would start. He gradually became aware of a soft, gentle snoring coming from the back seat, and realized just how far his thoughts had run away with him. Noticing this reminded him of something he'd first read in one the Buddhist books he'd borrowed from a chaplain in Iraq; it was the same thing his new Zen teacher in Chapel Hill kept reminding him to do. *Let go of thinking!* He decided to give it a try. He turned his attention to his own breathing, and to the sound of Cade's.

He managed to keep his focus for about twenty minutes. By the time he saw the green and white exit sign marked "Buildwell Estate," he found that, not only was he relaxed, he was actually happy to be where he was—about to visit "America's Only Palace." His family's annual pilgrimage to this place was a Christmas tradition that went back as far as he could remember. The idea of sharing his tradition with Cade brushed away any remaining worries about meeting the people who had raised the young man capable of taking Alan's breath away with a mere word or glance.

Keeping his eyes on the road, Alan reached over, blindly, into the back seat and groped around until he found what he was pretty sure was a shoulder. He gave a squeeze and a little shake.

Cade grunted.

When there was no further sound or movement, he squeezed again and shook a little harder. "Cade!"

A grouchy, "What?" was followed by a series of moans and groans.

"And here I thought I was the old man in this relationship," Alan said with a grin. When they'd started seeing each other, he'd been bothered by the eight-year age difference. It felt good to realize he now felt comfortable enough to joke about it.

There was a snort from the back seat, and then a bleary-eyed, tousled head appeared in the rearview mirror.

"Even if I was awake, that wouldn't be funny." Cade looked out the windows. "We're already in Asheville? I thought you were going to wake me up before we got to town."

"The way you were sawing logs, I don't think Armageddon would have woken you."

"I do not snore!"

Alan could see that Cade was wide awake now. He pulled the car into a parking space in front of the gift shop near the gatehouse and looked around. "Everything looks familiar, but Dad always took care of this part. This is where we pick up the tickets, right?"

"Yup," Cade confirmed. "We're lucky my dad was able to call in a favor. You have to buy tickets in the summer if you want to come on Christmas Eve or Christmas Day."

Alan couldn't help frowning at this reminder of yet another way he was sure Cade's parents would find him lacking.

The morning sun had warmed the air outside, but he felt a small shiver as he followed Cade inside and waited while he picked up their tickets. He looked at the price on his when Cade handed it over. "Is this with the military discount?" Cade nodded. Alan whistled. "How did my folks manage to bring all seven of us up here every year?"

"That was a long time ago," Cade suggested, "and the children's price is much lower."

They returned to the car, with Cade now in the front passenger seat. Alan drove the two-mile narrow winding road through thick forest and then took a deep breath, holding it when he recognized the curve ahead; rounding it would reveal their first view of the house.

"You're really excited about this, aren't you?" Cade asked.

The house appeared and Alan emptied his lungs in a long, silent whistle. "I am. I really am!" His grin felt like it went from ear to ear. "I was a senior in high school the last time I was here. It was such a big part of Christmas that it hasn't really felt like Christmas the past twelve years without it."

All his childhood memories crowded in at once. He felt a tug in his chest and moisture forming at the corners of his eyes. Over the last few years, he'd worked on himself long and hard to get in touch with his emotions—mostly. He'd been proud of the fact that, for an ex-Marine, he was comfortable with crying when he needed to. Still, this didn't seem like the time or place for a big *boo-hoo* moment.

He took a couple of deep, calming breaths and reached over to rest his hand on Cade's thigh for a moment, until he needed it again to maneuver the Mercedes into a parking space. He switched off the engine. "Ready?"

"Sure." As they got out of the car, Cade added, "Looks smaller than I remember it. 'Course, I haven't been here since, like, third grade?"

"Are you kidding me? I thought you grew up right around the corner?"

"Well, almost. It's a few miles. But, you know how it is—the same way nobody from Anaheim ever goes to Disneyland. Besides, like I told you, this place isn't that much bigger than our house, so why bother?"

He knew Cade was joking, but his gut gave a little churn anyway, reminding him of the meeting looming before him.

Cade must have noticed, because he reached out a hand and said, "I'm sorry, Alan. You do know I'm kidding, right?"

"Right." Alan forced a smile and took Cade's hand. "Shall we?"

They walked together toward the huge, yellow stone structure before them. The walkways crisscrossing the gigantic front lawn were lined on both sides by luminaries—small, white paper bags, each with a candle inside. Alan remembered how his parents had always planned their annual visit so they arrived in the afternoon and spent a few hours touring the inside of the house, so that when they came out it was dark, and the acres of front yard glimmered with soft flickering lights. It was like looking at a starry sky. He regretted he wouldn't get to enjoy that part of the tradition this year. But, maybe next year. Maybe a year from now he could stand in this spot, holding Cade's hand and sharing the magic of those lovely lights. Maybe he'd even kiss him, right here in front of everybody!

He thought about how much he'd like to come back in the spring, when the gardens were in bloom. He'd seen plenty of pictures of the famous gardens, but he'd only ever visited in December, so he'd never seen them in person. If the reality was even half as beautiful as the photographs... He wondered if they rented out the gardens for weddings. Probably not for gay weddings—*Whoa! Where did that thought come from?* he asked himself, his eyes scanning side to side. He looked down at their joined hands as they continued walking. He gave Cade's a little squeeze and, when Cade looked over at him, he used his eyes to direct Cade's gaze down to their hands. Looking around, then back down to their hands, he said, "I think we should..."

Cade stiffened, narrowed his eyes, and tightened his grip on Alan's hand. "Are you kidding me? This is Asheville. Straight people have been in the minority for several years now!"

Alan laughed. "Yes, but like you pointed out," he looked over to the people moving in and out of the house, "these people aren't from Asheville. They're from all over the place. I bet a lot of them are from little country towns where folks still get freaked out about it."

Cade sighed. "You're right. I do love attention, but maybe not that kind of attention." He let go of Alan and shoved his hands in his front pockets, then turned and started walking toward the house again.

Alan trailed behind, afraid he'd done the wrong thing.

They stopped outside the front doors, looking at the giant wreaths and the pine garlands which seemed to be strung everywhere. There were throngs of people visiting the house that day. Alan figured it was probably the busiest day of the year for the grand old mansion. Couples and groups of parents with children milled around in the entryway. His childhood visits had always been a

159

little earlier in December, and Alan was used to seeing school groups, bussed in to learn the history of the Gilded Age and America's mega-wealthy. There were no yellow buses in the parking lot today, though, it being Christmas Eve.

They crossed the entryway and went into the solarium, which was known as the Winter Garden. Bright sunlight spilled through the glass ceiling, and the central fountain was overflowing with red and white poinsettias. Cade began to walk toward the far side of the room, but Alan caught his arm. "Let's save the Dining Hall for last. That's where the tree is!"

"It's your show, big guy."

"Let's do the Tapestry Hall and Library, and then go upstairs through the bedrooms."

"Lay on, MacDuff!" Cade winked and motioned with a sweep of his arm. Alan was grateful for the gesture, because he had no idea who this MacDuff was, or what he was supposed to lay on him.

They went from room, to room, to room. Cade seemed to take only a mild interest in his surroundings. He certainly wasn't experiencing any of the awe Alan felt as his eyes met sights that had bowled him over as a child. The house, and all the antiques, and the holiday decorations, still seemed mighty darned impressive, even in light of all the things he'd seen during his twelve years in the service. His rifle platoon had spent a few nights in one of Saddam Hussein's palaces, and even if it hadn't been wrecked, it could never have held a candle to the grandeur he now saw everywhere he looked.

Each room brought fresh memories—the way his four older sisters always seemed to operate as a single unit, making him feel like an only child; how his parents always knew exactly where he was, and never let him stray too far; but especially the pure joy he saw on his mother's face every time she laid eyes on another beautifully decorated room. The flood of memories brought a smile to his lips and an ache to his chest at the same time.

Cade nudged him with an elbow. "You're awfully quiet."

"Lost in my thoughts, I guess," Alan admitted. He also noticed he was starting to feel a little tired. He figured it must have been their early start, combined with all the strong feelings this visit was stirring up. "Whudduya say we head on down to the Dining Hall and have a look at that tree?"

"We're not going through the basement?" Cade asked as he leaned over and rubbed his shoulder against Alan's.

"I forgot there was one. I don't think we ever went down there."

"I was wondering whether or not they decorate the scullery maids' chambers for the holidays." When Alan didn't say anything, Cade raised an eyebrow. "I can live not knowing."

He could tell Cade was trying to cheer him up, which meant he must really look like he needed cheering up. Knowing that Cade could pick up on his moods so well made him feel like crying again. But, dammit, he was here to enjoy Christmas! He steeled himself and vowed not to ruin the day.

They made their way downstairs and to the far end of the house—to what Alan remembered as the largest indoor room ever built. Well, in a house, he meant. Of course stadiums were bigger. They walked into the Dining Hall and his breath caught in his throat. He couldn't even guess how high the ceiling was, but it was huge, and it was curved like the roof of a cathedral. It was so tall it made the three fireplaces at one end of the room look small by comparison, but each fireplace was tall enough that you could walk right into it. The massive dining table was, as always, set and ready to receive thirty or more guests in gracious elegance. He turned to face the far end of the room, and there it was—the biggest Christmas tree in the world! At least, that was how he'd always thought of it. He'd seen pictures of the one in Rockefeller Plaza, and he didn't know which one was actually bigger, but he'd put his money on the Vanderwells over the Rockefellers any day. Comparing the wealth of those families to the pitiful sum in his bank account struck him as funny, and he was about to share this "hilarious" thought with Cade, but remembered in the nick of time how his jokes tended to go over.

"Alan?" Cade rested a hand on his shoulder. "You look tired. Are you okay?"

"I think maybe I'm a little overwhelmed," he admitted. "You know, lots of memories here. It's making me think a lot about my mom. I guess I am pretty tired."

"Do you want to stay longer? If we head on to my folks' place now, you could probably get a nap before dinner."

"A nap." Alan snorted. "Now I know I'm the old man in this relationship." Cade still looked concerned, so he smiled and said, "I'm kidding, okay? But I've seen what I wanted to. Let's go."

Regret

Cade gave Alan directions for the short drive to the house he grew up in. As the car glided past sights he hadn't seen in years, an intriguing idea crossed his mind. "Could we make a little detour before heading to the house?"

A look of relief leapt to Alan's face. "Fine by me," he said.

Alan hadn't mentioned the whole meet-the-parents thing since the diner, but Cade was becoming convinced he was more nervous than he'd let on. "Take the next left," he said.

"Where are we going?"

"I was thinking... I'd kind of like to see the high school. I haven't been back there since..."

Alan reached over and took Cade's hand. "Since that night?"

Cade swallowed. "Right. Since that night. I mean, of course, I wasn't at school that night, but you know what I mean."

"I know." Alan squeezed his hand. "Are you sure you want to?"

"Yeah. I am. After all, it's just a bunch of buildings. And nothing bad happened there. You know...I mean, I don't freak out at the house...in the foyer, where he raped me... So, yeah, I'd just like to drive by, see what the old 'hallowed halls' look like these days." He turned and looked out the window at the houses going by. "Not this right, but the next one."

Alan rounded the corner and the school came into view. He turned into the parking lot and pulled into a space facing the main entrance.

Cade scanned the old, familiar, brick buildings, surrounded by playing fields, against a backdrop of mountains. He'd expected to feel something when he saw them again. Regret? Some kind of nostalgic pang? The best he could come up with was a vague sense of ennui. Alan had been so emotional, looking at an old building from his past. Cade felt a kind of relief that mere architecture seemed unable to vex him. But it did stir memories.

"It's funny"—he looked out the passenger window—"you know, this is where I lost my virginity."

"At school?" Alan sounded incredulous.

"Yeah, in the locker room." He glanced back at Alan in time to see his eyes getting wider. "It was after school one day. The coach had made me come back after classes to do an hour of clean up. I don't remember what crap he'd accused me of, but he was always after me for one thing or another.

"I'd been there about a half hour, gotten all the towels into the hampers, and mopped the shower room. I started some tidying up, when I noticed the door to Eric's locker was open a little way. I'd been sneaking peeks at him ever since school started that year. He was gorgeous, and built like a linebacker. Which, I guess, is why he was a linebacker."

Alan gave a nervous-sounding laugh.

Cade continued, "I couldn't help myself. I opened his locker and right on top of a pile of clothes, there was his jockstrap. I didn't even know what I was doing; I just picked it up and started sniffing it. I'd never smelled anything so glorious. It was like I'd died and gone to heaven." His attention snapped back to Alan. "Am I grossing you out? I've never told anybody this before."

"Not grossing me out." Alan's smile was genuine. "I'm fascinated. What happened?"

"Well, I hadn't been sniffing long when I heard a noise and turned around and there was Eric! And there was his jockstrap in my hands! I panicked. I tried to bolt, but he spread his arms and leaned on the lockers on both sides so I couldn't get by. He said if I'd blow him, he wouldn't tell anybody. I couldn't believe my ears! It was what I'd wanted for months, and there he was actually asking me to do it."

"And how'd it go?"

Cade felt like he was on thin ice. He didn't want to shock Alan, or have Alan think less of him, but it also felt so freeing to be telling another person about this. And not just any person—Alan. "It was great. It was everything I'd dreamed it would be. I mean, I knew I was gay, but up to that point it had been kind of…theoretical. Once I was doing it, well, it just felt so right."

Alan nodded. "So, Eric became your boyfriend?"

"Well, that's a whole other story." Good as it felt to get this off his chest, he wasn't sure how far he was ready to go all at once. "He insisted he wasn't gay, but he kept coming back for more. We started spending more and more time together, you know? Going for pizza, watching movies. I was out, and he wasn't, but he knew I'd never go into the closet, so we just kept it casual, and nobody seemed to notice. Or, if they did, they didn't care. This is Asheville we're talking about.

"So, we just carried on that way for almost two years. He wanted to take things further, but I wouldn't. I knew I didn't want to go all the way till it was with somebody I could at least imagine being with long-term. I hadn't necessarily ruled him out on that, but I knew he'd have to change a lot before I could think of him that way, and…I guess I was hoping against hope, you know?"

"Yeah," Alan nodded again, "I do."

Cade reached over and stroked Alan's thigh. "Hey, thank you for indulging me…and for all the driving! I think we should get you to the house so you can lie down for a while."

Alan's smile looked pasted on. "If you insist."

"Take a left out of the lot, and we'll be there in a few minutes."

Reunion

Alan followed Cade's directions, driving through neighborhoods of larger and larger houses. He turned a corner, and they passed between a pair of huge stone pillars, each with a small, discrete sign identifying the Country Club. No houses were in view from this street—just trees on either side, interrupted here and there by a gated driveway.

"It's the next one on the left," Cade said, as they rounded a bend in the road.

Alan turned the car and drove the few yards to a large set of black wrought iron gates. He stopped and lowered the window. There was a keypad at the end of a pipe extending from the stone wall. "Code?" he asked, reaching out.

"Oh seven, one four." Cade replied with an impish grin. "Ring any bells?"

"Your birthday?"

"That's right, Mister, and don't you forget it. Again."

"Cade! If you hadn't waited till the fifteenth to tell me, I wouldn't have *forgotten*."

Cade smiled. "You know I just like teasing you, right?" he asked, as the gates swung open at a glacial pace. Pointing up the hill, where the driveway disappeared around a curve, he said, "Don't worry, it's only about another hour from here."

Alan grimaced. "Seriously?" he asked, driving forward.

"No. You just seem so worked up, I'm trying to lighten the mood."

"Epic fail." Alan turned and gave Cade a weak smile. As he turned back, the house came into view. "Holy shit!" Alan felt like his eyes were about to pop right out of his skull. "You gotta be fuckin' kiddin' me!" The house was huge. Gigantic. Gargantuan! He thought his brain might short circuit as it searched for every word he knew that meant large. It was nowhere near as big as Buildwell, but it had to be ten times bigger than any house he'd ever seen where people actually lived. He let out a sound he'd never heard himself make before. It was some kind of whimper.

Cade groaned. "This is why we went to Buildwell first. I thought it might soften the blow."

"Nice try." Alan appreciated Cade's attempt to ease his worries, but his mouth formed a thin line as he negotiated the long driveway, each turn revealing more and more of the Bishop Estate.

"Alan?" There was a troubled look on Cade's face. "I knew you were a little anxious about coming here, but...I just realized, I've never heard you drop the f-bomb before. You've got to try and keep calm."

"Calm! Calm? That's fine for you to say, you grew up here. Me? I'm like a fish out of water! Like a teeny-tiny fish in…in…" He let out an exasperated sigh. "I dunno, in way too much water." He could hear how ridiculous he sounded, but he couldn't seem to do anything about it.

He looked at Cade and saw genuine concern—maybe worry. It dawned on him that his own bad mood was infecting his boyfriend. He knew he had to try harder. "I'll be okay, Cade. And I'll try to calm down."

Cade reached across and gave his thigh a firm squeeze. "Oorah!"

Seeing Cade actually try for Marine macho made Alan laugh, but he could tell it sounded flat, maybe false. He took a deep breath. "Oorah!"

He brought the car to a stop at the foot of the massive stone stairs leading to the front porch. Porch wasn't the right word. It was twenty feet deep and ran the entire width of the house. It looked plenty big enough to throw a party for an entire rifle company. He switched off the engine and took a few deep breaths, telling himself he could do this. He fumbled under the dash, looking for the trunk release.

"It's on the left, just below the air vent," Cade offered.

They both got out and met at the back of the car. As Alan lifted their overnight bags from the trunk, movement caught the corner of his eye. He looked up to see an older woman in a gray dress and white apron coming through the giant pair of front doors. Her silver hair was done up in a bun, and she pushed a pair of wire-rimmed glasses to the top of her head as she stepped onto the porch.

"Cade! *Mon petit!*" she cried out as she came down the steps with her arms stretched wide. Cade rushed to meet her halfway and they embraced in a fierce hug. "*Quel plaisir de te revoir! Ça fait si longtemps!*"

"*Ma chère Agnès, je vous prie de m'excuser. Vous m'avez manqué terriblement!*" Cade murmured into her neck as he snuggled close. They both leaned back and beamed into one another's faces. There was such warmth in her eyes as she looked at Cade that Alan felt the knots in his neck and shoulders loosen just a little.

As he started up the steps with the bags, she turned her head to face him, still beaming. "And you must be the Alan I've heard so much about!" Her English was perfect, but he noticed her accent was a thick combination of French mixed with a southern twang.

"Alan, this is Agnès. Don't tell Mom I said this, but Agnès is the one who really raised me."

She gave Cade a playful swat on the shoulder. "Don't even think such a thing, young man!"

"It's true, my dear." Alan had never seen Cade's face so bright. "Everything important I know about life, I learned from Agnès," he said, as he turned her toward the house and led her up the stairs on his arm.

166

Alan followed.

As they crossed the porch, a beautiful woman in a form-fitting red dress appeared. Her thick, shiny auburn hair reached almost to her shoulders and framed a heart-shaped face. "Darling!" she exclaimed, as she stepped through the door and ripped Cade from Agnès's arm.

Her embrace looked even more powerful than the one Alan had seen a moment before. She let go and took Cade's shoulders in her hands, leaning in to plant a kiss on his lips.

"Mother!" Cade protested.

But before he could scold her any more, she turned, reaching both hands to Alan's shoulders and taking a firm grip. She smiled. "May I?"

"Um…" He looked down at the bags in his hands. She let go and he crouched to put them down. "Of course," he replied as he stood, and he was instantly wrapped in her arms.

"Alan! I am so happy to finally meet you!"

Despite the crush of her hug, he was able to reply, "I'm happy to meet you, too, Mrs. Bish—"

"Oh, no!" she interrupted, slackening her grip and leaning back to look him in the eye. "Didn't Cade tell you? I'm Marilyn. Please!"

Alan smiled. "He did tell me. I'm sorry. It may take some getting used to."

"That's quite all right, dear. Take your time." She put an arm through his and turned him toward the door. Looking back over her shoulder she said, "Cade, darling, you and Agnès take your bags upstairs and then meet us in Lew's study. I want to introduce Alan to your father."

As Marilyn stepped forward, Alan looked over his shoulder at Cade and mouthed the words, "Help me!" When Cade only shrugged, he steeled himself to face his doom.

She led him through front doors almost as big as Buildwell's. He heard Agnès's voice behind him—hushed, but full of animation—saying something to Cade in French. The words were a foreign blur, until he distinctly heard the word "hottie" just before Cade cried out, "Agnès! Shame on you!" Alan couldn't help shaking his head.

Marilyn led him down a long central hallway toward the back of the house. She was talking a mile a minute, and he lost track of what she was saying as he tried to glance through the open doors they passed. He only got glimpses of large rooms filled with what looked like lots of expensive furniture and art. He felt that tightness returning to his chest. At the end of the hall, they turned left into yet another large room. This one was also filled with expensive furniture and art, but somehow, it had a cozy feeling about it.

A man sitting behind a desk in the center of the room looked up and smiled as they came in. He stood and came around, looking like an older, taller version of Cade. As he approached, he held out his hand. "Alan!" His handshake was warm and hearty. "It's so good to finally meet you. Call me Lew."

Alan saw the same twinkle in Lew's eyes that he'd grown so fond of in Cade's.

"Have the women got you settled in yet?" Lew asked.

Marilyn answered for him. "Cade and Agnès are taking the bags up." She turned to Alan. "Cade can show you to his room when he comes back down."

"Oh!" Alan's brows furrowed; he hadn't thought this through.

"Is something wrong?" Marilyn asked.

"No, no. I just thought there'd be a, er, guest room, or…something?"

"Oh!" Marilyn looked shocked and raised a hand to her breast. "I'm so sorry, Alan! I wasn't thinking! I didn't have a room prepared. I mean, I just…I assumed you and Cade were sleeping together. Please forgive me." She turned toward the door. "I'll have Agnès make up the Blue Room."

"No. Marilyn, please. It's fine." He felt the heat rising to his cheeks. "I'm the one who made assumptions. I'm sorry. Of course I'd like to be with Cade."

Just as he was wondering if the moment could get any more awkward, Cade walked in.

"Hiya, Pop!"

Lew took him in a firm embrace. "It's so good to see you, Cade. I miss you, son."

"I miss you, too, Lew. You really should try to get down to Durham once in a blue moon. It's not that far."

"We do need to make more of an effort," Lew agreed, looking at Marilyn. She nodded her head.

Cade turned to Alan and said, "Can I interest you in the nickel tour?"

Alan hesitated—he knew better than to try humor with relative strangers, not to mention strange relatives—but he had to break the tension somehow. "Considering what they charge at Buildwell, this place has gotta be worth at least fifty bucks!"

The three Bishops looked back and forth among one other for a moment, then they all turned to Alan and laughed politely.

Cade took Alan by the hand and led him from the room.

"That went over like a lead balloon," Alan admitted once they were out of earshot.

"Don't worry about it. Sometimes I think the whole money thing makes them a little uncomfortable. Well, Mom anyway."

Cade led him through a series of rooms on the main floor—Music Room, Library, Billiard Room, Sitting Room. He was starting to feel overwhelmed again when they reached the front of the house and turned a corner. "And this is the Great Room," Cade said as they stepped into a space that looked about the size of a football field to Alan.

The ceiling must have been twenty-five feet high, and one wall was made entirely of glass, looking out onto dark green forest. The Christmas tree was almost as tall as the ceiling, and it was a thing of beauty. It was…what was the word he was looking for? Tasteful. The Troxler family tree had always been short and stocky, with big lights in every shade of the rainbow. Hung with a rag-tag assortment of ornaments, it had been a bright and blinking symphony of color. This tree was slender and perfectly tapered from base to tip. Thousands of tiny, white lights illuminated hundreds of small glass balls in silver, purple, and turquoise. A strand of broad silver ribbon wound its way around from top to bottom in a single spiral.

"Nice tree," he tried.

"Yeah, well, that's Marilyn's thing. It's completely different every time. I guess purple and green is this year's black."

Alan wasn't sure what Cade meant, but he decided to let it go.

Cade took his hand. "I think the kitchen's the only thing you haven't seen." He gave a tug and Alan followed him.

Like every other room in the house, the kitchen was huge, with giant windows looking out onto the back yard. Beyond the cooking area, the room extended into another large space with a dining table and chairs. It looked to him to be about the size of his condo, and he figured they probably called it their "Breakfast Nook." He walked over to check out the view from the windows.

"I don't think I've ever seen a yard so perfect. It's so green! Your folks must have a full-time landscaper." He could see Cade was trying to suppress a laugh. "What?" Alan asked. Cade giggled. "Would you please tell me what's so funny, Cade?"

Cade stopped laughing and cleared his throat. "You're right, Alan. It *is* green. In fact, it's *the* green." Alan scowled. "It's the eleventh green of the golf course, silly!"

Marilyn and Agnès came into the kitchen, each with a list in hand. Agnès looked a little worried. "Let's review where everything is, and what you'll need to do when, shall we?"

Marilyn nodded, but then turned to the men. "You must be tired from your drive and all that walking around Buildwell. Dinner's not till eight. Why don't you two go upstairs and settle in?"

Cade walked over to Agnès, put a hand on her shoulder, and looked at her with grave concern. "Will your evil overseer be granting you a holiday reprieve so you can be with your family, or are you stuck here for dinner?"

"No, dear. I'm going home in about twenty minutes—as soon as I finish setting the table and making sure everything else is on autopilot for Her Royal Highness."

Alan could tell this was a running joke between the two of them. From the moment he met Marilyn, it was obvious she was very down-to-earth, with a warm, giving heart. He was sure she must be an easygoing and generous employer.

Marilyn clucked her tongue as she cracked open the oven door and peered in at the turkey. The aroma, which had been enticing before, now overwhelmed Alan's senses and reminded him he hadn't eaten since breakfast. Turning to Marilyn, he said, "If by 'settle in' you mean take a nap, that sounds really great."

"I'll walk you up," Cade said, as he wrapped his arms around Agnès and squeezed her tight. She made a sound somewhere between an "oomph" and a sigh of satisfaction. As he released her, he said, "I can't believe this is all the time we get together. I'll have to come back soon so we can visit. *Je reviendrai bientôt, ma chère, Agnès!*"

"You know I'd like that, Cade." She reached up and brushed the backs of her fingers across his cheek. "*Reviens vite me voir, d'accord?*" Tears pooled at the corners of her eyes.

"Or, you could come visit us! We've got plenty of room, and there's lots of interesting stuff to see in The Triangle area."

She smiled and ran her fingers through Cade's hair. "Perhaps, my dear. *On verra.*"

Cade stepped back, taking both her hands in his. He gave one last squeeze and then turned, wrapping an arm around Alan's waist as they walked from the room.

Cade led him up a back stairway and down a long hall. He swung open the last door on the right and stepped inside. With a sweeping gesture, he said, "This is it. Welcome to Chez Cade!"

Alan walked in, fascinated to have his first look at the room where Cade Bishop had done his growing up. He wasn't surprised to see posters from plays and musicals on the walls, or to not see trophies and posters of athletes—the things Cade would have seen in Alan's old room, if it was still there to see. "You really were into theater," he observed.

"You have no idea." Cade beamed. "Like I told you, Marilyn was an actress and a dancer before she and Lew got married. She keeps everything!" He pointed out how every horizontal surface in the room was covered with various objects. "These are props and costume pieces from every show I was ever in."

Alan walked over to a dresser and picked up what looked like a very small crown. It felt like cardboard under the shiny gold fabric. There were fake jewels sewn to it. "Is this some kind of crown?"

"Ah." Cade came over and took it from him, perching it on top of his head and securing it with the elastic chin strap. He struck a regal pose, with his arms crossed over his chest. "From when I was Prince Phra Bat Somdet Maha

Chulalongkorn," he said in a deep voice. He must have seen Alan was lost. "The Crown Prince of Siam?" He was still clueless. "I was in *The King and I*."

"Oh. I liked that movie."

Cade smiled. "Actually, it was one of the shows we did together. Marilyn played Anna."

"The teacher?"

Cade nodded.

Alan yawned. "You know, I really could use that nap."

"Under the covers, or on top?" Cade inquired, slipping the crown from his head.

"I'm too tired to do anything but lie down," Alan said, as he fell onto the bed, using each foot to push off the other sneaker. He rolled over onto his side, pulled a pillow out from under the covers, and adjusted it for comfort. Cade snuggled up from behind, spooning him and wrapping an arm over his chest. Alan took Cade's wrist and pulled him in tighter. Then he kissed the back of Cade's hand, closed his eyes, and allowed himself to drift away.

Repast

It took a moment for Cade to understand what was bothering him. Someone was knocking on his bedroom door.

"Cade!"

He rolled away from Alan. "Mom?"

Her voice was muffled by the door. "Dinner's in about a half hour, sweetie. I thought I should warn you, in case either of you wants to take a shower or anything."

"Thanks, Marilyn. We'll be down!" He turned to see Alan rolling onto his back and stretching out his arms, yawning.

"Wow! I was really out."

"I think we both were," Cade said. "It's been quite a day. Do you want a shower before dinner?"

Alan crossed his arms behind his head. "Not really, unless—" he sniffed at his pits "—you think I need one."

Cade buried his face in the nearest pit and nuzzled, sniffing and licking. "Nuh-uh! These are just the way I like them!"

Alan laughed and pulled away. He grabbed the pillow and smacked Cade over the head with it. "Leave my pits be, young man. We have a dinner to get ready for!"

They got up, grabbed their bags, and threw them onto the bed. Sorely as he was tempted, Cade managed to keep it all business as they changed out of their jeans and tee shirts into slacks and button-down shirts. They headed down the stairs and into the dining room.

When they entered, he was relieved to see that all the removable sections of the table had been taken out. The room could accommodate twenty for dinner, but now the table looked as if it might seat only six or eight. There were just four chairs—at the head and foot, and one on either side. Not exactly intimate, but at least it wasn't like that scene in *Citizen Kane*, where the two characters are at either end of a forty-foot table. In fact, if the table were any smaller, there wouldn't have been enough room for the countless trays, bowls and platters spread out in the spaces between the place settings. Agnès—*um, he meant, Marilyn*—had outdone herself this year. He was enjoying an internal chuckle over his mom's love of entertaining and her total reliance on Agnès, when Marilyn and Lew walked in.

"Gentlemen, please be seated," Marilyn said, moving to the foot of the table. Lew followed and pulled out her chair.

Cade headed for the near side of the table and was surprised when Alan grabbed his chair and pulled it out.

"May I?" he asked.

"*Bien sûr, mon cher.*" He seated himself.

Alan helped push the chair in. As he went around to take the opposite seat, he said, "Marilyn, this all looks so wonderful. You must have been preparing for days."

"I can do some of it, but it would never happen without Agnès. She's a genius in the kitchen."

"The turkey looks like something out of a storybook, and is this green bean casserole?"

Cade couldn't help notice the way Marilyn's smile slackened as she leaned toward Alan. "Yes. We don't ordinarily eat food that comes in cans, but when Cade was nine, he had this at a friend's house, and he's insisted I make it every year with the authentic original recipe."

"I don't really ask for much, do I, Mother?"

Her smile returned, full force. "No, dear. You really don't."

"And...what is this?" Alan asked, pointing to a platter between him and Marilyn.

"That!" Marilyn beamed with pride. "That is a special holiday recipe I inherited from my mother. Margaret's Famous and Delicious Lime Jell-O Mold."

Lew piped up for the first time. "Or, as it's known around here, Marilyn's Infamous and Possibly Dangerous Lime Slime."

Cade giggled and chimed in, "Don't go near it, Alan. It's got carrots and celery and nuts and...Dear God help us all, cottage cheese!"

"You men really should try to show some holiday spirit." Marilyn pouted, but it was clearly all in fun.

"We men really should try to keep our holiday dinners down, which won't be happening if that comes within three feet of me!" Cade retorted.

Apparently Marilyn had had enough fun with the annual derision of her Jell-O. She turned to Alan. "Would you say grace?"

For a moment, Cade was stunned. Prayer had never been part of their holiday tradition. But then, it occurred to him that on the handful of occasions over the years when they had prayed before a meal, it had always been when there were guests, and those guests were religious. He realized that while his mother had no particular beliefs of her own—or, at least, none she'd shared with him—she cared about her guests being comfortable, and she did her best to make them feel at home. As much as he'd always loved her, this insight deepened his appreciation for who she really was.

Alan reached out, and the four of them joined hands.

Cade closed his eyes and listened to Alan's rich, melodic voice. "We venerate the Three Treasures and give thanks for this food, the work of many people, and the suffering of other forms of life." There was a long pause. "Oh! Amen."

Cade felt a pleasant shiver as Marilyn squeezed one hand and Lew the other. He opened his eyes to look across the table at Alan. It was a beautiful sight. He had wanted so much for Alan to be a part of his family and now it was happening.

"That was lovely, Alan," Marilyn said. "Is it Buddhist? Cade mentioned that you're Buddhist."

"Yes, ma'am—" her eyebrow shot up "—Marilyn, sorry. Yes, it's the meal verse they use at the temple where I've been going for a while now."

"And, what are the Three Treasures it mentions?"

"That's the Buddha, the Dharma, and the Sangha."

"Well," she replied, "I know a little about the Buddha and, if I'm not mistaken, I believe the Dharma means his teachings, no?"

"That's right."

"But, what's the Sangha?"

Cade jumped in before Alan had a chance. "It's what they sing-uh!" He cackled at his own joke. Three steely glares turned in his direction, but only for a moment before they all joined in the laugh.

Lew sliced and distributed the turkey while everyone piled their plates with food and began eating.

Marilyn put down her fork and turned to Alan. "You weren't brought up Buddhist, were you? I think Cade told me your father was a minister?"

"That's right. Lutheran."

"Isn't it quite a leap from Lutheran to Buddhist?"

"Well, I guess you can thank the military for that. The first time I found myself in a combat zone, all the things I'd learned from the Bible just didn't seem to make sense anymore." A worried look crossed Alan's face. "Oh!" he said. "I don't mean any disrespect, if you're—"

"Don't worry, Alan." She smiled. "No one's going to take offense here over anything to do with religion."

"Oh, good." He looked relieved, and then a little concerned as he watched her raise a spoonful of jiggling green salad to her mouth. "Well, I started reading about other religions, and the Buddha's teachings just seemed to make a lot of sense. So I started studying, and then I started meditating—which isn't always easy in the middle of a war."

"You were over there a long time, weren't you?"

He put down the roll he'd been buttering. "Twelve years, between Iraq and Afghanistan. I mean, they shipped me home between deployments, but never for long, and never close enough to spend much time with my family."

"My goodness. The things you must have been through. Cade said you were injured?"

"Yes, ma—Marilyn." He gave her that sheepish grin Cade found irresistible. "A couple of chest wounds, but they're all healed now."

"Your family must be delighted to have you home."

When Alan didn't respond, Cade looked up to see him again staring in fascination at the trembling blob of brilliant green, orange, brown, and white dancing on the end of Marilyn's spoon as she lifted it to her mouth.

"Well…" Alan tore his eyes away from the Jell-O and wiped his mouth with his napkin.

Cade wondered how far he should let his mother go on with this third degree, but Alan continued.

"Most of them are. Dad passed in oh-eight, and my mom's in a nursing home. She has Parkinson's and dementia. But I've got four sisters, and the middle two always seem happy to see me. Rachel's closest to me in age, and she's thrilled to have me home. Sarah—she's the oldest—she's not taking the whole gay thing very well."

"Yes. I'm so sorry about your mother. And Sarah. I know it must be stressful."

"She's a good person. I'm hoping she'll come around but, for now, I'm not pushing."

"Cade said you started a new job last summer."

Cade was beginning to regret how many things he'd said to her over the last few months. He felt like Marilyn was putting Alan under a microscope—though Alan didn't seem to be troubled over talking about himself, which he sometimes was with Cade.

"Yeah. It's not much really. Just working in a coffee shop, but it's part of a service organization for vets that was started by a vet and run by vets." A shadow clouded his eyes. "Veterans, that is—not veterinarians!"

Everyone laughed, and Marilyn reached over and patted the back of Alan's hand. "We knew what you meant, but thank you for being clear. I can see why Cade likes you so much. You know, it just occurred to me. He's never told us how you two met!"

Cade had had enough, and he certainly wasn't about to let the conversation veer into those waters. "I'm sorry, Alan. It was unfair of me not to warn you. Marilyn taught Barbara Walters everything she knows about aggressive interviewing techniques!"

"Cade!" The look on Marilyn's face reflected not only surprise, but maybe a little hurt, too. She recovered quickly, though, and turned her warm smile back on Alan.

"If I'm being nosy, I apologize, Alan."

"No, it's fine," he said. He turned and gave Cade a look he couldn't quite interpret. Perhaps he had come to the rescue when none was needed. But, whatever it was, he was glad he had headed that last question off at the pass.

The silence was only slightly awkward as they finished their meals.

It was broken by Lew, who said, "I think I'm ready for dessert."

Marilyn stood, hefted the remains of the turkey from the table, and put it on the sideboard. She replaced it with a large cherry pie and a stack of dessert plates. "I'll be right back with ice cream." She smiled and went through the swinging door to the kitchen.

Lew sliced the pie and handed out plates. Marilyn returned and the ice cream was passed around to the great pleasure of one and all.

When everyone had finished, Marilyn stood and picked up her empty plate. As she turned and picked up Alan's, she asked, "Would you mind helping with these in the kitchen?"

Alan was on his feet the moment she'd said the words. "Yes, ma—Marilyn." He chuckled and took the plates Lew and Cade offered him, trailing through the kitchen door behind her.

Recognition

Alan rolled up his sleeves and took a towel from the rack, while Marilyn stacked the plates next to the sink and began filling it with hot water. He noticed the two dishwashers under the counter to her right and realized this wasn't about washing dishes.

"Alan," she said, as she handed him the first soapy plate, "I want to thank you for the difference you've made in Cade."

He felt the color rising in his cheeks. He rinsed the plate, then turned away as he rubbed it dry. He'd never had an opportunity to discuss his sexuality with either of his parents, so he couldn't know if they would or wouldn't have accepted the real him. He liked to think they would have been okay with it but, if Sarah was anything to go by—well, you could never tell in advance how a person was going to react, especially when that person was your parent. Cade had told him that when he came out, Lew and Marilyn hadn't just been supportive, they'd become activists for equal rights. Still, it seemed strange that he was about to have the conversation he was apparently about to have with her. "Your son is a very strong person, Marilyn. I don't think I've done anything to make him—"

"Oh no, Alan." She handed him another plate. "Don't sell yourself short. I agree, Cade is a strong person, but after the—I know he's told you about this, at least some of it—when Eric attacked him…it was like his world ended." She continued to scrub a plate that he could see was already clean. "As a little boy, Cade wasn't just happy, he was exuberant. You've never seen anyone with such zest for soaking up every moment of life. There just wasn't anything that failed to bring him joy." She set the plate down in the soapy water and looked at it. "When he first regained consciousness in the hospital, of course I was relieved. But for all his injuries, the thing that really worried me was his eyes." She looked up at him. "Not the bruising… It was…" She paused for a moment, trying to collect herself. "The light was gone from his eyes, Alan. My beautiful, precious child was looking up at me, but the person I loved wasn't there. For four years, I did everything I could think of to bring my little boy back.

"And, he has gotten better. Gradually. But I still kept looking for that glint in his eye. That…ebullience. It always used to just pour out of him. Alan, today is the first time I've seen it. Being with you has brought my Cade back to life. For that, I can never thank you enough. It's like you've given me my heart back."

Hard as it was for him to let it in when other people said nice things about him, Alan had to admit the change in Cade over the last eight months was noticeable. He couldn't deny that he must have played some part in that. The feelings of insecurity which had been bothering him all day melted as Marilyn handed him the next plate, and he saw the glimmer of unshed tears brimming in her eyes. They held each other's gaze for a moment.

"Am I interrupting something?"

Alan was startled by the sound of Cade's voice behind him, but Marilyn calmly turned and smiled. "Not at all, son. In fact, feel free to join us. Alan doesn't know where things go—you could put away after he dries."

"Mmm...you two look like you've got things under control. I think I'll check on Dad and make sure he's not getting into trouble."

Marilyn watched Cade retreat from the kitchen, and turned back to Alan. "You know, I never did find out what the Sangha is."

"Oh. It just means the community of people."

She smiled and rested a damp, soapy hand on his forearm. "Well then, I'm very happy to have you as part of our Sangha, Alan." She took a step closer and stretched up on tiptoe to kiss him on the cheek. "Thank you for giving me my son back."

She squeezed his arm and then turned back to wash the last plate.

Rejoice

Cade left Alan and Marilyn to their work at the sink and wandered the house, aimless until he approached the doors to the Music Room. He hadn't touched a piano since his last visit home, and he felt a sudden urge—in part to find out how rusty he'd gotten, but mainly to bathe in the rich, sonorous voice of the instrument he'd grown up playing. He stepped into the room and his heart warmed as he took in the familiar sights.

One entire wall was lined with books of music and books about music. The other walls were covered with framed posters from operas, ballets, and—of course—musicals. In one corner stood the austere pedestaled busts of the Three Bs, which Llewellyn had given Marilyn as a joke, but she had liked them and displayed them prominently. Groupings of string, wind, and percussion instruments were placed tastefully in the other corners and, there—in the center of the room, standing proud as if holding court—was his great-great grandmother's Bösendorfer.

Some of his earliest memories were of his mom helping him stack books atop the bench, and then steadying him as he climbed onto the perch he'd built high enough to reach the keys. A smile crossed his lips as he reminisced about how patient she'd been helping him to pick out simple melody lines, like "Twinkle, Twinkle Little Star," with one finger. How they'd struggled together as he developed the two-handed coordination needed to play "Chopsticks," the rush of victory when he finally mastered it, and the sudden thrill of delight when—as he played it through for the twentieth time—she suddenly joined in at the bottom of the keyboard, adding a bass accompaniment. That was the moment which had sealed his fate as a devotee of music in general and the piano in particular.

He lifted the dust cover, exposing the keys, and brushed his fingertips up and down the keyboard in a fond caress. He pulled out the bench and took a seat before his old friend.

He noticed Marilyn had set several books of Christmas music to the side, and placed one on the stand, open to her—and his—favorite. His upbringing hadn't included any established religion, though both parents made sure he knew he was free to explore, and that they would support any decisions he made in what they referred to as "the spiritual realm." None of the faiths he'd investigated had held any particular appeal for him, so he ended up practicing nothing at all. The one exception to the "no appeal," however, came in the form of Christmas carols. He loved them all—no matter whether they were secular romps through wintry wonderlands, or sacred hymns laden with angels, and wise men, and alleged virgin births. He could play and sing any and all of them over, and over, and over again, and never grow weary.

The book spread open on the stand made it clear he and his mom were still on the same page, as it were—that she was as eager to hear as he was to play their mutual favorite. He leaned back and interlaced his fingers, turning his hands around and pushing them away as if to make his fingers crackle and crunch. They didn't. They never had. Sometimes, he was jealous of guys who could crack their knuckles.

He scanned the pages of music and then rested his fingers lightly on the keys. He took a deep breath and began playing the simple introductory passage. The chords washed over him like a balm for his soul. He took another breath, and started to sing.

> *Oh, holy night, the stars are brightly shining,*
> *It is the night of our dear Savior's birth!*

It felt like truly coming home.

> *Long lay the world in sin and error pining,*
> *Till He appeared and the soul felt its worth.*

He was feeling his own worth in a way he hadn't in years—if ever. It was so clear that Alan had been the key to his awakening sense of well-being.

> *A thrill of hope, the weary soul rejoices,*
> *For yonder breaks a new and glorious morn.*

He took a breath to start the next line, but startled at the sound of a deep, rich baritone—an octave below his own range—booming out behind him.

> *Fall on your knees!*

Alan! How could he have known the man for eight months and never heard him sing?

> *Oh, hear the angel voices!*
> *Oh, night divine, oh, night when Christ was born!*

A shiver ran up Cade's spine.

> *Oh, night divine,*

182

Alan held the high note for a long time and then let his voice slide dramatically down the next two notes, the same way Cade always did when he sang it. A tear slid down his cheek.

Oh, night, oh, holy night.

. . .

Alan felt, more than heard, Marilyn and Lew step into the doorway behind him.

"Oh, Alan!" Marilyn exclaimed. He turned to face her, feeling a flush of heat rise to his cheeks. "You have such a beautiful voice!"

"Thank you, Marilyn." He turned back to look at Cade and was surprised by the tear glistening on his boyfriend's cheek.

"Cade must make you sing for him every day," she said.

Cade looked as surprised and confused as Alan felt. At the same instant Alan was saying, "No, he—" Cade was replying, "I didn't know—" They stopped speaking at the same time, and simply gazed into one another's eyes, smiling.

Alan looked back at Cade's parents. Marilyn raised one eyebrow as her lips formed a knowing smile. "Looks like you boys still have a lot of 'Getting-To-Know-You' to do."

He turned back to Cade and didn't miss the twinkle in his eyes at her words. He knew visions of *The King and I* were dancing in his head.

Cade turned toward his parents and said, "How 'bout we all sing some carols?"

Alan and the Bishops moved over to the piano and stood on either side of Cade. "What shall we start with?" Marilyn asked, leaning back against Lew's chest and resting her head on his shoulder as he wrapped her in his arms.

"Sleigh Ride," he replied, tipping his head and kissing the top of hers.

Cade flipped through one of the books, found the page, and began playing. Marilyn sang the first verse, and the three men joined in for the chorus.

Surprised by how comfortable he felt, compared to the edgy mood he'd been in earlier, Alan gave himself over to the music and lost all track of time.

After an especially raucous rendition of "The Twelve Days of Christmas," he noticed Cade flexing and extending the fingers of both hands and shaking out his wrists. He was shocked when he looked at his watch and discovered it was almost midnight. Holding out his left wrist to Cade, he gazed into his eyes and said, "Look at that, it's almost Christmas."

"Jeepers!" Cade replied with a smirk. "We'd better be getting to bed, or Santa might not visit!"

Marilyn turned to Alan. "Christmas is the one morning of the year we don't have to set the alarm clock. Cade, you'll be in to wake us up when you're ready to open presents?"

Cade's expression went flat and serious. "Marilyn. I am not three. I'm twenty-three." He cracked a grin and bounced up and down on the piano bench. "And, of course I'll be in early to wake you!"

The four of them hugged and kissed and said their goodnights. Then the two couples made their way upstairs.

Renewal

Consciousness crept over Cade like the lifting of an early morning fog. The first thing to catch his awareness was a furry heat where his cheek and hand rested on Alan's chest. But, something was wrong about the shape. Alan's pecs didn't curve that way. He cracked open one eye, and saw it was a thigh, not a chest. Alan wasn't lying next to him like usual. Instead, he was sitting up, leaning against the headboard. Cade opened his other eye and let a small moan escape him before saying, "Merry Christmas!" He smiled as he rolled over to look up at Alan's face, and was stunned to see it wet with tears. He scrambled to sit up and brushed his fingers across a damp cheek. "Alan! What's wrong?"

Alan reached up and took Cade's hand in his own, giving it a gentle squeeze. "I woke up thinking about my mom."

"Oh." Cade cast his eyes down. He knew Alan had been struggling to come to terms with his mother's gradual deterioration. He wanted to help, but he didn't know where to begin, because he'd never been through anything like that himself. But seeing Alan in pain was more than he could bear, and he knew he had to try! He looked up again. "Can you talk about it?"

Alan met his gaze and took a deep breath. "Sometimes I just get...it's just too much." He grimaced. "I'll be going along thinking I'm okay, and then something reminds me of how she used to be."

Cade felt Alan's shoulders tremble. "Is that what happened yesterday, at Buildwell? Too many reminders?"

"Yeah. I think so."

He slipped an arm behind Alan's back and pulled him in tight.

"Every room we went in...there was some memory there. And I'd be happy for a minute, but then I'd look around and see how nothing there had changed. Twelve years and everything looked exactly like it always had. And I'd think about her again, and how much she's..." His shoulders shook again and Cade squeezed him tighter. "She's gone, Cade!" His lips twisted, and tears streamed down his cheeks. "But...she's not. She's stuck in between." His voice quivered. "Sometimes, when I look at her, I get the feeling she's in there, and trying to get out, but she can't." He pressed his face into the crook of Cade's neck. "And then...meeting your mom..."

"Uh-oh." Cade was afraid of where this might go.

"No. No—she's wonderful! But she's so young, and so beautiful, and...vibrant!" His shoulders shook in earnest now. He drew in a raspy breath and sobbed.

Cade wrapped his other arm around Alan's chest, joined his hands together, and hung on for dear life. "I get it, Alan. I do." He rubbed his cheek on the top of Alan's head. "It's the contrast. It's so unfair."

Alan lifted his head and looked into Cade's eyes. "I thought I was beyond expecting life to be fair, but it's just so…it just makes me so sad." He dropped his head back to Cade's shoulder. "I wish you could have known her." He gasped and looked up again, another wave crashing into him. "Oh, God…" He bit his lower lip. "Oh, Cade, I wish she could have known you!"

Cade freed a hand and stroked Alan's cheek.

"Your mom is so happy about us being together…" Alan sighed. "My mom won't ever know how happy I am."

Cade rocked them gently back and forth as Alan's breathing steadied. He was taken by contrasts of his own. The man is his arms was so big and strong, yet here he was, able to let it all hang out and show his weakness as well.

"I'm sorry," Alan reached up and wiped each eye with the back of his hand. "It's Christmas." He cleared his throat and looked into Cade's eyes. "I'm supposed to be merry."

"Oh, Alan. Don't you know that's one of the things I love most about you? You don't try to be any way other than how you are. I'm trying to learn that from you."

"You? Learn from me?" Alan smiled through the last of his tears.

Cade arched an eyebrow. "Stranger things have happened!"

Alan let out a tiny laugh, shaking his head. "Not much stranger." He leaned in and pressed his lips to Cade's.

When he pulled away, Cade said, "I'm not kidding, Alan. There's something about you. You're so open. It makes me feel like…like I don't need to hide anything. Been a long time since I felt like that."

There was a gentle rapping at the door. "Cade?"

"Merry Christmas, Mommy!" he squealed. He could hear her muffled laughter through the door.

"Breakfast's ready whenever you two are."

"We'll be down in a few!" he hollered back. "Sorry I didn't wake you…" his voice trailed off as he heard her footsteps retreating down the hall. "Well. Speaking of nothing to hide…" He arched that eyebrow again. "How's about a shower, big guy?"

"Sounds great!" Alan's smile was wide, and maybe just a bit lascivious. Cade could see the crisis had passed. He climbed over Alan and jumped to his feet, taking Alan's hand and pulling him up off the bed.

He felt bad about keeping his parents waiting, but cuddling in the shower felt so good that he did his best to prolong it. Eventually, they stepped out of the steamy enclosure and dried each other off, then slipped into sweatpants and tee shirts.

Alan took Cade's hand and led the way downstairs, inhaling deeply as they descended. The heavenly aroma of fresh-baked bread permeated the house.

"Wow! That smells great!" Alan said.

"Yeast rolls! Another one of Grandma's Christmas traditions. Only, this one's actually good."

Alan chuckled.

Lew and Marilyn were seated on stools at the island in the center of the kitchen, sipping from steaming mugs and whispering to one another, their heads bent at a conspiratorial angle.

When they looked up, Marilyn said to Cade, "Well! It's about time, lazybones."

"Sorry, Marilyn," Cade rejoined. "I guess I didn't realize how tired I was." A wave of nostalgia swept through him. "This is the first time you ever had to wake me up on Christmas morning."

She raised the back of her wrist to her forehead and sighed. "My little boy is finally growing up!"

The humor intended by her melodramatic gesture was clear, but the truth in her words didn't escape him.

Alan squeezed Cade's hand and boomed out a hearty, "Merry Christmas, Marilyn! Merry Christmas, Lew!"

They replied in unison and Marilyn stood, reaching out both hands. "Come, you two. Let's get some breakfast and open presents!"

A tray in the center of the island held the results of Marilyn's early-morning baking. The rolls had been arranged in the oven so they'd baked into one another forming the triangular shape of a Christmas tree. A light green glaze had been drizzled over the finished rolls, and a fine dusting of glittery red sugar sparkled in the sunlight streaming through the kitchen windows.

"I don't know, Marilyn." There was a playful glint in Alan's eye as he spoke. "Cade warned me about you and your green foods. But these smell way too good to resist." He picked up a plate and pulled a roll away from the others.

Lew moved to the counter for the coffee pot and filled the two remaining mugs. "Cream and sugar's there," he indicated with a nod of his head.

Cade heaped in spoon after spoon of sugar and poured in cream nearly to the rim. He watched Alan take a sip from his unadulterated mug—"The way God intended it," he'd often said.

Lew led the way as the four of them carried their plates and mugs into the Great Room.

As the other three seated themselves, Cade put his things on the coffee table and bounced up and down on the balls of his feet. "I may be all grown up now, but I get to keep my title as Chief Present Distributor!" He felt like he was about to bubble over, but when he looked at Alan, there was still a trace of sadness in his expression. He decided right there and then he would channel his excitement into making sure Alan had a real family Christmas. When Alan looked up, Cade asked, "Who shall we start with?"

"Marilyn." Alan smiled and looked at the gifts under the tree. "Definitely Marilyn!"

Cade bounced his way over to the tree, snatched up a small package, and brought it over to her. "This is from the two of us."

He feared his grin might break his face as he watched her delicately unwrap her gift. She peeled away the paper to reveal a jeweler's box covered in black velvet. She opened the box and gasped.

"Oh, Cade! It's beautiful!" She carefully lifted out a small cloisonné brooch in the shape of the masques of comedy and tragedy. It was fashioned from gold, but the enamel-plated faces were striped in the colors of the rainbow flag. "Where on earth did you find such a thing?"

"We had it made. There's a fabulous custom jeweler in Durham. You really have to come and see the things she makes."

"It is fabulous! I've never seen anything like it!" She held it out to him, and he pinned it to her dress. "Thank you so much, darling. It's just wonderful!"

"Lew's turn!" Cade crowed, as he raced back to the tree, returning with a slim parcel roughly the size and shape of a manila folder. His father ripped off the paper and held up a brown leather case, zippered on three sides. On the front, his initials were monogrammed on a rectangular gold plate. He unzipped and unfolded it; the interior was a maze of pockets and pouches and slots, with further zippers and snaps. "Is this for travel documents?"

"Exactly!" Cade beamed. "You're overseas so much these days, it seemed like the perfect thing!"

"This is very thoughtful, son. Thank you so much."

"Actually," Cade said, "it was Alan's idea."

Lew glanced down at the folder and ran his fingers over the surface. He raised his eyes and looked back and forth between Cade and Alan. "Well...Thank you, sons."

Cade bit his lower lip when he looked over at Alan and saw him lowering his eyes, a flush of pink rising to his cheeks. "Alan's next! Alan's next!" he cried as he dashed back to the tree. The box he retrieved was cubical in shape, about ten inches on each side, and it was heavy. Very heavy. He tried to imagine what his parents could have dreamed up.

Alan undid the wrapping carefully and set the paper aside on the sofa. He put his ear to the box and jiggled it. He cocked an insouciant grin at Marilyn. "Paperweight?"

She smiled, sphinxlike.

"Doorstop?"

"Oh, for goodness sake, Alan!" Cade could barely contain himself. "Would you just open it, already?"

Alan slipped open the box top and extracted a statue of the Buddha. It was dark gray—almost black. The figure was seated atop a lotus blossom, with one hand pointing up and the other reaching down past its knee, touching the earth. Alan stared at it intently, and then looked up. "Thank you, Marilyn, Lew. This is…"

Cade had rarely seen Alan speechless.

Ever the consummate hostess, his mother kept the conversation rolling. "We had it sent from Japan. Cade mentioned that your temple is a Zen Center, so I did some research. You know, Buddhas come in all sorts of poses, but this one is the most prevalent where your tradition started."

Alan looked back and forth between Marilyn and Lew and the statue. "I don't know what to say. It's… Thank you. I already know right where I'm going to put it."

"We're glad you like it, Alan," Lew said. "Now, Cade, I think it's your turn."

Cade clapped his hands together, and then rubbed them. "Finally!" He walked to the tree and carried back a box as tall as Alan's, and as heavy, but narrower. He plopped down onto the sofa, jabbing his knee into Alan's as he tore away the paper. He ripped open the box and slid out a large crystal obelisk. He was no expert, but he knew Baccarat when he saw it. The face of the crystal was etched with a small replica of the Tony Award, and his name below it. After that, were the words "Best Actor" followed by *The Perfect Detonator* November 13–23, 2014." It had been his first leading role in the Duke University Theatre Studies Program. It had also been the first time ever that Marilyn had not seen a show he was in.

He stared and stared at the object in his hands. His lip trembled when he looked up at his mother. "I…umm…"

"I'm so sorry I didn't get to see you, my darling." She shook her head.

"No! You couldn't…" He knew it had broken her heart to miss his opening night. Instead, she had rushed to Florida that day because Grandma Margaret had been hospitalized due to a stroke, and she'd felt she had to be at her mother's side. He'd sent her a copy of the dark, grainy video a fellow student had made—so at least she'd gotten some idea of his performance—but they both knew it wasn't the same.

He looked down again at the obelisk. The reflection of the lights from the tree glimmered off its surface. He felt the weight of it in his hands. His breath came quick and sharp. He needed to break the tension. "First time for everything, I suppose." He looked up at her and grinned. "Hey! I guess we're even now!"

She gave him a quizzical glance.

"For me not waking you up this morning?"

They both laughed.

From the corner of his eye, he caught Alan sneaking a peek at his wristwatch. "Oh, gosh!" Cade said, looking at his own watch. "I can't believe it, but we have to get going."

"Are you sure you can't stay a little longer?" The look in her eye was heartbreaking.

"No, we've really got to get back to Durham."

Alan interrupted. "I'm sorry, Marilyn. This is my fault. My family's all gathering at Rachel's, but…it's my sister, Sarah. Her husband is a preacher, and he's a big-time fundamentalist. They won't come if Cade is there, so we're working it out in shifts. Cade and I are going for a late lunch, and then Mary and Ruth are coming with their families around three, so we can all visit, and then Cade and I will clear out by five-thirty before Sarah and her crowd show up at six. I'm sorry it's so complicated."

"Don't apologize, Alan," she said as she rose from her seat. "It means a lot that you're willing to be flexible, even when others aren't. We'll just have to plan for a longer visit soon."

Cade and Alan both stood as she came over. She hugged Alan and then turned and wrapped Cade in her vice-like grip. "I love you so much," she whispered in his ear.

"I love you, Mom."

. . .

Alan watched the two embrace. He was glad they were both so young and had plenty of time ahead of them. He also knew how easily things could be taken away. He remembered his years in the service, when visits home were few and far between. Each time, it had been so hard to tear himself away from his family, especially from the look in his mother's eyes that said she knew she might never see him again. He promised himself he'd never let Cade take Marilyn for granted.

He turned to Lew. "I'll just run upstairs and grab our bags."

When he came down, the three Bishops were gathered in the back hallway.

"We'll walk you out," Lew said, taking one of the bags. Alan fell in step and walked beside him. "I'm a man of few words, Alan, but I want you to know… Cade couldn't have picked a finer man."

He knew he should say something, but the feeling of being so totally accepted in what he had imagined would be a foreign, or even hostile, territory was more than he could process. He swallowed around the lump in his throat.

As they walked in silence to the car, he thought about the fact that he hadn't heard more than twenty words out of Lew in the time he'd been there, but Marilyn was never short of something to say. It brought a smile to his lips, knowing which side of the family Cade got his talkative streak from. He opened the trunk and put the bags in, then turned to see Cade and Marilyn at the top of the steps, their foreheads pressed together as they murmured quietly to one another. After an intense hug, made awkward by the gifts in their hands, Cade took the boxes and carried them down the stairs.

For a moment, Marilyn followed Cade's progress with her gaze. Then she looked at Alan and called down, "Thank you for coming. It's so good to finally meet you, and...welcome to our family!"

For the umpteenth time in less than twenty-four hours, he could feel the heat rising to his cheeks. "Thank you, Marilyn. I'm glad to finally meet you, too. Please come see us soon." As Cade put the boxes in the trunk, Alan turned and gave Lew a hearty handshake.

"Drive carefully, son. Traffic's going to be bad today."

"Yes, sir." He gave Lew's hand a tight squeeze, walked around to the driver's side and climbed in. Watching in the rearview, he saw father and son embrace. Cade waved and blew a kiss to his mother as he got into the passenger seat and fastened his belt.

The engine roared to life, and Alan navigated the curves of the driveway. When they got to the street, he stopped and looked to his left to check for oncoming cars. "So...I guess that went okay?" he said.

"Are you kidding? They love you!" Cade enthused.

Foot firmly on the brake, Alan turned and looked to his right, but not to check for traffic. Cade's eyes were shining, and the expression on his face was angelic.

Cade reached across with both hands and took one of Alan's from the steering wheel.

"I love you, too, Alan."

Fin?

KISS ME
AT KWANZAA

L.L. Bucknor

For my crazy family. Love you guys. Happy Holidays!

. . .

"What are your plans for the holidays, Ish? If you're here the day before Christmas Eve, you must be staying local," Freddy asked as he leaned on Ish's cubicle wall.

Ishmael Cutter, or "Ish" as he was known, liked having workday chats with his coworkers...usually. But holiday celebrations weren't his go-to topic of choice. He didn't hate Christmas or the other major holidays, but having to deal with snowflake-encrusted jingle bell decorations, the bulked-up shopping crowds on the weekend (and weekdays, as it got closer to Christmas) or the god-awful Christmas music, made him want to shove a candy cane up someone's nose. Forget torture devices, you wanted to break a man, force Christmas music down his throat until gingerbread goo bled from his ears.

Music which Freddy, the office nice guy, played non-stop in their office from Thanksgiving onwards, and Ish didn't want to be the office Scrooge by asking him to change the station. He was the newbie. Well, he should say, he and his cubicle-mate, friend and secret crush, Adan Flores, were the newbies in the office. They were hired as human resources generalists, two weeks apart, a little over a year ago. *Adan.* Ish stole a glance at the other side of the shared cubicle. His friend wasn't back yet from lunch, but before he got lost in wondering what new place Adan had discovered on his lunch adventures, Ish tried to pay attention to Freddy and his Christmas cheer, and attempted to keep the inner holiday cringing to a minimum.

"My family goes all out for Christmas."

Ish would never have guessed.

"We're talking a winter wonderland, snow globe come to life. The entire house has so many Christmas lights, I'm sure it can be seen from space."

He could only imagine. "Ugly sweaters too?" Thankfully, his family never subjected him to the ugly Christmas sweaters phenomenon.

"And the matching socks. This year, we all got monogrammed footed pajamas in matching colors to wear on Christmas Eve. We have gingerbread decorating competitions. Sing carols the entire night. And I love every hokey, cheesy minute of it."

Ish tried not to visibly shudder in front of his jolly coworker who, now that he thought about it, looked like Santa Claus in a business suit, but slimmer.

"Freddy, don't get me started on family holiday celebrations. I am pretty sure mine will outdo yours," Adan called from over Freddy's shoulder. Ish, along with Freddy, turned to face Adan as he unwrapped the scarf from around his neck. "My family celebrates all the holidays. And Christmas Eve is my youngest sister's birthday, so it's even double the fun." Adan shook his head in amusement and slipped past Freddy to put away his messenger bag and outer garments.

Nothing hotter than a man in a suit, Ish thought, as he watched Adan unbutton his suit jacket and loosen his tie. He'd love to see him out of the suit too, but for now he was happy inner-perving on his coworker. Adan, with his hazel-green eyes, tan complexion and compact stature, had been Ish's ideal for too long.

"It's good to see a fellow Christmas fanatic," Freddy said, glancing at his watch. "If you're back, Flores, it must mean break time is coming to a close. I need to call my wife to remind her about a few last-minute arrangements. If I don't see either of you for the rest of the day, have a wonderful Christmas."

"And Kwanzaa," Adan chipped in.

Freddy looked back, amused. "Happy Kwanzaa to you too. Never really hear that one much, but why not?"

Adan sat down in his office chair and turned to face Ish. "Sucks you brought lunch, Ish. I found a Cuban food truck nearby. Had a great Cuban sandwich. We have to go there together next time."

"Thanks for telling me about it," Ish muttered. He'd had to brown bag it for the last week, since he'd dipped deeply into his funds with Christmas presents for his family and friends—including Adan. He knew his friend would love the tickets to the comedy show he'd got him.

"With that attitude, I should maybe reconsider sharing with you." Adan slid a still-warm sandwich in front of Ish.

Could he be any sweeter? He'd kiss him right now, if he ever thought his feelings would be returned. Just because they were both gay, the same age and currently single didn't mean Adan would automatically reciprocate his interest.

He took the foil-wrapped sandwich and put it next to his computer. He'd probably munch on it while working. "You're the best, man."

"Yeah, yeah. I'm sure you say that to all the boys. You don't fool me. You can get me the next time."

Damn right he'd get him next time. He'd also like to get under him next time, or right now if possible. He sighed; if only he dared say it.

"Were you mentally cringing at Freddy's Christmas talk?" Adan asked.

Ish didn't think he was that obvious. God, he hoped not. Adan had teased him for the last couple of weeks any time someone got extra festive at work, especially at their office Christmas party. Ish might grumble to bait him, but he secretly enjoyed the attention. "I see how you're, enjoying my suffering."

"Every time," Adan smiled. "It's a novelty to know someone so anti-Christmas. The Williams-Flores-Coleman-Benson clan love the holidays. Sometimes I think my mother searched for the most obscure holidays just to have a reason to party. And since my older brother has finally been discharged from the service, my mother has been extra celebratory. It's Damien's first Christmas home in a few years, and she's turned the house into Santa's Workshop. Littlest sis thinks it's the best thing ever."

Ish studied the pictures of Adan's large family on the shared corkboard. He'd never seen a more diverse bunch. He couldn't wrap his head around their different backgrounds, much less picture the utter madness of having so many people in a family. Adan's mother had been married three times, and had five children, ranging between twenty-nine and five years old. From the stories Adan told, his upbringing was an interesting, yet close-knit one, nothing like Ish's family who preferred order and monotony. His little family of four—which consisted of him, his parents and older sister—never changed routine, just vacation destination. Of course, he was considered the oddball, with his tattoo sleeves and piercings.

"What are you doing for Christmas, Ish?" Adan asked.

"Oh. Nothing special. My family isn't really one of those Christmas jingle bells types. We usually have dinner at my parents' house and then travel on vacation for a week. This year, I can't, since we have to work this weekend. My plan is to veg and catch up on my DVR until Saturday."

"So that means you're free on the twenty-sixth?"

"Yes. Why?"

"Would you like to come over? Meet my family? Celebrate the first day of Kwanzaa with us?"

Ish's stomach dropped at the question. Wasn't it a big step to meet the family? "I think that's my first time ever of being invited to celebrate Kwanzaa."

Adan laughed. "You're the first person I've ever invited over for Kwanzaa. We celebrate everything, like I said. Besides, my mother likes to incorporate all of our cultures. Tall order for an Irish-Honduran-African-American-Jewish family. My mother and stepfather won't mind. We could bar hop afterwards, together or with a few pals. It's up to you."

He could only process one thing at a time. He didn't even know what one wore to a Kwanzaa...party? Day? He didn't even know what to call it. "You're sure it wouldn't be an imposition? I don't even know what to bring."

"Yourself. And an empty stomach."

Too many thoughts were racing through Ish's head, all at once. He'd heard about Adan's family, seen the pictures and even accidentally video-chatted with Adan's teen sister, Natasha—well, he might have squeezed a few words in between her flirtatious chatter. Luckily, Adan was there to see that it was all one-sided.

Adan shrugged. "So will you come over? It'll be fun."

. . .

Adan was nervous as hell. He watched Ish, anxiously awaiting his response.

He'd been crushing on the guy since the second he set eyes on him thirteen months ago. But Ish was in a relationship when they first met, and Adan had an "ex thing" still going on, so the timing wasn't right. Neither man was unattached, until now.

They'd hung out as coworkers and become buddies. Ish was a great friend—certainly not classically handsome, with his big ears that stuck out like satellite dishes, and his long, slightly crooked nose. Yet, paired with a set of wide, brown eyes, inky-black hair that was slightly longer in the middle, a nose piercing (which he sadly never wore to work), and his lanky, taller frame, it worked for Adan. It worked far too well. At times, he thought his friend might've been checking him out in return, but perhaps he was projecting, and it was just wishful thinking. But if Ish didn't see him in that kind of light, maybe he could slowly try to change his mind. They got along so well when they hung out, dating should be just as easy.

Adan was still watching Ish, waiting for an answer.

Ish narrowed his eyes. "This isn't a pity invite, is it?"

Pity? "No way." Although he might have to apologize after his boisterous family were through with Ish.

"In which case, I'd love to come."

Adan internalized a groan, and hoped that the very dirty thoughts he was having didn't show on his face.

"We could go to Tino's together afterwards. Ogle that hot bartender."

"That sounds cool." Going out, that is. He wasn't keen on Ish checking out the hot bartender.

"His name's Mateo—hot name for a hot guy, though I heard from a friend he's off the market. Still, doesn't hurt to look."

Damn it. Adan would need to step up his game before Ish got his hooks into someone else. He wanted it to be him. He made a noncommittal grunt and went over his plan for that night.

Taking Ish to meet the family—he'd mentioned his friend to them, *a lot*. He blamed it on them all being so close, and having a young mother. His mom had his older bro when she was fifteen, and him at twenty, so sometimes it was more like she was his best friend, as lame as that sounded. His Honduran father, whom he never met, died before he was born, so he and his older brother were closer to their mom than most. At twenty-four, he was a proud mama's boy, And when his mother mentioned that Ish was more than welcome to come—winking when she said Ish's name—that was when he realized he might have been talking about his friend just a little too much. He had it bad.

"What should I wear? Business casual? No visible piercings?"

"Please don't hide yourself on my family's account. We are not the type to discriminate."

When Ish was away from work, he'd wear his eyebrow and nose piercings, uncover his tattoos from beneath the stuffy business clothes. That's what Adan loved the most—when Ish could be himself.

"Wear whatever you like. I'd say you could even come over naked, but there will be little eyes present."

"That's more *after-party* attire, anyway."

Adan couldn't hold back a grin. "So will you come over? Meet my fam?"

Ish rested his head on his arm and—Adan was sure it was on purpose—slowly licked his lips, before giving him an answer. "I'd love to come to your party."

"Eh, more like a feast."

"I'm going to have to remember to search on the internet 'how to Kwanzaa.'"

. . .

Ish smoothed down his wool coat, picked up the cake he'd bought from a local bakery, and walked to the front of Adan's family home. It was a holiday spectacle. There were blinking lights dripping from the roof, around every window, and even a moving Santa Claus on their lawn. Ish could hear one of the figures make noise. It sounded like *ho, ho, ho!* He'd seen the house from the end of the block—his friend hadn't been exaggerating.

Ish hesitated before knocking. He didn't understand why he was building the moment into something far bigger than it was, but he couldn't help it. Meeting family was a new experience; he'd never met any of his boyfriends' parents. Add in that he wanted to ask Adan out and he could feel himself start

197

to sweat with panic. Taking a deep breath, he tried to calm down. It was too late to chicken out. He was already at the house, and it was only a family celebration, not a date. Later, when they went to the bar, Ish would put his cards on the table and ask Adan out properly. Of course, if he wasn't interested, it could be very awkward come Saturday morning. But he'd take a chance. His best friend was tired of hearing him discuss all the excellent qualities that Adan possessed and even joked that if Ish wasn't going to make his move, he'd have to stop by at his job and ask Adan out himself. Ish would *not* let that happen.

Ish quickly pressed the doorbell before he lost his nerve. He heard high-pitch giggling as the door opened. At the sight that greeted him, Ish nearly dropped the cake box.

Adan wore a green sweater that brought out the same hue in his eyes. His close-cut brown hair was brushed to the side and he wore the biggest smile. Ish even liked his one slightly crooked front tooth.

"Ish! Thanks for coming. You brought something? You didn't have to!" He picked up the little girl crowding in the doorway with him and held her on his hip.

"Adan ran so fast to see you!" she said.

"Quiet, squirt." Adan tickled her and put her down as she laughed out loud. "This is my friend Ish."

"Hi, Ish! I'm Avery. Everyone calls me AJ. It was my birthday the other day and I'm five! Did you bring us more cake?" She looked hopefully at the white box in Ish's hand.

"I did bring more cake—apple spice cake. Happy Birthday!"

"It's not my birthday anymore, silly. It was December twenty-fourth. You have to save it up for next year! I'll be six then! Bring more cake for my party!"

"You're inviting me already?"

"Do you like unicorns?" she asked solemnly.

"Yes. I do."

She beamed. "Then you can come to my party. It's going to be a Christmas unicorn birthday party!"

Before she got too carried away, Adan intervened. "Say, AJ, how about we let my friend in since it's cold outside, and then we can close the door."

He beckoned Ish to come inside, and helped AJ close the door. She tugged Adan's pant leg to get his attention and he kneeled down. She looked at Ish as she whispered in her brother's ear. Adan whispered something back that made her giggle, and she jetted out of the foyer. Laughing, Adan turned to look at Ish, who was holding out the cake box like a war prize.

"It's a secret," Adan said, "but AJ told me it's okay to tell you. She thinks your nose ring is pretty. Glad you wore it. You look less like work Ish and more like my Ish."

Ish chuckled. "Thanks."

Adan nervously cleared his throat and took the box from him. "I mean my friend Ish. Not that I'm implying you're my Ish. You're your own person. I don't own you."

Ish touched Adan's shoulder to quell the babbling. "Adan, I got it." He watched Adan's tan skin get red around the cheeks. *Interesting.*

"Let me introduce you to my family and I can take your coat. You don't have anything valuable in the pockets, do you?"

"Er, no?"

"I ask because my mom invited my great aunt Pearl and great uncle Hubert over tonight. And, uh, Aunt Pearl has sticky fingers. Sweetest ninety-three-year-old you'll ever meet, but she'd lift all your valuables in the blink of an eye."

Ish thought he must have misheard. "Pardon?"

"Yeah, she likes shiny things, mostly. Cell phones are safe, surprisingly, but the silverware…never is if she's around."

"How much can an elderly woman steal?"

"You'd be surprised. Thankfully, Damien is on Pearl and Hubert duty this time. He'll pat her down when he brings them back to senior living tonight. It's something we're kind of used to, but newbies are fresh meat."

"And your great uncle? What is he? A bank robber?"

"No, just very grumpy. He's gotten less offensive in the last couple of years. He's actually here celebrating Kwanzaa with us…though my money is more on his wanting a home-cooked meal. He didn't bat an eyelash with me or Damien being gay, though he then proceeded to tell us about his wild days as a soldier—don't even ask, because I'm still trying to erase them from my brain. So if he scowls at you for the night, please don't take it personally. He's been warned to keep the more colorful comments down to a minimum."

Ish couldn't help raising his eyebrows. He had a feeling this would be a most interesting Kwanzaa feast. He gave Adan his coat and watched him walk to the kitchen, staring at his ass all the way. The dress pants were fitted and he got a great view. It wouldn't be friendly of him to ignore a great bum. He'd like to bite and—

"Ish! I'm so glad you made it!"

Ish shook himself out of it, as Adan's oldest sister, Natasha, slinked down the stairs to greet him. He wondered if there was something wrong, but then noticed she was moving awkwardly due to her dress being too tight. *How did she breathe?* She grabbed his hand and held it close as she grinned. *Hmmm, looked like trouble with a capital T.*

"It seems like ages since we talked, Ish. Did I ever tell you that I think your name is the coolest thing ever? O-M-G! Is that a tattoo on your wrist? What is it? It looks like a snake's head. Can I push up your sleeve to see it?" She flipped her long hair over her bare shoulder and thrust out her chest. "You need to come over more often," she said, as she pushed his sleeve up to his elbow. He couldn't even get a word in. "It's a snake. But a cute one." She winked.

Time to cut this chat short, Ish thought, but she continued.

"I was thinking of getting a tattoo too. What would you suggest?"

He tried to pull his hand back without being obvious, but she held on tightly.

"Aren't you too young to get a tattoo?" he asked.

"I'll be eighteen in twenty-three months."

Now he didn't care if he was being obvious. He snatched his arm back and took a step away for good measure. "Well until you're eighteen, I guess picking out tattoos would be a moot point." He pushed his sleeve back down. "Maybe I should help out your brother. Can you point me in the right direction?"

"I'm sure he's fine. I love your nose piercing." She moved to stand closer. "Are you pierced anywhere else?"

"Natasha." An older guy, who looked to be in his early fifties, walked in from another part of the house and joined them. *Hello, silver fox.* "Honey, I love your dress—especially the print—but did it change in the hour since I've seen you?"

"I made some minor adjustments, Daddy. I think it's more flattering, don't you think?"

"I thought the longer hemline looked much better. This one is fine, but the other version was more classic. Your pinning skills, though, are something to applaud, honey."

"I got the message, Daddy." She shuffled away, barely able to lift her legs high enough to climb the stairs. The man turned to Ish with a smile.

"I'm Ruben Coleman—Natasha and her twin brother Nathan's father. My fashionista is a handful. My gray hairs grew in the day she started puberty." Ruben looked to the direction of the stairs and shook his head. "Adan sent me to bring you to the dining room. Janet—their mother—needed help in the kitchen with something. Follow me. Do you have your pen and paper, Ishmael?"

He froze. "Call me Ish. I didn't know about the pen and paper, sir?"

They walked past a huge Christmas tree that was filled with decorations of every color and shape known to man. His family usually would pull out the artificial tree from the attic, change the lights if a few bulbs burned out, but kept it simple. Adan's family tree had personality. Ish had never seen anything like it. He passed a fully lit electric menorah next to the tree. He should have guessed their family celebrated Hanukkah, too.

"Please, call me Ruben. I'm just kidding. Then again, it might be tough remembering who's who. We're sitting around the dining table, waiting for the Umoja celebration to start." Ruben grinned at him. "You look so lost. Don't worry, we'll help you out. You're wearing the same look I had when Janet first invited me to celebrate Kwanzaa. That was five years ago. It was a culture shock but very interesting. I'm Jewish, by the way. Never knew what an Umoja from Nia was, but I'm very familiar now." They arrived at the dining room and Ruben stepped to one side so that Ish was in plain sight. "Everyone, this is Adan's friend from work, Ish."

A collection of *hellos* was called back at Ish. An elderly man whom he assumed was Uncle Hubert just glared at him from his seat. Ish glanced away and checked out the table filled with all types of covered food dishes and pans. He saw Adan appear from behind a door with the cake he'd brought. Adan winked at him and went to put it down next to a mat piled with fresh fruit and a wooden candelabra with black, red and green candles. There was a black, red and green flag on the wall and a list of principles next to it. He hoped that the list included whatever Ruben just told him about Kwanzaa or he was going to be lost. He'd forgotten to search for Kwanzaa information due to worrying about the perfect outfit to wear for meeting Adan's family. He'd settled on a red sweater, black pants that accentuated his good bits, and a green belt to try and incorporate the Kwanzaa colors.

"Adan! Mommy gave me bananas for the mat. May I have a banana when we can eat it, please?" AJ held up her little bunch of bananas proudly to Adan.

"Okay, but I put a green apple in the bowl especially for someone who loves green apples. Should I take it out?"

"I love green apples! May I have it?"

"Yes, you may, squirt," said the redheaded hottie with a buzz cut, in the corner.

That must be Damien, Ish thought. *Wow*. If he didn't have the hots for Adan, he certainly would for Damien. Tall, muscular and handsome definitely described Adan's older brother. Ish watched as Damien stood to lift AJ up to the fruit bowl. She dropped the bananas next to an ear of corn and pointed at the green apple. "I'm gonna have that soon."

"Are you going to share with me? Green apples are my favorite too."

"Okay! I'm going to go tell Mommy! Be right back! Don't go nowhere!" AJ and her wild mass of curls ran from the room to wherever her mother was.

"She's been super excited Damien is home instead of having to talk to him on Skype," Adan explained once AJ left. "He's her new favorite person."

Adan stood close to Ish and rested a hand on his shoulder. Ish swore he could feel it in his toes. He smelled so good. *Get it together, Ishmael!* He didn't want to embarrass himself in front of Adan's family. He tried not to stare too obviously as Adan continued. Ish was taller by maybe four inches, but that put Adan's head at the perfect distance away from his. If they were alone, he could just have leaned over ever so casually and brushed his face against Adan's, before he sucked on that bottom lip. Adan barely had a top lip, but his bottom lip? It begged to be played with and teased. Ish would suck on it until it...

Ish blinked and mentally shook his head. He was doing it again. He looked around to see if anyone had noticed. Adan was talking to Ruben across the table but didn't remove his hand from Ish's shoulder. Ish glanced over and caught Damien's green eyes staring back directly at him. *Guess someone noticed.* He couldn't tell if Damien was upset about it or not, since the soldier had a poker face. Adan saved him from further examination.

"Let me go around the table and introduce you, Ish. This is our great aunt Pearl. Aunt Pearl, this is my friend, the one I told you was joining us."

A little silver-haired senior citizen wearing the biggest pair of eyeglasses smiled up at him and tried to stand. "Let me hug you, young man. Properly greet you."

Adan coughed something that sounded like "cover your pockets" as the little old lady who barely reached Ish's elbow surprisingly gripped his hips and sides tightly. He kept his arms at his sides by default. She held on for a few more seconds and let go.

"Welcome," she said, and promptly sat back down.

Adan nodded and moved to the next chair, where a dark-haired teen was texting on a smartphone. "This is Nathan. You'll probably be seeing him from only this angle, since his phone became his life. Hm, I wonder why? Is it because a certain cheerleader has finally returned his calls?"

"Cheerleader, you say?" Damien asked jokingly. "Our little bro has a girlfriend? Say it isn't so."

Nathan did not look away from his screen to reply. "Shut up! You guys are just jealous I'm the only brother in a relationship. How the lonely love to mock."

"Relationship?" Damien and Adan called out together with devious grins.

"Look at you, Nathan. You used a big boy word," Adan said, and affectionately rubbed his brother's head.

"Fu—er, shut it. Just because you and Damien don't have boyfriends at the moment, don't take out your frustrations on me. Hi, Ish. Nice to meet you. My sister and brother can't stop gabbing about you." He rolled his eyes. All the siblings had various shades of green eyes, it seemed.

Adan shoved Nathan's shoulder. Nathan flicked Adan back and returned to hovering over his phone. *And Damien was gay too? What are the odds on having two hot gay brothers?*

"I do not gab about you," Adan protested. "I might have mentioned you once or twice."

"More like a million times," Nathan snorted.

Adan ignored the last comment. "You met Ruben—my mother's ex-husband and dad to the twins."

Ruben waved from his conversation with a man with coffee-bean colored skin. Ish knew he was AJ's father from the smile.

"This is my mother's current husband, Derrick," Adan explained.

Ish shook Derrick's hand in greeting.

"Thanks for coming over to celebrate the first day of Kwanzaa with us."

"A damned United Nations in this house!" Hubert announced loudly, glaring at Ish.

"And you're a member. What country do you want to represent tonight, Uncle Hubert?" Damien asked.

"Sass from the Marine!" Hubert harrumphed and took a swig from his glass while glaring at Ish.

Nathan, Ruben and Derrick tried to smother their laughter. Watching Adan's family in bemusement, Ish felt a little overwhelmed. This was a definite one-eighty from the Cutter family. He could imagine his father fainting with confusion from all the various conversations going on at once. The colors of everything would probably frighten his mother. His parents were a little on the staid and conservative side; it had taken them years to accept his nose piercing. Being gay? Not a problem. But the moment he altered his body, his mother had a conniption. He still couldn't figure it out.

"Hello, Ish," greeted a woman with curly red hair cut in a pretty, modern bob. She was wearing a green African print kaftan, and had AJ in tow. "I'm mother to a good number of this group. It's so nice to finally meet you. Call me Janet." Her green eyes twinkled. She walked toward Damien; there was an empty chair next to him. "I guess I can sit down now."

"No, Mommy, no! I get to sit next to Damien. I asked him and he said yes." AJ climbed in the chair and grabbed her eldest brother's arm for good measure.

Janet smirked from behind AJ's chair and winked. "Everything okay, Uncle Hubert?"

"What?"

Janet moved directly behind the old man and leaned over his shoulder. "Okay?"

"Fine. Waiting for you to start with the coronation! People are hungry, you know!"

"You want to represent Hungary, Uncle Hubert? Great choice," Damien chimed in. "I'm sure you'd have the entire population in tip-top shape." Everyone laughed—except for the crotchety old man, of course, and AJ, who was glowing and holding Damien's hand.

"Janet, sweetie, you should have said you needed help in the kitchen, dear. I could have lent a hand," said Aunt Pearl.

"I'm sure you could've," Adan's mom said very quietly.

"What was that, dear?"

"There was no need. I had more than enough hands on deck," she said, loud enough for her aunt to hear. "Ish, thank you for the cake. It looks delicious, though you didn't have to bring a thing but yourself. I've enough food to feed an army and then some." She put a wooden cup and a bottle of sparkling grape juice next to the candelabra. "I think I butted in while Adan was introducing you around the table, right? Natasha's in her room still?"

"Trust me, Janet. You want her there," Ruben said.

Janet sighed. It was the kind of long-suffering sigh Ish's mother usually aimed at him when he did something outrageous. "Do I even want to know?"

"Know what?" Natasha came in, wearing the same dress but it reached her knees, which were covered in leggings. She squeezed in between Ish and Adan. *Fantastic.*

"Going to miss the news tonight at this rate!" Hubert announced.

Adan didn't miss a beat. "The ginger Marine is my big bro, Damien. The squirt next to him, you already met."

AJ giggled at the introduction. "Damien, that's Ish. Adan talks about him all the time! He's his friend. He's my friend too. He's coming to my birthday party!"

"Invited him already? You must like him," Damien said.

She giggled again and whispered loudly, "He's going to bring cake. And he likes unicorns too!"

Ish was enjoying learning about Adan's family, but he was more excited at the increased contact from Adan. His friend left his hand on his shoulder, the prolonged touch just giving more credence to what he felt. Tonight, he was going to ask his friend out. No matter what. He prayed Adan wouldn't turn him down.

. . .

Natasha sauntered past both of them, brushing Ish's arm before sitting down between her twin and her father. Thankfully, she'd asked Adan about tonight's seating arrangements before Ish arrived. Adan had shut down Little Miss Happy Pants' plans to sit next to *his* friend, and was relieved she'd stuck to the arrangement. One never could tell with Natasha, even if she knew she didn't have a chance in hell.

But enough worrying about Natasha's antics; Ish smelled really great. His shoulder was so warm and firm under the red sweater, Adan could have kept his hand there all night. Except it would be too obvious and he was trying to play it subtle. He'd still have to work with the man if his plan backfired. But there was something about the way Ish was looking at him tonight…maybe he wouldn't turn him down. He just didn't need his nosy family in on the plan or, God forbid, helping him get a date.

He guided Ish toward the two empty seats between Aunt Pearl and Nathan. Unfortunately, that put Ish directly across from Uncle Hubert and his death glare. Adan motioned for Ish to take his seat. Then, as Adan sat down, their legs accidentally touched. Both froze and looked at each other.

"Sorry about that," Adan whispered.

"Don't even mention it," Ish whispered back.

Adan glanced at Damien and caught his stare yet again. His brother wouldn't call him out on it but he knew he should expect the third degree sometime in the near future.

"Let's get this show on the road then," Janet said. She clapped her hands once and walked over to the fruit on the mat. "I'd like to thank family and friends for coming to celebrate Umoja, the first day of Kwanzaa with us."

"Umoja means unity," Adan explained quietly into Ish's ear.

Ish leaned closer. "Thanks. I left my notes at home." He lingered for a few seconds, though it felt like hours to Adan. His arm felt a little colder when Ish finally did pull away.

"We're very happy to have new faces and reunited ones today. There are seven guiding principles of Kwanzaa. We celebrate each principle for seven days. Normally we'd have a drum solo, but the bongo seems to be missing. I think it might have been the summer solstice barbecue. Jury's still out." Adan's mother shrugged. They usually made their own traditions, anyway.

His mom continued reading from the list on the wall. Feeling it was his duty to check Ish was following—what kind of host would he be otherwise?—Adan turned, and once again found himself momentarily lost in those wonderful brown eyes.

They *were* flirting, damn it. Adan liked it very much and wanted more of it. He tuned out the rest of his mother's speech while he and Ish played a tame version of footsie underneath the table. They pressed their legs together, neither moving, while stealing shy glances in between his mother's words. Adan had completely forgotten about explaining what it all meant, until he heard the loud pop of the bottle being opened: it was time to drink from *Kikombe cha Umoja*: the wooden chalice.

His mother poured the drink into the cup for everyone to take a sip in honor of the day. AJ got the first sip, and Adan realized his mother had lit the first candle already. How long had he zoned out? He wasn't sure. He watched AJ pass the cup to Damien, and returned his gaze to his mother, who gave him a thumbs-up sign as she walked to her seat. He knew she was referring to Ish. He rolled his eyes but she just smirked.

"Not drinking any of that!" Uncle Hubert complained loudly. "Fizzy drinks give me gas. It's the chemicals! Not natural!"

"You should only do what's natural, Uncle Hubert. You should make that your first decree when you're in charge of Hungary," Damien quipped, passing the wooden chalice to his mother. She took a sip and passed it to Derrick. He did the same and passed it to Ruben. The twins were next and then it was Ish's turn.

He kept his eyes locked on Adan's, licking his lips seductively before he took a small sip from the cup. Adan didn't know if he could take any more without embarrassing himself at the dining table. He hastily took the wooden cup, sipped, and passed it on to Aunt Pearl.

"Oh, fiddle sticks. This cup is almost empty. I can get some water from the kitchen instead—"

"There's enough for one more mouthful, Aunt Pearl," Adan cut in.

"Oh it looks like there is. Thank you, dear." She peered at him over the rim and took her sip. Once she was finished, Damien took the chalice. Crisis averted.

"I'll get the roast from the kitchen, Mom," Adan suggested.

"Kitchen?" Aunt Pearl chimed in. "I could help the boy." She smiled and moved to stand.

"No! I mean, thank you, Aunt Pearl. I think I have it."

"I could help," Ish offered. Adan was about to tell him he was a guest, but Ish continued, "After you show me where the bathroom is. Please."

"I can help with that, Ish," Natasha said from next to her father. Ruben and Derrick both shook their heads.

"Appreciate it, sis. But I'll show him." Adan grabbed Ish's shoulder before anyone else offered. Janet and Damien were busy with uncovering dishes. Nathan and the dads were chatting—Adan had no idea what about. He was no longer paying attention. He got up and led Ish past the pouting Natasha, to the hallway, pointing out the bathroom door, but Ish grabbed his hand and walked both of them inside.

Ish closed the door and steered Adan backwards, until he was pinned against the sink. Ish kept a hold of his hand. "I never imagined doing this here but I have to."

"You mean having conversations in my family bathroom is not the ideal?"

"Adan, I'm serious. It really isn't ideal but I can't hold back. I want to be with you. So much."

Adan froze.

"And if you tell me the touches and the looks tonight were just a part of my imagination, I'm going to call you on it. I've dug you since the day you walked onto the Human Resources floor."

"Me too."

"Why haven't we dated?"

"Our timing was off. You had Wes, and I was doing that idiot loop with my ex."

"Let's fix this, then."

Ish moved closer, cupping his hands around Adan's face as he breathed him in. Adan placed his hands over Ish's and waited to see what his next move was. Ish took his gesture as acquiescence and tilted his head to the side, his lips closing in, his gold nose-ring tickling the side of Adan's nose as they tried to get the angle right.

They teased each other with small kisses, pulling back each time to smile at each other, then pressing their lips together again. Adan pushed his tongue deeper, licking around Ish's teeth. Ish returned the gesture, the sweet kisses quickly picking up a spicier, more intense vibe. Adan leaned closer, lifting his hands to hold Ish's shoulders. Ish moved one hand up and down Adan's side, grazing gently across his body and driving Adan crazy. The body contact left Adan in no doubt; Ish felt the same as he did. He was already aroused, and if they kept this up there was no telling where it would end. He moved to rub himself against Ish's thigh, as they continued making out, for a moment forgetting where they were and desperate to take it to the next stage.

A knock from outside the door barely broke through their haze, but as soon as AJ announced, "I have to go potty, please," both men broke apart, breathless and panting. *Bathroom.* They were in his family's bathroom, and Adan had temporarily lost his mind to the thought of what he wanted to do to Ish. He reluctantly let go.

"I'll be right out, squirt," he said. Ish was straightening his clothes and Adan the same. They grinned at each other.

"Rain check?"

"Yeah." Adan ran his finger across Ish's cheek and smiled. "We could go back to my place, instead of Tino's."

Ish pouted dramatically. "No hot bartender ogling?"

"I'd rather ogle you."

"You say the sweetest things." He winked and opened the door.

Thankfully, AJ was nowhere to be seen, and Adan decided she must have gone to use the other bathroom, which was a blessing because he didn't know what excuse he could offer for being in the bathroom with Ish. AJ was terrible at keeping secrets and he wouldn't lie. "I'll go get the roast for real this time. Meet you back at the table."

Ish kissed the side of his neck and left.

Adan practically floated to the kitchen. He couldn't believe how things had progressed, but he wasn't complaining.

He was searching for the pot holders when he heard someone clear their throat.

"So? You like Ish, huh?" Damien asked with folded arms.

"Was it that obvious?"

"Considering the two of you have been staring at and touching each other for most the night, not to mention the mysterious disappearance and your red lips, I think you moved a long way up on the 'I dig Ish' scale."

Adan groaned.

"Oh, and AJ telling me the delightful story of how you nearly knocked her over when you heard Ish at the door. That was the deciding factor. He's cute."

"Back off, Williams. He's off the market for the time being."

"Is that so, Flores?"

"Yep."

"Guess I shouldn't ask about catching up with you after I drop Aunt Light Fingers and Uncle Grump home?"

"Nope. No third wheel for tonight, thanks."

"Wear a condom."

"I don't know if sex is even on the menu."

"I've been eyeing you guys tonight. So, you know…condoms." Damien raised his eyebrows in warning and then turned to leave.

Adan found the holders in a drawer and brought the hot dish into the dining room. Natasha had taken his seat while he was away. He didn't know what she'd cornered Ish about, as he only caught the tail end of the conversation.

"I appreciate the offer," Ish said. "I'll still be gay in twenty-three months, though."

Adan pointed his thumb toward Natasha's chair and she rose, then stopped to wink at them. Adan shook his head in despair and reclaimed his seat next to Ish. "I apologize for whatever she said."

Ish shrugged and squeezed Adan's fingers. "Can't knock a girl for trying."

Adan looked around the table. AJ was sitting next to Damien, waving her hands animatedly. Aunt Pearl was shiftily eyeing the cake server. Nathan was teasing Natasha about something, but she ignored him to smile flirtatiously at Ish. Ruben was discussing something with his mother and stepfather, all three laughing loudly. And here was Ish, in the thick of things, and ready to start something with him.

Adan had a lot to be grateful for this Kwanzaa.

LION'S HERO

Alexis Woods

MY OVERFLOWING THANKS:

To my beta readers Francú Wulf Godgluck, Eric Alan Westfall, Jacob Lagadi and Victoria Milne. To Shayla Mist for *Judgement Day* and Jacob Lagadi for *Six Wing Soldiers*.

. . .

DEDICATION:

To my own little *Etan Ari*. Roar, mighty lion, roar.

Prologue

His awe-inspiring presence filled my room. The air around me grew heavy and overpowering. I struggled not to drop to my knees, for He did not care for that.

A light hand, like a breath of spring air, brushed over my hair, calming me, filling me with warmth. I stood with my head bowed, ready to go wherever He needed me to go, do whatever He needed me to do.

"Ari," He said.

"Yes, my Lord."

"It's time."

"I'm sorry, my Lord. It's time for what?" Nervously, I shuffled my feet. His aura pulsed strongly when He was this close, walking around me. Studying me. It had been a long time since my Lord Father—*Baali, Adonai, God*—had approached me directly. His actions were always purposeful, He did nothing without meaning. I stood a little straighter under His scrutiny, and felt a caress to my back, between my wings, to settle me.

"To claim your other half, my brave lion."

"O-other half? Mine? I don't—"

"Yes. Your other half is *My* hero; he's a man of God."

I was surprised by His turn of phrase. "My Lord?"

"A figure of speech, Ari. He'll be yours and yours alone, but he finds faith in Me. Do you understand?"

I wanted to just say no, and started to shake my head, but caught myself. I knew that if I remembered my Lord's words, eventually I would come to understand what He meant. He only ever hinted, made all of us journey for the knowledge. I nodded instead.

"When do I leave, my Lord?"

"Now. Oh, and Ari?" He paused, and I listened raptly. "Call me Father."

An overly bright flash of white light filled my vision and, as my sight slowly returned, loud noise filled my ears. *Dear God, I'm not in Heaven anymore.*

On the first night of Chanukah

Ari stood facing a black door. Music raged on the other side, the sound seeping heavily through the cracks. He took a deep breath in and braced himself before pushing it open and found himself in a dimly lit corridor. In front of him, a line of humanity, mostly women scantily dressed, stood waiting to be allowed to enter by a brute of a man checking small cards as he was handed them. He marked their hands, unhooked the rope and let them enter the room to his left. Here the hallway opened up into a large room jammed with bodies, the music deafening, lights flickering, humans singing and, *is that dancing?* A huge, pulsating sign caught his attention. *Club Haven* flashed in colors of purple and green.

Running his hands down his body—his very *human* body—Ari took in his clothing. He wore a black logo shirt and tight dark jeans, along with boots on his feet and a silver ring adorning his left thumb. Sliding his hands over his head and ears, he discovered a short, spiky hairstyle and pierced ears. Fingering the earrings, three on one side, five on the other, Ari mumbled, "Really, my Lord?"

A long-haired girl dressed in black and silver spun in front of him as she walked by and ogled him. A silver bar ran through one eyebrow and a ring through her lip.

"Nice shirt," the girl threw his way, before twirling around to her friends.

"Thank you," he replied to her back. Ari slapped his hands to his face to check for further piercings. "Well, thank you for that, I guess."

He pulled his shirt away from his body to see what was imprinted on it. *Satan's Thorn*, the shirt proclaimed, complete with rampant lion brandishing a wicked-looking stake.

"Funny, my Lord," Ari muttered with a laugh. An answering chuckle filled Ari's mind, followed by a reminder of *Father*. "So, do I get a hint?" The profile of a man with dark hair, the ends curling at the collar of a white shirt, sleeves rolled up displaying an array of colors on his skin, filled his mind. The club's bar was in the background.

Ari gasped and fell back against the door in surprise, palming his face. Father's words came back to him: *He's a man of God, he finds faith in Me, he'll be yours...* He's, he, he'll. Ari sucked in another long breath. He knew of angels sent to Earth to meet their other half—his mentor Leo, was one of them—but he'd heard they were always women. Never had a man been chosen as an other half.

"Are you alright?" a deep voice asked, coming from his right.

Ari cautiously spread his fingers to see a white button-down shirt, the top two buttons undone. A thick gold chain bearing a Star of David sat atop golden skin. He looked up at a scruffy oval complete with solid chin, straight nose, and warm brown eyes he immediately wanted to get lost in. *Oh God! Oh God! Oh God!*

I'm right here, Ari. No need to yell.

Those let-me-drown-in-you eyes came closer. Ari jerked his head back, knocking it into the wall. "Ow!" He grabbed it and began rubbing the sore spot. With his head down, Ari didn't realize the stranger—*my other half?*—had stepped closer. When the man tried to pull his hands away, Ari stepped to the right, his military reflexes kicking in, moving him away from any unknown. Ari's brain was in overdrive. Was this the one promised to him? This man had him in figurative knots, tongue-tied and dizzy.

"Skittish," the man mumbled, obviously mistaking Ari's step back. The man glanced to the side briefly, just long enough for Ari to see his profile and the bar in the background. Ari internally acknowledged that this man was Father's choice for him.

"Head okay?" the man asked, leaving the space between them.

"Yes, thank you."

"Mind if I take a look?"

"Um…alright." Ari lowered his hands and bent his neck, allowing the man to run his fingers through his hair, feeling for a bump. The soft touch was almost as calming as—

"Got a name?"

Ari was pulled from his previous thought before it had a chance to fully form. The fingers continued to gently probe. He winced when the lump was found.

"Ari."

"Well, Ari, you'll survive. Only a small bump." Hands were removed, and Ari felt the loss tugging at his core. He continued looking down, his mind registering the dress shoes and dark slacks. Moving upwards, Ari noted a bulge, a braided belt, a white tucked-in shirt, and then he returned to the man's groin. Ari chewed on his bottom lip.

A chuckle above and a spiral of Hebrew letters on an arm swept into his vision. Ari grabbed the arm, twisting it to read the words. He gasped when he realized what it said.

The man stepped close again. "Can you read it?"

"Yes," Ari breathed, meeting those soul-searching brown eyes again—this time seeing streaks of gold radiating out from each iris. "It's beautiful. You bound them as a sign upon your hand?"

"Yes," the man replied. His expression asked questions that Ari knew he wouldn't have—couldn't give—the answers to.

"Are you faithful?" Ari asked.

The corner of the man's mouth twitched up. "Always. Are you?"

"Completely."

Eyes widened in response to Ari's reply. "I see." The man's gaze flicked up and down Ari's body. "Interesting shirt. Are you a thorn in Satan's side?" he teased.

Ari grinned. "Most definitely, and any chance I can get."

This time, the man laughed, the joy lighting up his features. Ari could feel the instantaneous pull to latch on to this man and never let him go, but a surge of anxiety had him looking away, briefly, then back up. The man was studying him thoughtfully.

He glanced at his watch. "I'm sorry, little lion, I've got to go." He reached forward with his other hand to touch Ari, but pulled back before making contact. "I hope to see you again."

Ari nodded, but as the man tried to retrieve his arm from Ari's grasp, Ari tightened his hold. "Wait, please. You never told me your name."

He smiled, and Ari's breath caught in his throat. "It's Gabriel."

"Well, goodbye, Gabriel," Ari said, finally releasing his hold on Gabriel's arm.

"Goodnight, little lion." And he was gone. Ari leaned back against the wall, his heart racing.

Are you going to let him get away?

Ari raced after Gabriel, exiting the club and looking around for him. A white shirt disappeared to the right and he took off after it, dodging humans in his way as he threaded past… *What is this place?* Humans were dropping coins into flashing machines and pressing buttons or pulling levers. Ari spotted Gabriel getting into an elevator marked for the parking garage. By the time he reached it, the doors had already closed. Twisting his fingers, he waited to see what floor it stopped on. He thanked the One Above that it was only two floors as he sprinted up the nearby stairwell.

Ari wasn't expecting Gabriel to be standing just in front of the exit door when he slapped it open in his rush to reach him, and he ended up bumping hard into his back. Gabriel turned around, surprised.

✿ ✿ ✿ ✿

"Ari?"

"I'm sorry, I'm sorry." The man stared at his feet, absently rubbing one wrist, but there was no mistaking the flaxen, spiked hair or those cuffs on his ears.

Gabriel, his heart pounding, took in the nervous gesture of his little lion. *His? Where did that come from?* He shook his head, clearing his thoughts and tried to focus on the boy—no, man—in front of him. "What's wrong?"

Ari looked up, confused. "Wrong? Um...there's nothing wrong." He refocused his attention on the ground.

Gabriel tilted his head to the side and crouched down, trying to get into Ari's view. The height difference was a bit of a problem, and he ended up with one knee on the ground. He put his right hand on Ari's, stilling his nervous motions. "Ari."

Vivid green met his. Cat-like in their color, the wide-open stare caught Gabriel off-guard. *Scared? Of what?* Gabriel's social work skills with teen runaways crept to the fore. He kept his hand steady on Ari's, but otherwise made no further moves.

"What can I do for you?" Gabriel didn't want to assume anything. Ari might look young, but he must have had an ID saying he was twenty-one to be in the club. When only silence prevailed, Gabriel chose to ask the age question. "How old are you?"

Ari looked deep in thought, and then he smiled. "Twenty-one."

"Good. You live around here? I've never seen you at Haven before."

This time a frown and a shake of Ari's head.

Kicked out? Homeless, maybe? Gabriel flipped through options in his mind. *Shelter? Which one? The Atlantic City Rescue Mission would chew him up looking like that. Covenant House would take him, but it's late. I could just take him back to the clinic, we've got extra beds there.* "Do you have someplace to stay tonight?"

Ari's eyes grew large and he stepped back from Gabriel. "I've got to go," he muttered, looking away. Ari's body twitched in what looked like a moment of indecision before he turned and fled down the stairs.

Gabriel sighed and stood. He debated going after him, but from past experience knew it would probably freak Ari out more. Instead, he walked in the general direction of where he thought his car was, a click of his key fob reminding him. The short drive home to his little row house in Gardner's Basin was filled with images of a shy, green-eyed lion and a little prayer that perhaps they might meet again.

✿ ✿ ✿ ✿

Ari found himself curled on his right side on a bed. Shrugging his shoulders, he felt the weight of his wings shift and he sighed. He brushed a hand along his left ear and found only a single small stud. A check of the right turned up none. Before Ari could even fathom the meaning of this new development, He appeared in a gradually widening spray of light. Ari quickly swung his legs over the edge of the bed and stood, head respectfully tilted down.

"My Lord," then Ari remembered and added, "Father."

"You ran away, Ari."

"I know, Father." Ari shifted nervously. "I got... I'm sorry. I panicked. I don't know how you...I mean, how did you expect..." Ari clenched his fists in frustration. He knew it wouldn't do any good to be angry with Him. It'd drive you madder until you realized that the problem wasn't with Him, but with yourself. Ari sank onto the bed, slapping his hands on his thighs.

"How do I fix this?"

"Tonight check the wallet I gave you. It contains everything you need. You have seven more nights."

"Seven, my Lord! I mean, Father. What...what happens if I don't complete my mission in time?"

He chuckled. "Your *mission*? An interesting choice of words, Ari. Hmm. I suppose if you don't complete your mission this Chanukah, there will always be next year, or the year after that."

"Oh." Ari let that sink in. Eight nights of Chanukah, and already he'd let one slip away.

"Are you ready to return, now?"

"Yes, Father. I'm ready."

On the second night of Chanukah

This time Ari arrived in an empty bathroom stall. He quickly pulled out the thin wallet from his front pocket. Thumbing the twenty-dollar bills, he counted five. Next he extracted the lone card, a picture staring back at him. The fiery emerald glare in the boy's eyes and the piercings had Ari astonished as he recognized himself in the picture.

The top of the card read: New Jersey Identification Card. It continued with his name, Ari MacCabe. *MacCabe, Maccabee. Descendant of Judah, then, my Lord?*

Of course, Ari.

The address read 21 Seaview Lane, Galilee, New Jersey, and a date of birth of December sixteenth, 1993.

Today is the seventeenth.

Ari chuckled, realizing that yesterday was his "birthday." *Guess I was celebrating.*

Sliding the card back inside, and the wallet into his pocket, Ari exited the stall. His reflection in the huge wall mirror stopped him. He ran his fingers through the thick, short, tawny brown hair, softly spiked on top. He leaned closer and opened his eyes wide to take in the bright green irises. Ari turned his head back and forth to examine his ears, admiring the colorful array of studs and cuffs. Stepping back, he checked out his clothing. He wore the same tight, dark-wash jeans as before, topped with a new T-shirt—this one proclaiming *Serpent's Destruction*. A large writhing serpent was impaled on a wicked-looking bright silver sword, upright like a cross.

He took a deep breath in, then stepped to the door, and pushed it open, finding himself inside the casino, just outside Club Haven. The line to get in was already snaking around the ropes. He slid into line, quietly stepping forward with the rest of the queue. He was barely paying attention to his surroundings as he advanced, nervously pulling out his wallet to pay the cover charge. He startled when a hand was placed on his shoulder. Ari found he couldn't turn around with the solid grip of the hand holding him in place.

Warmth pressed against his back, and an arm adorned with Hebrew letters curved around his body to tap his wallet.

"Put that away, I've got this."

Ari breathed a sigh of relief at Gabriel's presence. Although he knew the concept of money, he'd never actually used it before. He watched the exchange with rapt attention, filing the information away for another time.

Gabriel turned, replacing his wallet, and snagged Ari's elbow, leading him away from the cashier. The hallway before them was filled with eager patrons awaiting their turn past the bouncer. The club music was already loud, and Gabriel leaned in to speak.

"I was hoping you'd be here."

A little shudder ran through Ari. "I was hoping you'd be here, too." He glanced up, briefly making eye contact with Gabriel, before dropping it down to the floor. "I'm sorry I took off yesterday."

Gabriel's hand cupped his cheek, his thumb gliding softly across the surface. "It's alright. I'm sorry I scared you off."

Ari blinked slowly, leaning into Gabriel's touch. He spoke softly, just loud enough to be heard over the music.

"You didn't. I, uh, panicked. Sorry."

"Don't be." Gabriel dropped his hand, and they stepped forward as the line shortened in front of them. "You looked a little lost last night, and you surprised me, following me like that. I work with a lot of runaways and young men with no place to go."

Ari glanced up, surprised. "And you thought that I was…"

Gabriel raised his eyebrows. "And are you?"

"No. I mean, um, actually you're sort of right. I live with Father, but," *Sorry, my Lord*, "he pushed me out yesterday. He said I've got to find my… He gave me eight nights and some money. I can return after that, tail between my legs, if needed. I'm hoping it's not, but it's hard…" Ari swept his hands down in front of himself.

"And you're spending your money here?" Gabriel frowned.

Ari squeaked, his mind racing. "I got in free yesterday because it was my birthday, and I was hoping to find you tonight." Ari dropped his head, saw the empty space, stepped forward and found himself in front of a much taller and very broad man wearing a Club Haven shirt with an expectant expression on his face.

"ID?" he said, holding out his hand. The guy was huge, and Ari reflexively stepped back, bouncing into Gabriel. He spun around, and found himself staring at a blue cotton covered chest. Hands grasped his arm, and Ari looked up to find Gabriel smiling at him.

✿ ✿ ✿ ✿

Gabriel was staring down at Ari when a new voice interrupted them.

"Ari?"

"Thelial," Ari said on a breath of air.

"In the flesh." He opened his arms wide, and Ari quickly moved in to hug him.

Gabriel gaped at Thelial's breathtakingly beauty. Easily six foot four, he was a blond-haired, blue-eyed Viking God. Gabriel wasn't aware his face showed his longing to be the one holding Ari. Glancing up, he saw Thelial looking back, and was alarmed to realize he'd been caught staring.

"Hi, I'm Theo," he said, extending one hand in greeting, the other arm wrapped protectively around Ari's shoulders. Gabriel ignored the hand, frowning at the offending arm. *Damn, there's no competition if Ari wants him over me. And look at that smile.*

"I'm Ari's half-brother."

Thank God. Gabriel grinned in relief, and, stepping forward to get out of the way of the other patrons, he reached out to shake Theo's still offered hand. "Gabriel."

"Did he send you?" Ari asked Theo, his shoulders hunched, his hands stuck in his pockets.

"Yes and no," Theo answered. "He told me you were in town, but I didn't expect to see you *here*. Should have known you'd show up at Club Haven. The whole family does at some point."

Gabriel was puzzled by Theo's response, but Ari nodded as if he expected it. "So, Ari's not staying with you?" he interjected, his mind reeling from this familial turn of events.

"What? No." He glanced at his brother. "Father didn't set you up anywhere, Ari?"

"No," Ari replied. "My ID and a hundred dollars."

Theo appeared displeased by his father's actions. "And how long?"

"Seven days."

Theo glanced back at Gabriel, looking him over, top-to-bottom, and then he nodded.

Gabriel chuckled, spreading his arms wide. "Do I pass muster?"

"May I see your tattoo?"

Gabriel stepped closer and held his arm up. Theo cradled it with his hands, gently turning his arm and reading the words inked into his skin. *And into my soul.* The tension Gabriel had been feeling drifted away at Theo's touch, a calm replacing the rough sea inside his mind.

Theo nodded and was about to release Gabriel's arm when Ari delicately took hold of it.

"How long ago did you have it done?" Ari asked, his fingers tracing the words.

"I had it done in bits and pieces whenever I could afford it and had the time. Started when I was twenty-five. Five years later, I finally had it completed over this past Thanksgiving break, so about three weeks now."

Ari let a fingernail drift over Gabriel's skin, and he sighed at the soft touch. Theo cleared his throat, bringing Gabriel back to reality. The music suddenly seemed too loud.

"Here." Theo held up two free admission passes. "Take these for another time, and go on and get out of here. You won't be able to hear each other inside." Gabriel slid them into his wallet as Theo opened the line barrier to let them out.

"Thank you, Thelial." Ari said, beaming up at his brother.

"Yes, thank you. I really appreciate it. Ari…" Gabriel held out his hand, hoping Ari would take it.

Ari looked at Gabriel's hand, then glanced back at Theo, who gave a single nod. Ari's smile grew wide as he turned back to Gabriel and joined their hands.

✿ ✿ ✿ ✿

Gabriel sat Ari down outside the little coffee shop located inside the casino, and asked what he'd like to drink. Ari shrugged. He'd never had food before. It wasn't necessary on his plane of existence. A night of rest in Heaven was all he needed following a battle. Ari frowned at himself internally. *How can I be so confident on a battlefield, yet a simpering fool here?*

"I know just what to get you," Gabriel said, patting his shoulder. Ari watched him as he went to stand in line.

You're no fool, Ari.

I know, my Lord, but I'm lost here. I know nothing! I feel like an idiot, bumbling around the battlefield, randomly striking out and hoping I hit the enemy and not my compatriots.

I sent Thelial to help.

Yes. I'm sorry for my anger. Tomorrow I'll need to meet with him earlier to gather his knowledge.

It will be arranged.

Gabriel placed a white paper cup in front of Ari. "Are you alright? You looked a little lost in thought there."

Ari met Gabriel's gaze as he sat. "Yes, I'm fine. Thank you for asking and for this." He indicated to the cup. "What is it?"

Gabriel bequeathed Ari one of his heart-stopping smiles. "Hot chocolate."

Ari watched as Gabriel pushed back the little tab on the lid and secured it in place. He did the same to his own cup, and inhaled the sweet aroma.

"Oh, this smells good." He wrapped his hands around his cup, mimicking Gabriel, and took a tiny sip. He jerked his head back at the heat in his mouth. "Hot!"

"Um," Gabriel murmured, watching Ari as intently as Ari was watching him. "That is why it's called *hot* chocolate."

222

Ari frowned at the slight, then realized Gabriel's little smile was because he was making a joke, and he brightened. *I really need that crash course.*

"So, Ari, do you attend college?"

"College? Oh, you mean university? No, I teach."

"Really? You're so young. What do you teach?"

"Battle tactics, weapon forms, like sword and shield, spear, arch..." Ari trailed off at the peculiar look on Gabriel's face. "What?"

"Is that some sort of military school?" Gabriel wore a distinctly displeased expression.

"Oh! I shouldn't have told you that. I'm sorry. I think I'd better go." Ari began to rise from his chair.

"Wait, please." Gabriel placed his hand on Ari's arm, and Ari could feel the warmth travel into him. He sank back down.

Ari raised the cup to his lips, and blew away the steam before trying another sip. This time the flavor rolled over his tongue. He savored it a moment with eyes half-closed, before taking another sip.

"Do you like it?"

Ari nodded. "Yes, it's very good." He paused a moment. "Um, so yes, I'm a military trainer, and if needed I'll lead on the battlefield."

"Really? I didn't take you for armed forces. Definitely explains those lovely muscles you have. You must be a military brat in order to have moved so fast through the ranks."

"Brat?" Ari asked, blushing. No one had ever told him he had lovely muscles.

"Your father's military too, right? So you grew up with it."

"Oh, yes. Father's the Commander."

"Well, that explains the harsh 'go out there and make your way in life' deal he threw you."

"What? No!" Ari was aghast at the thought. "Father is most generous and kind, but He is sometimes set in His ways. He does what He thinks is best for his children."

"You have a lot of brothers and sisters?"

"Brothers, and yes, there are quite a few of us." Ari sat quietly a moment recalling his comrades in arms. God's Army was many, and bonded together, they fought off the devil's evil forces.

"So," Gabriel said, interrupting Ari's reverie, "could you take me?"

"I'm sorry. Take you?"

"You know, in a fight. Could you beat me?"

Ari studied Gabriel, surveying his height, his body mass, and then, realizing this body wasn't his normal body, he shook his head. Ari figured he'd better give a vague, yet truthful, answer and decided these questions were touching a bit too close to home.

"I don't know. Right now, I'm not myself. It's late. I'd better go." Ari stood once more. "Thank you for the drink." And he quickly walked away.

✿ ✿ ✿ ✿

Gabriel was stunned. Again, Ari ran. This time he figured he'd better go after him. He scooped up the cups and discarded them, then took off after Ari. He saw him turn down a corridor, but when he got there, Ari was no longer in sight.

After a search turned up nothing, Gabriel sighed and returned to his car. Tomorrow was another long day of damaged and misguided teens and other lost souls, all needing the help he could provide. He sent a little prayer heavenward, asked God to watch over and protect his own little flock, and to do the same for Ari. He brought the star he wore to his mouth and kissed it. *Amen.*

✿ ✿ ✿ ✿

Ari sat up in bed, trying to process all the implications of his mission. He'd never really given much thought to having a mate, partner, whatever. All he knew was any angel lucky enough to find their special other half, wasn't seen again in Heaven. He'd lost his closest friend, one he truly called brother, that way.

So, this is it. My last few days in Heaven. Am I ready to leave? Have I accomplished all that I am supposed to do? Who will take over for me, and what will I do once I'm human? Gabriel had seemed upset about the battle training and military issues, but what else was Ari trained for?

Gabriel worked with runaways, perhaps he could too? Ari growled with the many problems plaguing him, and he ran his fingers through his mane of hair in annoyance.

"I'm glad to see you awake," Thelial said as he strode into the room. Ari rose to greet him and smiled at their nearly identical heights.

"It seems Our Lord is playing a cruel joke on me, Thelial."

"Why do you say that, Ari? He does go about things in an unusual manner, but who are we to question Him? We are here to serve Him."

Ari sat back down heavily onto his bed, his wings fluttered out to the sides. "I know, I know. Yet… Still… I don't know. He says Gabriel is my other half, mine alone, and I feel the pull when we are together, but what do I have to offer him? I'm a nervous wreck as a human."

Thelial chuckled and stepped closer. Of course, an angel of love would think the whole situation was funny. He wasn't living it. Thelial ran his hand over the top edge of Ari's wing. It was a soothing gesture, one he certainly appreciated at the moment.

"Let me help you, Ari."

Ari looked up at him. Thelial's face was glowing with inner peace.

"Close your eyes," he said. Ari did and felt Thelial's calming influence run through him. "Good. Now pay attention, and I will tell you everything you need to know."

On the third night of Chanukah

Running late, Gabriel sprinted through the casino towards Club Haven. Not paying attention to who he was zigzagging around, he stumbled to a halt when he heard his name being called loudly.

"Gabriel!"

He back-tracked to find Ari and Theo outside one of the buffets popular with the gambling community. Theo was dressed for work in a club logo shirt, standing a full head taller than Ari. Gabriel smiled, taking in Ari's spiky hairstyle and skin-tight jeans, but when he took in the image on his shirt, his smile fled.

"What's wrong?" Ari asked.

"I'm not a particular fan of that shirt." The image was a collared demon kneeling before an angel, a lion reclining at the angel's feet. *Devil's Due* titled the picture.

A cocky grin emerged on Ari's face as he looked down at his shirt. He chuckled. "Sorry. Father is having a bit of fun with me."

"Your father designed the shirt?" Gabriel asked in disbelief.

"Yes," Theo replied. "Father has a particular love for angels, especially those that fight against the demons among us. Ari tells me you help teenagers." Gabriel nodded. "Father will be very happy to learn that you help them in their fight against their inner and outer demons."

"I guess that's one way to look at my work, but still," Gabriel pointed at Ari's shirt, "it's collared and kneeling. Is it better to be forced to submit, or to die for your beliefs?"

Theo held up his hands in defeat. "Now you're talking Inquisition, and war history is so not my thing. I'd better get going to work anyway. Ari, I'll see you tomorrow."

Ari nodded, and watched Theo as he walked towards the club. Once he was lost from view, he turned back to Gabriel, shyly smiling.

"Do you think we could get more hot chocolate? I really liked it."

"Sure," Gabriel agreed, and swept his hand out to indicate for Ari to precede him. They walked side-by-side in silence, until Ari stopped him with a hand on his arm.

"It really bothers you?" he asked, chewing on the side of his bottom lip.

"What? Oh, your shirt. Yeah, it does." Gabriel didn't like seeing Ari upset. He reached up and thumbed Ari's lip loose from his teeth. He slid his palm quickly across Ari's cheek to soothe him before dropping it down and stuffing both his hands in his pockets, unsure if he was allowed to touch.

"I work with a lot of kids and young adults that haven't had it as good as you and me. Maybe they were raised by a single parent who worked all the time, or were bullied or beat on by their dads."

"Father would never!" Ari interrupted.

"I didn't say he did, but collaring and controlling—not my cup of tea. It brings up too many stories of the nasty things people can do, and then say they do it in the name of love or honor."

Ari opened his mouth, but Gabriel overran him. "Yes, I understand it can be done in a loving manner if both partners want that, but we can just get this cleared up now—I'm not into *that* stuff."

"Okay," Ari said with a smile, a little bounce and a shrug. "No collars, no controlling, but," he leaned in close to Gabriel and whispered, "what if I want to call you Daddy?"

Gabriel's mouth dropped open, and Ari laughed. He spun around on one foot and did a little crazy hip swivel dance.

"Who are you, and what have you done to my shy, little lion?"

"Your little lion learned how to roar today."

Gabriel grinned, Ari's mood was infectious. "Really? And who do I have to thank for teaching you?"

"Thelial. Now can we get some hot chocolate?"

✿ ✿ ✿ ✿

Oh, my! I can't believe I said that. To Gabriel. Ari's mind was racing, almost as fast as his heartbeat.

When they reached the little shop, Gabriel said, "Sit," and Ari sat, only realizing it afterwards he'd done it without hesitation. He sat there with his elbows on the table, chin resting on his fists, and studied his other half.

Gabriel was shorter than Thelial, but still he was many inches taller than Ari. His hair was dark brown, cut short. His body filled out the button-down shirt quite nicely. And those muscles... Ari was quite taken with those large forearms and stunning gold-flecked brown eyes.

Gabriel's vehemence about Ari's shirt surprised him, but he was glad to see some backbone where before he'd seen only the sweet side of Gabriel. Ari knew he needed a strong-willed partner. Father was always full of advice and support whenever Ari needed a bit of guidance. His daddy comment wasn't far from the truth. Still, Ari had to wonder what he could offer Gabriel in return. *No opportunity like the present.*

Gabriel placed a cup in front of Ari, and he pulled off the top to allow it to cool quicker. He waited for Gabriel to take his seat next to him before he spoke.

"So, can I ask you a question?"

"I'd be surprised if you didn't," Gabriel replied.

A feeling of apprehension stole over Ari. "What's that supposed to mean?"

"Just that this is the third time we've met up, and there hasn't been a whole lot of time for getting to know each other."

Ari's expression placed the blame firmly only his own shoulders.

"Hey," Gabriel said, nudging Ari's leg with his knee. "None of that."

"How can I not?" Ari implored. "It's my fault."

"I'm not blaming you."

"But you should."

"Why? And really, why are we arguing about this? Shall we make this our first official fight? Be good to get it out of the way now, I suppose."

Ari looked horrified. "We're fighting?" His breath quickened. Things were definitely not going as planned.

✿ ✿ ✿ ✿

The look on Ari's face panicked Gabriel. Determined not to let this night be a repeat of the prior two, he placed his hand on Ari's thigh and squeezed gently.

"Stop," he said firmly. "Stop that right now, and listen to me." Gabriel inwardly laughed at his statement. *God, I sound like my father.*

Ari stared down at Gabriel's hand on his leg, and he gradually calmed.

"This okay?" Gabriel asked quietly, adding another little squeeze with his question.

"Yes," Ari whispered.

"Look at me."

Ari slowly complied.

"Now, ask me your question."

"Oh, um…" Ari bit his lip, momentarily taken aback. "I was just wondering if I stayed in the city, is there someway I could be of use to you…at your job, I mean?"

Continuing to speak in softer tones, Gabriel responded with a smirk, "I'm sure I could find a use for you…at my job, I mean." Gabriel was thrilled to see Ari's face flush pink as he broke off eye contact. It was a rather endearing quality in the boy.

"You're really cute when you blush," he murmured. This only reddened the glow of Ari's skin further.

Gabriel couldn't believe he called Ari cute. *Like he's a child, when in reality, twenty one was an adu—* He cut off the thought. *Maybe, I do have a daddy-kink.* It would explain why he couldn't get any of his prior relationships to work. They had all been men his own age, or older, with established careers. They didn't need his help or his guidance, not like Ari seemed to.

Gabriel slumped back in his chair with this new revelation. Ari looked over at him puzzled.

"Are you okay, Gabriel?"

229

He met Ari's gaze, and his smile grew as he lost himself in those big green eyes. "Yeah, I'm good. Really good, in fact. Did you mean what you said about staying here?"

"I think so. I'd like to, but I'd need to find someplace more permanent to stay and, of course, I'd need to find work."

"Where are you staying now?"

Ari looked down again. "I can't tell you," he mumbled.

"Can't or won't?"

"A little of both. I want to tell you, but I'm not allowed to. Maybe someday, it all depends."

"On what?"

"A couple of things, but I can't really tell you them either."

Gabriel was starting to get annoyed with this conversation. It was hard to get to know someone when they withheld information and talked in riddles. He was a straightforward kind of guy and didn't like secrets, especially not with someone with whom he was trying to make a connection. What kind of relationship would this be if it started with what was essentially lies and omissions? Gabriel decided to bite his tongue for now and try another avenue.

"Okay, why do you need a job? You told me yesterday you were in the military. Are you already done with your service time? Seems kind of quick, only three years, assuming you joined up at eighteen."

"I'm a trainer, not really in the military."

"You said you led troops. I wasn't aware the United States Military let outsiders control their forces." Gabriel watched as Ari fidgeted, his fingers tapping the table, but his leg stayed still. Gabriel guessed Ari didn't want to dislodge his hand, and he figured his hand might be the only thing keeping Ari from running.

"Um... I..."

"I'd like the truth, Ari. Don't lie to me."

Ari's head snapped up, stunned, his mouth a thin line. He stared hard at Gabriel for a moment, before dropping it down again.

"I can't," he mumbled.

"Can't what?"

Ari stood abruptly, Gabriel's hand sliding off his leg. He snagged onto Ari's wrist instead. Ari, in turn, stared at Gabriel's hand.

"I'm sorry. I'm not allowed to tell you the truth. Not yet, anyway. Please... Let me go." The last came out in a choked up whisper.

Gabriel released his hold on Ari, who raced off. Again. He smacked his hand down on the table, almost toppling the cups. Growling low in his throat in frustration, he lowered his head into his hands.

✿ ✿ ✿ ✿

"You're making a real mess of things, aren't you?" Thelial said as he entered Ari's room. Ari rose from the bed, his restlessness manifested in red-rimmed and puffy eyes. Thelial enveloped him in a hug.

"I just don't know what to do. Tell me what to do, Thelial. Please." Ari wasn't above begging at this point.

Thelial released him and reached up to the top of Ari's wings. He let his hands glide down the edges. "Sit," he said.

Ari settled himself back onto his bed and watched Thelial pace the small confines of his room. A small writing desk sat in one corner, a globe of the Earth upon it. Ari watched as it rotated all on its own, glowing on one side, mimicking the Earth's rotation of the sun. It was approaching evening where Gabriel lived.

Ari stood and walked over to the globe. He let his fingers drag along, ghosting the East Coast of the United States. New Jersey was tiny compared to most of the other states. He wondered again what he would do once he lived there. Was there a place for him in a place like that?

Atlantic City was full of sinners. Perhaps he could be an officer in their law department. But working with young kids, like Gabriel did, sounded much more fun. Fun he rarely had here in Heaven. He was always busy training or off fighting some demon. He was sure living outside Heaven would have its sad moments and be hard work, but he would be with Gabriel, and really... *that's all that matters, isn't it?*

He turned to face Thelial. "I have to tell him the truth."

"He won't be pleased."

"No, I suppose *He* won't, but I've got no back story, Thelial. I'm a ghost trying to become real."

"Don't you mean an angel trying to become human?"

Ari chuckled. "Yes, you're right, of course."

"How do you think Gabriel will react?"

"If I'm lucky, he'll think I'm crazy, but he'll believe me. If I'm not..." Ari shuddered, his wings fluttering. He rubbed his face and, his hands sliding back to his ears, fingered the three piercings. "If I'm not, I guess there's always next year." He finished with a sigh.

On the fourth night of Chanukah

Ari pushed open the door to *Young Heroes*. He liked the name; it suited Gabriel. He was stopped by a second door; this one locked. Ari peered through the glass door to see Gabriel moving around the room, straightening chairs and restacking magazines.

He knocked on the glass, the sound loud in his ears. He watched Gabriel spin around and glare at him. Gabriel visibly sighed, gave his head a little shake, and then he turned around and disappeared out of sight.

Ari paled in shock. He placed his hands flat on the door and began slapping its surface, yelling Gabriel's name. When he didn't return, Ari's forehead joined his hands. The cool glass did nothing to ease the heat of his face. He closed his eyes against the pressure building there.

I've lost him already, my Lord, haven't I?

Have you lost faith in Me already, Ari?

No! I just… Am I doing the right thing?

You have your plan, Ari. Now you must follow through and deal with the consequences of your actions.

A soft tap on the glass brought him back to himself. Gabriel was standing on the other side of the door, a suit jacket on, and a backpack slung over one shoulder. He motioned for Ari to step back. Ari moved to the side of the vestibule, but when his back hit the wall, his legs buckled and he sank to the floor.

Gabriel yanked the door open and squatted down in front of him. He brought a hand up to Ari's cheek and gently used his thumb to smear the wetness there.

"What are these for?"

Ari touched his wet cheeks with his fingertips. "What are they?"

"Tears?" Gabriel tilted his head, "Have you never cried before?"

"Never."

The singular reply surprised Gabriel. He shifted to sit next to Ari, pulling his knees up and resting his wrists over them. He stared at his hands thoughtfully.

"I find that hard to believe, Ari. Nothing has ever made you so sad or mad or upset in your life that you cried? And yet, here you are crying." He turned to look at Ari, who was still fingering his cheeks. "So, what has you so upset now that you finally are?"

Ari peeked over at him. His mouth twitched and another tear fell.

"I'm afraid. I've never been afraid before. Not once. Not even when I had to fight my first... You'll not believe me when I tell you the truth. You won't believe me, and then I'll be gone."

"Where will you go? Home?"

"Yes," Ari whispered, "but it won't be home anymore. Just a holding place, I think."

"A holding place... That's an odd way to describe your home."

"I'll have to wait another year."

"To what?"

Another sob, this one wracked Ari's body. Gabriel threw his arm around Ari's shoulders and pulled him into his body. Ari's head fell against his chest, but his hands still lay in his own lap. *He's afraid to touch me.*

"To what, Ari? What will you have to wait another year for?"

"To come back. To find you. To try again."

Ari's whispered, stuttered words crashed into Gabriel's heart, along with a thousand questions. One rose above the others: *why does he need to try again when he already has me?* That question brought another, perhaps even more important: *Does he? Does he have me?* Gabriel's heart screamed "Yes" while his mind was wary. There was still this unspoken "truth" to discuss.

Gabriel's fingertips gently caressed Ari's bare upper arm.

"Come with me tonight?"

"Where are you going?" Ari asked.

"Temple. It's not far." *I could do with a little guidance tonight.* Gabriel held his breath.

Ari swiped at his face as he sat up. "Yes. I'd like that."

As Ari came around the car, he could see a frown pulling at the corners of Gabriel's mouth.

"What?" he asked, then realizing where Gabriel's gaze was drawn, Ari looked down at his shirt. Tonight's was again black, emblazoned with a stylized sun. Over the sun were the words *Celestial Transcendent*, and pictured were three symbols: a Star of David, the Cross of Jesus and the crescent moon and star of Islam.

"I'm not dressed correctly for your temple, am I?" They moved towards the entrance.

"Well, I don't usually make a habit of wearing jeans and a T-shirt to temple, but on occasion I have, and there are plenty who do on a regular basis. We're pretty relaxed here. Rabbi Cohen will certainly be amused.

"Why's that?"

"He's young, about my age, and definitely progressive. You'll like him."

"If you like him, I'm sure I will, too."

They'd reached the front doors and Ari stopped, staring at the many people inside the foyer. The rabbi was welcoming the congregants as they arrived.

"Ari?" Gabriel stepped in front of him.

Ari turned his attention back to Gabriel. "I'm sorry." Then he smiled, a cocky little smile. "I know I'll like your rabbi very much." He stepped around Gabriel and entered the building.

"Ari!" the rabbi exclaimed upon seeing him and, ignoring those in front of him, pushed through to embrace Ari.

When Gabriel eased up next to Ari, the rabbi finally noticed him, his brows rising in surprise.

"Gabriel." They shook hands. "*Shabbat shalom.*"

Gabriel responded in kind, following with, "How do you two know each other?"

"Malachi's family," Ari answered at the same time Malachi said, "Cousins." He smiled fondly at Ari. "How long are you here for?"

"Another four days at least, then we'll see." Ari glanced over at Gabriel, indicating his reason. "Hopefully longer."

"Ah. Well, inside with you both. We'll be starting soon. Come see me after?"

Ari nodded and allowed Gabriel to guide him towards another room, the double doors wide open and inviting. Ari could feel the room beckoning him, and he readily stepped inside. Gabriel's hand on his lower back directed him down the aisle towards the bema and into a row of seats.

Gabriel settled beside him in the aisle seat. Ari watched as he reached into his jacket pocket and withdrew a round piece of fabric which he placed on his head.

"So," Gabriel began in hushed tones, "a rabbi in the family, and you can read Hebrew. Can I assume you're Jewish, too?"

"I…" Ari began, then stopped. This was a heady discussion, so he quickly gathered his thoughts before speaking. "I don't identify with being Jewish or Christian or Muslim." He chuckled, patting the picture on his chest, then sobered. He had to make sure his following words were construed correctly.

"I believe in the one true God and the existence of angels and demons. I believe there is a heaven. I believe in 'do unto others as you would have them do unto you.' I often ask my Lord for guidance and wisdom and strength, and sometimes He answers and sometimes He requires me to puzzle out the answers for myself.

"And does He lend you His strength?" Gabriel asked sincerely.

"Not often, but once or twice, when I faced a particularly nasty demon, I could feel extra power in my sword arm, and I knew it was because my Lord was with me."

"You sound like you know God personally."

Singing erupted from the rear of the room signaling the end of the conversation. Still, Ari whispered softly, "I do."

✿ ✿ ✿ ✿

Gabriel sat frozen, disbelieving what his ears had heard. How could Ari claim to know God? That was impossible. And crazy. And yet it seemed somehow believable or, at least, Ari believed it to be true.

He could feel Ari relax as music and song filled the room. The cantor and the rabbi walked to the front of the sanctuary, cajoling everyone to join in. Ari did not participate much in the service, he just seemed to take it all in. At the point when Rabbi Cohen instructed everyone to take a moment and pray silently, Ari closed his eyes. Gabriel was enamored of the peaceful expression gracing his features.

He'd caught sight of the rabbi watching Ari periodically throughout the service. A tiny flare of jealously emerged, and it unnerved Gabriel a little. Another man, even if it was a cousin, looking at his little lion. *And there I go again, calling him mine.* Gabriel tamped down that green spark, telling himself that Shabbat was a time for peace and reflection and a renewal of body and soul. And how much he'd like to get his hands on Ari's body.

Gabriel must have made some small sound, because suddenly Ari was peering at him, one side of his mouth quirking up as he reached over and placed his hand into Gabriel's.

The service continued with song and prayer until, again, Rabbi Cohen raised his hands and the congregation rose. Ari's attention was riveted on the ark, while Gabriel's was insistent on not moving from Ari. The Torah was removed from the ark and placed into the arms of a congregant who began a slow progression around the room. The rabbi approached Gabriel and Ari and held out his hand.

"Ari?"

Ari looked over at him then reached out to clasp his hand. Gabriel barely suppressed a growl as he watched Ari's cousin pull him up onto the bema. A whispered conversation took place with Ari shaking his head. The rabbi placed his hand on Ari's shoulder probably assuring Ari he could do whatever was being asked of him. Ari finally nodded.

The Torah was disrobed of its ornaments and mantle and laid reverently onto the podium, and Rabbi Cohen motioned with his hands for everyone to sit. He waited a moment for everyone to take their seats before speaking.

"It is with great honor that I invite my cousin, *Etan Ari ben Baali*, to bless our congregation with the reading of tonight's *parsha*. And I'd like to call forth his beloved, *Gabriel ben Yahuda*, for the *aliyah*." He held his hand out towards Gabriel. In shock from the use of the word beloved, he didn't immediately rise. A tap on his shoulder from behind finally prompted him to movement.

Gabriel walked to the front of the sanctuary trying to clear his throat of the lump that had formed. When swallowing failed to work, he took a deep breath and glanced up at Ari. He found a pale man staring back at him, rocking slightly from side to side. A nervous man who needed his strength. With that thought, Gabriel leapt up the steps to stand to Ari's left and placed his hand on his lower back. Ari leaned in, seeking more contact, so Gabriel reached across his body to take Ari's hand. The unexpected death grip he received made him wince, and immediately it let up, but Ari didn't let go.

"Alright, boys," the rabbi whispered to them, "make me proud." Ari let out a small huff of a chuckle and a lot of tension from his body. Rabbi Cohen picked up the corner of his prayer shawl and pointed out the starting words to Ari, who placed the pointer there. Ari took a deep breath in, and then he nodded for Gabriel to begin the prayer before the reading of the Torah.

Gabriel did his part, adequately chanting the blessings before and after, but Ari was magnificent. His rich, tenor chant held the entire congregation in rapt attention. In fact, Rabbi Cohen had to stop him as he far exceeded what was supposed to have been read this evening. After Gabriel chanted the final blessing the rabbi pulled them both back from the Torah, calling out to the congregation, "A moment's indulgence, if you will."

He turned them to face each other, placing a hand atop each of their shoulders. Ari reached out and took Gabriel's hands in his.

The rabbi and Ari began speaking to each other in Hebrew, but Gabriel didn't understand any of it. It was one thing to recite and know the blessings, another to actually know the language. He quickly tuned it out, as he often did when surrounded by other languages at the market or other stores, until a sharp retort from Ari snapped him back. Whatever had been discussed, Rabbi Cohen was reluctant to let go of the conversation. Another curt *"Lo"* from Ari, and it was done. The rabbi nodded, moved his hands to their heads, muttered what sounded like a quick prayer, and then he gently urged them back to their seats.

Ari took Gabriel's hand, leading the way, but they didn't return to their seats. Ari pulled him right out of the sanctuary. The muttered, "Hell," was all Gabriel needed to pull Ari back, encircling him in his arms, pinning him to his body. Ari pressed his face into Gabriel's chest, wrapping his arms around Gabriel's waist.

"Tell me," Gabriel insisted.

"He doesn't agree with me that I should tell you."

"I really don't understand what's so bad. What has you frightened you'll scare me away? I work with runaways and kids that have tried to kill themselves; kids that are living on the streets, working the streets, kids addicted to some nasty stuff. I've seen it all."

"But you haven't seen it all. I'm an angel of God who only knows how to do one thing: kill demons. God sent me here to find my other half—you—and fall in love. And I've only got four more nights to do it."

Ari pulled in a long breath and slowly let it out. "Now you think I'm crazy. Which is okay. I know I sound crazy. It's a hard thing to be—"

"Stop. Please, just stop." Gabriel pushed Ari out from his body, but kept a hold on his arms. Ari was staring at the ground, his body limp. Gabriel was sure he would drop if he let go.

"I should go. I'm sure you think—"

"Stop telling me what I should think, Ari. I can't even think with you going on like this." A tinge of anger laced Gabriel's voice, which he knew he shouldn't let out, but it was awfully hard in the face of what Ari was telling him.

Ari fell quiet. He slowly raised his head to meet Gabriel's gaze.

"For an angel who kills demons, you don't seem to have much confidence in yourself."

"I know. I said the same to Thelial."

"Your brother."

"An angel of love."

Gabriel sighed. "Your half-brother, Theo, is an angel of love?"

"Oh! I wasn't supposed to tell you that, just the part about me."

"I see." Since Ari seemed a little more steady on his feet, Gabriel let go of him and moved over to a nearby bench because his own legs didn't quite feel up to standing anymore. *Four nights to fall in love.* He let his body sink down, and leaned back against the wall. His hands lay folded together in his lap.

Ari stared at Gabriel's dejected form. He knew he'd messed it all up. It wasn't supposed to happen like this. He should have listened to Malachi. Should have waited until the last possible moment. He hadn't even gotten to kiss him other than a little peck; barely touched him other than holding his hand and arm. A few hugs where he'd felt safe, wrapped up in those strong arms. Already, Ari felt unprotected, his shield gone, his sword missing. But how to fix this?

"Gabriel." Ari moved closer. His glare was intimidating, and Ari almost took a step back, but he knew he could be strong and hopefully set things right with his other half. Ari sat down next to him, pausing, uncertain how to tell Gabriel what he needed to say. Ari's thoughts ran wild, his emotions felt ragged as his mind fought this previously unknown entity of doubt. Still unsure what to say to make him understand, his words stumbled out.

"Gabriel, I… I was given eight nights. Eight nights…to find you, and convince you I'm the one for you, but I've been going about it all wrong, running away when I should have been…trying to stay. Your world is not my world. I know so little about it. If I'm ever to survive here, I'd need your help—your guidance, your strength—because once I leave Heaven, there's no going back."

The sanctuary doors opened, and the congregation began filing out. Malachi caught Ari's attention and mouthed, "Everything okay?" Ari shrugged slightly in reply.

Gabriel rose and looked down at him. "I'm gonna go, Ari. Can Rabbi Cohen get you home?"

"No, Gabriel. I will take myself home…until the day you do."

Gabriel nodded, before turning away. Ari watched him go. He wasn't sure if Gabriel understood what he was implying, but he prayed he did.

✡ ✡ ✡ ✡

Ari lay on his side upon the bed, a pillow covering his face. Pressure against his shoulder startled him.

"Giving up, Ari?"

Ari pushed the pillow off, but didn't move to rise. "Not sure there's any point, Father. I've made quite a mess of things."

"Hm. I'm not sure it's as bad as you think it is." His hand glided down Ari's arm before being removed.

Ari held in a sigh at the loss and rolled onto his stomach, keeping his face turned away. "Pretty sure it is."

"Ari." The note of disappointment in His voice was evident and Ari winced. "You only have four more nights."

"I know. I just can't. Not tonight."

"You're going to waste a whole night? No. You're a warrior, my brave, fierce lion. You need to fight. I'm going to send you to Leo. He'll help you."

Ari pushed to his elbows and shifted his sight towards the floor. *Leo.* He could see His long colorful robe beside him.

"Raiding Joseph's closet again, my Lord," Ari teased.

"Ari!"

"I'm sorry." He paused and drew in a deep breath. "Yes, I'll go see Leo. Perhaps he can help me. If nothing else, it will be good to see him again."

And once again, light filled his room.

On the fifth night of Chanukah

Ari pushed open the door in front of him. A man stood stone-faced and motionless in the middle of the room. He wore a simple karategi: a white wrap-around jacket, tied with a black belt and white baggy pants; his feet were bare. Over one shoulder peeked the hilt of a sword, while in his hands was another sheathed blade and a rolled up pile of fabric. The man looked up as the door squeaked shut, and Ari's breath hitched.

"Leo," he murmured.

A huge, toothy grin transformed Leo's face into one of utter joy. He dropped the blade and fabric and hollered, "Brother!" before bounding across the room and crushing Ari in his embrace.

Upon release, Ari moved to hold Leo at arm's length, beaming. "I've missed you."

"Hey. What's going on out here?" came from behind Ari. He turned to see a petite woman, her long, dark hair pulled up into a high ponytail, striding towards them. Her tank top and shorts revealed olive-toned skin and toned muscles. Leo turned Ari by his shoulders to fully face her.

"Nina, this is my brother, Ari." The note of pride in his voice boosted Ari's self-esteem. He whispered in Ari's ear, "My other half."

"*Dios mio*! I'm so happy to finally meet you." She held out both hands in greeting, and Ari grasped them. "Leo has often spoken of you, but I didn't ever think I would get to meet any of his family."

Ari was confused. He silently looked to Leo for an explanation.

"How did you find Leo?" Nina continued. "He said he broke off all contact with his family. Said his father kicked him out."

Ari grimaced. "Actually, it was Father who sent me."

Nina's eyebrows rose in astonishment.

Leo chuckled. "Father has his ways of knowing. I'm sure he always knew where I was." He explained to Nina, "He's always hovering around somewhere, and makes his presence known when he wants to."

Ari laughed. It was the most generic, yet true, statement about Him.

"So, what brings you here now, Ari?" Leo asked, probably for Nina's sake, since Ari was sure he already knew to expect him. Ari's smile faded.

"Oh, um…" Ari glanced over at Nina. "My other…person…has me… Let's just say I'm a bit unsettled." Ari swallowed hard, his fingers drumming against the side of his leg.

Nina looked from Ari to Leo. "I'll just leave you two to talk. Don't be a stranger, Ari, okay?"

Ari nodded and waited until Nina was back in her office. "Leo, it's not going as planned. Father thought you might be able to help."

"It's not a battle mission, you know. This sort of thing takes finesse."

"Yes, and I've none of that."

"Sure you do. Think of it like sword practice. Each twist of wrist, push of muscle, thrust of arm, is an intricate dance. You need finesse for that."

"I suppose."

"Come. Let's get you changed. Then we'll practice."

✿ ✿ ✿ ✿

Theo must have been watching for Gabriel because, when he spotted him, Theo's stare was boring into his body. Gabriel looked around as he approached, hoping to spot Ari.

"He's not here," Theo told him.

"Do you know where he is?"

"Of course."

"Are you going to tell me?" Irritation laced Gabriel's question.

"No."

"No? Why not? I'd think an angel of love would be jumping at the chance to add another notch to his belt."

"I don't appreciate the analogy, Gabriel. Besides, what I do doesn't work on angels and their human halves." Theo's eyes narrowed. "Wait! You believe him about us?"

"Actually, I'm still deciding. For all I know you could be in on the same deception."

"Deception is a rather harsh word to use, Gabriel." Theo's voice had a hard edge to it that almost had Gabriel backing down. Instead he chose to stand and fight.

"Well, Theo, if you and Ari aren't going to provide proof then, I think, it's exactly the right word to use. You're both deceiving me with, if not outright lies, then certainly omissions. Now, tell me where he is."

Theo smiled, further aggravating Gabriel. His body was practically vibrating with anger. When he didn't get an answer, Gabriel huffed and spat out, "Fine. Perhaps Malachi will know where to find him."

Gabriel turned away, only to be stopped by Theo's hand on his shoulder.

"Wait. Please. I'm sorry my smile angered you. I smiled because I think you are absolutely perfect for Ari. He needs someone strong-willed, someone to give him purpose. I believe Father was right when he chose you."

Gabriel blinked, and his mouth dropped open, but no words came out.

"Tell me," Theo continued, "how do you know Malachi?"

This was a question Gabriel could answer and, perhaps, learn an answer to a question that had plagued him last night. "I see Rabbi Malachi Cohen every

242

Friday night. He's my temple's rabbi and supposedly Ari's cousin. But, I guess, it's just another deception to add to the list."

"Gabriel," Theo pulled him closer so he could speak in a softer voice, "Father instructs us to use these words—brother, cousin, father—because they are words you understand. We are all family. All brothers—family. Besides, never once did Ari lie to you. I told you I was his brother. Who called Ari his cousin?"

"Malachi," Gabriel breathed out, some of his anger fading. "But what about the weapons training and the demon fighting?"

"All true. Here." Theo reached into his pocket and withdrew a folded piece of paper, offering it to Gabriel.

"What's this?" Gabriel unfolded the note.

"Ari's current location."

✿ ✿ ✿ ✿

Gabriel could hear the clanging of metal on metal before he even pushed open the door to Tribunal Training Academy. He slipped inside and sat in one of the chairs located along the outside of a large practice mat. At its center, separated by a few yards, were two Aris: his and another without the spiky hair and ear piercings. Truly, this other man—*another angel?*—must be related to Ari. Gabriel soon noted a few other differences between the two of them.

Suddenly, Ari and his twin raced towards each other, their weapons swiftly attacking and defending. Their steps were sure and cat-like. *No, lion-like.* A dance of movement with the ringing of steel the song.

They separated again, and their swords spun in slow, intricate, identical arcs. Faster and faster, they spun, until only a blur indicated the path of the blades. As one, their swords slowed, then stopped, and they raised the blades in front of their faces. Ari bowed to his twin, but when the twin reciprocated with an even deeper bow, Ari gasped.

"Truly," the twin said, standing upright, "the student has surpassed the teacher."

The smile that split Ari's face was breathtaking. Gabriel held his own breath, waiting to see what would happen next.

Ari knelt down on one knee and laid his sword on the floor. He then leapt up and flew towards his twin, wrapping him in his arms.

"Thank you, Leo."

"You're welcome, Ari. Now, how do you feel?"

"Better. I needed that. I've missed your guidance."

"But now you have another to help you."

"I'm not sure that's true. I don't think he will accept me." Ari's chin dropped to his chest.

Leo planted a finger under Ari's chin and gently pushed upwards. "I think you are wrong."

"How can you be so sure?" Ari asked. Gabriel could hear the pleading note in his voice.

Leo turned to look at Gabriel. When Ari followed Leo's gaze, Gabriel rose from his chair.

Ari turned slowly and began to stalk towards Gabriel, running a hand through the top of his hair, spiking it up, making him even more lion-like. Gabriel's heart was pounding, and he flexed his hands nervously.

Once Ari stood before him, Gabriel raised his right hand and combed his fingers through Ari's mane. With his fingers threaded in the thick hair, he pulled Ari towards him. Gabriel tilted Ari's head back, his breath warm on Ari's parted lips.

"I'm going to kiss you now," Gabriel said.

All Ari managed was a quick, "Ye—" before Gabriel's lips were on his.

✿ ✿ ✿ ✿

Sweet, sweet Gabriel. Ari followed Gabriel's kisses, mimicking his movements of lips and tongue. Gabriel tasted delicious. *Better than hot chocolate.* Ari giggled and Gabriel pulled back.

"What's so funny, little lion?" Gabriel whispered.

Ari smiled shyly. "I was just thinking about how your kisses taste."

"Well, if you have time to think then I haven't kissed you well enough." And he dove back in for Ari's lips.

Gabriel wrapped his left arm around Ari's waist, pulling their bodies closer together. Ari placed his hands on Gabriel's chest. He could feel Gabriel's strong heartbeat beneath his fingers—*beating for me.* Gabriel licked at Ari's lips, and Ari opened. The driving kiss was strangely soft and breathtakingly violent at the same time. A pleasant shudder ran through Ari's body, unfortunately ending the kiss.

"Are you alright?" Gabriel asked.

"Yes," Ari breathed. He pressed his ear to Gabriel's chest between his hands. Each *da-dum* of Gabriel's heartbeat pulsed through his body.

"Does your heart beat for me?" Ari asked.

"I think it must because every time I think I've lost you it aches."

Ari lifted his head. The sincerity he saw in Gabriel's eyes stole Ari's breath. He raised his hand from Gabriel's chest to his cheek. Gabriel leaned into the touch.

A cough sounded behind Ari and they separated. Ari turned to find Leo standing a short distance away with his arm around Nina's waist.

They stepped forward. Leo held out his hand and introduced himself to Gabriel.

"And this lovely lady is my wife, Nina."

Nina lightly smacked Leo on the arm before also extending her hand to Gabriel.

"Gabriel," he replied. "It's nice to meet you both. So, Leo, what's your relation to Ari?"

"Brother," Ari and Leo replied at the same time, and then they reached out and clasped forearms.

"Now, this relation I believe. You two look enough alike to be twins."

"No, Leo is definitely older," Ari teased. "He taught me everything I know about weapons and fighting."

"Until Father booted me out," Leo finished.

"Oh," Gabriel responded, his finger pointing between Leo and Nina, "so, you two?"

Leo frowned and looked intently at Ari. "He knows?"

Ari nodded, stepping closer to Gabriel, who put an arm around him.

"And do you believe, Gabriel?"

"I'm still undecided, but Theo makes a pretty good argument."

"You spoke with Thelial?" Ari asked.

Gabriel looked down at Ari. "He's the one who told me where to find you."

"Thelial is here?" Leo inquired.

"Yes," Ari answered.

"Who else?"

"Malachi."

Leo sucked in a deep breath through his teeth. "This is not good, Ari."

"What? Why?"

"Joseph came to see me yesterday. He said he had a vision, and that help was coming, but he refused to give me any more information."

Ari groaned, sinking into the closest chair. He placed his elbows on his knees and his head in his hands.

Gabriel knelt on one knee next to him and placed a hand on Ari's thigh. "Tell me."

Ari dropped his hands, but left his head hanging as he shook it.

"Ari." The bite of command in Gabriel's voice startled Ari into looking up. Ari leaned back in the chair, putting some space between them, and sighed.

"It's never good when Joseph has a vision. Something is going to happen, something bad."

"Well, we'll need to gather," Leo said. "How long, Ari?"

"Three more nights."

Leo's lips formed a tight thin line as he nodded. "I'm sorry, but we'll have to take care of this."

"I understand."

"We'll meet tomorrow. Is Malachi bound?"

"I'm not sure what you mean."

"Is he married?"

"Yes," Gabriel answered for Ari. "He's married to the cantor."

Leo turned to Gabriel. "Are you able to contact him?"

"Yeah. I've got his number. He helps me out at the clinic sometimes."

"Clinic?"

"Young Heroes."

Leo grinned. "I know the place. You do good work there."

"Thank you."

"Judah is here too," Leo said, getting them back on topic. "He's on the police force. I'll contact him and see if he's aware of anything going on and have him meet us tomorrow. Gabriel, if you'd please contact Malachi, then that just leaves you, Ari, to contact Thelial. Can you also see if you can get any more information from Joseph? I suspect he'll confide in you since you're still technically in command."

"Okay," Ari agreed.

"Good. Let's go."

"Wait." Gabriel said. "Now? But we just—"

"Fine," Leo cut him off. "You have one hour."

✿ ✿ ✿ ✿

Ari rose and took Gabriel's hand, pulling him to his feet. Gabriel's knee was not at all happy at having been pressed to the wooden floor, and he winced.

"You okay, Gabriel?"

"Just a little rusty. Nothing a little lube won't fix." He huffed and laughed at his own joke, while Leo snickered along. Ari looked between the two of them.

"I don't get it," he said beginning to pull Gabriel towards the locker room.

"What's not to get? Lube…sex?"

Ari pushed open the door. "I don't know those words, Gabriel."

Gabriel pulled Ari up short and stared at him in amazement. "How can you understand the concepts of collars and control and kink, and not know about sex?"

"Thelial used a lot of words, and I only understood half of what he told me. Like intercourse…is that something between meals?

Gabriel's hands flew to cover his face. "Oh my God, Ari. Are you seriously telling me you never…" He paused and peeked out through his spread fingers. "Are you a virgin?"

Ari smiled. "That's what Thelial said I am, but I thought that word was for a woman who hadn't birthed any children."

It was Gabriel's turn to groan and sink down onto the freestanding bench in the room. He closed his eyes as he gripped the edge of the bench.

Ari knelt down on both knees between Gabriel's spread legs, and placed his hands on Gabriel's thighs.

When Gabriel opened his eyes and saw Ari kneeling before him he growled, "Ari, you're killing me here."

"What? How can I?" Ari's face registered shock. "I've got no sword or knife here. I'm barely touching you."

Gabriel moved quickly to reassure Ari, stroking his hands along Ari's arms. "It's just an expression. Come, sit here." He patted a spot next to him on the bench. Ari rose and stepped one foot over the bench, straddling it when he sat. Gabriel turned his body, sliding his own leg over the benchtop so they could face each other. Their knees were touching as they studied one another.

Gabriel held his hands out to Ari, palms up. When Ari put his hands into Gabriel's, he lifted them to his shoulders, instructing Ari, "Hold on to my shoulders." Once Ari's hands were in place, Gabriel leaned over and placed his hands on the back of Ari's legs, at the top of his calves. He lifted Ari's legs and pulled him forward until Ari's legs were over the top of his. Gabriel slid his hands up Ari's thighs and grabbed the belt tying Ari's gi.

"This okay?" Gabriel asked.

"Yes."

Gabriel inhaled deeply as he thought about how to phrase his next question.

"Ari."

"Yes."

"Do you know how a person loses their virginity?"

"Of course. They fall in love and then they 'make love,' whatever that means."

"Fuck," Gabriel muttered.

"Make love and fuck are the same thing?"

Gabriel chuckled at his inadvertent use of the words. "Yeah, they are."

"Um, I thought making love was like making each other feel good. Your kisses make me feel good." Ari's lower lip snuck into his mouth and Gabriel drank in the sexy sight.

"Kisses are only the beginning, Ari." Gabriel reached up and ran his thumb over Ari's lips. "Perhaps you'd like to learn the next step?"

"Yes. Please."

Gabriel began working to undo the knot in the belt around Ari's waist. Their foreheads came together as they both watched Gabriel's fingers worry the knot loose. Gabriel unwound the belt and dropped it on the floor. He leaned back and raised one hand to Ari's cheek, trailed his fingers over Ari's lips, feeling the hot exhalations of breath.

He continued down the side of Ari's neck, rapid pulses of blood coursing under his fingertips, before moving into the hollow of his throat where softly placed touches garnered quick inhalations. Down further, fingers traveled on bare skin until they met the V of the overlapping lapels. Gabriel flattened his hand against the rise and fall, twisting until his thumb was pointed down. He inched under the fabric, his hand pushing the jacket open and exposing golden skin.

Gabriel began again at the hollow, his lips parted as he drew in short bursts of air, ghosting his fingertips over the exposed skin. Down, down, down and he heard Ari's breath hitch. Up, up, up and over Ari's throat until Gabriel cradled his chin in his hand. He held Ari still while he leaned in and kissed him tenderly.

Gabriel shifted so that he could place feather-soft kisses on Ari's cheek, He placed his other hand on Ari's back, between his shoulder blades, feeling the heat of his skin through the fabric. Gabriel slowly rose up, tipping Ari, easing him to lay flat on the bench.

Ari's gi fell further open, revealing an unfinished tattoo over his heart. Gabriel gasped and immediately traced the letters inked there.

Gabri. Five letters for five days. Each letter was inked within a candle, with the candelabra already fully tattooed below the letters. He could easily picture the completed Chanukah menorah complete with candles spelling **Gabriel's** when it was finished.

Ari's whimper refocused Gabriel. He glanced up to see Ari's head tilted back, and his back slightly arched, Ari's chest was pushed up as if trying to seek more contact. Gabriel raised his right hand to Ari's cheek, and let it glide down over his throat, continuing along the center of Ari's chest, stopping only when he reached the waistband of Ari's pants. He spread his fingers wide and slid them to hold onto Ari's hips.

Leaning forward, Gabriel nuzzled Ari under his chin, pressing kisses to his throat. Gabriel swirled little figure eights with his tongue to Ari's neck, and then blew cool air on them, stringing Ari along with each new sensation.

"Gabriel?" Ari whispered breathlessly.

"Yes, my little lion?" Gabriel replied as he continued the gentle assault of kisses to Ari's flesh.

"Are we making love?"

Gabriel chuckled. "Not yet, but we're getting there."

✿ ✿ ✿ ✿

"Okay," Ari said, wondering how long until they were *there* because Gabriel was making him feel really good. Ari drifted in the feel of Gabriel's lips on him until an errant thought arose that Gabriel wasn't getting any enjoyment out of this, so he asked, "But what about you?"

"Hm?"

Ari contracted his abs and reached up to Gabriel's shoulders, pulling himself into Gabriel's lap, pressing their groins together. Ari gasped at the contact and looked down to where their bodies met.

Gabriel ran his nose along Ari's jawline. He skimmed his left hand up the length of Ari's arm, taking hold of his wrist. He pulled Ari's hand down and placed it on Ari's own thigh. *Where's he going with this?* Gabriel placed his own hand on top of Ari's and pushed their hands up Ari's thigh until they reached his—

Ari gasped at the contact.

"Feel that, Ari?"

"Yes."

Gabriel molded Ari's hand around it, and then again placed his hand on top. Ari allowed Gabriel to manipulate his hand into small up and down movements that sent little spikes of pleasure into Ari's belly.

"Technically, it's called your penis, but us guys like to give it other names, like dick or cock. Some guys give it pet names or nicknames like Little Willy or babymaker. I've even heard it referred to as a joystick."

Gabriel swiveled his hand again and, moving it slightly lower than Ari's, he made contact with another very pleasurable area. As Gabriel's fingers traced imaginary lines, each touch sent a shiver up Ari's spine.

Gabriel chuckled softly. Ari stopped watching their hands, and their eyes met briefly before Ari slid his hand up to Gabriel's neck and leaned forward into a slow, lazy kiss.

Ari ended the kiss and whispered into Gabriel's mouth, "Tell me."

"Isn't that my line?" Gabriel asked, nuzzling Ari's nose with his own.

"Tell me more, Gabriel. Teach me."

Ari would have asked for more, but he was cut off by Gabriel's fierce attack on his lips. Gabriel's hand replaced Ari's on his dick, and all Ari could do was hang on and enjoy the ride.

A sharp rap on the door startled them apart. Leo's voice called into the room, "Time to go, boys."

Gabriel began a sort of deep grumble that resonated through Ari's body. Ari placed his fingers on Gabriel's lips, a shudder running down his spine.

"You have to stop that, or I'll never let you up."

"That's the point," Gabriel growled and snapped his teeth, pretending to bite him.

With Ari's hands on Gabriel's shoulder, he pulled himself to his feet. Gabriel grabbed hold of Ari's ass and pressed his lips to the bare flesh of Ari's abs now before him. Ari held still as Gabriel's tongue traced the paths between muscles and giggled when it dipped into a small indent in his body.

Ari contracted his stomach muscles, jerking back, and slapped his hand over the hole to protect it. He cupped his hand underneath and looked at the spot.

"What's this called?"

"Your belly button," Gabriel said smiling. "God, I'm going to have so much fun teaching you."

Ari frowned. "You can't say His name like that."

"Whose? God's?"

Ari nodded and whispered. "He hears everything, and I…" Ari licked his lips. "I don't want Him to know about *this*."

"I'm pretty sure He already knows about this."

Ari grimaced and stepped backwards until he was clear of the bench. He turned to an open locker and pulled out his T-shirt. Ari shrugged the jacket off, letting it slip down his arms into his hands. Gabriel's quick inhale had Ari turning back to face him.

"What?" Ari asked sharply. Gabriel's furrowed brow had him immediately regretting it.

Gabriel stood and stepped over to a large mirror. He held out his hand to Ari. "Come here."

Ari paced over and put his hand into Gabriel's, who then turned him so his back was to the mirror.

"Look," he instructed, taking the T-shirt from Ari.

Ari looked over his shoulder and gasped. Reflected there, on his skin, were black-inked wings covering most of his back.

Gabriel ghosted his fingers over the wings. "Each little thing, Ari, makes me believe just a bit more. Here," he held out Ari's shirt, "get dressed." With one more quick press of Gabriel's lips to his, Gabriel left the locker room.

Ari didn't immediately dress. Instead he turned to face the mirror to inspect his human body. Ari fingered the unfinished tattoo of Gabriel's name. He rotated his shoulders to see a stylized lion on one upper arm and a sword embedded in a snake on the other. Ari's fingers traced the paths that Gabriel's tongue had taken. When he reached the edge of his pants he pushed them down to the floor. Another bit of tight-fitting fabric covered him. Ari pulled the stretchy band away from his body as he stared down at the still erect flesh inside.

Ari decided he liked the way the word dick sounded. Short, sweet, with that hard click at the end. He liked the way it rolled on his tongue when he thought about how it sounded. "Dick," he whispered to himself and smiled. But another rap on the door had Ari wincing as the band snapped back into place.

"Let's go, Ari," Leo called in.

Ari quickly pulled on the T-shirt and tugged the pants back up, knowing it didn't matter what he was wearing once he returned to Heaven for the daytime hours. One last glance in the mirror had Ari laughing. His shirt showed two griffins crossing swords. *Winged Warriors* was printed along the bottom.

Fitting, my Lord, he thought, but not expecting an answer, Ari turned and walked out of the room.

On the sixth night of Chanukah

Ari strode through the hallways of Heaven in search of Joseph. He found him staring into one of the many reflecting pools scattered around their home. Once again, Ari was struck by the thought that this wouldn't be his home much longer. But he couldn't dwell on that now; he'd been given his instructions: find Joseph and learn about the vision.

He knelt down beside Joseph and bowed his head. Ari took some cleansing breaths to slow his heart rate as he waited for Joseph to acknowledge him.

Father's arrival disturbed Ari's attempt to center himself, and Ari fought the desire to prostrate himself before Him.

"Abba," Joseph said in greeting. *Father.*

"Joseph," Father replied. "Ari." His hand stroked over Ari's hair, and he instinctively leaned into the touch, his heartbeat slowing as a feeling of rightness settled through him. "Tell us your vision, Joseph."

"Of course, Abba. In my vision I saw a young boy, weak, tired and lost. Many men surround him, taunting him, frightening him. I saw you, Ari, in your warrior form with others, angels and humans, trying to save him. There was red blood flowing, but I could not see who was wounded or dying. The vision ended with several candles wavering in brightness, seemingly fighting for air to breathe. At least one candle was totally extinguished."

Ari shivered. He did not care for this vision at all. A human life would be lost and he would be helpless to stop it.

✡ ✡ ✡ ✡

Gabriel pushed open the door to Tribunal. Already inside were Leo and Nina, Rabbi Cohen and his wife, Miriam, and a uniformed police officer Gabriel assumed to be Judah.

Gabriel smiled thoughtfully. He had spent a good portion of last night and today writing down everything that had happened, and everyone's names, and had drawn some interesting conclusions: Ari and Leo both meant lion, and with their similar appearances he assumed they held the same position of warriors. Malachi's name meant "messenger of God," and Cohen the shortened form of *kohein*, the Jewish priests of old. Suitable for a rabbi. Miriam, Malachi's wife and the cantor, was the name of Moses' sister, known for leading the women in song following the exodus from Egypt.

Judah could only be Judah Maccabee. It was Judah, the "Hammer," who led the Jewish people against the Syrians, reclaimed the great Temple and rededicated it with one little bottle of oil which miraculously lasted eight days. Now that little miracle is celebrated with a festival of lights, Chanukah. Gabriel even wondered if Ari's last name of MacCabe meant that he was related to Judah, or had it been chosen because of the holiday?

As if the thought of Ari made him appear, so he did, pushing through the locker room door, Thelial at his heels. Ari grinned and ran at Gabriel, colliding into his chest. They wrapped their arms around each other. Ari jumped up, his legs encircling Gabriel's waist, his hands around Gabriel's neck. Gabriel grabbed him and held on tight while Ari proceeded to kiss all previous thoughts from his mind.

Awws from the women followed by laughter from the men had them ending the kiss. As Ari's feet returned to the floor, they turned towards six pairs of bright eyes and six indulgent smiles.

Ari dragged Gabriel over to the police officer with his left hand. He clasped right forearms with the officer.

"Hammer! It's wonderful to see you again. How are your brothers?"

"Everyone is doing well, *Aluf*. It's good to see you too, although I wish it was under better circumstances. Leo said Joseph had a vision."

"He did. It's bad, and I'm nervous."

"Let's sit down," Leo interjected and pointed out a circle of chairs on the far side of the room.

Judah nudged Gabriel as he walked beside him towards the chairs and introduced himself, asking Gabriel to call him Jay.

"What's that you called Ari? Aluf?" Gabriel asked.

"It means 'General.' He leads us in battle, you know."

"So he's told me."

"Gabriel." Judah laid a hand on his arm, stopping him a moment. "Leo said you're Ari's. I have to admit I'm surprised—never seen Him pick a same-sex half before." As they moved to rejoin the others and sit, he smiled. "My brother will be happy to hear of it."

Gabriel was curious. "Which one?"

"Nate."

Gabriel was puzzled; there was no brother by that name. He was sure he knew the correct names of Judah's four brothers. "I'm sorry. This might sound strange, but aren't your brothers: John, Simon, Eleazar and Jonathan."

Judah smiled as he sat. "You got 'em. But here we go by John, Sy, El and Nate."

"You're all here?"

"Here, there. Wherever we're needed. I've called them to come help. Joseph's visions are never a cause to rejoice, only to gather your weapons and steel yourself for the fallout."

252

A small shiver rocked Gabriel as the implications of Judah's words echoed in his mind. Ari's hand squeezed Gabriel's shoulder before he stood and paced the small circle. He noticed Ari's T-shirt today was white, which was different from the usual black ones he'd been wearing. The front of the shirt read: *Enemy of Dark*, and when he turned, there on the back, almost identical to the inked ones on Ari's skin, was a set of angel wings.

Gabriel listened as Ari recounted Joseph's vision. He didn't realize he'd been fisting his hands tightly until Ari squatted down in front of him and placed his hands on top of Gabriel's.

Ari stared into Gabriel's eyes—*searching his soul?*—before Gabriel turned away. Judah stood and stepped away, pulling out his cell. The others were gathered together, trying to dissect the information, organizing and reorganizing it, in hopes of bringing something more useful to light.

Gabriel frowned. "I hate to admit it, but I'm out of my league here. Everything you said is crazy scary and my heart is racing. I'm angry that it's going to happen, that He is even letting it happen, even though He has given you forewarning. But I'll do anything to protect the boy." Gabriel turned back to him, pleading, "Tell me what you need me to do."

✿ ✿ ✿ ✿

Ari was momentarily at a loss for words. Gabriel referring to Father as He, his anger at the situation, and that look on his face…wanting, needing, to help in any way possible. Ari's heart beat furiously, and he knew right then he could never be without Gabriel. He tightened his hold on Gabriel's hands, the corner of his mouth turning up.

"Father chose well when he chose you for me. Your fierce protective nature, your righteous indignation, your willingness to put yourself into a dangerous situation. You have a warrior's spirit, Gabriel, to match my own."

Ari rose, pulling Gabriel to his feet.

"First," Ari continued, "I demand a kiss from my beloved, and then we shall see what Judah and Leo have to say. Then, I would like to see if I learned well what you taught me yesterday."

"What I taught you?"

Ari's eyes drifted to the locker room door, and Gabriel followed his gaze.

"Oh!" Gabriel said, understanding brightening his features. "I think I like your plan, *Aluf*," and he pulled Ari in for that demanded kiss.

On the seventh night of Chanukah

Another new door. This one blue with little rectangular windows etched with a geometric design. A *mezuzah* was attached to the right upper corner of the doorway—parchment wrapped in frosted glass, with the Hebrew letter *shin* on it; Ari raised his hand and touched it. *A sign upon the doorpost of your house.* Ari knocked on the door.

Through the windows, Ari saw the light from inside suddenly blocked by a large individual. When the door opened, Gabriel stood bare-chested, blue-jeaned and damp. Ari greedily absorbed the vision before him.

He started with the naked feet, watching toes wiggle, panned upwards over thickening legs, a growing bulge, a waistband riding low on Gabriel's hips. Strong arms rested comfortably, crossed on Gabriel's fine-haired chest. Ari had quite enjoyed running his hands through it last night, thrilled to find hard pectoral muscles had been hidden beneath those button-down shirts. He realized Gabriel was watching him, a wry smile on his lips.

"Do I pass inspection, *Aluf*?"

Ari licked his lips, remembering just how forceful Gabriel's kisses had been. "With flying colors."

"A rainbow flag, certainly," Gabriel laughed, but Ari's blank look at the joke forced Gabriel to explain as he ushered him into the house.

"So this is where you live?" Ari asked, looking around. He desperately wanted to inspect Everything Gabriel, but managed to hold himself in check, knowing soon this would be his home, too.

"Shall I give you a tour?"

Ari nodded and followed Gabriel as he walked around the downstairs, pointing out the living room with a tiny office tucked into a corner, a half bath and a large kitchen with a table and chairs. He glided his hand along the banister as they ascended the stairs. Up here was a room with weights and a stationary bike, a full bath, and, "My bedroom," Gabriel said, pushing the door fully open.

Brown wooden furniture adorned the room. The headboard of a quilt-covered bed was embossed with beautiful Celtic knot work. A long dresser sat opposite the bed, and atop it was a large mirror, framed in wood of the same design. An assortment of small figures and pictures were arranged on the dresser. Ari stepped closer to inspect them.

As he picked up a picture, he was enveloped in Gabriel's arms.

"That's me and my dad several years before he got sick." Gabriel sighed, before placing a kiss to the side of Ari's neck. "I'm lucky I've still got him, and my mom, but I wish they lived closer. Florida is way too far."

"You miss them."

"Yeah. In fact, I talked to my mom today. Told her I met someone. I was a little vague on telling her how we met. We are *so* going to have to come up with a good story for them. The truth is a bit unbelievable."

Gabriel nuzzled into Ari's collar, as Ari watched him in the mirror. "Mmm. Forgot to see what shirt He picked for you today. I like this dark green on you."

The shirt had an open book decaled on the front of his shirt. Swirls of mist rose from its pages of squiggle lines. On the top of one page was printed the words *Judgement Day*; on the other was *Who shall live?* Ari was helpless to suppress a shiver of fear. Gabriel tightened his hold, whispering, "I've got you."

Ari turned in Gabriel's arms and pressed closer. Hearing his beloved's heartbeat was enough to cause all of Ari's worries to rise to the surface, and he inadvertently gasped. Gabriel stepped backwards, pulling Ari towards the bed. As he sat back against the headboard, Gabriel tugged Ari into his lap.

Once Ari was settled between Gabriel's legs, he leaned back. Gabriel's comfortable chest warmed Ari's back and he tried to relax.

"Tell me," Gabriel said, speaking softly into Ari's ear as he nosed it playfully. Ari knew the act was to get him to loosen up, but thoughts kept intruding of how badly things could go wrong, or how Gabriel's name might be written in His book. *But then why put me here? Why bring us together, only to lose each other?* Ari's fears manifested as a shuddering sob.

Gabriel manhandled him, turning him to the side and holding him tightly, cradling Ari's head with one hand, and his body with the other.

"*Kfir.* Little lion. Tell me what's wrong, please."

✥ ✥ ✥ ✥

Ari's shaking body was scaring Gabriel. He couldn't figure Ari out. One second he had confidence in abundance, the next he was a nervous wreck. Gabriel was worried he wasn't strong enough for Ari, but not knowing what was setting Ari off... Well, how could he help if he didn't know what the problem was?

Gabriel palmed Ari's cheek and lifted his chin. If there was one way to stop someone from crying, it was kissing. Gabriel skimmed his lips softly across Ari's, who responded by crushing his lips to Gabriel's. The kiss was hard and fierce, like Ari was trying to devour him. Gabriel relished the taste of the salty tears on Ari's lips. He would lick those tears away and make his beloved happy.

Laying Ari down on the bed, Gabriel slid on top of him. Feasting on the taste, he spread his kisses around to Ari's cheeks and chin, an earlobe, and finally a softer kiss to each closed eyelid.

As Gabriel pulled back, leaning up on his elbows, Ari opened his eyes, and Gabriel could see glassy green surrounding large black pupils. A slow smile grew on Gabriel's face, and Ari reciprocated with his own.

"How can I have known you only seven nights, and already I don't think I can live without you?" Gabriel whispered, gazing intently at Ari, willing him to see the truth in his words.

Ari raised his hand to Gabriel's cheek. "You are mine, *yadid*. My beloved. We are meant to be together. Only *Adonai* can tear us apart. Do you trust Him? Believe in Him? Have faith in Him that He is making the right decision for you...for us?"

Gabriel pushed up and tumbled to Ari's side, sliding his legs off the bed to sit on the edge. Ari knelt behind him, putting his arms around Gabriel and laying his head on Gabriel's shoulder.

Like the little flask of oil somehow lasting eight precious days, finding Ari was a miracle. Gabriel wanted to believe in the unbelievable. Wanted to believe that Ari and Thelial and Judah were truly who they said they were—even if it meant truly believing God existed and played in the affairs of humans. Yes, he had faith in God, but one could have faith without believing in the existence of Him. If only he could see it for himself, but he felt it was too much to ask. Ari would want him to believe without having to reveal his true form. *So the question remains, do I trust God to make the right decision for me?*

"You called me *kfir*, young lion," Ari continued, "and perhaps I am. Here, at least, walking on this earth, I am young, and you will teach me. But there, Gabriel, I am *Aluf*, the general, and His warriors follow my lead. Never before have I been afraid of losing someone. Father's soldiers are triumphant in battle." Ari moved off the bed and came to stand in front of Gabriel. He cupped Gabriel's face, making sure his gaze never wavered. "I am afraid of losing you. One candle will be extinguished and many others will flicker. What if that one candle is you?"

Gabriel could see the fear and concern written so clearly on Ari's face. He gathered Ari to him, pressing the side of his face to Ari's chest as he wrapped his arms tightly around him. Emotions welled up in Gabriel, stealing his breath. There was no way he was going to lose Ari. The candle wouldn't be Ari, either. He'd do everything in his power to keep him safe.

"Stay with me tonight?" Gabriel asked.

"We need to check in with Leo and Judah."

Gabriel nodded. "Okay."

"I can stay till dawn, then I must return." Ari smiled. "Perhaps I could get a few more lessons."

Gabriel's heart lightened. "I'm pretty sure that could be arranged."

On the eighth night of Chanukah

"We found him," Leo said, as Gabriel approached the group outside Club Haven.

"Where?" Gabriel asked.

"Steel Pier."

Gabriel grimaced. Frustrated, he dragged his fingers slowly down his face, looking upwards. He shook his head. *I'm looking towards Heaven for answers when they are right here in front of me.*

A hand was placed lightly over his heart. Gabriel focused on Ari. Same black jeans, same spiky hair, same piercings, different shirt. Black again, with six flying, sword-bearing white angels. *Six Wing Soldiers.* Perfectly apt for Thelial, Judah and Judah's four brothers. Beneath the angels stood four humans and a griffin. Gabriel reached out to trace the figures on Ari's shirt.

"You?" Gabriel asked, touching the griffin.

Ari nodded, then took over naming everyone, except Gabriel, so, of course, he needed to ask.

"Everyone, but me. Have I no part in this grand rescue? No place in your plan for me, Ari?" The last words were barely choked out. Anger warred with tears. *Is God reneging on His promise? Why else not include me? How can I allow Ari to put himself in danger without taking the risk myself? Am I to lose Ari once the boy is saved?*

After last night's "lesson," Gabriel knew Ari had his heart. They'd spoken long into the night about themselves, trading stories. No one could have made up the things Ari spoke about, and Gabriel inwardly shuddered again thinking about the demons. They had practiced more kissing and touching as they explored each other's bodies. Gabriel had traced every one of Ari's tattoos with his fingers; Ari had traced Gabriel's with his mouth and tongue. The taste of Ari, like ambrosia, and hearing those sweet sounds spill from Ari's lips when he came was like his own personal Hallelujah Chorus.

Ari's hands took hold of his upper arms.

"No," he said firmly. "There is no place in our plan for you, but, *yadid*, you are my plan, my future." Ari made sure Gabriel was looking at him. "I must keep you safe. Promise me you will stay behind us, let us handle these demons as we were trained to do. I don't think…" Ari's voice faltered, and he paused for a breath. "I don't know what I'd do if something were to happen to you. You are my beloved one, the other half of me, and you have my heart."

"As you have mine," Gabriel replied, lips tilting up, as he placed his right hand over Ari's heart. He cupped the back of Ari's head with his left hand and hauled him in, their lips moving soft and sure against each other's. Gabriel ended the kiss, but kept them close as he whispered into Ari's mouth.

"I know I don't want to live without you, little lion. My heart refuses to let you go walking into danger without me by your side. So what are we going to do?"

"Let's talk to Judah," Ari suggested, taking Gabriel's hand and pulling him along. "As an officer, he must have dealt with this type of situation before. We've fought together many times, and I trust his judgement."

Judah listened carefully to their concerns and suggested how Gabriel could be of help. His expertise working with teens would be beneficial once the threat was eliminated, but, in the meantime, he was to stay back and let them handle the fighting. Gabriel wanted to argue about his strength and ability to fight, but hard stares from the others stilled his tongue. They had to work as a unit, and Gabriel's inexperience would disrupt their cohesion.

Plans were finalized and they threaded their way through the gamblers and party-goers of the casino in an effort to reach the boardwalk. They were met outside by three of Judah's brothers. Sy was already in place, keeping a careful watch on the boy. Gabriel was introduced to each of them, and the hug received from Nate had him grinning. Ari's growl of discontent was duly noted.

The brothers handed out mics and earpieces, and they split up into teams. Gabriel was placed with Malachi and Miriam at the entrance to Steel Pier. They were to keep watch for the thugs who hadn't yet been spotted, and also to catch the boy if he should run their way.

Gabriel blanched at the word "catch," and he voiced his concern. He told them it would scare the boy more, that they should instead follow him discreetly and make sure he stayed safe. Judah, in his uniform, and Gabriel could then approach him later. Their agreement, and Ari's smile of approval, gave Gabriel's ego a much needed boost.

They tested their hardware, asking Sy some questions and listening to his responses, until everyone was ready. Gabriel walked next to Ari as they made their way along the rows of shops, pointing out his favorite places to eat or buy treats. Taffy and fudge were popular here at the shore, and Gabriel looked forward to sharing them with Ari. The wind blowing cold off the ocean, had him rubbing his hands up and down his arms to keep warm; the long-sleeved shirt and sweatshirt were not enough to stave off winter's chill.

Gabriel had been looking off towards the water when Ari's arm suddenly blocked him and he stopped. They'd almost reached Steel Pier, but right in front of them were several punks in black leather jackets. They were sitting on the boardwalk's railing, hurling insults at pedestrians as they went by. Gabriel frowned, and then his eyes narrowed as he studied them. Before he could think better of it, he raised his voice.

"Tyler!"

They all turned to him.

"Hey, Ga-a-a-abe," drawled one boy, hopping off the fence and approaching. "What's up?" Tyler stopped in front of Gabriel and Ari, shoving his hands into his jeans' pockets. Gabriel drew himself up and put a little edge into his voice as he spoke.

"I'm disappointed to see you here. Thought you said you were breaking it off with this crowd." He'd been meeting on and off with Tyler for close to two years now. Gabriel had high hopes that the twenty-three year old would have had enough conviction to drop out of his gang, complete his GED and maybe take some college courses.

"Yeah…well. I tried, but it's hard to say no to the guys."

"Who's your friend, Ty? Your boyfriend?" one of the boys hollered, laughing and knocking fists with the others.

Ari's rumble of anger was hard to miss, and Tyler stumbled back, staring. Gabriel placed his hand on the back of Ari's neck, and traced some small circles there with his fingertips, but not before the damage was done.

As Tyler turned and ran through the entrance to the pier, the punks dropped off the fence and followed him.

"Think I found our thugs," Sy said, his comment transmitted directly to their ears, and Gabriel blushed. Figured he'd be the one to screw things up already.

✿ ✿ ✿ ✿

Ari knew Gabriel wasn't the only one who had reason to be embarrassed. *If only I could have had a little more control. Not acted like a stupid, green-eyed idiot.* But beating himself up over it wasn't going to stop those boys from hurting the one they needed to protect. Ari needed to get them moving forward again.

He'd taken only a few more steps before Sy spoke again. "Damn! Our boy's just taken off like a demon-out-of-hell and is running towards the Showboat Casino. There's at least a dozen humans and others after him. I managed to snag two humans, but get going."

Ari was already moving, Leo right beside him. *Others,* Sy had said. *Hell.* They could see the boys diving through the railing and scurrying under the boardwalk and pier.

"They went under the boards," Leo yelled into his mic before the two of them leapt over the railing, rolling as they landed on the sand. Once under the boards and shrouded in the shadows, Ari shifted into his griffin warrior form. His lion body was eight feet long in tawny length with another three feet of swishing tail. His eagle's head was white feathered, his orange beak sharp, and his front claws deadly. Four feet of folded white wings were tucked into Ari's sides. With his pupils blown wide open in the darkness, and Leo with his knives drawn, they stalked their prey.

They were soon joined by Judah, El, John, Nate, and Sy. They had also shifted from their human forms. Now each stood seven feet tall, cloaked in white robes, their white angel wings outstretched. *Six sets of wings,* Ari thought as Leo questioned Sy about the two boys he had already caught. Ari clicked his beak, inclining his head towards the enemy. The angels drew their swords, and let Ari lead the way.

They could hear the punks taunting the boy, and his answering pleas to be let go. Ari stepped slightly in front of Leo and the angel brothers, growling low and loud. The dozen gang members in front of them, spun around, drawing knives and in one case, a gun. As Ari lifted up onto his hind legs, pawing at the air, Leo opened his mouth, a surprising roar coming from his lips. They hoped to frighten the human teens and young men into dropping their weapons and running. It worked on a few of them, and a couple more when the Maccabee brothers rounded Ari and Leo, wings spread, swords held at the ready.

Seven were left, hell-born all. Imps brandished knives and wing-backed demons held two-handed swords, swinging them menacingly at the Heavenly warriors, but Ari knew they would be no match for the angels and Leo.

Pairing off, Ari took on a demon who shifted into the form of a bear. They circled each other warily, but the impatient demon quickly closed in. Ari dodged and snapped his beak, closing hard on the bear's neck. The demon's form went limp, and Ari tossed the body away before turning to check on his warriors.

Ari watched the battles between angel and demon, ready to leap in if needed. Leo struggled briefly with an imp, before finding an opening and sinking his knife deep in the imp's chest. The Maccabee brothers dealt long cuts and killing blows to each of their attackers. The demon bodies melted away where they lay.

A shout caught Ari's attention. Gabriel was approaching fast, stumbling through the deep sand.

"Hey! Stop!" Gabriel was yelling past him.

Ari spun around. There was one demon left, with just enough seeming humanity left that Ari recognized him as Tyler. He had one black skeletal arm around the boy's neck and held a gun firmly against the temple of the obviously frightened young boy they were sent to protect. Ari shifted to his angelic form.

"Let him go, Tyler," Ari commanded. Unfortunately, this only resulted in Tyler spreading his tattered black wings as he turned the gun towards Ari. His tighter grip on the boy's neck caused the boy to gasp in pain.

"Tyler! No!"

Ari turned back towards Gabriel's voice and watched his beloved's mad dash to place himself between Ari and the demon. The loud report of the gun firing had angel white flying past him. Ari stepped to the side to see Tyler pushing the boy away so he could face the angels unencumbered. The intended shout to warn Gabriel away lodged in Ari's throat as Gabriel slowly fell to the ground. His legs buckled with Leo's scream echoing in his ears. The fight forgotten, Ari crawled on hands and knees to Gabriel's side, tears clouding his vision, repeating, "No, no, no..." over and over again.

A red stain was already blossoming over Gabriel's heart by the time Ari reached him. He quickly covered the hole with his hands as his body sagged forward. Ari touched his forehead to Gabriel's.

"You promised," he choked out. "You can't leave me." He pressed his lips to Gabriel's, and then slumped over, his head on Gabriel's shoulder as he closed his eyes.

✿ ✿ ✿ ✿

The hand stroking lightly over his hair had Ari opening his eyes to the bright white of his room. He pushed away violently from the lap he'd been resting on.

"You promised!" he yelled, daring to be angry at Him, but not brave enough to look at Him. Ari curled his legs under him and pressed his forehead to the floor.

"Did I, Ari? Did I promise you?" His voice was stern, but Ari could also hear compassion there.

"You said he'd be mine, mine alone, and I need him."

"You need him, Ari?"

Ari suddenly knew what was expected of him. He pushed to his feet and drew the sword from the sheath on his back. He then knelt on one knee, placing the sword before him on the ground.

"I need him, Father. He is truly the other half of my soul, and he has my whole heart. I could not bear to be here, if he is there." Ari paused and stood. "I relinquish my role as *Aluf*. I can no longer serve You when my love for him is greater than my love for You."

"I accept your resignation, but what if he does not return your love, my lion?"

"I am Gabriel's lion now, Father. He is *my* hero. He risked his life for a boy he doesn't even know. Placed himself between a man with a gun and me. He was protecting his beloved. Me. I have faith that he loves me. Please send me back."

The light in the room grew brighter, His chuckle suffusing Ari with warmth. "Go with grace, my warrior. I have faith in him, too."

✿ ✿ ✿ ✿

"That was fast," Leo commented upon Ari's arrival. Ari immediately dropped to his knees beside Gabriel. Thelial's hands were over the wound. The boy knelt by Gabriel's feet.

263

"Put your hands under mine," Thelial said to Ari. He quickly did as instructed. "Now breathe your love into him."

Ari looked up, startled by Thelial's words. "Breathe my love... Oh!" He quickly bent over Gabriel and pressed their mouths together. He slipped his tongue out to push Gabriel's lips open and began alternating breaths with words, speaking from his heart.

✿ ✿ ✿ ✿

Gabriel stood in the doorway. The room was piercingly bright and he squinted to try and see who was there. An angel lay prone speaking in Hebrew. Gabriel could not understand, but when the angel stood and drew his sword, saying *Aluf*, he gasped, realizing it was Ari before him. The room grew suddenly brighter, and Gabriel threw his arm up to protect his sight.

As the light dimmed, Gabriel dropped his arm and could now see a shimmering figure before him.

"Who are you?" he asked. "You don't have wings like the other angels."

"No, I don't," the figure replied kindly. "I have no need for wings."

Gabriel glanced around the little room, then back at the one before him. He was curious. "Why not?"

"I should think the Creator wouldn't have need for such things."

"The Creator?"

"Yes, you know it I'm sure, Gabriel. Genesis, Adam and Eve?"

"Of course. In the beginning, Adonai created the..." Realization dawning on Gabriel, he dropped to one knee, bowing his head. "Am I dead, then? Is this Heaven?"

"Yes and no. You are in limbo at the moment, and this is but one rung on the ladder to Heaven. I brought you to this place to ask you a question, My hero. Shall I keep you here, beside Me, or return you to Earth? I believe you would be a benefit to both."

"And where will Ari be, Father?"

"Ah," God laughed, "calling me Father already. Thank you, Gabriel. As for your question, Ari has chosen to remain on Earth."

"Then that is where I need to be. He holds my heart. I could never be happy here without him, my need for him is too great. Please send me back."

"You have put your faith in Me, Gabriel. Now I shall put my faith in you. Care well for our mighty lion."

"I will," Gabriel replied as the light grew brighter and he closed his eyes.

✿ ✿ ✿ ✿

"I love you. You are my heart as I am yours. I'm not leaving you. I know you love me, our love is meant to be...come back to me." Over and over Ari spoke, his arms growing at first tired, then unexpectedly warm. He glanced to his and

Thelial's joined hands and watched in wonder as a soft, white light engulfed them.

"Your love is healing him, Ari. I am just augmenting the power with Father's love. You must keep going," Thelial explained. Ari's sight now roamed over Gabriel's features as he spoke lovingly to him. He noticed the moment Gabriel's eyelids fluttered and he gasped for air.

"Gabriel…" Ari dived for his lips, forcing a whimper from his beloved. He drew back to watch as Gabriel's eyes blink open, a tiny smile forming on his lips.

"Ari," he whispered, "come closer."

Ari leaned down again.

"You love me?" Gabriel said, and Ari laughed, his eyes sparkling.

"I do."

"That's good." Gabriel reached up and tangled his fingers in Ari's hair. "You were a beautiful angel, and such a fierce griffin, but I'm happy to call you my *kfir*, my little lion." And he pulled Ari's lips to his.

When he released Ari, Gabriel added one more thing.

"I love you, too."

Epilogue

Tonight, as I watch Gabriel and Elijah light the first candle of Chanukah, I pinch myself. Just a little reminder to myself of what I have lost, but also all I have gained. White wings no longer grace my back; instead I bear the reminder outlined in black ink.

No longer am I sent out to search for and destroy demons. Leo's taken me on at Tribunal Training, and now I help to train others in hand-to-hand combat and knife and staff techniques. We offer our services free to anyone in law enforcement wishing to learn, knowing this is the best way to help humans keep the demons at bay. Judah keeps harping on me to take the entrance exam for the police force, but right now, I'm happy where I am.

Heaven is no longer my home because I live with Gabriel now, in that same little row house. At night, in place of a single cot, Gabriel's adorned bed greets me whenever I enter our room. He still gives me lessons in life and love and, of course, practice really does make perfect.

Elijah—the boy we saved—was placed into our custody just after the start of the new year. When Passover rolled around in the spring, Gabriel reminded me that the people of Israel believe, one day, the Prophet Elijah will come, and he will be a herald of peace. I can't say much for the world, but he has been a wonderful addition, making, as Gabriel likes to say, "our couplehood into a family."

Now, the three of us are regular attendees at Friday night worship services under the ever watchful Rabbi Malachi and Cantor Miriam. Malachi even has me helping out Sunday mornings at Hebrew School with the children. I love to get the little ones all riled up, roaring and growling. It doesn't matter what day of the week it is, though, because whenever I step inside our temple, I sense His awesome presence. I close my eyes for just a moment and let the feeling sink into me. I am at peace. *Ve'imeru*—no, not let us say, let me say—amen.

~ ✿Shalom✿ ~

ONE
NIGHTSTAND

Rick Bettencourt

He rolled off me and onto his back, breathing in rapid staccatos, which I hoped was a good sign—testimony to my skill in bed. The backdrop of my bedroom window lit his chiseled features, and I pretended I had just been with a movie star.

The sweat on my chest, damp from having been pressed next to his, cooled in the stale air as the ceiling fan above us thumped in time, piercing the silence between his sighs.

I looked to my right, away from my casual encounter. Something about our new acquaintance made me feel as if I needed to give him time alone to recompose in the rawness of our afterglow. Or maybe I needed to gain some self-control. To the right of my closet, a Native American painting hung—a gift my grandfather had given to me for my thirteenth birthday several years ago. I could barely see it in the dark. The furnace whirred on, and I pulled the blanket up over my torso.

The metal headboard rattled, like it does whenever I move alone. Just a few minutes ago it clanged like the set of bells from that Salvation Army collector in front of the mall. The heat of our passion had my old bed banging against the wall louder than a Christmas hoedown. I looked over to him, sitting up, his back to me.

Through the window, the streetlight at the end of the road mixed with the stark-white snow fluttering outside and cast a subtle glow upon the room.

Watching him catch his breath as he sat on the side of the bed, gave me a chance to take in the perfection of his physique. He inhaled and slowly let it out. Damn, I must've been good. His back looked firm and muscular, or maybe it wasn't so much how it appeared, but how I remembered, having gripped him at the shoulders as we made love.

Love? Was it really making love? Maybe. This one felt diff—

He reached down and fumbled for his jeans. "God, snow's really coming down." His voice was low and sexy. His Levis were by the nightstand atop his work boots. I knew. I had peeled them off and left them there. He went on, "Guess, we're gonna have a white Christmas after all."

Propped up on an elbow, I leaned closer to him. "I guess we are." I could smell his musky scent, which was also on my hands. I breathed it in.

He put his feet into his Levis, stood, yanked them up and buttoned the fly some. "I love the snow." He sat back down on the edge of the bed and reached for his boots.

I wanted to touch his naked back. My right hand strained under the sheet, wanting to reach across, but that would have been too forward, too affectionate. This was, after all, just a one-night stand. Yet, I bit my lower lip, and mustered up the courage. "Maybe you should stay." I didn't know why I said it. Well, I knew why. I didn't want to be alone, not during the wee hours of Christmas Eve morning—actually any morning.

At twenty-three, living by myself, in the family cottage—with neighbors who were old and thought I needed Jesus to save me from my ways, and field mice that would stop in for a nibble and some warmth—life could get pretty lonely. Sure, I worked at the mall, a few towns over in Peabody, but...

Maybe it was just me. Being gay and having a traditional life seemed an oxymoron.

"Gay men just want to screw around," I would tell Shelly, my co-worker and friend. To which she would reply, snapping her gum and rolling her neck, "Sweetie, it ain't just the gay guys." She'd then launch into some show tune, or quote a line from a production she'd been in. As a theatre major, she had this thing for being overly dramatic. I wondered what she'd think of Kirk, and if she'd have gone up to him, like I did, and asked him to dance.

Rolling over on my side, I imagined us being real lovers. This time, when I spoke, I added his name—at least what I remembered it to be. "Kirk?" I cleared my throat and looked out the window again. "You don't have to go, I just—"

"Stay?" He combed a hand through his thick, blond hair. He turned around, and those soft, brown eyes made me remember why I went out of my way to talk to him at Skeeter's—practically the only gay bar north of Boston and south of Montreal. Approaching another guy, let alone messing around with him, was not in my general nature. But like I said, Christmas begot my loneliness.

It looked as if his eyes glistened with a bit of hope, but I wondered if I was making it up, and the darkness offered no confirmation. He strapped his watch to his wrist, after having retrieved it from the room's only nightstand. "I thought you had to work in a few hours?"

I sighed. The store opened at six a.m., and being Christmas Eve, I had to assist those last-minute shoppers. "But, you don't have to go, yet." I looked over at the alarm clock, which was on his side of the bed. "It's only two."

"It's getting late."

The scrap of optimism I had sank like my grandfather's skiff did that time Gramps and I planned to play Cowboys and Indians and row our way to Salem. The family cottage—technically a two-bedroom, yet more like an overweight studio—was the last house on a dead-end street in Conant, Massachusetts. The house had been my grandparents'. With their passing, my mother inherited it and I moved in, shortly after, to be closer to campus.

From my head, I shook away the thoughts of me standing by that brackish stream, holding onto my Tonto feathered headband, and watching my grandfather pull the boat to the shore.

I looked back at the painting Gramps had given me. Perhaps my eyes had adjusted to the dark—or maybe I still had a spark of radiance in me that somehow lit the room with hope for Kirk and me—the Native American Thanksgiving feast appeared clearer.

Kirk kneeled on the bed, and sat down on his haunches. He took a deep breath, and I heard it exit through his nostrils. "You...know..." he stammered, and paused for a few seconds, let out another breath, this one through his mouth, and flopped down onto his back. "I hate being alone too." His feet dangled to the side, as he lay in a rather contorted manner to, apparently, avoid dirtying my bed with his boots. We lay there for what felt like twenty minutes, but was probably no more than just a few seconds, when his arm touched mine.

The soft patch of hair on the back of his hand grazed and tickled mine. It felt more erotic than what we had just done with our private parts. I couldn't help but inch closer to him.

Another round of silence, this time punctuated by a snowplow in the distance scuffing its blade along the road.

"I'm not real good with these," I admitted.

He cocked his head in confusion. His features were striking, like one of the models I'd seen on the cover of a fashion magazine at the grocery store checkout. The sharp angles of Kirk's face cut a shadow on the bed linen. I wanted to memorize its placement on the sheets, so I could recall exactly where to touch when I would, no doubt, be home alone later on and reminisce.

"Not real good with what?" he asked.

I let the shadow go, and went back to his eyes. He had moved in. I could smell the subtle hint of alcohol on his breath—a vodka tonic with lime. "One-night stands," I said and licked my lips. I could almost taste the tang of his drink. Yet, I really wanted his mouth back on mine. There was something about him, more than just good looks.

"Who said it was just one night?"

My heart jumped to conclusions and I quickly sat up. "I bet you say that to all da boys," I said in my best East Boston accent.

Shelly's lessons in street smarts came to mind and I heard her telling me not to be so easy, to play a little harder to get. She thought my get-married-white-picket-fence dreams were for old folks. I pulled my arm away.

He shook his head, and grinned. "So, you'll be at Macy's, right?"

"Yup. I work in Men's."

He nodded. "Of course you do."

Shocked by his boldness, I elbowed him playfully. "Hey!" To hell with Shelly's hard-to-get rule. I like this one.

"Well, I've got a little shopping still to do."

"I knew it. You struck me, as one of those last-minute types." I bit my lower lip, as if trying to take back my words. I didn't want to offend and wasn't sure how much joking to do.

He lifted a hand, palm up.

I said, "Twenty to fifty percent off tomor—well, today."

He let out a soft chuckle and scooted onto his elbows. "I've got to get a gift for my mom and dad."

With a hand under my pillow, I pushed myself up further. "What do they like? Do you get them one gift to share? Or do you get them each something separately?"

He sat up and got his shirt from the edge of the bed. "Definitely separate gifts." He let out a heavy sigh. "They haven't been together since I was in…eighth grade."

"Oh." I felt a little funny for invading. "Well, there are sales galore. I'm sure you'll find something." I watched him stretch out the neck of his thermal. "What do they like?" I asked. I didn't care about privacy invasion. I wanted to stop him from dressing any further.

He popped his head through his shirt and put an arm through the sleeve. "I don't know. My dad's a businessman. Mom teaches and raises my little brother." His left pec disappeared under the pull of his shirt, and he put his other arm in the opposite sleeve. "I usually get my dad a tie, or something. My mom, she likes cooking."

"Oh, well Housewares is…" I had to think. It wasn't my area. "Forty percent off," I said, with a hint of uncertainty. "I could definitely help you pick out something for your dad. Doors open at six."

He rubbed the back of his neck.

I was coming on too strong. Shelly? Gay men seemed to only want a quickie, and there wasn't much quick about me. I threw the bed linen back, put my feet on the cold wood floor and reached down to grab my clothes. They were in a heap on the floor. I usually slept on the other side, his end of the bed—after all the nightstand and lamp were there, as well as a small area rug to soften the cold blow when getting out of bed on those chilly winter mornings. I shook my head, cursing myself for being too nice, again, trying to make a good impression and leaving the good side of the bed for him. I thought of my grandfather, who always put himself last.

The light went on. I cleared my throat, turned around, squinted and patted down my hair for fear of it sticking up like it often does.

He was standing, with his hand still on the old, cracked lamp. "Sorry." He righted its crooked shade.

"Don't be." I felt for the cowlick on the back of my head and tried to flatten it.

"I just wanted to get a better look—"

I drew my head back in surprise.

"Oh, no! I didn't mean it that way." He must've read my mind.

The buoyancy in me floated to the surface, again. I took my Red Sox cap from the bedpost and put it on. "My hair's a mess. I have the thickest head this side of Milwaukee."

He scratched his jowls. "I'll say."

I stood there for a moment, and suddenly remembered I was naked—except for the baseball cap. "Kirk!" I turned my back to him, grabbed my 501s and shimmied my way into them. I left the top button undone, for good measure—sometimes you have to lure the catch. I wasn't sure what else to say, which was a first for me. I wasn't bad looking, at least from what I'd been told. Shelly thought I was all that and a low fat bran muffin. She was always making up some silly saying. Even though I despised the gym, I kept active. I hiked the fields in the summer, ice-skated, or cross-country skied in the winter.

Kirk was back at the window, perhaps giving me my privacy to dress. "It's really snowing hard," he said.

"Hmm." I walked over to the front of the bed, and leaned a hand on the foot rail. The brass felt cold to my touch. "Maybe you should have a cup of cocoa or tea before you leave." I traced a finger along the green-patina bar.

He came over and met me between the bed and dresser. "You need to get some sleep. You have to go to work..." He looked at his watch. "In less than four hours."

Shrugging my shoulders, I said, "That's okay. I don't get much sleep this time of year. I'm used to it." I had just gotten off work at eleven, had been too keyed up to go home, and stopped by the club for a drink.

He put a finger through the loop of my jeans and pulled me toward him. "Thank you."

Surprised, I leaned my head back. "For wh—"

He kissed me.

I felt a little like the Jell-O cake my nana used to make for the holidays. I wobbled in his grip. Stiffen up, I thought, hoping I wasn't drooling from the side of my mouth. I was about to slip him some tongue when he stopped.

He let go of my beltline. "Sorry."

I wiped my mouth, for fear of a river of embarrassment pouring out. Nothing. "No, don't be—"

He grabbed me at the waist again—this time the Jell-O mold held firm—and his lips met mine, but much more tenderly.

Nana's cake moved to my arms, which fell to my sides in a bouncing jerk. He pulled back. When I opened my eyes, he was staring deeply with those warm chestnut irises of his. "There's something about you," he said, and kissed me one more time, a quick peck on the upper lip and a little nibble with those perfect, orthodontic model-like teeth.

My mouth slowly slid open, while he went to the window. "Wow," I muttered to myself. I didn't think he heard me, at least I hoped, for I didn't want to come across as needy. It wasn't just his striking good looks that attracted me. There was something else I hadn't felt before. I felt lightheaded, almost nauseous.

He pulled back the curtain to, apparently, get a better look at the street. "Man, my truck's got about an inch of snow on it already."

I walked over and slipped up behind him. I wanted to rest my chin on his shoulder, but he was too tall. Instead, I leaned in toward his upper back and breathed in the clean scent of his shirt. Downy? Or Snuggle? I was about to nuzzle closer when he turned around. My nose met his triceps.

"Oh! I didn't know..."

I was embarrassed and held a hand to my nose. "I was just..." I put my hands up in the air, and walked backward. "I was looking at the snow...at your truck. Yeah, the truck...I just wanted to make sure..."

He flashed those gorgeous teeth.

It was cold without my shirt on, and I folded my arms across my chest.

"That's OK." He started toward me. "The truck's fine."

"No worries." I waved a hand at him and walked over to my closet. Doug, you are just downright pathetic. I grabbed a hoodie from the middle rack, put it on and zipped it up. "This house is old and drafty." When all else fails, talk about the weather.

"I think it's kinda cozy."

I caught his reflection in the mirror above my bureau. He was leaning a muscular thigh against the footboard—looking cute, innocent, hot and tender all in one. I turned to face him. "So, you want some cocoa or what?"

. . .

274

My grandparents' kitchen hadn't been renovated since the fifties, when they bought the cottage as a summer camp. It had a black-and-white checked linoleum floor, worn down in little paths that led from the stove to the sink. The kitchen's red metal cabinets took a good pull to open them, and some of their steel handles were missing—having been replaced with stark white ones from my mother's house. The room looked like a jumble of *Happy Days* meets *Growing Pains*.

"This place is a gem," he said. "It's your parents'?"

I shook the packages of hot chocolate so that their contents would settle to the bottom. "Technically my mom's. She lets me stay here. My parents are divorced, too." I tore open the envelopes, both at the same time. "She doesn't have the time to watch over it, or have any interest in selling. 'Too many childhood memories,' she says." I poured the cocoa into the mugs, and left the empty, white-with-blue-lettering envelopes on the counter.

Chair legs and the bottom of his boots scraped the tired linoleum. "Works out well for you," he said.

"It does." I turned around to see him leaning back, with the front two legs of the chair off the floor. The water rumbled to a boil. I went over to the stove—practically the size of my mother's Prius—took a mitt off the oven handle, and lifted the cast iron kettle from the flame. "The place needs some work." I clicked the burner's knob off and the blue, orange and purple flame sputtered out. "But I can't complain." I poured the hot water into our mugs. The powdered chocolate popped to the top.

"Can I help you with that?"

"No, I got it." I put the kettle back on the burner. The metal on metal sound gave me chills. I took a couple spoons from the drawer, placed them in the mugs and stirred. "Would you like some Fluff?"

"Some what?"

While keeping an eye on my stirring, I looked over my shoulder. "You're not from around here are you?"

"Chicago, originally," Kirk said. "Moved here during high school when my mom got the position at U Mass."

I let the spoon go. "Kirk from the Windy City." The utensils clattered along the sides of the ceramic mugs, as I lifted and carried them to the table.

"Windy City indeed," Kirk replied.

"Well, I was born and raised here. I go to school over at North Shore." North Shore was the name of the community college, the next town over.

"Yeah, I've heard of it. A friend of mine goes there."

Friend? I didn't want to ask. It was a large school. I probably didn't know who anyway. Plus, I didn't want to know about a potential relationship. I went back to the cupboard, yanked it open, took out the jar of Fluff and held it out for him to see. "Marshmallow. You've got to try it." I put the jar on the table and sat down across from him. "It's excellent in hot chocolate."

He let the chair down so that all four legs rested back on the floor, reached across the table, grabbed the Fluff and looked at the label. "Hmm." He flipped it around. "It's pure sugar."

I shrugged. "Most good things are." It felt so right just having a mundane conversation. I didn't want it to end.

He unscrewed the lid. It made a hollow sound as it came off. "If you say so."

"Just take a dollop."

He took his spoon out from his mug, wiped it on a napkin, and scraped some of the marshmallow out. "Looks like melted sugar."

"It's good. Trust me." I folded my hands in a steeple-like manner and leaned my chin on them.

He smiled, and for the first time I noticed his dimples. "A shot of whiskey would be good too," he said.

I didn't keep booze in the house. I wasn't much of a drinker, and only did so when I went out to the club. "I'm sorry. I don't think I have any."

"I'm only kidding." He put the marshmallow-smeared spoon into his mug. "Wow." The spoon, with the jar's sticky contents still on it, rose to the top and almost fell out of his cup.

"If you just hold the spoon down for a little bit, the marshmallow will melt off." I watched him follow my instruction and chuckle as the iceberg of Fluff bounced to the top, causing hot chocolate to seep down the sides of his mug. "That's okay," I said. "That's what napkins are for."

He lifted the cup and gave me a half-hearted toast.

I did the same.

"To a good Christmas."

"To a good Christmas," I repeated.

He took a sip. "Ow, that's hot." He darted his tongue across his lips, trying to cool his mouth.

I chuckled. "Yes, it is—hence the *hot* in hot chocolate."

"It's good though." He blew into the cocoa, and this time took a small slurp.

"Pass me that canister." I pointed to the jar.

"Oh, sorry. I didn't mean to hog it." He slid the Fluff over.

"You like, huh?" I asked.

"Who wouldn't like a hunk of sugar?"

"A hunk, maybe." I felt my face flush. I couldn't control it.

He smirked and flashed an incisor.

"So…" I needed to divert the attention from my silly statement. "You're twenty-five?"

"Next month."

"Wow, a quarter of a century."

276

"I know." He took another sip. "And still living with my mom." He shook his head. "It's funny, when I was kid I thought I'd be so much further along than where I am now." He put his mug down. "Oh, don't get me wrong. I'm not a freeloader. I pay board and shit." He took a napkin from the holder at the edge of the table, near the window, placed it down and then put his mug on top of it. The wind howled outside and he looked over at the frost-covered window. "It *is* a little drafty in here." He held a hand out toward the sill.

"Sorry. Would you like to move to the living room?"

"Oh, no. I'm fine. I didn't mean to criticize. I was just agreeing with what you had said earlier."

I nodded. "No problem."

We sat for a few moments, listening to the wind whip outside and whistle through the cottage's slats. I thought about going to turn on the Christmas tree. My mother had always done so on Christmas Eve day, and didn't shut it off till after we opened presents the following morning. But I decided against it. Besides, I didn't want to wake up the mouse I had seen scurry across the floor the other day.

Kirk cleared his throat. "I should let you go."

I looked back at him, the mouse thoughts erased from my mind. "You don't have to. Besides the weather…"

He glanced at his watch. "My mom will be pissed." He straightened his back. "She's a light sleeper and will hear my truck pull in."

My chair shifted and shuddered along the floor as I rose. "Well, I guess I should catch a few hours before work."

"You should." He took another sip of his cocoa. "Damn, that is good." His chair inched back and he got up. "Thanks for—" he pointed to the table, "—the North Shore version of hot chocolate."

I sighed, reached out and put a hand on his shoulder. "I had a good…It was nice to meet you."

There was an awkward laugh, on both our parts, and then silence, broken only by the sound of a snowplow scraping another street.

I retracted my hand. I didn't know how to allude to our earlier intimacy without sounding trite. "Like I said earlier, I don't normally do this." *But I'd do you again in a heartbeat.*

A wry, half-smile curled the right of his mouth. "Do what? Share your Fluff?"

I couldn't believe he said that and I laughed. "In a manner of speaking."

He looked down, and kicked lightly at the leg of the table. "Well, for what it's worth, this was the first time in a long time."

I'd thought I was just another notch on his bedpost, but maybe not. The realization warmed me and made my stomach knot in anticipation. "It's hard meeting people sometimes. Isn't it?"

His gaze remained on his boot. "Yes." Those damn chestnut-colored eyes glanced my way and I felt Nana's Jell-O cake wobble in my knees again.

"It was nice meeting you, Doug."

There was another moment of awkward silence. The hum of the plow's engine sounded as if it were getting closer. I wasn't sure whether it was appropriate to kiss him. "Let me walk you to the door?" It shouldn't have been a question, but I asked it nonetheless.

"Oh, sure."

We walked toward the living room and past the stairwell that led to the basement, from where the mouse had come the day before, and scared me witless. I stopped and stared at the door, with its old skeleton keyhole practically painted shut.

Please, God, don't let that rodent scurry out now.

The furnace roared to another start. I jerked, half expecting to see the mouse.

"You should turn your tree on," Kirk said.

I faced him. "Oh, I was going to. My mom used to put it on all day Christmas Eve and into the morning."

"Mine too!"

We exchanged a smile that warmed my heart. As we moved deeper into the living room. I reached out to him, but he quickly went to the tree. "Where's the switch?" he asked. "Let's put it on."

I pointed to the wall socket near the floor. "The plug's in the back."

He was already on his hands and knees reaching behind the tree skirt for the cord. "What, no presents down here?"

"Santa hasn't come yet."

"True." He plugged the cord in and the tree blinked its colored lights. He looked up at it, while sitting on his legs. "Nice. You decorated it yourself?"

The memory of having put the tree up alone came to mind, but I quickly erased it. "Yes, I did."

The colored lights danced in Kirk's eyes. "They're festive. I like them better than the clear ones." He moved a hand to one of the ornaments and traced the white beads upon the sphere of blue glass. I had purchased a whole box of them, getting twenty-percent off with my employee discount. "Very nice," he said.

"Thanks. My mother always liked blue and white."

He looked over at me, not bothering to get up from the floor. "Hanukkah colors. Are you part Jewish?"

"No, but she was from West Peabody. There's a large population of Jews there. She absorbed some of the culture. Used to sneak into Temple with her best friend Esther, when they were kids." I watched him stand. "She wanted to be like Barbra Streisand in *A Star is Born*."

He glanced my way, and went back to some of the ornaments I made when I was in elementary school. "Barbra Streisand, huh? And who did you want to be?"

"When I was a kid?"

He touched the pinecone cowboy I made for Gramps when I was eight. "Yeah, we all wanted to be someone, or something, when we were growing up." He went over to the snowman I made out of an old spool of thread for my grandmother.

"An Indian. I wanted to be a Native American." I felt silly for admitting it. Me playing with my gramps like he was my best friend. It seemed weird telling it to someone I just met.

He looked back at me. "You'd be a good Tonto."

"I would?" I laughed and put my hand to the zipper of my hoodie. Something about him recognizing Tonto warmed me.

"Well, I wanted to be a vet." He pointed to the brown and red construction paper cutout I had created in Mrs. Johnson's art class. "I loved animals, and still do."

I edged closer to him. My shoulder brushed against his. "That was supposed to be Skippy, our cocker spaniel." I chuckled. "It looked nothing like her. In fact, I was mad when my father said it looked like a rat."

"It ain't a rat." He pulled it off the tree and gingerly held it up to the window. "Nah. That's definitely a cocker spaniel." He smiled at me, his eyes sparkling.

Those damn dimples.

He hung Skippy back on the tree. "Maybe it was the whiskers that threw him off."

Smirking, I looked at it one more time. "Yeah, it is a bit reminiscent of a rodent."

He took a moment with it. "Yeah, a bit." He nestled it back into the crook of a branch. "I love homemade ornaments. These are really cool."

"Oh, thanks."

"You can tell someone special takes care of them." He glanced my way and went back to the blue and white spheres from Macy's.

"It takes someone special to appreciate and notice them."

He moved over to the other side of the tree, out of my view. "It does, does it?"

"Yeah, I think." I slipped around front. The scent of the pine filled the air. It reminded me of Christmases as a kid. I loved the smell of real trees.

I leaned down to see if I could tell which ornaments he was looking at, and caught a glimpse of the Indian ornament Gramps had made for me. My grandfather's gravelly voice filled my head. My little Tonto, he'd say. It was during one of the many times when my grandparents and I were decorating the tree with new ornaments to commemorate the year. Nana was in the kitchen, and he'd kept an eye on her from the living room.

"Your grandmother—she's a fine lady," he'd said to me, pointing her way. "There's not a thing in the world I wouldn't do for her." He'd rubbed a hand across his chin, and the dark stubble of his jaw sent out a rasp. "One day, you'll have a lady just like her."

Despite being no more than ten at the time, I knew I would never have a "lady" like he thought. But I got his point. I'd have someone special, whom I too would sacrifice my needs for.

A rustle from below broke me from my thoughts and Kirk sprang up from the Christmas tree's lower limbs. We were face to face. My lips parted.

He moved closer. "Someone special, huh?"

For a moment I wondered if he'd read my thoughts, but then I remembered we'd been talking about "special people" and admiring homemade Christmas ornaments, when a crash on the front porch shook the house—no doubt, snow sliding off the tin roof. I was used to it, but Kirk jumped back. "What was that?"

"The roof is metal. It can only hold the snow for so long, before it comes careening down."

He moved back in toward me. "Careening?"

I inched closer. "Careening."

He kissed me, and I closed my eyes.

. . .

Later that morning, standing amid a crowd of shoppers pushing me out of the way while I tried to make some semblance of the rack of socks in front of me, I thought back to my encounter with Kirk. I could almost smell the scent of pine that hung in the air as I sat alone by the tree after he left. I had felt so empty.

"Doug! Register seven. Stat!" Shelly's voice pierced through my fog.

"Going over!" I yelled, not sure if she could hear me above the combined din of Bing Crosby and frantic customers bustling about.

A gentleman dressed in a full-length tweed coat asked me where the men's watches were. I pointed behind me, noticed the wedding ring on his left hand, and imagined he was shopping for his husband. It pushed home the point that I had no one.

"Excuse me!" a high-pitched voice shouted to my right. I looked over to find a plump woman with bright red lipstick, some of it painting her front teeth. "Do you have these in extra-large?" She held up a pair of boxers from the clearance bin.

I shook my head. "That's all we have. Been out for weeks."

She huffed, threw down the smalls and stomped away.

I headed to register seven. Along the way, I righted a package of cotton T-shirts, ripped open at the top. I was a bit obsessive when overtired.

"Seth!" a mother yelled, grasping her son—who looked all of ten—by the hand. "How many times do I have to tell you? No straying from Mommy."

"But, Mom!" he said, in a sing-song whine. "I wanna go home."

Bing Crosby segued into the overly-upbeat instrumental of "Sleigh Ride" I'd heard a gazillion times from the store's piped in music.

A crash rang out from behind me and an avalanche of Hanes underwear fell from an end cap. "Son of a—," I muffled.

The rascal ran out from the aisle and went to his mother, who glared at him. She put her hands on her hips. "Seth Goldstein!" she yelled. "Did you do that?"

Shaking my head, I got down on my hands and knees and started picking up the packages of men in tighty whities.

"Doug!" yelled Shelly. "I told you! I need you on the register!"

"There's been an incident!" I yelled back, adjusting the metal shelf that had unhinged. "I'm picking up nearly naked men off the floor."

"What!?!?" she asked. "Sleigh Ride" was at full gallop.

I sighed and stood up.

Seth and his mother were by my side helping to pick up the mess.

Shelly looked at me and threw her hands out in a what-the-hell manner.

"The Hanes display toppled," I said, with an edge in my voice.

She smacked her forehead with the palm of her hand and walked over to the register.

"Seth," the mother said. "This nice man is trying to work and you're—

The second shelf came down as Seth leaned on it to get up. A slew of mediums slid down.

"Enough!" I yelled. My eye twitched. "Get out! Just leave! I can take care of it myself."

Seth's mother stood, mouth agape and grabbed her son's hand. "Let's go."

The jangle of "Sleigh Ride" seemed louder, but it was probably just me growing more irritated. The high-pitched bells went right through me. I knelt back down and started picking up more packages of near-naked men.

A pair of black shoes trotted to my right, practically nipping my fingers.

A woman's high-heel boot kicked a packet of underwear. "Oh, for goodness sake," its wearer said. "This place is a mess."

"God, help me," I said, bobbing and bending to stuff packages under my arms as fast as I could.

Finally, the song ended and I placed a few of the *men in white* onto the bottom shelf. A different version of "Sleigh Ride" started. I stood up. "No effin' way!"

A woman in a blue coat glared my way.

"They just played this!" I said to her.

She looked over one shoulder, then the other and quickly walked away.

"Giddy up! Giddy up!" sang a deep voice behind me.

I turned to see an elderly man with dandruff in his eyebrows, snapping his fingers and tapping his foot to the song.

"Stop being so happy," I said to him, but he didn't pay me any attention. I took one of the dangling shelves that Seth had unhinged. I tried to snap it back into the end cap, but it slid from my hands and thundered to the floor.

"Doug!" yelled Shelly. "What are you doing?"

"This place is a madhouse," I heard a customer say.

I grabbed the top shelf and it too clamored to the floor.

"Doug!"

Tears swelled. I quickly wiped my eyes with my sleeve and looked around to see if anyone noticed me crying. I was so tired. I just wanted to go home and go back to bed. I gripped fistfuls of my hair as if to yank it out. *Why me?*

"Let me help you with that," said a gravelly voice to my right. A man with a striking resemblance to my grandfather picked up one of the racks. "I used to work at this store when it was called Jordan Marsh," he said. "You're probably too young to remember." He balanced the shelf on his raised knee, lifted the bracket and snapped it into the back of the end cap. "These things were always a pain." He grabbed the second shelf.

"Thank you," I said.

He secured the other one and turned to me. "Merry Christmas."

Tears wanted to swell again, this time in memory of Gramps, but I held them back. The kind stranger reminded me so much of him. "Merry Christmas," I said and swallowed a lump in my throat.

He smiled and walked away. I watched him disappear into the crowd of shoppers.

Next, the soft timbre of a piano filled the store and things appeared slightly out of focus. Feeling faint, I held onto one of the shelves that the old man had put back up. "Sleigh Ride" had changed to a melancholy rendition of "What Are You Doing New Year's Eve?" I'd never heard it before.

The subtle pitch of the singer's voice sent a shiver through my body. I trembled and the nostalgic melody rewound my thoughts: Gramps dancing with my grandmother—him, all smiles, holding her hand, and she, all dreamy-eyed—looking back at him, like they'd just met instead of having been together for decades.

I knuckled a tear away from my eye, but it didn't help wipe away the memories: just a few weeks ago, setting up the tree, with only a cup of cocoa by my side, and feeling as if I'd always be living a life alone.

The singer belted a high note—the type you'd see on TV that'd make an audience stand and cheer—and my goosebumps intensified. There I sat with my gramps, the two of us, watching the ball drop on New Year's Eve—the first after Nana died. He'd held a tissue, looked away from me and dabbed his eye.

My lower lip quivered. It all hit me just right, or just wrong, and I burst into tears. I mopped my eyes with the back of my hands.

Then, from where the guy who'd helped me with the end cap had disappeared, out came Kirk.

My mouth fell open.

The bustling sound of customers returned and practically masked the song, but I could still hear it.

A surge of hope awakened me and washed away any dizziness I'd had. Despite Kirk being across the way, I could see his dimples form as he looked my way.

I too smiled, and hoped I had enough time to remove any evidence of crying before he got too close. I spun around, grabbed an opened package of T-shirts, tore one out, blew my nose into it, wiped my eyes and threw it to the floor.

"Nice song," he said.

A grin developed, and I turned. "It is." I kicked the tee down the aisle.

"You got plans?" he asked.

My palms started to sweat and I dried my clammy hands on my pant leg. "What? For New Year's?"

Somehow his smile got wider. "Yeah. But first, I need to take you up on that offer to help me find a tie for my old man…"

. . .

One year later, to the day, Kirk appeared in the store again. I loved it when he visited me at work. I felt special when my guy came to see me.

I grabbed his hand.

"Break?" he asked.

"Are you serious? It's one of the busiest days of the year."

"Register seven!" Shelly yelled. I could hear her strumming the counter with her acrylic nails. "Please, before Mother Mary starts singing Happy Birthday to her newborn baby." She'd been promoted to supervisor, and her Broadway theatrics were now being put to good use in sales. After last year's Christmas rush, she and I had gone into Boston so she could audition for *Funny Girl*. "Don't you just love the way life hands you lemons?" she said on the train ride home, after not getting so much as a chorus part. "Well, how would you know?" she added, before I could answer. "Now that you're dating Kirk, everything's coming up roses for you."

Leading Kirk toward the ties I smiled at him. "But never too busy for you." I waved to Shelly, and pointed to my man. She rolled her eyes and went over to the register herself.

Kirk waved back to Shelly, but she was too busy logging on to the register to acknowledge him. "She still hates me."

"She's just jealous," I said. "Now, back to your shopping list, Stranger." We were reenacting, for posterity sake, the setting of our first *real* date. "Does your father like blue?"

"You know he does. Oh, wait!" he quickly added.

"You're not playing right," I said.

"I know…sorry." He looked at the tie selection." Oh! Hold on. You've got to see this." He fumbled through his black-mesh shopping tote. "I wanted to show you this." He pulled out a Christmas ornament. "Look what I found."

My mouth fell open as I held a hand to my heart and clutched my name badge.

He held it gingerly by the little gold string on top. "It's an anniversary present. One of them anyway." He lifted it in front of his face, as if getting a better look at it, and glanced back my way while it twirled around. "Ain't it cute?"

It was a miniature jar of Fluff. "I can't believe…no way. That's awesome. I didn't know we carried those. I hadn't seen—"

"You like my Fluff?"

I chuckled. "Very much." I leaned into him and whispered, "I like more than your Fluff."

Kirk cleared his throat. "Now how about you helping me pick out a tie for my dad?" He put the ornament back in his bag, and adopted his play voice again, as if we hardly knew each other.

"I'd be happy to." I put my hand on his shoulder and led him across the aisle. "Just like last year?"

He put his thumb through my belt loop, like he always did. "You're supposed to play along. And over there…" He pointed to the watchcases. "That's where I'm supposed to ask you to dinner."

"You better take me someplace good…again."

"62 of Salem work?" The 62 was my favorite, albeit expensive, restaurant.

"We don't have to go there. It's too much money."

He shrugged. "I don't care. You're worth it."

I looked at him and continued to walk. "Merry Christmas, babe." I lowered my voice, and leaned into him. "And I got a special present in store for you." I cocked an eyebrow.

"In this store?"

I hip checked him playfully. "No, silly, at home." I glimpsed over my shoulder, and said, even more softly, "in our bedroom." I went over to the tie rack, selected a Tommy Hilfiger, and handed it to Kirk. "What about this one?"

He took it without even looking. "Oh, and I left the Christmas tree on."

"Perfect." I navigated us around stacks of unopened boxes that neither Shelly nor I'd had the time to unpack. "I've got to get back to—"

The high note to "What Are You Doing New Year's Eve?" played overhead. I hadn't heard it since the year before.

"What?" Kirk asked.

I faced him.

His brows knit. "You OK?"

I nodded, swallowed the lump in my throat and held out my arms.

Again, he scrunched his face. "What?"

I took his hands, and led him aside—to a clearing where we'd have more room.

Under the glare of fluorescents, with our song continuing to play, we danced amid boxes and Christmas apparel strewn about the floor—and ignored the hubbub of shoppers bustling about.

THE END

SHINY THINGS

Amy Spector

ACKNOWLEDGMENTS

I would like to thank my beta reader Kristen and editor Debbie McGowan for
making this story better than it would have been.
Al Stewart, who encouraged me in ways that he likely didn't realize.
My husband Aaron for his child wrangling efforts.
And my sincerest thanks to all the members of the Jellie Bellies group for their
friendship and encouragement.

. . .

This book is dedicated to Patrick.

Chapter 1

Nathaniel Avery stood in the small entry of Gallery Nocturne just long enough to shrug out of his jacket, and for the warmth to seep back into his fingers.

It had been more than a decade since he had set foot into the space. Back then, it had been called something a little less pretentious—something like *Shiny Things on High*—and had specialized in art constructed of salvaged metal. Now, it focused on night scenes portrayed in oils and gouache and interpreted by, what Nathaniel supposed were, modern day Whistlers and Rembrandts.

Not really his thing. But cherubim, made entirely of bottle caps, hadn't been his thing either.

Even as he walked deeper into the labyrinth of the gallery, he could still hear his team as they carried in the scaffolding and supplies for the renovation project. The space was small, in the grand scheme of things, but they had made good use of floating walls and smaller, more intimate rooms, and in the end had created a space that felt far larger than he knew it was in actuality.

Taking rough measurements in his head, it only took a moment for him to realize that something was wrong. He slipped the work order and estimate from the satchel he had kept slung over his shoulder. As he expected, it had been prepared by his father. And, by the looks of it, not too many weeks before the pleading call he had received from his younger brother. Sadly, it had become a familiar scenario since his father's failing health had brought Nathaniel back to Ohio, two months ago.

He needed to talk to the owner about the additional time needed and reassure him, or her, that they could still be out of everyone's hair before the, in his opinion, terribly timed charity fundraiser scheduled for the evening of Thanksgiving day.

He probably needed to confirm the color swatches too, just to be safe.

He could fix this. He *would* fix this. Even if it meant he had to spend more evenings working himself than he would have liked.

The crew would spend the first day removing and wrapping canvases for temporary storage, start the plastering and preparing walls and ceilings for painting. Instead of assisting, Nathaniel would verify the job's specifications, re-measure, and recalculate the quantity of paint needed for each color. Then Caleb could arrange the order and delivery.

Nathaniel was just happy that his brother had waited until the team was on-site before having the paint order filled. No doubt, Caleb had learned that lesson the hard way.

Lost in his own thoughts of how to manage too large a project with too little time, and absently following the sounds of murmured voices, Nathaniel nearly collided with a slight, ginger-haired man as he turned into one of the smaller gallery rooms. He looked down to apologize, and froze, the apology forgotten.

Nathaniel had only been sixteen years old the last time he set eyes on Vincent Cooke. It didn't surprise him that he recognized the handsome redhead. And, even after all that time, it didn't *completely* surprise him that the sight of the younger man stirred up so many of the same emotions the sight of the boy had.

When Nathaniel said nothing, only continued to stare, the redhead smirked, pushing heavy bangs from his eyes, and lifting a brow. "Can I help you?"

"I'm looking for…" Nathaniel finally managed, forcing his eyes away to scan the work order he still held in his hand. *Vincent Cooke.* "You," he finished lamely. His voice sounded strange to his own ears, not that his old high-school crush would know the difference. The man didn't even seem to recognize him, which just made Nathaniel angry. Irrationally so, he knew. But hell, here stood the man whom he had spent years blaming for being booted out of his home and sent to live with his father's sister. The man had no right *not* to remember him.

"*You* kissed me." The words escaped him before he could stop them. His tone sounded accusatory, and he knew, in all likelihood, psychotic.

Vincent Cooke's smirk split into a wide, wicked, grin.

"Oh, honey, I kiss a lot of people."

Chapter 2

Despite the initial embarrassment of having to spend his afternoon with the man, it had gone unexpectedly well. Cooke wasn't particularly disturbed by his outburst, almost like it happened every day. Without so much as a word about it, he led Nathaniel on a tour of all the public spaces, comparing what Nathaniel had on his floor plan comp with the swatch colors Vincent had stored on his iPad—a complete professional.

There were seventeen different color mixes, which Nathaniel felt was excessive, but the other man was adamant.

"Are you familiar with Claude Bäcker?" Vincent asked him, looking a little surprised when Nathaniel shook his head.

"Well, he was an up-and-coming artist. As of now, he has arrived. Mad talented—" He gave Nathaniel that smirk again. "Mad being the key word."

Nathaniel couldn't help but laugh, which seemed to please Vincent immeasurably.

"He's one of those crazy geniuses that never leaves the house and never shows their work. Anywhere."

Vincent looked at him expectantly, and Nathaniel didn't know what his line was supposed to be.

He finally asked, "Then how does anyone know he's talented?"

Vincent let out a laugh. "That is the secret of genius. It finds a way. So," Vincent continued as they worked their way through the gallery, quicker now, "he has agreed to show here." Vincent indicated his gallery with a little spin, arms flung wide.

Nathaniel worriedly watched the tablet the man held in his hand. By some miracle, it did not fall.

"I had approached him about a show a dozen times, easily. Calls, letters. I was this close," Vincent indicated an inch or so with his thumb and forefinger, "to offering a blow job."

He grinned, seeming pleased when Nathaniel's eyes went wide and he, no doubt, blushed. "But apparently the fundraiser made the difference.

"Still," Vincent went on, and Nathaniel couldn't believe how much one man could talk, "the list of requirements is as long as one of those massive arms of yours." Vincent gave him a wink. "Specific colored walls for each of the pieces. Lighting. And, oh God," Nathaniel watched as the man rolled his eyes, "a different temperature for two of the smaller rooms. One hot, like in the nineties. The other, low forties."

Nathaniel figured his facial expression must have been disbelieving, with the delivery of Vincent's next words.

"I. Shit. You. Not."

There was something amusing about seeing the slender man, with his angelic looks, say *I shit you not,* and Nathaniel laughed. And he marveled that he had laughed more in the last twenty minutes than he had in the last two months.

Vincent Cooke continued to talk. He talked and talked, like maybe he didn't normally get to talk to anyone most days, and to Nathaniel's immense relief, his uncharacteristic outburst of less than an hour before hadn't seemed to matter at all.

. . .

When Nathaniel had finally returned home, it was already dark, having worked the entire team a few extra hours in an effort to make the deadline.

Happy to see his father already sleeping peacefully in his room, Nathaniel relieved Katherine almost as soon as he walked in, shooing her out the door with a kiss on the cheek, all his thanks, and payment for a week's work.

It had been rather heart-breaking. When his brother Caleb had called with their father's diagnosis of third stage Alzheimer's, Nathaniel had dropped everything to drive back to Ohio, to find the nineteen-year-old Caleb struggling hard to try and hold together the household, their father's business, and take care of a fragile old man that Nathaniel barely recognized.

All of it, without help.

He had been angry, overwhelmed with guilt, and demanded that his brother tell him why he hadn't been called earlier. Of course, he had already understood the reason, even before Caleb's very telling refusal to talk about it. Nathaniel's father didn't want to see him. It still hurt.

The old man had shipped him off to live with his aunt less than twenty-four hours after discovering him kissing his tenth-grade biology partner. It hadn't mattered how hard he'd argued. His father had no plan to raise a gay son. So he hadn't.

He and his brother's first decision together after Nathaniel's return had been to find nursing help. Katherine had been a Godsend: a retired nurse who had the patience of a saint, in Nathaniel's opinion, and who was also willing to work for, if not cheap, then a reasonable rate.

Katherine made it possible for the two of them to focus on the other things that needed their attention. Most especially, their father's business—the one that was currently paying the man's medical bills.

Nathaniel made himself scrambled eggs, eating them directly from the skillet to minimize the wash up, wanting as little as possible between him and sleep. Even with the lights on the kitchen was dark, any illumination easily swallowed up by the mustard walls and the dark wood cabinets he remembered from being a kid. It still had the same yellow and brown vinyl covering the floors that had been part of the house when his parents had purchased the place. When life had been simple. Before his mother had passed away.

The only thing that was different from the house he had been sent away from all those years ago was the refrigerator, its modern stainless steel in direct contrast to the decor, which looked as if it had been vomited up by the 1970s.

Despite his best efforts not to, as he ate his mind replayed his day, which he supposed was better than dwelling on being twenty-six and living in his father's guestroom. He wondered momentarily what Vincent would think of that. What he would think of how Nathaniel had left behind every dream he'd ever had years ago, while Vincent himself seemed to be living his own.

It was almost enough to make him not want to return to the gallery in the morning. But the project was key to the fundraiser. And the fundraiser was to benefit a local youth shelter with what Nathaniel had been told was a great LGBT program. He would focus on that. He would focus on the shelter and the children it helped. He could so easily have been one of them—if his Aunt Mary hadn't, albeit begrudgingly, agreed to take him in.

He was scraping the remains of his eggs into the disposal when his brother entered the kitchen, suitcase in hand.

"What's all this?" Nathaniel asked, indicating the bag with a nod of his head.

"Mags has the weekend off," his brother told him, an unbelievably bright smile on his face.

"And, what? You two running away?"

Caleb's laugh was almost musical, and Nathaniel couldn't help but grin.

"I thought we'd drive somewhere for the weekend." After a moment, his smile waned. "That's okay, right? I just wrapped up the Miller project. And you're handling the gallery. And there isn't anything else on the schedule until after the first. And," Caleb added, as if still trying to sell the idea, "I even made arrangements with Katherine to work the weekend if you needed her. She needs the cash for Christmas."

Nathaniel appreciated how Caleb never said anything about Nathaniel's avoidance of their father. Never judged him—just quietly made the arrangements needed to lessen their interaction.

"Yeah. Of course it is," Nathaniel assured him. "I've got it all under control." Turning to lean back against the counter, and crossing his arms over his chest, Nathaniel studied his brother. "Well, I guess we finally need to have that safe-sex talk."

Caleb laughed again, and to Nathaniel's surprise his brother dropped his bag and came across the kitchen to hug him tight. Nathaniel couldn't stop himself from stroking his brother's inky black hair, so similar to his own.

Caleb had only been nine years old when Nathaniel was sent away, and he could still see that child when he looked at him. Caleb may have been nineteen now, a grown man, but he was still a boy in so many ways. He certainly seemed far younger than Nathaniel had at the same age.

Caleb's whispered, "Thank you, Nate," made Nathaniel's chest constrict.

He continued to stroke Caleb's hair. "Hey, you need a break. I get that. Take some time off with your girl. Don't worry about any of this for a few days."

Caleb tightened his hold for a moment before releasing his brother's shoulders and pushing himself away, self-consciously wiping at his eyes with the back of his hand. "I'm so glad you're back. You saved me, you know?"

He said it with such sincerity that Nathaniel wanted to reach out and hug him again.

"No, you'd have figured it out yourself." Nathaniel cleared his throat. "Listen, just let me know if you need any more money for the trip and I'll deposit it into your account tomorrow morning. And give Mags a kiss for me."

After Caleb left, Nathaniel washed the skillet and utensils, putting them away. Clicking off the light, he made his way, as quietly as possible, past his father's room. He peeked in to confirm the man was still sleeping and not in want of something, before picking up the receiving end of a baby monitor and heading to the guest room.

By the time he crawled under the sheets of the undersized double bed the exhaustion had set in, and sleep only took moments to come.

Chapter 3

Vincent was just wrapping up the last of the trinkets that lay in the front display case when he heard Kyle.

"Good God, it's cold," the man said, as he made his way through the door setting off a soft chime. A lidded paper cup in each hand, he took a moment to stomp the damp from his boots on the rug that sat just inside. "How in the hell can you afford to keep this place warm?"

"That's easy," Vincent answered. "By losing money."

"Hand over fist, no doubt," Kyle said. He leaned in to press a quick, chilled kiss to Vincent's lips before handing over one of the steaming cups.

"Now you're just talking dirty." Vincent grinned.

The gallery was closed, and would be for the duration of the repairs and painting, not opening its doors again until the evening of the fundraiser. Vincent was happy for the company.

Watching Kyle drop cross-legged in his expensive jeans to the dusty floor, back against the floor–to-ceiling plate-glass window, Vincent felt a flutter of happiness. Kyle's easy-going nature helped him not to worry as much about the man being so completely out of his league. They had been dating for nearly four weeks, and Vincent was beginning to think that the relationship might have the potential to go somewhere.

"Hot chocolate?" Vincent asked, popping the lid off the cup to peek inside.

"Mocha."

Now that was tragic. Vincent hated coffee—would have sworn he had told Kyle that fact more than once, but still he appreciated the gesture—and took a few polite sips before setting it aside.

He fought to hide his grimace.

"So, what do you think?" he asked, dropping down beside Kyle and indicating the empty walls with their thick smears of fresh plaster.

Kyle smiled. "It's going to look amazing."

"You are a man of vision." Vincent laughed, pleased. "I need this to go off perfectly." He watched as Kyle drank from his own cup and picked at the label between sips, and wondered what was on his mind.

"What you need is publicity," Kyle eventually said.

Vincent nodded. "I do. I've run ads in the smaller local arts magazines, and I've contacted the newspaper and the local news stations, but haven't heard anything yet, so no guarantees there."

"Well, that makes me feel a little better then," Kyle said, standing up again.

Vincent narrowed his eyes. He followed Kyle's movements, only then noticing that he had started to look a bit nervous.

"What is it?"

Kyle was quiet for a few moments, appearing to pick his words carefully. "I was hoping to ask Michael Flemming out." He was quiet again for a moment before continuing. "And I wanted to know if that would be okay with you."

Vincent raised an eyebrow and studied the man he had been dating. Kyle was flushed and animated, and Vincent realized that he was excited. Maybe a little nervous but definitely excited. "He's that hot editor from that gay magazine, right?"

"Yeah." Kyle started to pace the floor in front of where Vincent still sat. "I could bring him to your Claude Bäcker exhibit, and I bet I could get him to cover it in *Loud*."

Vincent wasn't sure he cared how Kyle justified it to himself and held in a sigh. "Of course," he said, fighting to keep any disappointment out of his voice. "We aren't exclusive." Even if technically he hadn't seen anyone else since he and Kyle had started dating. "You really like this guy, don't you?"

"Yeah, I do. I ran into him at a club a couple of weeks ago. He came up to the bar when I was waiting on my drink. We talked awhile, and I could have asked him out then, but I wanted to check with you first."

Vincent had it under good authority that Michael Flemming didn't date writers, but he didn't mention that to Kyle. He had also heard from more than one guy that he could plow you into the mattress. He didn't say that either.

"Well then, I say go for it." Vincent forced out the words and pushed himself up to standing, brushing off the back of his dark wool trousers. He needed Kyle out of the gallery so that he could sulk in privacy. "Listen, I've got a ton to get done," he said, in his best, optimistic voice. "But it's going to be a great event."

Vincent walked forward, subtly herding Kyle toward the exit. "So, shoo with you. And good luck with that Flemming guy."

Kyle smiled, relieved, and Vincent realized that the man must not have known him at all. At the moment, with the restless night he'd had the night before, he felt transparent, like his emotions were on display for all to see. Yet the man in front of him didn't seem to see him at all.

"I'll leave you to business then. And I'll see you on Thanksgiving," Kyle added, giving Vincent a quick hug and pushing his way back out the door, letting a few leaves find their way inside.

The orange and gold leaves swirled for a moment from the gust of wind and the closing of the door before settling on the aged mahogany floor, still, in the now quiet gallery. Vincent stared at them for a moment, feeling the beat of his heart in his chest, a heavy, reassuring rhythm, and sighed. It wasn't broken, though somehow that was worse. He felt empty and more tired than he'd realized.

He gathered himself up to face the day, straightening and smoothing his gray sweater, tugging at the white cuffs that peeked out from under its sleeves. He still had things to do. He could dwell on his inner turmoil later.

He turned to head into his office, only to stop short when he caught sight of Nathaniel Avery. The man stood just inside the room, his pale eyes full of sadness or sympathy. Maybe pity. Vincent didn't know and didn't care, but the mere idea that Nathaniel saw him as someone to pity put steel in his spine. And finally, *finally*, Vincent started to feel like himself again.

. . .

Nathaniel watched the vulnerable look in Vincent Cooke's eyes turn cold, a smirk creeping onto his lips. "Are you lost, Mr. Avery?"

That tone was back—the same tone as their first moments together yesterday, which had become warm and gentle, and sometimes teasing, as the afternoon had worn on.

"I wanted to see if there was anything you needed help finishing up." Nathaniel looked around the room at the empty display cases and the various boxes—some nearly full—of carefully wrapped items. "We'll be wanting to cover anything that needs covering shortly. And I was hoping to make arrangements to come in myself tomorrow, to get on with the sanding."

Vincent let out an exasperated sigh. "Do you always work on Sunday, Mr. Avery?" His voice was snippy, but with no real heat behind it.

"Every chance I get," Nathaniel answered very seriously, and watched Vincent fight a smile.

"Fine." Vincent waved a hand in the air dismissively.

Nathaniel watched him take another deep breath and stand, hands on his hips, scanning the room. He was all business then, and it reminded Nathaniel of the kid he had been. He was far more attractive now; not that he hadn't been attractive before. No, Vincent had always been beautiful. Creamy complexion, a spatter of pale freckles across his nose and cheeks that Nathaniel had loved but remembered that Vincent had loathed. He still had the same warm hazel eyes and plump lower lip that had kept Nathaniel up at night when he was sixteen, just figuring out that it was boys, not girls, that did it for him.

But a twenty-five-year-old Vincent Cooke was something to behold. His shoulders were broader, and his cheekbones more defined, having lost the fullness of youth. And that look in his eyes, right before he had slipped on the tough facade, was one that Nathaniel had nearly forgotten from all those years ago. It made him want to tug the younger man into his arms.

"I suppose I could use your help with these boxes."

Vincent's voice brought Nathaniel out of his thoughts and back to reality.

At his instruction, Nathaniel bent to grab one of the full boxes and trailed after Vincent to a small storage room, placing the box on a counter beside the smaller one the other man had carried. They made several trips, moving the boxes in a not-all-together awkward silence. They deposited the last of the boxes into the room and before Vincent could head back out the door, Nathaniel said quickly, "I'm sorry about that guy. Your boyfriend or whatever."

Vincent looked back at him, hesitating a moment before boosting himself up onto the counter. He crossed his legs at the knee and folded his arms defensively across his chest. "He wasn't my boyfriend," he said. He sounded weary.

"I'm sorry anyway." Nathaniel leaned back against the opposite counter, just a few feet separating them, tilting his head to study him.

Vincent studied Nathaniel right back, eyes narrowed, and Nathaniel found himself wondering if Vincent Cooke did, in fact, remember him after all.

"Yeah, well, no worries. I'm easily distracted by the next shiny thing," Vincent said with a smile, his eyes traveling the full length of Nathaniel's body.

Though Vincent's smile was wide, teetering on lecherous, his eyes just looked hollow.

Nathaniel frowned, searching the face for signs of the boy he had been, and hurt for him. "No. I don't believe you've ever been like that."

Vincent's wide grin vanished, replaced by an altogether more subtle, soft, curl of his lips. He averted his eyes, cast them down, his cheeks pinking just a little in embarrassment.

Nathaniel thought of a time when he would have reached out on impulse, to use his fingers to brush away the bangs that had fallen over Vincent's eyes—the bangs he still hid behind. But he forced his hands to stay down at his sides.

They were both silent for several moments, just the sound of their breathing and the lulling hum of the late afternoon traffic outside.

"You've gotten tall," Vincent finally said in a quiet voice.

Nathaniel smiled. "I hoped you'd noticed."

Chapter 4

Vincent was tired and wrung out from yet another restless night's sleep when he arrived early on Sunday morning. Nathaniel Avery's truck was parked at the curb, the man himself leaning against the rough exterior of the building, eyes closed like he was asleep standing up.

As Vincent approached, he felt himself reddening at the memory of the previous afternoon, the embarrassment of it making him short-tempered.

"I hope I didn't keep you waiting too long," he said, inwardly cringing at the irritated tone of his own voice. Vincent didn't like for people to see the vulnerability underneath the Vincent Cooke he worked so hard to present to the world—even as a part of him wanted nothing more than to be himself with one of the few people in his life he had ever been himself with.

The battling desire for both made him feel like an emotional pendulum.

Nathaniel, who was holding a thermos in his hand, gave a little jump at Vincent's words, making Vincent wonder if the man actually *had* been sleeping.

"Good morning," Nathaniel said, straightening and smiling sleepily, handing over the shiny metallic thermos once Vincent let them both in through the front doors. "I wasn't sure if you liked coffee, but I remembered you used to like Pop's peppermint hot chocolate."

Memories of sitting at Nathaniel's kitchen table, drinking hot chocolate while working on homework, flooded Vincent's mind.

He stared down, the heat of the thermos warming his chilled hands, and felt a sensation of sadness and regret slither through him like a living thing. It was not an emotion he normally let himself dwell on.

"Thank you, yes."

Vincent was hit with the strongest desire to apologize. And for so many things. Mostly for acting like a bipolar asshole, but also for having pretended not to have recognized Nathaniel the moment their eyes had met that first day. It had been stupid and petty, and what he thought the act was preserving, he didn't know.

Part of him even felt the need to apologize for the kiss from so many ages ago. He knew he'd forced it onto Nathaniel, certainly before either of them were ready. So what happened after, to Nathaniel Avery, had been his fault.

Vincent had wanted Nathaniel so much. Whether it was just teenage hormones or something more he couldn't say. But at the time he had thought himself in love. Madly. He had never even entertained the idea that Nathaniel had not been similarly inclined. But even if there *had* been any doubt, the question had been answered when Nathaniel's shocked hesitation had erupted into tongue and teeth, and hands exploring in a way Vincent had only ever dreamed about. When one of Nathaniel's hands had found its way to the small of his back, fingers lightly skimming under the waistband of his pants, Vincent had let out a sound loud enough to bring Nathaniel's father around the back of the house to investigate.

He hadn't seen Nathaniel since that day.

There had been any number of rumors about where Nathaniel Avery had disappeared to, labeling him as everything from a runaway to a suicide. Vincent would likely have never found out the truth if, after several failed attempts to speak with Nathaniel's father, he hadn't skipped class to hunt down Caleb at his elementary school.

Caleb had recognized Vincent from all the evenings he had sat studying with Nathaniel at their kitchen table and had told him that his father had sent Nathaniel to live with an aunt in Chicago. Caleb had cried. Later, Vincent had cried too.

Nathaniel Avery's absence had left a void in Vincent, and he had mourned the loss of his love life, or the potential of one, but until that very moment, hadn't realized the real loss had been the friendship.

. . .

Tuesday morning, Vincent sat in his office sorting unpaid invoices and filing away those he had already paid but hadn't gotten around to putting away. The rest of his office was pristine, as always, but the desk itself was a bit of a disaster. Gallery Nocturne had been short-staffed since mid-summer, when Campbell had turned in his two weeks' notice. Vincent was disappointed but completely understood. Campbell Price had been the perfect right-hand man, but he was also a talented ceramicist, with a chance to study under an even more talented one. Vincent would have taken the opportunity, too. But since Campbell's departure there just never seemed enough time for everything.

Even with the door almost closed he could hear the muffled laughter of the workmen and the loud rhythmic hum of the sanding machines with their dust vacuums. Oddly, that was not something Vincent had known existed and was disappointed that his visions of bulging biceps and sanding blocks hadn't come to fruition. He doubted anyone had ever needed to take off their shirt from the exertion of using a sanding machine.

Vincent was fighting the urge to hunt Nathaniel down. He knew his entire team was busy. Had been all morning. They certainly did not need interruptions. But Vincent was having a problem keeping his mind off the man.

He peeked at the clock on the wall and gave in. He grabbed his jacket and stepped out into the gallery proper. He looked around at the walls, with their haphazard dotting of freshly sanded plaster, and walked deeper into the gallery, back toward the small enclosed rooms and the back wall where the bulk of the work was being done. In some mistaken inspiration of genius, the previous owner of the space had made a half-assed attempt at a Venetian plaster technique that to Vincent's mind just looked cheesy. He would be happy to see it finally gone.

With directions from a short, barrel of a man in worn jeans and a baseball cap, Vincent headed to the largest of the gallery's small rooms. The entry had been covered, floor to ceiling, with plastic, keeping as much dust as possible confined in the enclosed space. Vincent knocked on the wall by the entrance before he pushed his way past the plastic sheeting.

He had to tap on Nathaniel's shoulder to get his attention.

Turning off his sander, Nathaniel leaned it against the wall, before pulling some sort of post-apocalyptic protective mask down, to hang around his neck. "Hey," he said, that tired smile making a reappearance. "Did you need something?"

"Yeah." Vincent nervously toyed with his bottom lip with a thumb and forefinger, feeling the small lump where a piercing had once been. "Would you like to grab lunch? It's nearly noon." He forced his hand back to his side and stood, trying not to shift from foot to foot. Twenty-five was a little old to be acting like a nervous kid, but Nathaniel Avery's presence had that effect on him. "I mean," he took a breath, "could I buy you lunch?"

Nathaniel flashed him another smile, this one wide. "Absolutely. I have a change of clothes, if you can give me a minute."

Vincent agreed, heading back to his office to the sound of Nathaniel giving out instructions. They met a few minutes later at the front door. Vincent letting them out and locking up behind them.

They decided to walk to the diner a few blocks up the street. The Short North, as the gallery district of Columbus was called, was littered with restaurants, from Japanese to Greek and everything in between. The 620 Diner was good and close—geographically, though about as far away from a place for a date as you could get. Vincent had thought it a logical choice, under the circumstances.

They had walked in silence for half a block, before Nathaniel spoke. "So, how is it that your dream of owning a gallery here came true so quickly?"

Vincent's smile was sad. That Nathaniel remembered pleased him, but it wasn't like they hadn't spent nearly eight months practically connected at the hip. "Well, shortly after I graduated from the university, Dad passed away. I inherited some money and the building was on the market." Vincent shrugged. "The timing was good."

And it had been. Vincent had just completed his BA at OSU with a major in art history and a minor in business. And, though he had always imagined working in a museum, he had every plan of one day owning his own small gallery. True, it wasn't exactly New York City, but Vincent thought he might like it more for that fact.

He had always envisioned the excitement of discovering unknown talent and selling pieces of art, shipping them all over the country. Since he was small, he'd dreamed of receiving deliveries in large wooden crates and using crowbars to force them open, exposing their contents while straw spilled out onto the floor.

Unquestionably, Vincent had watched far too many old movies.

"I'm sorry about your father. He would have been proud." Nathaniel's voice was quiet. "And I've got to admit, I am pretty impressed."

Vincent looked over to catch the man looking at him and felt embarrassed. "And how about you?" Vincent inwardly flinched the moment the words came out of his mouth.

"Well," Nathaniel said, pulling open the diner door and letting Vincent walk in ahead of him. "My plans have taken a bit of a detour."

The two of them walked to an empty booth, Vincent raising his hand in greeting to a family sitting in the corner.

"Detour?" Vincent prompted, once they were both seated in their respective sides of the booth.

"Dad got sick, so I came home," Nathaniel stated simply.

"I'm surprised you did." Vincent wasn't sure if he would have done the same thing for his own father, under the same circumstances.

Nathaniel laughed, but it wasn't a happy one. "I didn't do it for him. I did it for Caleb. He needed me. Hell, he needed me a whole lot sooner."

Nathaniel fiddled with his menu before speaking again. "How is it that you came to have my dad's company doing work for you?"

Vincent thought he almost looked hurt, and quickly shook his head. "I didn't know. Campbell handled it. He called the firms, got the bids." He shook his head again. "I didn't know until you nearly plowed me down."

Nathaniel chuckled at the memory and Vincent was unable to hold back his own laugh.

"Did you leave anyone behind?" Vincent gave into his desire to ask. In for a penny, in for a pound.

"A boyfriend, you mean?" Nathaniel asked to clarify.

"Yes." Vincent held his breath, not sure exactly why.

"Not really. I had been seeing someone on and off. More off, to be honest."

"And now it's off?" Vincent refused to feel self-conscious.

"Yes. Mason called it off officially when I told him I was coming back here for the foreseeable future."

"I'm sorry." And Vincent was. Sorry it had happened—sorry now that he had brought it up.

Nathaniel waved his apology away. "I'm not. It wasn't that serious. I think I miss the cat more."

They both laughed at that and the odd tension of the moment seemed to disappear.

They each ordered soup and a sandwich and for now avoided, as if by unspoken agreement, any more discussion of the past. Vincent was more than okay with that. At the moment, he wasn't completely sure he could handle finding out that Nathaniel's life had been anything but happy.

"So why Thanksgiving?" Nathaniel pulled a napkin from the shiny dispenser that sat on the table. "Isn't everyone already waiting outside of Walmart or something by seven p.m.?"

Vincent laughed. "Oh my God, Nate. I said those exact same words to Bäcker." He almost didn't register the slip. Everyone had always called him Nathaniel. Friends, teachers, his parents. Everyone. Everyone, that is, except for Caleb. And then Vincent.

But Nathaniel didn't say anything, just shrugged his shoulders and held his hands up in a *that's what I'm saying*, gesture.

Vincent shrugged. "I don't know. It's just one of his requirements for the show. Like the eight billion wall colors and the lighting. And everything else." He pushed his bangs aside and let out a breath. "But I think he's a big enough draw for it not to matter anyway. And besides, the shelter needs it. *I* need it."

And he did. The gallery did okay. Probably better than most of the similarly sized galleries in the area. But really, art was not normally high on the list for the vast majority of shoppers when the economy was a roller coaster. If you wanted to bring in big dollar buyers—the ones that were still spending, and not just the forty, fifty dollar variety—you needed an artist who sparked interest, and not someone whose work had already flooded the market. The kind of attention an artist like Claude Bäcker could bring to his little gallery could be game changing.

"And why the kids' shelter?" Nathaniel asked. "Was it your suggestion or his?"

Vincent could feel his blush. He didn't want to tell Nathaniel that after he had disappeared, Vincent had looked for him everywhere. That when Nathaniel's father wouldn't take his calls or answer his door, Vincent had called hospitals and had talked his sister, who at nineteen already had her own car, into taking him to shelters around town. The thought that Nathaniel might have had nowhere to go had haunted him. It had changed him on a fundamental level.

Instead of answering Nathaniel's question Vincent asked one of his own. "Why didn't you ever contact me?" Vincent saw Nathaniel's expression soften, as if his question was an admission in itself, and Vincent fought the urge to look away.

Nathaniel shook his head. "I tried." He shook his head again and started over. "No, at first I was mad at you." He held up his hand in a defensive gesture that almost made Vincent laugh. "Then, when I came to my senses, they wouldn't let me. I tried. I kept trying. For a while, anyway. Then I didn't try anymore."

They stared at each other, the quiet stretching between them. Vincent could see the apology there on Nathaniel's face, perhaps even some regret. But before he could say anything back, accept the apology that was being silently offered, crack a joke—everything about this moment felt far too serious—he heard a small chirp of delight.

Vincent looked up and, smiling, introduced the invading threesome from the corner booth to Nathaniel: Elijah and Jacob, and Abigail—a chubby little girl, with dark hair and blue eyes, whom the couple had flown halfway around the world to adopt. As everyone shook hands, and Nathaniel complimented Abby's bright red patent leather Mary Janes, Vincent wondered if Nathaniel had ever envisioned such a life for himself. *Maybe a life with Mason, a toddler held securely in his arms.*

When Nathaniel flashed him a happy smile, Vincent found himself smiling right back. He wondered if he had a single friend that would appreciate someone like Nathaniel and found himself mentally flipping through an inventory of people he knew.

He was only slightly disappointed when he was unable to come up with a single suitable match.

Chapter 5

Two days later, Nathaniel found himself sitting outside a picturesque red farmhouse surrounded by rustic barns and the excited sounds of small children.

"Why are we here again?" Nathaniel still wasn't certain how he had ended up here with Vincent, as opposed to working to finish the man's project.

"Remember me telling you how my father would take me and my sister for a cider run every year?" Vincent asked, opening the driver's door and climbing out. Nathaniel followed his lead, sliding out of the passenger seat and into the chilly breeze.

Nathaniel did remember. The odd little rituals of the Cooke family had always stuck with him. At sixteen, Vincent's family life had seemed like something from a television show. A father to make dinner in the evening, pumpkin picking, and cider from a local orchard. When Vincent told Nathaniel that his family went to a local farm every year to pick out and chop down their own Christmas tree, Nathaniel had actually accused the kid of lying.

But Vincent had never made him feel like less for not having a family like his. Instead, Vincent had just tried to include him as much as possible, happy and excited to share.

"Of course I do," Nathaniel answered and Vincent grinned wide.

"Well, I thought that you might enjoy it," he said, grabbing Nathaniel's sleeve and tugging him to the largest of the outbuildings. "I haven't come here since Dad passed."

Vincent let go once they entered through the large barn doors into what amounted to a little shop. Long tables ran the length of the interior, along the walls and down the center, most covered in large wooden crates of apples— reds, golds, yellows and greens, some even a mixture of all at once. Nathaniel hadn't even been aware that apples came in so many colors.

"So do we get to watch them being made into cider?" Nathaniel asked. He felt completely out of his element.

"Sadly, no," Vincent replied with a sigh. "They make their cider in October, but we can still buy it."

Nathaniel laughed. "Then why did we drive two hours to come here? There's a grocery store five minutes from my house."

"Because," Vincent said, beaming, "this is the best cider on the planet." As had always been the case, Nathaniel found the redhead's enthusiasm contagious.

Beckoning Nathaniel over, Vincent headed to the counter where he ordered them each a glass of cider and a warm, glazed doughnut and then led them to a bench just out back of the barn. The bench had a great view of the fields and of children playing, waiting for their parents. It was a little too cold perhaps, but Vincent seemed content, so Nathaniel pulled the collar of his coat up a little.

"My father brought us here every year when I was young," Vincent told him, holding out the paper plate so that Nathaniel could take one of the doughnuts. "Normally a week or two into October. They have this little hay maze that I used to love to run through and still love watching kids play inside. And they always have pens of farm animals to pet—goats, calves…bunnies, even."

Vincent looked over, smiling, the tip of his nose pink. "Now, bite the doughnut and then take a drink of the cider."

Nathaniel did. "Oh my God." It was perfect.

"I know, right?" Vincent bounced up and down a little on the bench, seeming to try and warm himself. "I cannot even walk by a bakery without longing to drive down here. I smell doughnuts and it's like I'm ten again." Vincent grinned. "And when it first starts to feel like fall? You know that first day in September, when logically you know that it is too soon but still, somewhere in the back of your mind, you're hoping that *this is it*? All I want to do is jump in my car and drive."

Nathaniel had always loved to hear Vincent talk about things like this. The little moments, those joyful moments that, in his mind, always separated Vincent from Nathaniel's own dark little world. Which, admittedly, Nathaniel knew was unfair. It wasn't like his father hadn't loved him, hadn't taken care of him. It was just that after his mother had passed, Nathaniel had always felt like he and Caleb weren't much different in his father's eyes than that old house— just something else that needed attention he didn't have time to give.

Nathaniel sat quietly next to Vincent, listening to him talk about the little things that he and his father and sister would do. Nathaniel liked that Mr. Cooke had tried to create these little memories for his kids. He thought that if one day he had children of his own, he would want to do the same thing. He liked the idea that someday after he was gone, his children would sit around, reminiscing about simple things, like a trip to a cider mill, or carving jack-o-lanterns or their father making peppermint hot chocolate for them and their friends.

"I bet my dad would like this," Nathaniel said, raising his near-empty glass.

Vincent studied him a moment, eyes squinting against the wind. "Well, I say we pick him up a jug."

They returned their glasses and wandered the farm a little longer, following a path from the larger barn to a smaller building with a long porch. The railings were already wound with little white lights and natural wreaths hung on every window. *A Christmas shop of arts and crafts style ornaments, no doubt*, Nathaniel guessed.

"Now, we can't go inside," Vincent told him. "It is against the rules to look at Christmas things until after Thanksgiving."

Nathaniel laughed. "That a Cooke family rule?"

"Nope." Vincent rolled his eyes. "Dad would have strung up Christmas lights in August if the neighbors wouldn't have complained. This is all me. I like to enjoy the holidays as they come."

They climbed the wooden porch, their steps echoing in the quiet of the morning, and followed the length of it as it wrapped around the side of the building.

"Perfect." Vincent grabbed Nathaniel's sleeve, pulling a little. "It's still here."

Vincent signaled Nathaniel to have a seat as he fished a phone from his pocket.

"Doesn't this fall under your no-Christmas policy?" Nathaniel laughed, sitting down on a wooden bench, already occupied by a life-size fiberglass Santa Claus, and throwing an arm around its shoulders.

"A picture of you with Santa trumps all rules," Vincent said, holding his phone in front of him to line up the shot. "Now you do me."

They swapped places—sort of. This time Nathaniel held Vincent's phone and Vincent climbed onto Santa's lap, grinning like he was eight. Nathaniel took the photo and told Vincent to wait as he swapped Vincent's phone out for his own, taking one for himself.

After, they walked back up the path, both bundled in their coats. It had grown warmer as the morning grew late, but under the canopy of red- and orange-colored leaves, with the sun behind the clouds, it felt colder.

The two of them grinned at each other, happy not to break the odd echoey silence that seemed unique to moments spent under a cold, gray sky, a silence that wasn't really silent at all. The crunch of leaves under foot, the occasional rustle of a squirrel dashing across their path, the sound of voices just out of sight.

Just as it had always been, being in the presence of Vincent Cooke made Nathaniel feel content.

· · ·

Twenty minutes outside of Columbus, Nathaniel fell asleep, head turned toward Vincent, hands tucked deep in the pockets of his pea-coat.

Vincent couldn't stop himself from stealing glances. With his face relaxed, Nathaniel almost looked as he had at sixteen. Younger even. Nathaniel had always had a serious bent, thinking through everything he did, doing what was best, not necessarily what he wanted. He didn't seem much different now.

Nathaniel had been the perfect counterbalance to Vincent's impetuousness. In return, Vincent was the only one who could bring out Nathaniel's playful side.

When he had smiled wide from the simple joy of cider and doughnuts, Vincent had to fight the urge to lean over and kiss him, which was ridiculous, he was aware. But Vincent knew himself well, and he knew that he could easily find himself as crazy about Nathaniel Avery as he had been all those years ago.

Vincent liked serious. He liked thoughtful.

And it didn't help the that Nathaniel was still gorgeous.

Vincent had instantly been jealous of the boy's dark-haired, blue-eyed good looks when they had first met, paired together for science class. He had been certain he would hear the same teasing and taunts he'd heard all his life for his red hair and his slight build. But Nathaniel had merely looked at him with a certain light in his eyes that Vincent only later recognized as interest.

As Vincent slowed to a stop at a red light only minutes from Nathaniel's childhood home, the man next to him—still with dark hair and blue eyes, and that same intense seriousness Vincent found so appealing—stirred, opening his eyes. "Sorry."

Nathaniel's voice was gruff, and Vincent wanted to purr. "No problem. I think you needed it."

Nathaniel continued to watch him from where he sat, and Vincent glanced over again at the next stop.

"Thanks for today. All of it," Nathaniel said when their eyes met. He wore that solemn look he always had when he had been thinking. That look had always made Vincent feel like Nathaniel only spoke words sincerely, which made them all the more precious.

"Anytime."

Chapter 6

"It's your turn," Vincent said from where he sat, cross-legged, on the floor.

"A-3," Nathaniel called over his shoulder. He was working to tape off the trim and molding at the front of the gallery, preparing for the painting to start. It would take one more day to finish the repairs to the length of the back wall, and then another three days of painting. If they wanted Vincent to have any time to prepare for the fundraiser, they were cutting it close.

"Miss." Vincent's word was muffled by the hand he held up to cover a yawn.

"How exactly is this game of Battleship even supposed to work?" Nathaniel laughed, shifting to sit on the floor, also cross-legged. "You have to keep peeking at my side of the board, to see if you hit."

"Oh, I was going to cheat anyway." Vincent grinned over at him. "This just makes it easier."

"You little shit." Nathaniel threw an empty cardboard spool from a roll of blue tape, at him.

Vincent just laughed, fighting another yawn.

Nathaniel shook his head. "You should go home and get some sleep. I promise not to steal the silver."

"And you should let me help," Vincent threw back, but Nathaniel paid him no attention. "See, it's like we are both in hell and are destined to have the same conversation over and over again, throughout eternity."

"So," Nathaniel said, mulling the idea over, "my hell is spending the evening hours with a man that cheats at children's board games and that I don't trust with masking tape?"

Vincent threw the cardboard spool back at him. It hit his chest, bounced off, and rolled out of both their reaches, safe.

This was how they had spent the last two evenings—sitting around, arguing and joking, while Nathaniel tried to accomplish just a little bit extra. He couldn't give Vincent the originally planned three days, but he was going to be able to give him the whole day before Thanksgiving, which would mean he had a whole day before the fundraiser itself, to set up for the event.

Nathaniel couldn't remember the last time he had enjoyed working more. Vincent was funny, irreverent, and apparently cheated at everything—Monopoly, Sorry and, of all things, Cootie. Nathaniel didn't bother to ask why a twenty-five-year-old man owned a copy of a preschool game.

"Do you still paint?" Vincent suddenly asked. It hadn't been something they had discussed, and Nathaniel felt a rush of embarrassment.

"No," he stated, not wanting to talk about it.

He watched Vincent toy with his lip; it was something he seemed to do when he was nervous or, like now, debating his next words. "Not since you came back?"

"Not for a long time." It was a difficult admission to make.

At sixteen, Nathaniel had loved nothing more than painting. He'd had plans to attend art school and had hoped to spend his life with a paint brush in his hand. It had been his love of painting and Vincent's enthusiasm over his skill—and he had been skilled—that had cemented their friendship all those years ago. It embarrassed him that, while Vincent had followed through on his own plans, Nathaniel lived a sad little existence in his father's guestroom and painted with polyester rollers, not sable brushes.

Vincent looked thoughtful. "Do you still think about it?"

"And what if I told you no?" Nathaniel asked, knowing it would have been a lie.

Vincent squinted at him, as if reading Nathaniel's thoughts. "I'd say that as long as you're happy it doesn't matter if you never pick up a paintbrush again."

You make me happy. The thought popped into Nathaniel's head but he didn't say the words, only grunted and got back to work.

"Look," Vincent said after a few minutes, turning his Battleship board around, looking proud that he had managed to construct a crude happy face with white and red pegs. "Tomorrow I should bring a Lite-Brite."

Nathaniel laughed.

. . .

When Nathaniel walked in the door, Katherine was putting a gallon of milk back into the refrigerator. She looked up when she heard him, and smiled.

"He's having a good day, Nathaniel," she told him. "He's been talking about you boys as children."

Nathaniel forced a smile. He was in too good a mood to spoil it with thoughts of his father.

"He told me all about Caleb getting caught toilet-papering some cheerleader's house," Katherine said, laughing. "Said he grounded him until school started again."

"Maggie. That was Mags' house," Nathaniel supplied, smiling at the memory. He remembered the early morning calls he had received from his brother throughout the entire summer, bored to the point that even talking to his boring older brother had seemed appealing.

"And about catching you with your hands down some poor boy's pants." She snorted this time and Nathaniel closed his eyes. He bit back a curse and felt his stomach give a nauseating roll that left him feeling sick.

"Don't you be embarrassed," Katherine said, patting his arm as she moved past to grab a kettle off the stove. "Gay or straight, boys are all the same."

"Why doesn't it bother you?" He wasn't sure why he'd asked, but he had, and now it was out there. Sometimes he soothed himself with the thought that his dad's rejection of him was generational, as much as anything else. Yet here stood Katherine, who couldn't have been too much younger than his father, and she didn't bat an eyelash at the thought.

"I grew up being taught that God doesn't make mistakes," she answered as she prepared her tea. "And I took it to heart. Of course, I was taught that by a grandmother that kicked her son out of the house for falling in love with a white girl."

Nathaniel felt the urge to throw something. "But isn't that nuts? How can people reconcile their words and their actions? How can they justify it to themselves?"

Katherine shrugged.

"My father wouldn't even talk to me. Shipped me off as quick as he could make the arrangements." Nathaniel felt his temper continue to rise, and he knew he should just drop the subject, but didn't. "What makes you inherently different from him?"

She sat down at the table, in one of the old, wooden chairs before she answered. "I'm not sure that's a fair question. I don't know that anyone knows how they would react in a situation, not until they're in it. As for my grandmother, I think she regretted it by the time I had come along."

"But it was too late," Nathaniel said. "By then, it was too late."

"Too late for whom?" Katherine asked pointedly. "Too late to apologize to her son? Yes, he was dead and gone. Died young. But not too late to change her ways, Nathaniel. The changing isn't always for the person you hurt. Sometimes we make our apologies to the people that come after. That's why the next generation is just a little better than the one before."

Nathaniel wasn't sure if that was true, so he just stared down at his shoes and at the ugly, scuffed vinyl. He idly wondered why his father had never updated the house, why he had continued to live in this dark, oppressive cave.

"He wants to talk to you, Nathaniel."

He heard the words and almost didn't answer. "I don't think I can forgive him."

He heard the scrape of the chair as Katherine got up, and after a moment, felt her hand on his shoulder. "I don't think he expects you to."

After Katherine had left, Nathaniel wandered to the doorway to the living room. He watched for a few moments while his father slowly flipped through old photo albums, stopping sometimes to run unsteady hands over the images nestled behind the clear plastic.

To Nathaniel, at that instant, his father looked positively ancient, though he wasn't yet seventy. Nathaniel wondered if it was the illness.

After a moment, his father looked up. His face was sad, but upon seeing Nathaniel, he smiled. "Do you want to sit with me?"

He knew it was coming, and still the question surprised him. Before he knew it, he had moved into the room and taken a seat.

His father turned the album so that Nathaniel could see its open pages. "Do you remember staying at that cabin?"

Nathaniel shook his head. "Not really. I remember the boat though." He found himself smiling. "I remember all of us loading into the boat one morning and you kept saying, 'Don't tip the boat. Don't tip the boat.'"

"And then," his father took up the story, "when I finally got in after your mother and both you boys…" His father laughed.

"You tipped the whole thing over yourself." Nathaniel finished, laughing too.

As the laughter died down, they both sat in silence, smiling a little at each other.

"You know," Nathaniel's father started, and Nathaniel had to fight the urge to hold his hand up to stop him from continuing, "I don't have a lot of time left. I can feel it slipping away. The memories—" his father waved a shaky hand in the air, miming memories being blown away on the breeze. "Soon you and Caleb will be putting sheets over the bathroom mirror because I'll be thinking some old man is watching me pee." Nathaniel could hear the impotent rage in his words.

Nathaniel thought what a nightmare it must be to know that your mind was failing and not be able to do anything about it. Only to sit and wait. He wondered if it was any consolation to know that when it happened you wouldn't actually know. He thought that would make it even scarier.

"While I still can, while I still remember, I wanted to tell you that I love you." His father wiped at his eyes. "Just know that. And that I'm sorry."

Nathaniel sat, the silence almost deafening. He thought about Katherine's words. But he also thought about the time he had spent under his aunt's roof and all those years he had felt unloved and unlovable. And he was unable to say anything. He didn't have it in him to accept *or* reject the apology, knowing that his father offered it believing he would likely be told it was too late.

Even after all this time, his father knew him.

Nathaniel smiled sadly and stood, preparing to leave.

"Maybe you should invite that little red-headed boy over for Thanksgiving."

Nathaniel stilled at his dad's words.

"His father died a couple of years back. I thought about calling you. I thought that maybe he needed a friend right then. But I wasn't sure how. How to talk to you again."

"Dad, I think Vincent is probably working that day. He has a fundraiser that evening." Nathaniel was surprised his voice sounded so steady. His father frowned. "That's too bad. He was a nice boy. Persistent." He gave a small laugh. "That must be a redhead thing. It reminded me of your mother."

Nathaniel made it to the doorway before he stopped and turned around to study his father.

"I love you, Dad." The words were out before he could stop them. And he was glad, because it was the truth. Whether he could ever completely forgive his father for what he had done to him he didn't know, but that didn't make it any less true.

His dad smiled and went back to looking at his photo album.

Chapter 7

With the paint dry on the walls of Gallery Nocturne, Nathaniel again sat in the passenger seat of Vincent's car, watching him as he drove them out to Claude Bäcker's place. He seemed to navigate the winding rural two-lane as if he had driven it again and again in some other life, easily taking the twists and turns through the shadow of dense trees and speeding up in anticipation of the as of yet unseen long, straight stretches of road, surrounded by farms with their fields bleached of color.

The hues of the leaves at this time of year had always reminded Nathaniel of Vincent, his hair a deep red in the muted light of the gallery, a beautiful fiery blaze outside in the sunlight, and nearly golden under a night sky. A remembered image of a younger Vincent, lying on a bed of fallen leaves, flickered through Nathaniel's mind, there and gone in the same breath.

The scenery of empty fields and fields still tall with long-dead corn stalks made Nathaniel think of the one and only Halloween the two of them had spent together, when Vincent's sister had taken them both to a local farm boasting a Trail of Terror, or Terror Trail, or some such thing. They had purchased their tickets, nervous and excited at the prospect of being chased by insane clowns and people in hockey masks wielding chainsaws.

It had been pretty much what they'd expected: stumbling in near darkness, adrenaline pumping—Vincent had been a much faster runner, reaching out to grab Nathaniel's sleeve, helping him to change course quickly, saving him again and again from a most horrific pretend demise. Vincent had been focused, fearless, quiet—except for his puffing breath and the occasional instruction yelled over his shoulder. Nathaniel had screamed like a girl.

God, it had been fun.

They had lingered after, in their overpriced *I survived* T-shirts, eating overpriced caramel apples, grinning stupidly at each other and trying vainly to stay warm by one of the electric heaters placed around and about. There had been a huge crowd of teenagers and adults, and he remembered a pretty little thing trying hard to make eyes at Vincent, but he had taken no notice of her.

"What are you smiling about?" Vincent asked, stealing a quick glance Nathaniel's way before focusing back on the road.

"Nothing." He didn't want to say, afraid somehow that voicing it would taint the perfect memory.

Vincent raised an eyebrow but didn't press. After a few minutes, he confided, "I'm almost certain Bäcker is stark raving."

They had come to a stop sign and, as instructed by the GPS, turned right. They were nearly there.

"Is that why you asked me along while you retrieve his artwork?" Nathaniel flexed his biceps.

Vincent grinned. "Not in the way you are implying. I don't need protection." He rolled his eyes at the thought. "But you can never truly enjoy the company of the insane without a friend to shoot looks at."

Nathaniel laughed at that, pleased. After ten years, they had practically picked up the friendship where they had left off. Vincent seemed more than content with just that. And it was friendship, Nathaniel was certain—he had overheard him on the phone the previous day trying to arrange what sounded like a date for the evening of the charity fundraiser.

If Nathaniel had felt he had more to offer, he would have asked Vincent himself. He had been strongly tempted to anyway. But he had nothing, and even though he'd been invited to attend, he wasn't sure he'd make it—not if Vincent was spending the evening with his date. Nathaniel would have liked to have seen him that evening, to enjoy his accomplishments at his first proper event, and for such a good cause, in a place that Vincent had created from the perfect storm of his passion and hard work. Nathaniel was proud of him, and part of him wanted to be there so badly, but he knew that he wouldn't have wanted to leave Vincent's side, while Vincent would likely prefer to spend his time with his date. Holding hands. Leaning in close to whisper in his ear. Sharing those secret looks only meant for each other.

"What are you doing on Thanksgiving?" Nathaniel asked. The words just spilled out, and Vincent glanced over, surprised at the abruptness of the question.

"Well," his answer came slowly, "my sister's in Texas, so I figured, if I didn't have all the prep for the party complete, I would finish up that morning. I have to meet the caterer there at five anyway."

"Come spend it with me." Nathaniel wondered if Vincent could tell how much he wanted him to say yes. "Come spend it with me, Caleb and Dad."

Vincent didn't say anything for a moment. "Can you cook?"

Nathaniel shook his head. "No."

"Can Caleb cook?"

Nathaniel shook his head again. "No, he's worse than me."

"So," Vincent summarized "You are asking me to come spend Thanksgiving with you and Caleb and a man who hates me? And the food will be terrible?"

Nathaniel laughed. "No, my father doesn't hate you. But, yes. The food will be horrible."

Vincent grinned. "I'd love to."

. . .

When they pulled up to Claude Bäcker's old farmhouse, the moving company was already there. The large white box truck, with *MacAlister Moving* displayed in large green and red block letters, and featuring a stylized illustration of a muscular man in a kilt and work boots, blocked the entirety of the drive so Vincent had to park the car on the street.

The movers stood outside the truck—three men, each wearing a black T-shirt and the same green and red patterned tartan as the illustration—waiting patiently.

"You picked them for their uniforms, didn't you?" Nathaniel asked quietly.

"You can thank me later," Vincent whispered back.

One of the movers extinguished a cigarette on the bottom of his boot before slipping the stub behind his ear and approaching, and Vincent flashed Nathaniel a wide-eyed look, biting his lip. Nathaniel snorted.

The three of them—Vincent, Nathaniel and the man apparently in charge of the moving crew—walked up the steps to the porch together. When the front door opened, they were greeted by the man himself.

Nathaniel found it slightly disappointing that Claude Bäcker didn't look raving mad. Not at all. He just kind of looked like someone's dad. His dark blond hair was sleep-mussed, his temples threaded lightly in silver. He wore a pair of thick-framed glasses, paint-splattered carpenter pants and a snug T-shirt imprinted with an obscure superhero logo that Nathaniel vaguely recognized but couldn't place.

He showed them to a large outbuilding nearly bursting at the seams with canvases, a few still blank, most already complete and leaning against the walls in layers of eight or ten deep. To the left of the doorway was a collection of canvases in a range of sizes, already wrapped and ready to go. Bäcker indicated them to the kilted man, staring at his legs a moment, blinking, like he had just noticed they were bare. Vincent grinned over at Nathaniel, and he thought the redhead looked like he was having the best time ever.

While Vincent stepped away with Bäcker, flipping through some of the other canvases together and chatting, Nathaniel leaned against the wall, well out of the way of the team of movers as they began carefully carrying the wrapped canvases out.

Nathaniel's eyes wandered between the movers as they came and went, and over the expanse of the workshop. It smelled of paint and of freshly cut wood from where Bäcker obviously stretched his own canvas, and of that wonderful smell unique to fall, carried in on each gust of the breeze coming through the open door.

As the artist walked into another room to retrieve something, Vincent turned around to hold up a medium-sized painting, the canvas no larger than twenty-by-twenty, to show Nathaniel. It was a study in oil of a young man's shoulders, long dreadlocked hair pulled up in a makeshift knot. The painting was beautiful, though the body it conveyed was not flawless and Nathaniel could almost believe that if he reached out and touched it, the skin would be warm beneath his fingers.

He met Vincent's eyes and the man silently mouthed the word *perfect*, the excitement of the moment seeming to light him from the inside.

In that instant, it were as if the world snapped into focus. Nathaniel's pulse raced in his ears, and he was unable to tear his gaze away from him.

When Vincent lifted a questioning brow and then his expression turned to concern, Nathaniel just shook his head and smiled. And in that moment, Nathaniel knew with complete certainty that if asked, years down the road, he would be able to describe in vivid detail the day he realized he had fallen in love with Vincent Cooke.

. . .

"Mr. Cooke?"

Vincent hesitated a moment when Bäcker called for him from the other room. He stole another last look at Nathaniel, who waved him on, still with that odd expression.

Vincent was hit with the thought that maybe Nathaniel found this place depressing. That this tumbledown shed full of beautiful art was a reminder of hopes and dreams he had long ago shoved away in a drawer.

He mentally kicked himself for not having considered that before dragging Nathaniel along on this stupid adventure.

Vincent had never had any real talent himself, and he had always been amazed by the amount of detail Nathaniel could get out of his paint and pencils. Even as an adult, he was still impressed with the talent Nathaniel had shown so young. He even kept, framed on one of the walls of his office, a small eight-by-eight piece that a sixteen-year-old Nathaniel had painted of Vincent's feet. He wondered if Nathaniel had noticed.

The next room was even more of a jumble. Stacks of canvases, teetering shelves, and barely enough room to move. The place screamed firetrap. Amongst the mess, Bäcker stood on one of those spinny office chairs, already shifting precariously from where it sat atop an old wooden desk, reaching to retrieve something from a ceiling mounted rack.

"Good lord, Mr. Bäcker," Vincent said, rushing forward as best he could to grab the chair's slowly revolving base before the man fell to his death. "You're going to kill yourself."

Bäcker just laughed. "Nah, I do this all the time." Vincent wondered why, if he had to reach that rack often, he didn't just move its contents somewhere easier to reach. "So, what's up with your guy out there?"

Vincent looked over his shoulder at the empty door and tried not to feel guilty about what he was going to say. "That's Nathaniel, an old friend. He's a very talented artist. Or was. It worries me a little that he doesn't paint anymore. He used to live for it."

"Well, art is emotion," Claude told him as he began his almost graceful dismount from the tower of broken furniture. "You do your best work when you are either coming from a place of joy or sadness. That in-between place? It's harder from there."

"From what place do *you* paint?" Vincent asked. When Bäcker didn't answer, Vincent figured that was answer in itself.

"I worry that he'll never pick up a paintbrush again," Vincent confided. Bäcker just shrugged.

"Would you be any less in love with him if he didn't?"

The words surprised Vincent and he quickly shook his head in denial. "It's not like that."

Claude Bäcker squinted at him—that same bug under a glass perusal he had given the mover's bare legs—and shrugged again. "Well, what do I know?"

The drive back to Columbus was a quiet one.

Chapter 8

From the outside, the Avery house was much the same as Vincent remembered, though perhaps smaller. It looked to have had a relatively new coat of paint, and Vincent liked the freshness of it, even as the place stirred up a number of memories best left forgotten. The last time he had been here he had spent half the afternoon banging on the door and pleading with the occupant inside.

He made his way to the back door, as he had always done, and pushed his way in, a pumpkin pie in hand. It felt like being a child again.

The memories inside were happier ones. Memories of all the months he had spent studying, watching television, sitting on Nathaniel's bed, reading while Nathaniel painted at an easel in the corner of the cluttered space.

As an adult the little house seemed small, cramped and dark. But as a boy it had been defined by Nathaniel's presence, and Vincent had loved being here.

Nathaniel stood at the counter, perusing an old cookbook, making what Vincent assumed were mashed potatoes. Vincent had never thought about mashed potatoes before, but he supposed that there would have to be more to them than just potatoes.

Another man, like a younger, smaller, version of Nathaniel, sat at the kitchen table placing rolls into a bright-blue bowl. It had to be Caleb. Vincent wondered if that was how Nathaniel had looked at nineteen. The thought made him sad.

But like the many other emotions the house was conjuring up, he wouldn't dwell on that now.

They both looked up and smiled, and Vincent felt the sadness of the place slip away.

"You're just in time. Turkey is nearly done," Nathaniel said before telling Vincent to put the pie on the counter.

"There's turkey?" He hadn't actually been expecting turkey. "I kind of envisioned popcorn and toast."

"And jelly beans," Caleb added, grinning.

Vincent laughed. He was suddenly starving.

He helped by setting the table for four, laying out matching plates and mismatched silverware, while the brothers finished pulling together the rest of the meal. There wasn't a full turkey, just a turkey breast, that smelled great but looked a little dry. Brown-and-serve rolls, stuffing from a box, potatoes and honest-to-God gravy—made from drippings—of which Nathaniel was extremely proud.

Caleb woke their father from where he was napping in front of the television and he joined them, sitting at the head of the table, Nathaniel opposite. They ate way too much in the dark little house—the gravy making even boxed stuffing taste good—and chatted happily, mostly about the present and very little about the past. Vincent kept catching Nathaniel watching him; he was smiling, relaxed, and seemed happy that Vincent was there.

It had been two years since Vincent had sat with a family on Thanksgiving, and as much as he longed to create a different kind of memory for Nathaniel— one that was bright and lovely and left no room for old, less happy, memories— he thought that maybe a moment like this was more important, a moment when Nathaniel could sit with his father and be a family again.

Mr. Avery made vague small talk with Vincent, and he was certain, at the moment at least, that the older man didn't remember him. He kept looking at Vincent, brows knit as if he was trying hard to place him, the memory just out of grasp.

Nathaniel had said that the medication had long ago stopped delaying the inevitable.

Suddenly Nathaniel's father asked after Vincent's sister, as if he had finally remembered who he was.

"She's good, Mr. Avery," Vincent told him. "She's married and has a little boy. Her family lives in Texas."

"She stopped by once and tore me a new one for sending Nathaniel away and ignoring you," he told him, laughing. Vincent stole a look at Nathaniel, who was staring at his father, obviously having never heard the story.

"I didn't know," Vincent said.

"You should tell her I said hello." Vincent nodded his agreement as he reached under the small table to squeeze Nathaniel's hand.

As they finished their dessert, Vincent checked his watch, aware his time was running short. He had to meet the caterers and would have preferred to make his escape with Nathaniel in tow. These few hours were only possible because Nathaniel had worked so hard, staying late into the evening to help reinstall the wall and ceiling track system, and install the canvases. He'd remained after Vincent's two employees and handful of volunteers had called it a night, switching out the plain clear bulbs for the color indicated by each piece, installed the hot and cold air floor units in two of the viewing rooms: a *winter* room and a *summer* room.

Nathaniel had done all that just so Vincent would have time and a place to sit down on Thanksgiving, so that he didn't have to eat his meal alone.

And that was when Vincent finally understood.

The two of them had stood in the middle of Gallery Nocturne, the rich black of late night sky outside the windows. In the low burnished gold of artificial lighting, surrounded by beautiful images of the same man again and again—a well-defined deltoid, the strained tendons in a sharply turned neck, the dip and shadow of a perfect glute—Vincent had realized something about Claude Bäcker. Claude Bäcker was not a mad genius. No, he wasn't mad at all. He was brilliant, devoted, and very much in love with a ghost.

Vincent had wondered then, standing with the grown version of a boy he had fallen so deeply in love with, if you could truly trust the feelings you held for a ghost, even when the ghost returned from the grave and seemed to feel them right back.

After saying his goodbyes, Vincent waited until he and Nathaniel stood alone, on the old wooden porch, and he hugged Nathaniel, holding on tight, hoping the action could convey all the things he didn't have the nerve to say, and had only just admitted to himself.

"Who are you taking?" Nathaniel called out just as Vincent reached his car.

"To what?" Vincent asked, confused.

"To the fundraiser," Nathaniel clarified with a small smile.

"No one at all."

As Vincent headed to the gallery, he had to fight the urge to turn the car right back around. Even knowing it was the most important night of his career, without Nathaniel by his side it hardly seemed to matter.

Chapter 9

Kyle was waiting outside the gallery when Vincent arrived.

"So," Vincent said as he unlocked the building's doors, "is your boyfriend going to make Gallery Nocturne a household name?" He meant it as a joke and felt bad when he saw the other man's stricken expression.

"Yes and no," Kyle answered, pushing past Vincent and in through the gallery doors. "He is going to cover it," Kyle told him. "He's actually coming himself."

The news surprised Vincent.

"I think he's hoping to interview the artist."

"Well—" Vincent continued speaking as he stripped off his coat and scarf, heading to his office and hanging them on the hook just inside the door. "The artist is supposed to be here but I'm not holding my breath." He sat behind his desk and leaned down to retrieve his tablet, needing to review the catering order.

Kyle bent down to catch his eye. "Are you still looking for a date?"

Vincent couldn't help but grin. "No, I'm good. I've met someone. I'm crazy about him, actually." It felt good to say the words out loud. "So, you and the editor didn't work out?"

"No." Kyle made an irritated noise in the back of his throat and dropped into one of the chairs opposite Vincent's desk. "Apparently he doesn't date writers. Can you believe that? It would be like me not dating…"

Kyle trailed off.

"Typists?" Vincent offered and Kyle just scowled.

"But you're still going to come, right? No date required." Vincent had a habit of always playing nice with his exes, even when his heart wasn't really in it.

"Of course," Kyle said, smiling warmly at him. "I wouldn't miss it." Now Vincent remembered why they had become friends in the first place.

"Besides," Kyle continued, "maybe I can score with the talent."

Vincent snorted.

. . .

Gallery Nocturne looked magical.

From where Nathaniel had parked on the other side of the street, he could see the warm glow from its large windows. The other shops along the street were closed, their windows dark. White lights lit the sidewalk, the city's understated holiday decorations having already been up for nearly two weeks.

The gallery was quite full, some patrons even spilling out onto the sidewalk, where they chatted and drank from flute glasses. Something nonalcoholic, Vincent had told him, but it looked real enough. It seemed like much the same crowd that he remembered from the monthly *Gallery Hops* when he was a kid—a monthly ritual that brought out adults and kids alike—on the first Saturday of every month. There were the older couples, with their tasteful clothing and money to spend, and the kids, college age maybe, with no money at all. The majority fell somewhere in between.

Nathaniel nervously looked down at himself. He was wearing a black sweater—new, so that it wouldn't look faded in the crowd of milling people—and his best pair of jeans. He wasn't sure if he made a very appealing picture, certainly not for the night he wanted to present his heart to someone who could do so much better.

Not sure whether he should leave it or not, Nathaniel slipped on his wool coat and patted the inside pocket, which held a small present for Vincent. He jaywalked, not bothering with the crosswalk. It was late, and the streets were slow. And, besides, it was almost a tradition on this strip of road to cross where you wanted.

He smiled and waved when he was greeted by the couple from the diner as he slipped inside, immediately spying the non-boyfriend—the man fool enough to ditch Vincent for a shot with someone else—making small talk with a couple of college-age kids.

Despite having seen it the night before, Nathaniel's breath was taken away by the first impression of the gallery, experiencing it for the first time as it was meant to be seen. As he stepped fully inside, the image that hung on the center wall—a wall painted a metallic bronze and lit by warm golden lighting—was powerful. This ornately framed oil was of the same man Nathaniel had seen in every other piece. The particular painting depicted the man's full body, back to the viewer, while he stared off to the right, looking at some unknown distant object.

Again, the man's long, dreadlocked hair was pulled up and bound at the back of his head, revealing the full length of his back, his buttocks and long, muscular legs. It was starkly realistic; even the calluses at the back of his heels looked rough to the touch, and there was just a hint of a tattoo, seen peeking around the side of the man's waist, just above a hip bone, but not enough for Nathaniel to make out what it was.

A large crowd lingered there, the image drawing people in, and Nathaniel slowly made his way around them. Vincent was nowhere in sight so Nathaniel continued to take in the exhibit, one piece at a time. Seeing each, even the ones he had hung himself, was a different experience when seen with the subtle lighting—a soft yellow, a warm amber, a faint blue—among the quiet hum of conversation.

Nathaniel stepped into the warmth of the *summer* room, as he and Vincent had started to refer to it. The heat was a comforting contrast to the cold temperatures of the late November evening. This room held images of the same man but younger, in his late teens or early twenties. His hair was shorter, his face fuller, but it was undoubtedly him. These images were less erotic, not that all the others had held that quality, but several certainly had.

Here, the man wore clothing and an open smile; he was leaning back on his elbows in a field of tall grass, smiling; a close study of a pair of feet, toes having wiggled themselves into the sand of some unknown beach; wearing low-slung trunks, as he bent to retrieve something from the damp left by high-tide, something hidden from view.

The room spoke of the freshness of new love. And the joy of it too.

When Nathaniel walked into the *winter* room it was empty except for Bäcker himself, and it confused Nathaniel for a moment, until he looked at the walls around them. Nathaniel had not been the one to set this room up, and hadn't been inside since installing the cold air unit in the early afternoon.

The cold was uncomfortable, but the paintings that adorned the walls, more so.

These were nothing like the images of the smiling boy or the virile man. These were images of a man in his last months. Weeks maybe. Wasting away from something unnamed. Like horror, recorded.

Nathaniel took a seat on the padded bench beside the artist; a lone man keeping vigil.

"What was his name?" Nathaniel asked.

He was starting to suspect that he wouldn't receive an answer, when Bäcker finally spoke.

"Patrick. Pat. I would sometimes call him Patty to piss him off." Claude gave a little laugh.

"How long were you together?" Nathaniel wasn't sure he should ask, but thought maybe, if the situation was reversed, he would have liked to talk about the person he loved, even after they were gone.

"Twenty-five years," Claude said, looking over at Nathaniel. "We were just kids, but I knew. I always knew."

Nathaniel thought about Vincent then. Vincent had said those exact, same words to him all those years ago, as he had pressed Nathaniel up against the side of his father's garage.

I knew. I always knew.

"I need to talk to Vincent," Nathaniel said and rose to his feet. Claude smiled up at him, like he had read his thoughts. At that moment, the artist didn't seem so much like a man grieving as a man with a very singular means to exorcize his demons.

"Good luck."

. . .

He spied Vincent standing at the northeast side of the gallery, speaking with an elderly couple, the two expressing an interest in a lovely oil of a torso.

"I'll need to record your information, process your payment, and have it tagged as sold." Vincent walked the couple over to his office, unlocking the door and leaving it open as he ran their credit card. "I only have one delivery spot still available for tomorrow, or we can look at the calendar and schedule a specific day."

Nathaniel waited patiently as they filled out the paperwork, and watched Vincent slip one of his helpers a *sold* tag to affix to the displayed work. "It's for a wonderful cause," Vincent said.

The couple agreed and left, talking excitedly about their purchase. Nathaniel stepped through the doorway just as Vincent looked up. The sheer joy that lit the man's face was staggering.

"You came," Vincent said, appearing unable to hold back a smile. "You're here. I've been missing you all night."

Fueled by the words and the affection he saw in Vincent's expression, Nathaniel used a foot to push the office door closed with a click, and at the same time pulled the redhead into his arms. He found Vincent's mouth with his own, swallowing the man's gasp of surprise. Surprise that turned to tugging and pulling, and fingers tangling in Nathaniel's hair. The sting of it making him groan.

Vincent broke the kiss, a murmured *please* escaping his lips and Nathaniel kissed him again, hungrier this time, and lifted him, allowing Vincent to wrap his legs tight around Nathaniel's waist.

They staggered clumsily together across the office, disturbing furniture and tumbling a stack of papers on the already messy desk. Only after depositing Vincent atop a low bookshelf, did they pull apart again, each trying to catch their breath.

They stared at each other, puffing in unison, Vincent blinking and a little flushed. Nathaniel, feeling incapable of communicating beyond grunts and groans, grabbed Vincent's palm and pressed it hard against his own chest.

See, this is yours. Please tell me you want it.

"I have something for you." Nathaniel's words, when he finally spoke, were a deep rasp, thick with the emotion he felt, and the desire that swirled inside him.

Vincent snorted with laughter. "Do you?" He laughed again. "If it's a rewind button, you might want to keep it for yourself."

Nathaniel laughed too, even as he lifted a hand to caress Vincent's cheek. "I meant that I had something in my pocket for you."

Vincent roared this time and Nathaniel had to kiss him again to quiet him down before a gallery full of people came to be let in on the joke.

This kiss was slow and deep, Nathaniel gently exploring with his tongue and allowing his fingers to do the same, brushing his thumbs over Vincent's cheekbones, trailing his fingers over his chin and down his neck and chest, around his sides, and to the bottom he hadn't been given the time to fully appreciate when they were younger.

When he pulled away the second time, Vincent followed him, trying to stop the kiss from ending.

Without a word, Nathaniel slipped a hand into the inside pocket of his coat and pulled out a small package. It was wrapped in thick, cream-colored paper and tied with a plain, black ribbon. He placed it in Vincent's hands.

"I think I've always known," he told Vincent, smiling. "Open it."

Vincent stared at him, his eyes soft and bright. The package was small, maybe five by six and only an inch or so thick, and it still took Vincent ages to open it. He removed the ribbon, setting it beside him, and unwrapped the box carefully, pulling the tape free without tearing the paper.

He lifted the lid to reveal a small, loose watercolor that Nathaniel knew Vincent had seen. He had painted it of Vincent only days before he had been sent away. It should have been long gone, destroyed with all the other reminders of their friendship that Nathaniel's father had taken away from him. But Nathaniel had saved it from his father, and had hidden it away from his aunt, like the treasure that it was—a reminder of the happiness he had left behind. The painting was a close-up of a younger Vincent, his eyes amused, resting his cheek on a hand with nails painted a metallic silver. Shiny and perfect. Like the man in front of him. Not flawless. But somehow perfect all the same.

Vincent looked at him, his emotions on display, as they had been all those years ago. "I love you, too."

Epilogue

"How about this one?" Nathaniel looked over to see what had caught Caleb's eye. It was tall. Way tall.

"Exactly how high do you think our ceilings are?" Nathaniel laughed, reaching out to snag Vincent's hand as he came stomping around another huge tree.

"And that's a pine," Vincent chimed in. "A scotch pine. You don't want one of those, they're pretty enough, but their branches don't hold heavy ornaments very well."

"They all look the same to me," Caleb said. His admission seemed to horrify Vincent. Nathaniel snorted.

"What kind do you suggest?" he asked, smiling at Vincent. The man looked so cute—bundled up in his wool coat with his knit hat pulled practically down to his eyebrows—that Nathaniel couldn't wait to be curled around him in bed that night.

"I think I might just have found the perfect tree."

They followed Vincent, a hundred yards or so, through the freshly fallen snow. It blew around their ankles, sometimes swirling high into the air between the closely planted trees. The sounds of it under their boots, and the scrape of the sled Nathaniel dragged behind him were the only soundtrack to the late afternoon.

"Here." Vincent waved his hands around like an appliance showroom model, adding his own *oohs* and *aahs*, to highlight his choice. "A blue spruce."

"Looks good enough," Caleb said, blowing on his gloved hands, obviously looking forward to getting out of the cold.

Vincent rolled his eyes.

"It is absolutely perfect," Nathaniel told his boyfriend, bending down to press a kiss to Vincent's lips. He didn't want to pull away. He could feel Vincent's mouth curve into a smile like the man was reading his mind. It always seemed like he could.

They chopped the tree down, documenting the whole thing with photographs on Vincent's phone, each of them posing, ax in hand—Nathaniel holding the ax, Caleb holding the ax, Vincent holding the ax. Nathaniel holding the ax, Caleb's prone body at his feet. On and on it went.

By the time they had the tree cut and secured to the sled it was well after dinner time, and the temperature was starting to drop.

The three of them stood huddled together while one of the men working the farm bound the tree up and fought to secure it to the top of the truck.

Nathaniel tried hard to memorize every moment of it.

"And you enjoy this?" Caleb asked Vincent, baiting him and making both Nathaniel and Vincent scowl.

At Vincent's insistence, once they got home, the tree was placed in its stand in the corner of the Avery living room, to set overnight; he was adamant about bringing the tree up to room temperature before decorating it. Nathaniel secretly wondered if that was like the rule of letting brownies cool before eating them. Which is to say, completely unnecessary. That night they cuddled in bed, feet entwined, kissing. Vincent still smelled slightly of pine and tasted of sugar cookies and the spiced cider they had shared after dinner. And the happiness of the moment was overwhelming.

Nathaniel remembered those nights in Chicago as a boy, wanting nothing more than to come back to this house. He thought about the emptiness he had felt there, even long after it had become his home. And he realized then that he wouldn't have changed a second of it. Because if he had, he might not have been here, at this exact moment, with the man he loved. A man he trusted to love him right back.

THE BARD AND HIS BOYFRIEND:
A TALE OF HOLIDAY HOMECOMINGS

Kathleen Hayes

As these words flow through my mouth, the breath of those tellers of tales traveling the spiral of time before and after me, expels from my lungs. As dawns break and seasons turn, the tales speak themselves and the world unfolds once more. When the space between this world and the Other is as thin as fog being broken up by the sunrise, as ephemeral as clouds whisking through a twilight sky, as changeable as the sands on the shore, we gather. As we approach this darkest day, we gather to be remade.

Hear then, and re-member.

I closed my eyes as the commanding words flowed over and around me. They echoed in my sinews and bones, rattled my flesh and made my soul feel like something tangible I could hold in my hand. They were the same words that concluded the celebrations on the first night of the week-long Winter Solstice rituals every year, but they were more than just words—they were *awen* spoken by a true bard and had power beyond measure.

Since the Celtic tribes first emerged in Eastern Europe, almost 5,000 years ago, my clan has been the caretakers of the *awen*. At each changing of the season, every member of the clan gathered for seven days and breathed life from the Otherworld into this one, remaking and re-membering the very fabric of existence.

We were the last clan of true bards and somehow we had ended up in the middle of nowhere in Sweet Briar Valley, North Dakota. To anyone outside the clan, the town would appear as if it had been abandoned a hundred years before. The exit from I-94 was marked "No Services," so rarely did a tourist or wayfarer take a wrong turn or get lost and find themselves wandering around a town that didn't exist.

That's why his arrival was such a shock.

Maddie ran up and grabbed my arm.

"Seth, come on. Mama said you have to come quick. There's a stranger, and he says he knows you."

Her voice was high with excitement and an edge of panic. Strangers didn't happen in Sweet Briar Valley. Ever. I had no choice but to run with her, or she would have pulled my arm out of its socket.

"Maddie. Slow down. I'm coming." Track had never been my strong suit, and I was already slightly out of breath.

"But, Seth, it's a stranger." The only sign that she had run all the way from the diner and then halfway back already was a slight pink tint to her cheeks. She had the same pine green eyes that just about everyone in the clan had, including me, even though she hadn't been born into the clan, and the stubbornness shining in them told me I had better just shove my concerns about breathing on the back burner and follow her as fast I could.

Despite my desire to cough up a lung, a slight smile played at my lips. Maddie was like a younger sister to me. It was really wonderful to see her settling into the community and running around like the little girl her parents never could accept. She slowed down about three steps from the door to Mama's Diner and flashed a not-so-innocent smile over her shoulder before striding inside.

The moment I followed her in I saw why.

Somehow, half the town had managed to make it into the diner before I had. To a one, they wore huge grins and were trying to shake the hand of a tall, tawny-skinned boy with sparkling brown eyes and a flop of curly black hair. It sounded like every single person was speaking at the same time.

And as soon as they noticed me, it got quiet enough that you could have heard a pin drop forty miles away in Bismarck.

"Seth!" he called, perhaps a little too eagerly. His eyes were wide and surprised behind his glasses. My heart seized in my chest and seemed to join my lungs in their revolt against breathing properly. My mind raced. If he was here, I knew what that meant. And I wasn't quite ready to deal with it.

"Alè," I whispered. I shook my head, cleared my throat and tried again. "Alè." It was slightly stronger this time. I couldn't seem to get much more than his name out.

However, before I could manage to shake off my paralysis, Mama's voice rang loud and clear through the silent crowd.

"Seth, why didn't you say you had met your Chosen?"

All eyes turned to me. Alè mouthed *Chosen?* at me and I groaned. Thankfully, it was enough to knock me back into action.

I tossed a glare in Mama's direction and closed the ten-foot gap between my very confused boyfriend and where I had been standing by the door. The crowd parted to let me through. I took Alè's offered hand and then turned back towards everyone else.

"Everyone, this is Alejandro. Alejandro, this is everyone. We'll see you later."

With that, I led him out the door, down the street and into my parents' house. They had kept my room the same since I'd left for college two and a half years ago, so I just kept on up the stairs and didn't look at him again until the door was firmly closed behind us. I leaned my back against it and closed my eyes for just a moment, trying to gather myself for the conversation to come. I wasn't sure where to start: the huge fight we had had just before I came home for the holidays, or the scene from the diner.

Alè took the decision out of my hands.

"I'm sorry," he said. And that just took the cake because I was the guilty one here. I sighed and pushed myself away from the door, but couldn't quite bring myself to look at him yet.

I guess he took my sigh as a signal to keep talking. "It's not like you had to say yes. I just thought you would have been willing to talk about it. But I overreacted. I shouldn't have gotten so mad."

I shook my head. This was all wrong. "No. This is my fault. I was being secretive, and I didn't want to talk about why I couldn't come home with you for Christmas break, so I just cut off the conversation."

Alè looked a little stunned by my blunt honesty. I probably should have just told him the truth before. But it's not an easy conversation to have. *I'm part of a clan of ancient druids who have to sing the Otherworld into this one four times a year or the fabric of reality will unravel* isn't really a great conversation opener with someone you are starting to fall in love with. Or if Mama and whatever mystical powers governed this town were correct, *starting to fall in love* with was long past, and I had already arrived at the *madly in love and want to spend the rest of my life with you* stage of things.

I took a deep breath. "Just...sit...and give me a second."

He nodded a little and perched on the edge of my bed.

After a good thirty seconds, I was no closer to a good explanation than I had been two days ago in our dorm room at the University of Mary. Since nothing seemed to be coming, I went with, "I'm a part of a clan of ancient druids who have to sing the Otherworld into this one four times a year or the fabric of reality will unravel. And I really don't know how you got here. I mean into the town. Because it's protected by mystical powers and only people who are part of the clan can find it. Although, I guess if you're my Chosen, then you're technically a part of the clan, even if neither of us really knew it yet." Pause. Deep breath. "Shit. That doesn't sound even remotely believable, but I swear I'm not lying to you. At the equinoxes and solstices, we all have to participate in seven days' worth of celebration and rituals."

Alè's stunned look from earlier was back again. I tried to lighten the mood a little. "But if you want me to come home with you and meet your family on Spring Break, I can totally do that." I finally looked him in the eyes and tried for a small smile.

I'm pretty sure I failed. I wanted for this not to matter. I wanted to be able to laugh it off if Alè didn't believe me or if he ran. But my heart was in his hands. I'm not sure I could have kept the fear and hope from my face if my life had depended on it.

We gazed into each other's eyes for what seemed like the longest time. Alè's face was maddeningly blank, and then he suddenly burst out laughing. I stared at him, confusion and horror warring for dominance within me, until he managed to get himself under control.

He met my gaze again without hesitation. "Seriously, Seth, that was the worst 'I have a secret identity' reveal speech I have ever heard. Sit and tell it to me like I have no clue what you're talking about 'cause that before was pretty useless."

He pulled me down onto the bed next to him, and then dragged both of us up so were leaning against the headboard, his arm around my shoulders.

It was a relief not to have to look at him as I talked. "Okay. I guess basics first is good. So we—humanity, animals, plants, whatnot—live here in the physical world. But there is also the Otherworld. Whenever you hear stories about people walking through stone circles and disappearing, or fairies kidnapping people only to have them return a hundred years later, not having aged a day, those stories are about people who have visited the Otherworld. It is woven with ours and you can sometimes go there, but it is more than that. It is like the paradigm or template for this realm. Things can only exist in this realm because the idea of them was created in the Otherworld. We have art and music and poetry here because the idea of beauty was created there. But over time the walls between this place and that one have grown thicker, harder to breach, as fewer people visit and there are fewer caretakers for the *awen*. Without the *awen*—the stories breathed through the true bard from the Otherworld into this one—this world begins to unravel itself from the Otherworld. And without that connection, our physical reality finds itself further and further from what it could be. Think about it. If the concept of beauty unravels from the Otherworld, then art and music and poetry and so on all cease to exist in this one. So that's why we gather to celebrate the changing seasons and breathe the *awen* into our reality."

Throughout my explanation, Alè's fingers rubbed circles on my shoulder and didn't stop as silence fell between us. It wasn't an easy silence, but it wasn't horrible and tense like it had been before.

Finally, I felt him nod his head. "Okay. It seems a little out there, but 'There are more things, in Heaven and Earth, Horatio, than are dreamt of' and all that so I guess I believe you. 'Cause I'm pretty sure you're not crazy. And you know when I stopped at the gas station and asked for directions, the guy had never heard of Sweet Briar Valley. And the GPS on my phone couldn't locate it either. So the whole bit about protected town seems to make sense. I'm not even really sure how I got here. The last twenty minutes of the drive is all really hazy."

I let out a breath I didn't even realize I had been holding. I felt tears of pure relief run down my cheeks. I turned in his arms and kissed him like I'd been wanting to since I stormed out of our dorm room two days ago. Alè returned the kiss immediately and my heart swelled with joy. I ran my fingers through his hair and reveled in the contact that I hadn't been sure I would ever have again.

Alè broke the kiss entirely too soon. He leaned his forehead against mine, his smile shining at me out of his eyes and every pore of his face. "So what's this about being your Chosen?"

I groaned and dropped my head onto his shoulder, shaking it a little. He leaned back and lifted my chin with his fingers so I had to look at him.

"Come on, I was okay with the whole ancient druid magics thing. How bad can it be?"

In my mind I screamed *Bad! Really Bad!* My mouth said, "It's not some destined mates thing, like what you read about in paranormal romances and whatnot. It's more like whatever is protecting the town can recognize when one of us has chosen someone to be a part of the clan—whether it be falling in love, or adopting a child, or whatever. Apparently, the mystical powers-that-be realized I was in love with you before I even did." I had glanced down, not able to say that last part while looking at him. I gathered my courage. I looked up again, "I do, you know. Love you."

There was no missing the joy that came off Alè in waves when I said that. His smile widened so much he could barely speak. But he managed, "I love you, too."

This time *he* kissed me and everything was perfect.

· · ·

Entirely too soon, we were interrupted by a series of knocks on the door, each one loud and solid, with an exaggerated pause before the next. After about five knocks, my mom's voice rang out from the hallway.

"I. Am. Going. To. Open. The. Door. Now."

Alè did a terrible job of swallowing a chuckle from beside me on the bed. I shot him a glare.

"Don't worry, Mom. No one's indecent."

I heard Alè growl an almost sub-vocal, "Yet," as Mom was opening the door. I was forced to elbow him. He went with it, rolling off the bed and standing up in one graceful motion. He clutched his side and plastered a look of mock outrage on his face.

"Alright, boys, I gave you as much time as I could manage. Dad's been chomping at the bit downstairs for ten minutes now. He just finished the pie Mama brought with her and won't be put off a moment longer."

I sighed. Mom, Dad and Mama. Mom and Dad would want to know all about Alè, but Mama had her nosiness skills honed to an art. Mama owned the local diner and everyone in town called her Mama, even those who were older than her, because that's what she acted like. She was a welcoming hug, a listening ear, and smack in the head, alternatively, to anyone who walked in her doors.

I looked back at Alè and reached out my hand. "Come on. We might as well get this over with. Don't worry. It won't be that bad." I shrugged. "At least there's pie."

At that, a smile flashed across his features and he grabbed my outstretched hand.

Downstairs, Mama already had a plate with a huge serving of her famous Key Lime Pie and a glass of milk set out for each of us.

Alè saw the pie and turned to me. "Is she the one who makes those care packages?"

He had tried to whisper, but failed, as everyone was paying such close attention to us.

Mama's joyful voice boomed across the table. "Of course I am."

Alè turned on his manners and smiled back. "Well, thank you, señora. I always enjoy sharing with Seth. Your truffles are my favorite."

Mama chuckled. "I like this one. Seth, you can keep him."

I replied wryly, "Thanks, Mama. I had kind of already decided to." I felt a blush spread across my pale cheeks as I realized what I had said. I stammered a bit, "I mean…I decided that I wanted to. If Alè wanted it, too."

Alè slipped his arm around my waist and whispered in my ear, "It's okay. I want to keep you too."

I'm pretty sure we looked like doofuses standing there in kitchen, smiling and staring into each other's eyes.

The moment was broken when Dad cleared his throat pointedly. "Sit your butts down, eat your pie and tell us about your Chosen."

I sat, but couldn't help responding with, "But, Dad, how can I eat my pie and talk at the same time?"

"You've managed for years, so I think you can probably soldier through at this point."

Alè didn't even try to smother it as both he and Mama burst into laughter.

He elbowed me. "I like your family."

"Yeah, yeah," I grumbled, but I couldn't help the grin that spread across my face. Happiness bubbled up inside my chest that Alè was here, and my family seemed to like him and he loved me. After our fight, I had anticipated a holiday break that would be long and miserable.

Everyone was looking expectantly at me, including Alè, as he took a bite of his pie. I stared back and put the biggest bite I could fit into my mouth. It was about a third of the whole piece of pie. Then I spoke.

"Wyphral roghmlemph argehlam."

I was prepared to keep going, but Mom broke me with her sincere face. She had a slightly exasperated air, yet was still beaming with happiness—at my having found a Chosen, I could only assume.

I swallowed as quickly as I could, washed it down with a sip of milk and looked back at Mom. "Sorry."

She waved a hand at me and told me to get talking.

"Alright, alright." I repeated what I had said at the diner earlier. "Everyone, this is Alejandro. Alejandro, this is everyone." Mama glared at me. I smiled and pointed at my mom, first. "That's my mom. She's the best mom I could ask for and is really nice—unless you leave your wet towels under all the other dirty clothes in the hamper. Then she yells at you about mold and gross smells. And, moving to the left, that's my dad. Enough said."

Dad grunted a greeting and went back to his second piece of pie. Not that he wasn't paying attention. He had the *I look like I am doing something else and don't have a clue what is going, but really I am watching everything like a hawk* thing down pat.

"And finally, that's Mama. She owns the diner, bakes the best pie there is, and you don't want to cross her or you will have a sore spot the shape of her kitchen spoon on your bum for a month." I smiled graciously at her and she nodded her head in agreement.

"Come on, child. Get to the good part," Mama encouraged.

"Umm, okay." I felt myself blush again and glanced over at Alè for moral support. He smiled at me. "Well, you remember that Adam transferred schools at the last minute 'cause he wanted to move with Larissa when she got that job in Michigan. So I found myself suddenly lacking a roommate. Alè was at

Williston State College for his first two years and transferred into UMary for his junior year. We got assigned to each other."

Mama threw a napkin across the table at me. "We already know all that. You know what I meant, when I said get to the good part. Go on now."

I threw the napkin back at her. "Fine."

. . .

Three Months Ago

I was lying on my bed hoping that letting my accounting book sit open on my chest would be enough for me to absorb the information. School had started almost three weeks earlier and I already knew this class was going to kick my ass. It didn't help that I couldn't stop staring at the picture of my roommate and his family that was sitting on his desk.

Alejandro was doing more to damage my calm than anything at this point. I'd dated before, but I'd never felt that immediate punch of attraction to someone. I found myself waxing poetic about caramel skin and toffee eyes and then shook myself for describing him like a candy store.

A stupid smile spread across my face as I thought about him. He wasn't just hot on the outside. He was a genuinely nice guy. He was great with his sister, and I loved how animated he got when they skyped together. His eyes would sparkle and joy shone out of every part of his body.

We'd bonded over being the only two people we knew who had ever used a Tumblr account. Up here in Bismarck, you got a sideways look and a confused, "Is that like Twitter?" whenever you mentioned Tumblr. It turned out we followed a lot of the same *Supernatural* fandom Tumblrs. I thought he might be queer of some stripe from some of the stuff he reblogged, but I hadn't gotten the courage to ask him about it yet.

I sighed and forced my thoughts away from my crush-worthy roommate and back to my accounting text book. An hour later, with far fewer pages read than I would have liked, my study time was ended by the welcome interruption of Alejandro coming back. I tossed my book melodramatically to the floor and groaned for good effect. I expected at least a chuckle from my usually cheerful roommate, but when I looked up he was still standing nervously by the door with his hands behind his back.

"Hey, what's up?"

He looked at the floor and then back up to me. It was hard to hear what he was saying at first, as he muttered, "*Hijo de perro.* This is harder than I thought." He paused, seemed to gather himself again, and continued at a more comprehensible volume, "I've never done this before. At least not with a guy. So I'm not really sure how to go about it. But here." He thrust his hands forward and shoved a bouquet of some kind of blue flowers into my hands.

340

Slightly confused, I replied with a drawn out, "Okay."

"*Mierda.*" He was mumbling again. "I mean, would you like to go on a date with me?"

Now, the flowers made sense. Suddenly, my heart seemed like it was going to beat out of my chest, and my palms felt slippery with sweat around the stem of the bouquet hanging haphazardly in my hands. My brain kind of stalled from surprise and possibly some almost unbearable hope. I think I must have stared at him for longer than I realized, 'cause when I finally refocused, he looked sort of wilted.

Hurriedly, I replied, again, "Okay."

He brightened noticeably. "Yeah?"

I grinned. "Yeah."

He threw his arms in the air and did a little jump. "Yes!"

My fast-beating heart stopped in my chest. All that joy I had admired from afar when directed at his sister was being directed at something I had done. It was breathtaking. Literally.

I couldn't help myself. I got up off the bed and pulled Alejandro towards me. Before he caught his balance, I leaned in and kissed him on the cheek. A deep blush spread from where my lips had touched his skin and his smile turned shy.

Still close enough that I could feel the heat coming off every part of him, I struggled to speak. I managed a hoarse whisper. "So where are you taking me on this date of ours?"

"Umm, if it's okay, there's this restaurant in town that's owned by a family from the same part of Mexico my dad is from. It's really good."

"La Carreta's or Arnaldo's?" In North Dakota, Mexican fare was pretty limited, but both places were delicious.

"La Carreta's," he replied

"It's a date!"

We both spent the next two days floating on clouds and smiling for no reason. Friday couldn't come soon enough.

. . .

Present

"And that's how Alè asked me out."

Mama cooed. "And I figured it would have gone the other way round, knowing you, Seth. Good for you, Alejandro."

"Yeah, yeah. Can storytime be done now? It's getting kind of late."

"Of course," Mom said, kindly. "Alè, how long are you staying with us?"

He glanced at me. "Is it okay if I stay until the twenty-second? Papa just said I had to be home two days before Christmas."

I startled at that news. "He knows where you are?"

Alè's shy smile was back. "Yeah. I told him I had to go and chase down my boyfriend."

I was stunned. I knew Alè had planned to come out to his dad and his sister—he would've had to, if I'd gone home with him like he'd asked—but he had done it over the phone and after we'd had our fight.

I leaned forward and planted a kiss on his lips. With my hands on either side of his face, I looked straight into his eyes. "I love you so much."

I waited a few seconds and then turned away. "Mom, is it okay if I go home with Alè after our celebrations are over?"

"Of course, honey. Just make sure it's okay with his father."

I grinned. "Thanks!"

Dad finally spoke up. "You boys get up to bed. It's a long few days ahead of us with the preparations and celebrations. Don't think you two are off the hook from all the hard work."

I walked around the table and wrapped my arms around Dad's shoulders. That was his way of approving of Alè—no guest in his house would ever be put to work. Family, on the other hand, that was fair game. I knew it was too soon to be thinking of Alè as family, but part of me couldn't help it.

· · ·

The week flew by. Mama had suggested Alè spend a lot of the day with the children who were learning all about the celebrations, the songs, and the rituals. It meant we had to spend a lot of time apart, but it was cool that he was taking such an interest.

Maddie had taken him under her wing. She had been brand new the year before, in a clan of people who had been learning these things since they were born. They bonded over it.

She'd run away from abusive parents. Mama had found her hiding by the water late one night. Apparently her family had come to camp by the lake and she'd taken her chances, not realizing how cold it got at night in the fall. Temperatures reached the seventies and eighties during the day, but fell to the low forties at night.

I'm not sure what kind of magic Mama worked, but she had Maddie out of her parents' custody and declared her foster child in under a month. I don't know much about how the system works but that seemed really fast, and Mama was in the process of adopting her.

I glanced across the barn from where I was separating kindling to where Alè and Maddie were braiding together evergreen branches. Alè noticed and smiled at me as he kept talking with Maddie.

I could hear what they were saying, but had been tuning them out until I heard my name.

"Sooo, tell me about your first kiss with Seth," Maddie said with all the subtly of a twelve-year-old.

Alè caught my eye again and I saw him blush. Without looking away, he began to speak. "Well, it was after our first date. Normally, you might walk a person to their door and have an opportunity for a goodnight kiss before you part ways. But since we lived together, we were both going to the same door. Seth didn't think that was any good. So he walked me to the main door of our dorms and said goodnight. I thought I was going to get a proper kiss then, but he just kissed my cheek and held the door open for me.

"I went upstairs and a few minutes later, he showed up as well. Apparently, to make it seem more real, he had walked all the way around to the back of the building and used that entrance to come inside. I threw a sock at him when he came through the door and joked, 'You call that a goodnight kiss?' He smiled and stalked across the room. Then he said, 'No, I call this a goodnight kiss.' Then he kissed me right on the lips."

"Was it a good kiss?"

Alè smiled and nodded. "It was the best."

My chest tightened a little at the memory and at hearing him retell it. I lost track of their conversation for a while. When I tuned back in, Maddie's voice was thick with emotion.

"I don't have a mom or a dad anymore. I had bad ones and they were taken away."

Alè's brow arched sympathetically as he looked at her. "That's hard."

"Yeah." Maddie seemed three times her age as she uttered that syllable. My heart broke for her and what she had gone through.

"I don't have a mom anymore either. Mine was good but then she died."

"Really?"

Alè nodded. "I miss her a lot."

"I don't miss my mom. Or my dad."

Alè looked a little stricken, like he didn't know what to say, but he managed, "That's okay."

"My mom used to say boys are born boys and stay that way their whole life. And she would hit me down there if I wanted to wear a dress." Tears were streaming silently down her face. "Seth says that sometimes girls are born that look like boys on the outside or boys are born that look like girls on the outside. And that's okay. Do you think a good mom would have loved me even though I'm a girl on the inside?"

Alè had tears on his cheeks at this point as well. He took Maddie's chin in his hand and tilted her head up so she was looking him in the eyes. "I had the best mom in the world. And I know she would have loved you. And now you have a mama. And, sometimes, mamas are even better than moms."

Maddie fiercely wiped the tears off her cheeks, smudging dirt all over them, and nodded her head. "My mama is way better than my mom was. She loves me all the time. Even when I get dirt in her pie pans."

Alè laughed wetly and sniffed. Maddie seemed to have moved on, and was back to braiding the evergreen branches together in a matter of moments.

Alè looked like he needed some time to gather himself. I raised my voice a bit and called across, "Hey, Maddie, is it okay if I steal Alè away from you for a little bit? I need some help carrying more kindling around from the back."

"Yeah, sure. As long as you don't spend the whole time kissing him and make me finish braiding all these by myself."

"I promise. No more than seven minutes of kissing."

She glared at me. "Five minutes."

I tried to keep a straight face and failed miserably. Through my chuckles, I said, "Of course, Maddie. You drive a hard bargain. Only five minutes of kissing."

However, when we got behind the barn, it wasn't kissing that I went for. I pulled Alè into my arms and wrapped him in the tightest hug I could manage. He cried against my shoulder for a few minutes.

"How could anyone treat a child like that?" he asked plaintively, tears still distorting his voice.

"I don't know. No one who should ever be called a parent, that's for sure."

We stood there, holding each other for a while longer.

I let my arms drop and placed a kiss gently on his forehead. "I think Maddie's allotted five minutes of kissing time is up. We should probably grab some kindling and get back inside."

He smiled back at me. "Yeah. We wouldn't want to get on her bad side."

. . .

Later that night, the Yule log had been successful lit and the last night of rituals completed. Alè had been great. He had participated with the elementary school kids in their part of the singing. They weren't part of the official tale tellings that the bards breathed life into with the *awen*. However, it was tradition that everyone participate in some way, even if they did not have the gift of the *awen*. Unlike my parents, I did not have the *awen* either. I usually played the ocarina, while Catherine and Steven, a brother and sister I had gone to school with as a child, did a fire dance.

Unlike the bonfires on the previous nights, the Yule log fire would burn for twelve days, and represented the victory of the light over the darkness as the days began to lengthen. It was surrounded by all the woven evergreen branches Maddie and Alè had worked on earlier in the day, sprinkled with locally brewed cider and then lit with a leftover piece of last year's log.

Alè and I were leaning against a smaller log that had been set out just for that purpose. We were wrapped in a warm blanket, and were sipping a mulled version of some of that cider. I sat between his legs and leaned against his chest. His chin rested comfortably against the top of my head.

It was one of those moments that you hope you'll remember forever.

Eventually, though, the cold got the better of us. We decided to head inside to be warmed by central heating and an electric blanket instead of the medieval system of a giant burning log. There was just one thing I wanted to do before we went inside.

"Wait just a minute." I fished around inside my coat's deep pockets. "I have something for you."

I handed him a slightly smushed but at one time well-wrapped box about the size of my palm. He smiled as he took it from me.

"Your present is at my dad's house. I had it shipped there, so you wouldn't accidentally open it or see it in the dorm room."

"It's all good. I want you to have this now though."

"Okay." He opened it quickly. An incredulous look crossed his face as he took the lid off the small box. I had gotten him a replica of Dean's necklace from *Supernatural*. "Really?" he said.

I tensed a little. I had wanted him to like it. "Yeah. I mean, we bonded over *Supernatural*, initially. And it's jewelry, which is kind of a dating-ish type gift, but still manly and whatnot. You don't have to wear it if you don't like it."

His face had cleared as I spoke. "Silly. Of course I love it. And I'd wear anything you give me. I'd just wear it under my shirt if it was really ugly."

I nudged his shoulder with mine. "Just you wait and see what I'm going to get you next year—something ugly that can't be hidden. And you just promised to wear it."

He nudged me back. "There are limits. Nothing that sparkles."

I laughed as we started walking back towards my parents' house. "All right. I promise. Nothing that sparkles."

. . .

The next day found us on the road for most of the day. While the drive from Sweet Briar Valley to Williston, ND might normally take less than four hours, in the winter, with the roads all covered in snow and ice, it took much longer. Instead of going the speed limit of seventy-five miles per hour on the highway, most cars were chugging along at about forty-five.

Thankfully, we were able to switch driving every few hours, and Alè was quite a good travel companion. We listened to an audio book for most of the journey, and our bladders seemed to be about the same size.

By the time we pulled into his dad's driveway it was almost eleven at night. All the lights were still on in the house, and before we had even opened the trunk to get our luggage out, a miniature teenaged version of Alè bounded out of the house and leapt into Alè's outstretched arms. Her legs wrapped around his waist, and if he hadn't leaned against the car at the last minute, I'm pretty sure they would have both been on the ground, covered in snow.

"Carmelina! *Ooof.* Get your feet on the ground before we both break our butts." A grin the size of the sun belied his words and he clung to the tiny person who I recognized as his sister, Carmen.

Eventually, she let go and stood back up on her own two feet. "*Sandro, vamonos.* If you stand out here much longer, your boyfriend's bits are going to freeze off."

I snorted in surprise at her words.

"Yeah, yeah. Let me be the one to worry about my boyfriend's bits, 'kay?"

It took a few minutes of gathering our bags and all the stuff that had somehow spread over the entirety of the back seat, but soon we were back in the warmth—with my bits thankfully intact.

Once we got all our stuff settled in Alè's room, we headed downstairs. I was more nervous than I wanted to admit. My family had loved Alè. I just hoped his family liked me.

While his sister was a petite version of him, his father was huge and had rugged features. It looked like he could bench press about five of me. Alè was not a small man. He was a few inches taller than my own five foot nine and he probably had about twenty pounds of muscle on me. His dad made him look as tiny as he made his sister look. Needless to say, I was intimidated.

Nervously, I broke out the little bit of Spanish that Alè had taught me on the drive. "*Hola, me llamo Seth. Gusto en conocerlos.*" I held out my hand to shake his father's hand first, intending to follow up with Carmen.

It was completely unexpected when I was pulled into an almost painful embrace and kissed on both cheeks, then unceremoniously left once more to my own balance. I barely had time recover before Carmen did the same thing, granted less painfully.

Carmen began to speak in Spanish, to introduce herself, I assume. Quickly, I interrupted. "Um, I don't actually speak Spanish. Alè just taught me to say that in the car."

His father actually laughed at that. "I know. It sounded like you were speaking German, not Spanish. Sandro will have to teach you better. You can call me Mr. Martinez."

"Thank you, sir." For some reason, I was still feeling intimidated.

However, my turn was over, and Mr. Martinez turned his penetrating gaze towards Alè. "So, Sandro, you are gay now, like Tio Juan?"

Alè blushed and I thought he would turn away but he didn't break eye contact with his father. "Sort of." I jerked in surprise and stared at him. "I think maybe I am pansexual. I just like people—gender doesn't seem to matter. I did some research. I think that's pansexual."

I breathed a sigh of relief.

Mr. Martinez looked slightly confused. "But you have a boyfriend, now?"

Alè also looked confused as to where this might be going. "Yes." He nodded in my direction. "Seth."

Mr. Martinez nodded, like that had explained something. "Okay. We will still go to Mass on Christmas. Best not to mention this pan thing to the Padre. He wouldn't understand." He turned back towards me. "Welcome to our home, Seth. Don't stay up too late."

With that, Mr. Martinez left us alone in the kitchen with Carmen.

She leaned closer to us and spoke, *sotto voce*, "I'm pretty sure *Papa* doesn't understand the 'pan thing.'"

Alè looked a little shell-shocked. I poked him in the shoulder. He snapped out of it and looked away from the door his father had disappeared through. "Wow. I thought it would be so much worse than that." He looked directly at me. "He really liked you."

Flabbergasted, I replied, "Huh?"

"When I brought the one girlfriend I had during high school home for dinner, he barely even greeted her in three whole hours. You, he spoke to directly. Welcomed you to the house, even. I can hardly believe it."

"Oh, Sandro," Carmen said with a sigh. "It's 'cause he can see how happy you've been these last few months."

I looked questioningly at Carmen. She seemed like a useful ally, especially if I wanted the good dirt on my boyfriend.

She glanced at me and then looked back at Alè. "In high school you were sad all the time. With Mom dying, and moving halfway across the country to follow Papa's job, it made sense. Then you started college and it was all work all the time. Do you know how many times you've mentioned homework or classes since you left for Bismarck? Not once. Every time we skyped, it was Seth this, or my roommate that. Papa was clueless, but I knew you were in love with him the third time you mentioned him."

She grinned at him and then turned and tackle-hugged me. "Thanks for making my brother happy."

I hugged her back. "He makes me happy too."

When she let go of me, I noticed a slightly evil glint in her eyes. "So," she said. "What embarrassing story do you want to hear first? Or should we go straight to naked baby pictures?"

"Don't, Carmelina. You know I'll get you back someday." Alè said, threateningly.

She was inching closer to the kitchen doorway. "Baby pictures it is!" she called back, as she dashed out of the kitchen.

"No!"

Alè chased her around the living room, and they ended up in a heap on the couch, laughing so hard they could barely breathe. I was standing at the side of the room, watching, basking in their happiness, when I noticed a suspicious silence. They shared a look before moving as one and tackling me to ground. I couldn't help but join in the laughter as I was tickled to within an inch of my life.

. . .

Midnight Mass was, inexplicably, at ten p.m. We'd gone with Carmen and Mr. Martinez, and kept a respectable distance from each other. I'm pretty sure the priest was busy enough we could have been holding hands in the front row and he wouldn't have noticed.

When we got back to Alè's house after the service, Mr. Martinez lit a fire, and we all sat around the Christmas tree and drank hot cocoa. Mr. Martinez turned in after a few minutes, with a gruff, "Merry Christmas." Carmen hung out and talked with us for another hour or so before she went to bed as well.

Midnight passed us by without our noticing. We were cuddled on the couch, watching the fire light dance on the walls, and I was reminded of the last night of the solstice celebrations. I wiggled a little so I could face Alè.

"Didn't you say you had a present for me?" I poked at him. "Gimme, gimme."

He smiled. "Hold your horses." He stretched his arm over the arm of the couch to the end table. He fiddled for a moment and then turned back around. He handed me a box that looked a lot like the box I had given him.

I grinned and took it from him. When I had destroyed enough of the packaging to get at the inside, I burst out laughing.

"Really?"

"Yeah. I mean, we bonded over *Supernatural*, initially. And it's jewelry, which is kind of a dating-ish type gift but still manly and whatnot."

"Shut up. I can't believe we got each other the exact same present." Nestled amidst the ruined packaging was a replica of Dean's necklace from *Supernatural*.

"Yeah, well. Great minds think alike."

"Can you tell what I'm thinking right now?" I asked, with a smirk.

He settled me back in his arms again, before he spoke. "You're thinking that you love me and that this is the best holiday you've ever had."

I turned my head and kissed his chest. "Hmm....you must be a mindreader."

The End.

THE
CHRISTMAS PRESENT

Larry Benjamin

Vi

Mama Black Widow sat at the table and waited. She was a powerful Obeah woman and fierce as a lioness in a cage. It was rare for Mama to visit a client. Usually they knew to present themselves at her kitchen door when they were in need. But when Vi had called and asked her to come, she had sounded different, desperate. And that was how Mama came to be sitting in Vi's vast white kitchen, with its heated limestone floors and wide cast iron range that had been handmade in a small village in France; waiting.

Through the kitchen's arched opening, Mama could see an enormous Christmas tree decorated with silver ornaments and gold lights, standing in a hall lined with gilt-edged mirrors. Vi followed her gaze. "Versailles," she said. "Have you been there?"

Distracted, Mama shook her head. No.

"That hall is modeled after Versailles' Hall of Mirrors."

Mama nodded again, a pained expression on her face. In the mirrors, she could see the reflections of rooms wrapped in antique wallpapers; rooms shimmering with gold dust and light; rooms so delicately balanced their designer forbade anyone to enter them while wearing perfume. The rooms were paneled and furnished with woods so rare, so impossibly beautiful, that were you to strip them of their priceless works of art, bibelots and objets d'art, you would have found yourself in an enchanted forest. It was these woods, kidnapped, split and stripped and nailed and twisted into grotesque shapes for human comfort that caused Mama to close her eyes and cover her ears; she could see their agony, in the elaborate grains of their woods; she could hear their anguished screams in the perfect silence of those rooms.

Mama closed her eyes and covered her ears. Vi stared at her. Mama looked different here, outside of the grimy gray light of her cramped, overheated kitchen in the cottage behind her brother's house. Her thick, coarse hair, twisted into dreadlocks, and laced with gray, showed here and there beneath the kerchief she wore, as she moved her head. She was dressed in black wool against the winter cold. Vi had only ever seen Mama dressed in black, except for once or twice when she'd seen her during the dog days of August. Then, she'd been dressed in dark gray, in deference to the unbearable heat of a New York summer: her only concession to the physical world.

Vi's father, the admiral, had trusted Mama implicitly—had insisted, in fact, he owed everything to the old Obeah woman. Now if the spell she was going to ask Mama to cast worked, she, too, would owe her everything.

"Mama? Are you alright? Do you need something to drink? I could make you a cup of tea." Her voice trailed off as she looked around the room and her eyes came to rest on the enormous locomotive that was her stove.

Mama nodded, turned her head away from the hall of mirrors and opened her eyes. "I'm fine. What do you need help with?"

"My son is in trouble. He has been asked to leave school because of…an *incident…*"

Vi hesitated and Mama's gimlet stare, contemptuous and cajoling at once, bore into her; the truth squeezed reluctantly out of Vi as if it were her last breath. "Because of an incident involving another boy. My son is *gay*," Vi whispered.

Mama waited.

"I don't want my son to be gay."

"Then you do not want your son," Mama said.

"What do you mean?"

"You cannot separate who he is from what he is. He is who he is because he is what he is. Do you see?"

Vi looked down at the table, admired the shape of her pale hands with their perfectly manicured light pink nails and flashing diamonds. "I suppose if he wasn't my only child I wouldn't mind so much."

Mama touched her hand lightly, pulled back, and looked into Vi's purple eyes. The screams of the barely formed girl-child rang in her ears, as the child was ripped from the one place she should have been safe. "You had another child," she said.

Vi started. "Yes. Yes, but I miscarried—"

"Violet! Lie to your husband, lie to yourself, lie to the world at large, but *do not* lie to me!" Mama was suddenly angry; her fury was as limitless and as uncontrollable as the wind.

Vi winced. "I—I had no choice—"

"Tell me what you want?"

Vi straightened in her chair. When she spoke there was steel in her voice. "I want you to free my son of the demons who are trying to twist him into something he is not!"

"Are you sure about that?"

"Yes," Vi said. "It will be my Christmas present to myself."

Mama pulled a deck of cards from within the confines of her layers of clothes and began to shuffle them. After a few minutes, she spread the cards in a fan across the table. She flipped them over one by one, then suddenly swept the whole lot onto the floor.

"Very well," she said. "It will be done. You will pay me ten thousand dollars."

Vi was shocked. Mama had never demanded such a high fee before. But she knew she would pay it. Without another word, Vi rose from the table and moved to the doorway. She knew from experience that she must not thank Mama for her spell.

Behind her, Mama cleared her throat. In the coarse sound there was a sharp edge of cruelty. "Vi!"

Vi felt her name pointed at her back like a knife. She stopped but did not turn around.

"Vi, having a second child would have made no difference. She would have been gay, too."

Aidan

"Oh! Clive! You're here," Aidan said, stepping into his dorm room and finding Clive, his father's assistant, inspecting his Christmas tree. How typical of his father to send his assistant, his *fixer*, he thought contemptuously.

Clive turned to look at him. A slender young man, Aidan was striking, with eyes green as new money, and long pale silky hair; there was something tentative about him, like candlelight caught in an evening breeze. Aidan held in his hand a small ornament. Clive could see it was a reverse glass painting of his school—*this* school—a Christmas tree at its front gates, its name and crest emblazoned across the top.

Aidan gestured at the ornament in his hand. "I stopped to buy this. It seems silly now. I should probably take the tree down."

"No," Clive said. "Go ahead and hang it. Someone can take the tree down later."

Aidan hung the ornament, stooped to plug in the lights, and stepped back to survey the effect.

Earlier, Clive had inspected the tree and had been surprised to see the tree itself was less a celebration of the season than a sort of memorial to the past, to loss. The only ornaments on it were the awkward, childish ornaments he had made with Nanny and which had never been allowed to hang on the family's glamorous tree; others commemorated lost pets, schools he had attended, nations and islands and continents his parents had been to without him. Watching Aidan, now blue, now green, now red, Clive cleared his throat, embarrassed to see something both heroic and tragic in him.

"I suppose we should leave," Aidan said.

"There's no hurry," Clive replied. "The jet is fueled and ready. We can leave whenever you want."

. . .

As the plane climbed, Aidan, buckled into the cream leather seat, felt like he was floating in the midday air, unloved, disconnected, tethered to nothing.

Flipping idly through the pages of *People* magazine, he came across a picture of his parents at some fête. His mother, pale, delicate, was resplendent in jewel tones and diamonds; his father, in requisite tuxedo, was equally dazzling, his silver hair swept back, his eyes glittering like pieces of ice. Surrounding them were other couples, the women equally fashionable and bejeweled, the men escorting them equally somber in black, looking preoccupied by other things, other thoughts. With a wave of sadness, Aidan realized theirs was a world he'd never know. He closed the magazine as the pilot announced their imminent landing.

Clive woke with a start, into the promise of the day, his dreams—dreams of skeletons, of treasure—falling away. He glanced tentatively at Aidan and saw hope and fear tumbling in his cool gray eyes. Aidan danced like a flame. Even sitting still, Clive could sense the turmoil raging within him. Aidan danced like a flame and seemed in danger of fading, of guttering and going out.

The quiet of the cabin was shattered by the cacophony of wheels lowering, and locking into place. The plane banked, turned, and descended from blue into green. Far below, Aidan could see glistening emerald mountains sloping down to the white shoreline and the turquoise crystal waters of the Caribbean at the shore's edge.

Aidan stepped out of the plane's door into the blistering tropical heat. Behind him, Clive, in his impeccable Savile Row suit, stopped to mop his brow. "Jesus," he muttered. "It's hot."

On the tarmac, a boy about Aidan's age leaned insolently against an ancient, battered jeep that was gunmetal gray beneath its coating of ash-colored dust.

The boy was shirtless and Aidan could see a sprinkling of curly, dark hair scattered like black pepper across his chest; a slick coating of sweat enveloped his muscled body like a polyurethane coating.

As they approached the jeep, the boy pushed himself upright and introduced himself. "Hi. I'ze Dale. I'm to take you 'ome."

When Aidan's eyes alighted on Dale and lingered on him a beat too long, Clive thought he saw hope, rising like smoke behind the cool gray-green irises, replace fear.

The road they traveled on—if it could even be called a road—was unpaved and badly rutted. As Dale capably changed gears, Aidan could see the muscles of his arms traveling up and down beneath his glossy ebony skin; sweat slid over his massive shoulders and danced between the great slabs of his chest, before pooling in his navel then falling onto the waistband of his low-riding jeans.

They passed a great many whitewashed houses built in the style of the plantation houses of the American South; low slung and broad, they seemed to clutch the ground tightly. The houses were genteel yet incongruous in their gentility, planted as they were in the savage landscape of beaches, fields of sugarcane and rain forest as alien as spacecraft. Each house they passed, Aidan noticed, had a name, and each name, he later learned, told its own story: Whim, Work & Rest, Peter's Rest, Princess, Jacob's Fancy.

At the foot of a road that began a sharp descent to the beach, stood a sign: Anna's Hope. Dale made a sharp right and followed the road in its downward spiral.

Dale swerved to avoid a magnificent mahogany tree that had been struck by lightning and now lay across the road, spilling its magnificent red blood onto the cracked earth. Jarred out of his thoughts, Aidan could just make out the house up ahead. Covered by a fine webbing of bougainvillea vines, it was a two-storied whitewashed structure with weathered shutters that lay crooked and flat beside the open jalousie windows. The brilliant blooms of the bougainvillea looked like blood stains, its whitewashed walls like bleached bone, its red tiled roof like blood caked upon its monstrous back. The house lay in the burning sun like carrion. A short distance away, the Caribbean Sea boiled.

In the middle of a broad open lawn was a flamboyant tree in full bloom, wearing a crown of blood-orange flowers. Long, feathery leaves pointed like accusing fingers.

The jeep skittered to a halt. This was it then. This was to be Aidan's home for the Christmas holiday.

Clive, seated beside Dale, turned to look at Aidan, who tried not to shudder at the lifelessness of the house, at its hopelessness. Anna's Hope? What had Anna found to hope for here?

Dale turned off the engine as a magnificent woman stepped out of the shadows of the veranda. Her skin was like cinnamon, and she had the regal bearing of a queen. "Hello," she called without the slightest trace of an accent. "Welcome to Anna's Hope." As they climbed out the jeep, the woman approached and offered her hand, first to Clive, then to Aidan. "I am Raeni, the caretaker."

Aidan took the hand she offered him; he was tempted to lean over and kiss it, so regal was her bearing. He caught a glimpse of Dale hauling their bags out of the jeep. Raeni followed his gaze. "And of course you've met my son."

Her son? Dale? This woman looked scarcely old enough to be anyone's mother, let alone the strapping muscular Dale. And yet, Aidan could see a resemblance; there was something of the prince in Dale.

"Come," Raeni said. "You must be tired and hungry. Supper is ready," she added, leading them into the house.

Supper, as Raeni referred to it, was a curiously formal affair, served in an octagonal dining room hung with an enormous crystal chandelier. The entire room looked as if it had been transported intact from regency England and plopped down in this tropical jungle. They ate batter-dipped flying fish and fried plantains off heirloom china and drank ice-cold Jamaican beer out of heavy crystal tumblers.

It was only slightly less hot inside the house where ceiling fans noisily pushed hot air from one end of the room to the other. The jalousie windows were all wide open in a vain attempt to catch a cooling breeze. Aidan could hear the faint murmur of the sea; in the distance, a faint drumming whispered back.

Clive, looking flushed and damp in his tropical wool suit and tie, excused himself immediately after supper and disappeared upstairs, leaving Aidan on his own.

. . .

Raeni discovered Aidan in a seldom used corridor that was hung with family portraits. He was standing in front of a portrait of a slender woman in white. Her hands were folded demurely in her lap, wrinkling the white dress. Her features were composed, inscrutable, yet there was tension about her eyes.

"She seems to be waiting for something," Aidan observed. "Who is she?"

"That was your great Aunt Anna. This house was named after her."

Aidan nodded, wondering again what she had found to hope for here.

Raeni continued to study Aidan as he continued to study Anna's portrait. His manner was not quite shy, not quite reserved. More hesitant. To Raeni he seemed...*bruised*. Like Anna.

"You look like her," Raeni said.

Aidan looked more closely at the portrait of his aunt, surprised by the resemblance which he hadn't noticed before. They shared the same light coloring and pale hair, the same cheekbones and gray-green eyes.

Next to Anna's portrait hung a painting of Aidan's grandfather, *the admiral*, the family patriarch. His stony face was without expression, his leonine head capped by a mane of white hair. "Grandfather, right?" Aidan asked, gesturing at the painting.

"Yes."

Yes, it was him. The great man himself: Olympian, bricklayer, millionaire, adored and adoring father, Raeni thought bitterly; his legend turned her stomach. She found the portrait no more tolerable than the man had been. When the house was unoccupied by family, she kept the portrait turned to the wall.

"Was he as mean as he looks?"

"A lot of people thought he was a hero," Raeni said carefully.

Aidan's mouth twisted into a half smile and he cocked his head as he looked at Raeni. "And you? What did you think?"

I, she wanted to say, *knew he was only another obeah fabrication!* Instead, she said, "I've said enough. I should not be discussing your family. Please forgive my lapse in judgment."

Aidan felt rebuked somehow. Her tone softened. "I've put you in Anna's old room. I hope that's okay. Goodnight, young Aidan," she said and left him alone with his thoughts and the sound of distant drumming, like the beating of his heart, in his ears.

. . .

Aidan was crossing the dunes on his way to the beach when he saw Dale sanding a small boat. Again he was shirtless and his sweat-covered torso shimmered in the sun like silk. Aidan longed to touch his hot shining skin.

"Hi," he called walking closer.

Dale glanced at him and then lowered his head dismissively, without answering.

"Can I help?"

Dale did not look up. "This is work, bwoy. Man's work. What you know about work?"

"Please," Aidan said. "I can help you."

Dale laughed. It was a malicious sound. His brilliant teeth tore a savage gash in his handsome dark face. "The only thing you can help me with is this!" He grabbed his crotch and thrust forward into his palm.

Aidan turned away. Tears pricked his eyes, and his cheeks burned scarlet as if someone had slapped him, twice, very hard across the face. He collided with Clive who placed his hands on his shoulders to steady him. Searching his face, Clive saw hope guttering in his smoky gray eyes.

355

Watching them sort themselves, Dale laughed and Clive aimed a warning look like a slingshot at him. Dale cursed and went back to his sanding.

Aidan pushed past Clive. Clive hurried after him. "Aidan… What happened at school?"

"Didn't Headmaster Brooks tell you?"

Clive trying to contain his exasperation, sighed. "He told me you were harassing—*sexually* harassing—another boy and one night the boy got drunk and you took advantage of him."

Aidan stared at him bug-eyed and dumb.

"I'm assuming that's not true, so would you like to tell me what really happened?"

"I didn't harass anyone—I mean, I wouldn't…do that."

Clive nodded, and waited for him to continue.

"There was a boy at school. He was a senior. He was one of the ones who used to bully me—"

"How do you mean bully?"

"You know—name calling and pushing me around—that sort of thing."

So he was a fisherman "Go on."

"I stayed at school over Thanksgiving—mother and father were away and it was only five days anyway. He was one of the few other kids who stayed, too. One night he came by my dorm room. I could see he'd been drinking. He asked me if I was bisexual. I started to laugh. Bisexual? *Me?* 'Hell no,' I said, 'I'm gay.' He laughed at me and then he tried to kiss me. I tried to push him away and that seemed to make him mad. He kept trying to kiss me and I kept fighting him, but he's bigger than me and he's on the wrestling team. Clive…he raped me.

"I went to Headmaster Brooks. I was so scared of Tom. I was afraid he'd come after me again. I could tell Headmaster Brooks didn't believe me. The next thing I knew, I was being kicked out of school. Clive, he hurt me. I—I bled."

"Did you see a doctor?" Clive asked, his voice shaking. Aidan shook his head, no. "Ok. We'll get you seen by one in town first thing tomorrow."

Aidan nodded.

Clive touched his arm, forced him to stop walking. "Aidan, I'll take care of this." Then, seeming to read Aidan's thoughts, he added, "I won't tell your father, but I promise I will take care of this. And Aidan, remember, I work for your father; I am not him."

Aidan looked at him, and saw, for the first time, not his father's evil factotum, not another weapon in the world's arsenal of cruelty, but a kind man, an ally.

"Thank you."

Clive dismissed his gratitude with a wave of his hand. As Aidan started to walk away, Clive called out, "Aidan, what do you want for Christmas?"

"A boyfriend."

Clive smiled. "I don't think I can help with that."

Clive turned back towards the beach, and Aidan noticed for the first time that he'd traded his impeccable suit for flawlessly tailored khakis, rolled at the cuffs, docksiders without socks and a hot pink polo shirt. "Clive—Clive, *does* it get better?"

Clive stopped and turned around. Looking at Aidan standing in the shadow of a Mangrove tree, he was reminded once again of candlelight. Like a candle's thin flame, Aidan burned bright, and guttered low, at the mercy of whatever wind blew his way, and was as impossible to hold. Clive removed his sunglasses before answering, "Yes, Aidan. Yes, it does."

. . .

Aidan had been gay as long as he could remember. Puberty had been most difficult and telling for him. As the other boys in his boarding school reached puberty and discovered girls, they'd sneak *Playboy* into their dorm rooms. They'd try to make him look at the lurid, leering women, but he'd always close his eyes. Not out of modesty or embarrassment but because to him these naked women had seemed alien, mutilated. He'd closed his eyes to keep himself from screaming at the horror.

He knew some of the boys, seeking relief, messed about with each other. A few times, he'd joined in but the others seemed to divine that for him, it wasn't about getting off and they mocked him and pushed him away. Eventually, he found it easier to leave them to their adolescent games and keep to himself.

. . .

Aidan woke suddenly. He'd been dreaming of a boy who looked a lot like Dale, only he had dreamed of this boy before, over and over. The boy was unknown, yet familiar.

Awake, he could still feel the boy's lips pressed against his own, could still feel the weight of his body on his. The beating of the drums seemed closer now, more insistent, louder, like a foreigner who, when confronted with a native who does not speak his language, simply speaks louder, hoping through volume alone to make himself understood.

The night air moved over his body like a lover's breath. He drifted back to sleep.

Dylan

Aidan had been leaning over the second floor balcony's balustrade, staring at the sapphire blue waters of Sir Francis Drake Passage, when he noticed the drumming. Normally, the drums were easy to ignore, their dull, steady rhythm like the hum of an electric fan. But, tonight, their sound was more intrusive, compelling, like the drone of a particularly persistent mosquito buzzing in his ear. He descended the stone steps and found himself propelled along the beach by the drums' steady beating.

Wave after wave stormed the beach like an invading army; the drums' irregular beating was like the crash of artillery shells. Suddenly, the beating of the drums stopped. Aidan found himself abandoned on a receding wave of sound. The sea grew still as tap water in the bottom of a basin, its surface like black glass. The sound of drumming started again as abruptly as it had stopped. The sea, which moments before had been quiescent, now raced towards the beach.

He erupted out of this seething, boiling cauldron of salt and water, cloaked in moonlight and sea foam like an ermine cape. He stepped out of the rioting sea with the easy sinuous grace of an eel. About Aidan's age, he was handsome, with broad shoulders and a narrow waist. His body, well-muscled and solid, seemed to vibrate with suppressed energy, seemed to contain all the fury of the sea, tightly reined. His beryl eyes, which seemed to hold all the colors of dawn, searched the beach, found Aidan standing stock still, his long flaxen hair plastered to his skull and shoulders by the sea spray.

"Hi, I'm Dylan," he called out casually, as if his sudden appearance had not been a cataclysm.

As they stood facing each other on that white sand beach, rimmed by trees, Aidan, who should have been frightened and was not, saw only a boy like himself. Yet he was different, too: as Aidan was light, he was dark; as Aidan was flame, he was water. Overcome with shyness, Aidan stared at his bare feet, which looked very dark against the white-white sand. When he gathered the courage to look at Dylan, he was overwhelmed by a desire impossible in its consummation. Dylan stared back at him and told him, with a look, that everything was possible.

They raced each other along the beach and swam to the nearest small island, where Dylan climbed a coconut tree and brought down a coconut. They shared its milk and white meat.

As the sun began its slow ascent, Dylan said, "I must go."

Aidan stretched lazily on the sand. "Will I see you again?"

"Yes, tonight. Come back here."

"What time?"

"Whenever you can get away, come. I will know you're here waiting and I will come to you," Dylan said before diving into the sea.

After he left, Aidan, reluctant to leave the spot where he'd briefly found happiness, settled against the sand. The image of Dylan standing at the water's edge held fast; Aidan slept.

A long finger of water reached him, tickled him awake. Dylan's voice in his ear: "Go. It's morning. Go home before you burn."

. . .

Dylan was a wonder. He tasted of salt and smelled of the sea. Twists of soft black hair fell from his scalp in delicate tendrils, seeming more like seaweed than hair. He swam as if he were part of the water and made love to Aidan as if he were a part of him.

When he touched Aidan's arm to point out a tiny gecko or a ghost crab scurrying along the beach, when he slipped an arm around his waist to guide him through the undergrowth in the rain forest, when he brushed a strand of his hair off his cheek, there was promise in his touch and tenderness in his eyes.

The days passed quickly. Aidan and Dylan met every evening. And every morning just before dawn, Dylan left Aidan for the sea.

"Where do you go in the morning?"

"I go...home."

"Where's home?"

"At the bottom of the sea."

When Aidan pressed him for details, Dylan told him a fantastic story, of an undersea kingdom, of a father who was God of the seas, of peace, of acceptance. As a child, Aidan's nanny used to tell him the most far-fetched and amazing stories. When he would accuse her of making these stories up, she would smile mysteriously and say with mock thunder in her voice, "Believe or don't believe. The choice is yours." Now as Dylan finished his own fantastic story, Aidan chose to believe.

"What are your people like?"

"We're a lot like humans. We age—though at a much slower pace. And we even die, though for us there is no disease or sudden withering. We gradually fade out, like stars, but once we die our energy is passed to those remaining so no one is ever truly gone."

"What else?"

"We are kind to each other. Always. There is no war, no hunger, no poverty."

"How is it that no one sees you?"

Dylan was holding his hand. He flipped their joined hands over and over in the sand. "We live in the blind spot of the human eye."

"Blind spot?"

"Have you ever thought you saw someone out of the corner of your eye, but when you turned your head you didn't see anything?"

"Yes."

"That's a blind spot. We live in that spot. Spirits live in that spot as well."

Aidan nodded.

"Everyone thinks spirits live in another dimension. They do not. Humans can only live in peace with what they cannot see so we remain hidden just beyond their sight."

"Why are you here?"

"I'm of the age to get married. I am here to choose my queen...or king...I kept seeing you in my dreams—"

"I dreamed of you, too—I know that now."

"That was no dream. I would visit you in that small space between sleep and wake. I couldn't help myself. I began to think you'd enchanted me. But then, after a while, I didn't care if I was under a spell. I just wanted to be with you."

Aidan grew quiet, was so quiet for so long that Dylan poked his shoulder and asked him what was wrong.

"Can I be your king? Can I come with you?"

"Come with me? Why would you want to do that?"

"Because, I love you."

Dylan sighed. "Do you? Do you even know what love is?"

"I do."

Dylan threw an arm around his shoulder. Aidan nuzzled his chest. "Tell me," Dylan said, "what love is."

"I can't."

"Why not?"

Aidan was beginning to regret starting this conversation. "Because...because love is an instinct. Like hunger." Aidan raised his head, looked Dylan in the eyes. "I mean how do you tell someone what hunger feels like? A newborn infant knows what hunger is. It doesn't have to be taught that. It recognizes hunger instinctively. And it recognizes a mother's love. Like I recognize your love—that *you* love *me* like *I* love *you*."

"I do, do I?"

"You do." Their lips met and Dylan gently bit Aidan's lower lip. Aidan bit back, then Dylan was rolling over him like a wave, both powerful and gentle.

The drums paused, and even the gods stopped to watch the mating of fire and water.

· · ·

Aidan and Dylan lay side-by-side on the sand, fingers entwined, watching the twilight sky. "I love you," Dylan said, still staring at the sky.

"I know," Aidan answered also staring at the sky. "And I love you."

"You know I am not of your world," Dylan said gently.

"I know. I know, and I don't care," Aidan said recklessly. "What do worlds matter when I have you—a world of my own?"

"If you go with me, you can never return."

"I don't care," Aidan said again. "I would rather be with you in your world than without you in mine."

"Very well. I will go back and tell my father I have chosen a mate. You."

"Can I go with you?"

"No. Not yet. I must tell my father, then you must ask for his blessing— You'll have to make him an offering which you must send into the sea—"

Aidan sat up. "Will I—will I have to sacrifice an animal?"

Dylan rolled his eyes. "No. He's not a barbarian. You need to offer his favorite foods—and Champagne. He loves Champagne."

Aidan nodded, making mental notes. "What else?"

"You'll need to build a raft so you can send his offering to the sea—I can show you where. And you'll need a conch shell to call him. And there's a prayer—I can teach it to you."

"Then what?"

"Then, we must wait for his answer."

"I should go," Aidan said, "so I can start getting everything ready." He stood and began dusting sand off his trunks.

Dylan laughed at his enthusiasm and reached up and pulled him back down to the sand beside him. "Wait! You can only make an offering and call him on a Thursday."

"A Thursday? That's perfect. Next Thursday is Christmas. You can be my Christmas present! I'll start building my raft tomorrow." Aidan rolled on top of Dylan and kissed him.

As they embraced, dawn's rosy lips kissed the cold shoulder of the night, leaving behind the greasy red imprint of a new day.

"I must go," Dylan said reluctantly as he rose.

Aidan stood as Dylan turned to leave. Planted on the beach, toes curling into the sand, hopelessly earthbound, flesh, he watched as Dylan, free, spirit, turned and plunged into the aquamarine sea.

· · ·

Aidan woke to rain, violent and white. Bolts of lightning, that seemed to come directly from the sea, tore at the cloud-ridden sky. The crack of thunder was like the striking of cane against unrepentant flesh.

· · ·

Aidan thought it would have been simple to build a raft. After all, he'd watched a video on YouTube, and Dylan had harnessed the power of the previous night's storm and lightning to bring him the logs he needed. Now, he just had to tie them together using the reeds he'd gathered. But his fingers were clumsy and sweat was stinging his eyes.

"You're not tying those properly," Raeni said. "They'll come apart before you get to the water."

Aidan jumped. He hadn't heard Raeni approach and he was supposed to be doing this in secret.

"Raeni! Hi! I'm—"

"I know what you're doing."

Aidan's eyes grew wide.

Raeni sat down cross-legged beside him. "Hand me those reeds, and I'll show you how to tie your knots."

Raeni's hands were sure and fast, Aidan's slow and slippery with sweat. They worked quietly until he asked, "Raeni, how do you know so much about building rafts?"

"Because I once helped your Aunt Anna build a raft very much like this one."

"You? You knew Anna?" Aidan asked, his voice full of wonder. "But how—"

Raeni lifted her hand to her mouth and Aidan's question—*How old are you?*—died on his lips.

Aidan shook his head, sure he had been about to ask a question. "What—what happened to Aunt Anna?"

Raeni sighed. "Anna was in love with a fisherman back in Boston. Your grandfather—her brother—thought him unsuitable and forbade her seeing him. She told your grandfather she was pregnant—a lie, but she thought then he would be forced to let them marry. Instead, he sent her here. I was to be her…prison warden, if you will. Instead, I became her friend."

Raeni's hands kept working the reeds she was tying so expertly as she told the rest of the story. "Anna and her fisherman were corresponding secretly. I, myself, delivered his letters and posted her responses. Anna was so sad. She loved him so much. And he loved her. I know because she showed me his letters.

"So he was a fisherman, and I told her about Agwe—that he would help them if she prayed to him and made him an offering."

Aidan gasped. "You know about Agwe?"

Raeni nodded. "I know," she said. Her hands moved faster. "I told her he would give them shelter in his kingdom."

362

"That's where I'm going—with Dylan," Aidan confessed excitedly. "Maybe, I'll see Anna when I get there. I can give her a message from you."

Raeni's hands stilled in her lap and she got a faraway look in her eyes. "Tell her—tell her I think of her often."

. . .

The new day touched his cheek, easing him from slumber. Aidan opened his eyes. Outside, the bright morning panted like a great white steed awaiting its mount.

Aidan struggled under the weight of a basket laden with the food Raeni had made—fried bananas and rice in coconut milk. There were also cornmeal fritters and melons as big as his head. At the water's edge, he dragged a wooden case of Champagne from its hiding place beneath a turpentine tree.

Sitting on the raft in the middle of pots and baskets and the wooden crate of Champagne, Aidan tried to row with the oar Raeni had given him, but he was anxious and his progress slow. He dove off the raft and slipped the reed loop that he had used to drag it into the water around his waist, then began to swim, towing the raft. It was heavy, and he was not strong. As he began to tire, a school of fish, red and green, swam up behind him, lifting the raft so that it seemed to skim over the surface of the sea as he swam. When he reached the spot where he was to leave the raft, he slipped out of the loop and thanked the fish who had helped him. With a flick of their tails the school swam away, a flash of red and green in the turquoise water.

Agwe

Aidan stood on the beach and blew into the conch shell as hard as he could. Then he recited the prayer Dylan had taught him.

Agwe, awakened by the trumpet call of the conch shell, and hearing the whispered prayer, made his way from the sea. Cloaking himself in a blue-green wave that crested over the beach, he stared at the pale youth whose tears stained the sand like blood. So this was Aidan. His son's beloved. He had come up from his oceanic kingdom expecting to find a dangerous boy, an experienced tempter, a polished seducer, and had found instead this delicate weeping Ganymede.

Why not grant his son and this...this *Ganymede*, their desire, as he had granted his beloved Anna and her fisherman their desire. Dear Anna, whose only hope had lain with him.

His green eyes flashed with decision.

363

Aidan and Dylan

Aidan watched as the raft in the distance sank and the sea turned from turquoise blue to deepest green. He drew a breath and waited for the raft to bob to the surface again.

Dylan rose from the sea. Smiling, he said, "My king," and offered Aidan his hand.

"My king," Aidan repeated taking his hand. Together, hand-in-hand, they walked into the sea, deeper and deeper into water the color of night. Holding Dylan's hand, Aidan tried not to be afraid, even as he felt the sandy sea floor fall away beneath his feet. A thatch of his pale hair spread and floated for a moment on the sea's surface, then disappeared as Dylan, the sea, embraced him.

The drums stopped beating, and the sound of church bells ringing, calling the faithful to Christmas services, rushed in to fill the silence.

Vi

"What do you mean Aidan is *missing*?" Vi asked.

"Just that," Clive said. "Aidan has disappeared—"

"Jesus, Clive! Like it's not bad enough it's not snowing on Christmas—you have to come in here and tell us this?" Thin, with features sharp as an axe, and silver hair, Aidan's father vibrated with nervous energy, cracking his knuckles, tugging at an eyebrow.

"Yes, Adolph. I'm sorry, but your son is missing; I thought you'd want to know that—even if it's Christmas Day and not snowing," Clive answered through gritted teeth.

Adolph flushed deep red. "How dare you come in here acting all self-righteous!" He began to pace, his cold eyes looked hard as diamonds, his brilliantined silver hair shining bronze in the apricot light of the lit Christmas tree. "People don't just disappear!"

"Your wife's aunt disappeared on that same island fifty years ago."

"People don't just disappear!" Adolph repeated. "Most likely he's shacked up with some island boy—"

Clive's mouth moved, but no words came out.

Vi sat on a leather chesterfield sofa, her impossible violet eyes wide, her mouth hanging in a little "O" of surprise. Her hands repeatedly traveled from her lap to her neck to claw at the pearl necklace there, as if trying to dislodge a lump in her throat.

"You think we don't deserve Aidan," Vi said addressing Clive.

"I think Aidan deserves better than the two of you. And I hope to God, wherever he is, he gets it."

Clive walked out of the room, and Vi started to cry. Adolph watched Clive leave. He folded his arms, then, unfolded them and looked out the window. Snow had begun to fall. It would be a white Christmas after all.

. . .

Vi, wrapped in fur and nerves, swung the kitchen door open with a violence that suggested she could, just as easily, rip it off its hinges. As it banged noisily closed behind her, she flung herself into a kitchen chair. "Mama, what have you done?"

Mama turned from the stove where she had set a kettle to boil.

"What do you mean, child?" Mama asked.

"My son is missing. What did you do?"

"What did *I* do?"

"Yes, you! *You* told me to send him to that godforsaken place⊠just as you told my father to send Anna there. *What did you do?*"

"I merely did as you asked. I arranged to free him from the demons who would twist him into something he is not." Mama placed a cup of tea in front of her, and sat down. Vi glanced down into the cup of tea and saw her son, swimming at the bottom. He was swimming with another boy who seemed carved of the water itself. It was dark but wherever Aidan, slender, glassine as a flame, moved, light seemed to follow him. It was a soft wavering light, but bright, like the light from a million and one candles. Aidan was smiling.

"Who—who were these demons?" Vi asked looking up from the cup.

Mama stood and with a finger as twisted as the hair on her head, beckoned Vi to follow her. In the hall, she pointed to a small mirror. It was egg-shaped and veined, opaque as an eye with a cataract, except at the very center where Vi saw nothing but her own reflection. Then she saw her husband's face. And her son's schoolmaster's face. And the scowling, bullying face of a boy she did not recognize whose hands were streaked with blood. And the pious, judging face of the newly elected Pope.

THE END

Xmas Cake:
A Modern Fairy Tale

Raine O'Tierney

[All Fairy Tales Need a Good Prologue...]

Once upon a Christmas season, in the snowy metropolitan city of Midday, there lived a rich prince, Kyle, and a poor baker named Riley. Mr. Kyle Prince resided in a grand high-rise apartment building with a view of the entire city, from the amphitheater to the art district. There was a doorman in white gloves, and Kyle was greeted by name as he walked through the lobby every morning. Businesspeople respected Mr. Prince; many took him into their confidence. He kept company with attractive people who lived in their own buildings, with their own doormen. Kyle was content and warm on snowy days.

Riley Harris, if you turn the page, was freshly graduated from college, and now contended with those hungry wolves: creditors. He faced overwhelming student loans and credit card debt, and found very little in the way of employment. Proud, and unwilling to be a burden on his parents, he had stubbornly left the small home the family shared when he started school. But making his way in the world proved difficult. Riley had three part-time jobs. He wouldn't have been able to fit attractive people into his schedule, unless they paid him for his time—but he hadn't quite sunk that far. There were no white-gloved doormen where Riley lived, because Riley's home was a beaten and rusted Volvo.

And so it was that Kyle and Riley's lives might never have intersected, if not for *A Yuletide Caper* being put on by the Midday Players in the old Jewel Theater.

...

[A Standing Date]

Kyle Prince had a standing date.

Looking out across the snowy sea of the parking lot, Kyle shifted, waiting for his date to appear. He didn't exactly know the other man's name—but regardless, it had become a nightly thing between them, something he expected without knowing how he'd even come to anticipate it. Once, twice, maybe, they'd exchanged a casual smile as Kyle stepped out the back door of the theater for some air. And then the third time, he'd gone outside, but not *only* to get air.

Would his date show tonight?

Almost as an answer, the lights in the small, nearby bakery began to flick off, one by one, until the entire building was still and dark. Oh yes, his date was coming.

They had never touched, never even spoken, but sometimes after a stressful board meeting, or when he was driving in to work in the morning, he'd remember that it was Wednesday or Friday, and his brother, Cameron, had a show at the Jewel Theater. Excitement would begin to prick behind his eyes. Whatever stresses he carried from the day would start to melt away because there was a smile in Kyle Prince's future.

Shivering a bit in the cold despite his heavy jacket, Kyle readied that smile now, readied his gloved hand, and waited.

As his "date" exited the back door of the bakery, he paused, momentarily hidden in the shadows. And then the man appeared in a pool of amber cast by the parking lot lights, and Kyle could no longer hold back his warm, welcoming, smile. The sameness of it was thrilling: the man would walk across the parking lot with a small bakery box tucked up under his arm. A red and green box, if it was the same one Kyle had seen in the window. Leftovers, perhaps, or something the baker made just for himself right before closing time.

How could one man eat so many baked goods? And—it was the season for it, after all—could his date be taking home Christmas cake every night?

For a moment there, he had a flight of fancy, the sort reserved for romance novels and bedtime stories. Kyle thought about leaving his post at the back door of the Jewel Theater, walking across the parking lot, and asking if the other man had Christmas cake enough for two in that box. He hadn't eaten day-old anything for as long as he could remember, but the thought that he might see the other man's smile more closely, or that his date might reply, say, "Why yes, I've had enough for two, but no one has ever asked!" sent a little shiver up Kyle's spine that had nothing to do with the cold.

Kyle smiled and waved.

. . .

368

[The Baker Stumbles]

Riley's vision blurred in and out as he tried to focus on his uncertain footing. Another inch of snow had fallen during his shift, and he wobbled and stumbled across the pavement. Was it snow? Or was it sugar? For a moment, he lost the thread as the blanket of white glittered under the light. Snow…or sugar…?

To an outsider, Riley might have looked like he'd stolen a few sips from the cooking brandy. Or popped in at one of the bars down the street on his break.

But being sloshed would have been fun, Riley thought, nothing at all like this. The violent upheaval of the ground and the pounding in his head—that would have been the aftermath of drinks with friends and laughter and the warmth of a bar. Those things were as much a fantasy as his thinking there were drifts of powdery sugar in the parking lot.

Riley had no drinking money though, and he had no friends, and there was no warmth—only the bitter chill of the evening and the wobbling, topsy-turvy movement of the earth. He blindly grabbed at the slick lamp post, his leftovers slipping from under his arms.

He'd felt funny the night before—just a tickle in the back of his throat—but then he'd woken up achy and worn, become bleary-eyed at his morning shift at the factory, found no available caroling work at the Ravenswood Shopping Center, and then hardly made it through his shift at the bakery.

Now, having miraculously survived until closing time, he was a single sentence from falling flat on his face. In fact, the man from across the parking lot was still smiling—hand raised in a friendly gesture—when Riley's knees gave and he crumpled to the pavement.

. . .

[A Prince and an Angel to the Rescue!]

It took Kyle a second to realize that something was wrong, because he'd been so lost in his fantasy of sharing cake with the other. But once he saw the young man double over, Kyle took off across the snowy parking lot, slipping and sliding as he went.

At almost the same moment, Cameron Prince—who could have been Kyle's twin, had they not been born a year apart—emerged from the back door of the theater, still laughing at a joke. Upon seeing his brother running across the pavement, Cameron sprinted after him—not out of any deep concern, but because his whole life Cameron had wanted to be where the action was.

"What are we running for?" he shouted happily across the silent parking lot, leaping through the snow. Cameron was reckless, and currently less encumbered (clothing-wise) than his brother, so they came together to a crashing halt, inches short of trampling over Kyle's date. "Oh."

"It's the baker," Kyle explained. "He's fallen."

"He's *drunk.*"

The man's cheeks were bright red and heat emanated from him like a convection oven, sweat rolling down his face before freezing.

This they could not have known, but when Riley looked up, he saw double—quadruple, actually—and he decided he must be dying, because two of the four men who stood over him were bare-chested angels with wings and cottony clouds over their privates. They even had halos. He reached for one of the Camerons, mistaking his costume (which was sewn by a design student and at that distance wouldn't have fooled anyone whose brain wasn't frying with a 102 degree temperature) for the real deal. He believed Cameron to be Kyle and Kyle to be the Angel of Death who had stood sentry for him every night outside of the community theater. Was that why he had always smiled?

Kyle caught his date under the arms as he lost that last bit of verticality and hauled him against his chest, feeling the blazing heat of his body even through his suit and overcoat.

"He's not drunk, he's sick. And you can't wear a jacket?" Kyle asked Cameron. Near-zero temperatures be damned, his brother would strut around in the wispy clothing whenever it suited him.

Throwing one of the man's arms over his shoulders, Kyle hoisted him off the ground.

"I don't...wanna...throw up in front of the angel..." Riley murmured, and nestled his head into Kyle's chest.

"Do you know how many phone numbers this costume has gotten me?" Cameron asked.

If not Kyle, the refrigerator certainly knew! Held up by a powerful set of holly magnets was a stack of phone numbers—most of them from actresses, stage hands, and audience members who had seen him in his ridiculous costume.

"We should get him to his car," Kyle said. He'd always been the planner. Cameron flew by the seat of his little cloud pants. "You can follow me to his apartment and we'll drop him off."

"You know where he lives?" Cameron asked curiously. "I didn't think you had any friends from Midday South."

Cameron was not wrong.

"Hey, kid, if I drive you, can you give me directions?" Kyle moved slowly, careful to keep them both from slipping and falling flat on their faces. The other shifted and murmured something incoherently.

"Go get my car," Kyle told Cameron, tossing the keys to his brother before returning his attention to the felled baker. "Hey, what's your name?" he asked

Riley softly, once his brother had walked away. He'd made the decision to take the stranger home seem easy—as if it were nothing more than Act One of the awful play his brother and the Midday Players were putting on. Kyle only slightly doubted his ability to pull it off, and his desire to help far outweighed that doubt.

Riley replied with his name, but it was slurred and incomprehensible, and Kyle couldn't understand it. It didn't matter, really; after a few dozen cautious, stumbling steps they were at the car. He needed the young man's keys. Kyle asked for them, nicely and then a bit more forcefully when the other didn't respond, and then, with the same cinema bravado he'd used to create this plan, he reached into the stranger's pocket and fished them out himself, unlocking the passenger-side door one-handed.

What he saw inside didn't immediately register. And why would it? Kyle Prince had never known anyone who was living out of their car. The sleeping bag, the cracked Dopp kit of hygiene products, the changes of clothes, the pillows—they could all be from a recent camping trip. And then he saw them: piles of pastry boxes in the floor board. They were crushed down and stacked neatly. Days' worth. Weeks' even. He'd always just assumed the young man went home, after their thrice-weekly "dates," to a warm loft and plenty of food. He was happy and healthy and well-cared for. Certainly not homeless. Certainly not fevered and delirious, and living out of the back of his car.

Without a word, without a thought, Kyle shut the car door, locked it and waited for Cameron.

. . .

['Not Kyle']

"Where's your halo?" Riley managed to articulate, letting his head fall back as he looked over the top of the angel's seventy-five-dollar haircut. This was the angel, wasn't it? He was wearing clothes now—a suit, but he was warm and firm, and Riley felt so safe against his side that he started to doze even before the last syllable had left his lips.

"My name is Kyle," Kyle said.

"I'm not..." Riley trailed off and sleepily nuzzled his head into Kyle's neck. In twenty-four years, he had never been so intimate with another person.

"We're waiting for my brother to bring the car," Kyle spoke gently, and Riley felt fingertips across his brow. "I'm going to take you home with me."

"I don't..."

Even so ill he couldn't think, Riley tried to proudly protest. He didn't go home with strange men, even if they were warm and handsome and possibly angelic, and he didn't accept charity.

371

Pride had driven him to this point—pride was all he knew. He'd been too proud to ask his parents for help with school, drawing on large loans after he lost his night job. Credit cards filled in the gaps. And after school was done, he'd been too proud to admit the debt he'd taken on. He got part-time work at the factory, and then another job as an assistant at the bakery, and then several weeks ago, since it was the holiday season and he had a relatively good singing voice, he started working a minimum-wage shift, caroling in full Victorian costume in the Ravenswood shopping district. But it wasn't enough and the creditors kept calling until they shut the phone off. And even when he came home to find an eviction notice on his front door and the locks changed, he was too proud to let anyone know he was out on the street. So he'd moved into his car.

But pride was no match against spending another night in the cramped backseat of the car. He gave in.

Kyle smoothed Riley's dark hair back from his brow, a little grin on his face. "All right, 'Not Kyle,' don't worry. You're not going to have to sleep out here tonight."

. . .

[The Nicest Apartment in All of Midday]

Cameron didn't think bringing Riley home was a bad idea. In fact, Kyle knew that his brother would have done the same thing himself if he'd had his own car and his own home and if he'd been the one to notice Riley in the snow. Even so, that didn't stop Cameron from being an ass about the whole thing.

"Guess you've got the couch tonight, brother," Cameron told Kyle plainly, navigating the icy Midday Bridge with ease. "That kid needs a bed, and I need my beauty sleep. I've still got six shows left to go."

Kyle sat in the back seat with Riley, holding him close, as if the young man might fall over and break. "And I guess you're going to have to pluck a number off the fridge and find somewhere else to stay tonight," Kyle mused. Maybe he could set up a cot next to his bed. Now he'd just need to buy a cot.

The heat in the car, the relatively smooth ride, and the warmth of human contact had lulled Riley into a blissful half-sleep, and he clung to Kyle in a way he never would have dared if he'd been in his right mind. He didn't want to make trouble for the angel, who was somehow driving the car and cradling him in the back seat at the same time, so he murmured, "I could share a bed with you."

Cameron burst out laughing. "Well, there's your solution, brother! That'll be a new one. We should contact the society page. *Kyle Prince Beds Homeless Man.*"

"Shut up," Kyle tossed at his brother. Of course they wouldn't sleep together…though his mattress was certainly large enough. He wondered if Ms. Miller was still at the apartment. She could help him get *Not Kyle* bathed and changed and into bed.

Kyle dialed the house number as the man lying against him half-hummed a carol.

"Are you sure he isn't drunk?" Cameron teased.

"There's presents in the trunk…I've got to get them into the mail…" *Not Kyle* said. "Have I missed Christmas?"

Kyle had to hold him still to keep him from struggling himself into a frenzy. He soothed the young man, promising that the presents would be fine. Everything would be fine.

If he'd been coherent, Riley most certainly would have delighted in the sight of the expansive high-rise condominium building, in the heart of Midday Proper. Lights ran up one side of the building and down the other, dancing, changing colors, giving the whole building a playfully elegant feel.

The doorman helped Kyle and Riley out of the car, held the door for them, and went ahead to call for an elevator.

The closest elevator was on the twelfth floor and it seemed to be stopping a lot, as if someone—child or mischievous adult—had hit every single button on the panel. Standing in the lobby, Riley held tightly onto Kyle and told him, in a barely-there voice, "I like you a lot."

"Oh yeah?" Kyle replied, puffing up just a little.

He was mostly disregarding everything the young man said to him, because he was, after all, running a brain-frying fever, but it still made him a bit proud to be liked. Perhaps Riley had considered their quiet exchange of smiles to be a standing "date" as well.

"Well, I like you too," Kyle said, and given the few facts that he had about Riley, it was the truth. The kid was obviously hard-working; even sick as he was, he'd still gone to work. He was friendly, with a charming, open smile. Most of all, he maintained these traits despite his living conditions.

"Did I leave my cake somewhere?" he asked, and Kyle shushed him again gently. He'd have Ms. Miller make some broth. Or, if she couldn't stay, he'd open a can of something himself. Surely he couldn't botch a can of soup too badly? No more stale Christmas cake for his patient.

Cameron caught up to them, having parked the car, and they got on the elevator together. They looked like quite the trio. Well-dressed Kyle, the fevered Riley, and Cameron in his little cloud and halo.

Ms. Miller greeted them at the door, a look of concern on her face. She immediately pulled Riley out of Kyle's arms, ignoring her employer as she shepherded him through the hall and into the living room. She spoke in low, soothing tones, telling him that she'd prepared a bath for him and that there was a pot of chicken and dumplings simmering on the stove. She'd have it ready for him just as soon as they got him cleaned up.

Kyle considered his housekeeper for a moment. She was not a mother, though still motherly. Usually, Ms. Miller had to settle for cooking and cleaning for the Prince brothers—whom he was sure she considered to be nice young men, but spoiled. The whelp she helped to the bathroom now was truly in need of her care and she became tearful with concern as she told him she'd chosen peppermint bubble bath for the water.

Where do you bathe on a normal night? Kyle wondered. *A quick shower at a friend's? Or a sponge bath at the library?* How opulent his bathroom seemed, as he and Ms. Miller quickly stripped off Riley's clothes to the tune of his weak insistence that he could do it himself. Kyle held him while Ms. Miller stepped over to the tub; she dipped a finger in the water and let a few drops fall onto her wrist. She ran a bit of cold water in and swirled it about with her hand. When she stepped back, Riley no longer seemed to have the energy to protest and they helped him into the water. He sank low into the thick bubbles, his chin disappearing beneath the froth.

"Where would you like him to sleep?" Ms. Miller asked, pushing Kyle back so she could make sure that Riley was settled and not in any danger of sinking under the water.

"My bed," Kyle replied without hesitation.

"And where are you going to sleep, Mr. Prince?" she wanted to know. Kyle sat on the closed toilet and watched Riley for a long moment.

"The same," he insisted firmly, with a look to tell her that he did not care to hear any opposition on that point. "If he needs anything in the night, I will be right there beside him and can get it for him."

"Of course," she agreed.

. . .

[Soup Is Not Cake]

Riley only ate half of his soup, too sick to appreciate the nuance and depth of Ms. Miller's recipe. The illness had stolen his appetite and despite the delicate texture of the dumplings and the perfectly tender vegetables and chicken, what he managed to get down sat heavy in his stomach.

The mere act of sitting at the kitchen table was almost too much, even when Cameron wheeled the super comfortable executive chair from Kyle's office. When he couldn't eat any more, Riley gratefully accepted the arms that guided him to the master bedroom.

Ms. Miller brought him cold medicine and a ginger ale, and at her direction he meekly climbed into the large bed, the sheets fresh and smelling of sunshine.

He let her tuck the covers up to his chin. When she put her cool hand against his forehead as he was drifting off to sleep, he found he missed his mother very much.

"Where's the angel?" he managed to ask, wanting nothing more than to snuggle up beside the man in the suit who had held him in the car. The angel without the halo. Sleep overtook him once more.

. . .

[The Prince Brothers]

In the living room, Cameron lay on the couch with the television remote in one hand, taking swigs from his post-play beer. The beer was the only indulgence he allowed himself during the run of *A Yuletide Caper*—there were certain standards one had to uphold when parading shirtless in front of an audience three shows a week. He put his feet on the back of the couch, just to antagonize Kyle.

"I'm surprised you took off the costume," Kyle said.

"Sorta itches."

"You can stick with the guest room, Cameron," Kyle said quietly. "I'm going to sleep in there with him."

"Well, he did ask you to," Cameron shrugged, flipping the channel. He had nowhere to be in the morning. "How could you say no to the feverish little mouse?"

"How did he end up living out of his car?" This thought had niggled at Kyle all evening. The Italian leather couch Cameron was disrespecting with his dirty feet would have easily paid three months' rent on a loft in Midday South. Sell the couch, house the young man. It didn't make sense to Kyle. How could one man—no, not *one man*—how could he, Kyle Prince, own a couch that would have cozily set up the other?

And the real question: how had he smiled and waved at the baker every night he'd come to pick his brother up from that dreadful play and not realized that something was amiss?

"He's living out of his car because he doesn't have you as a brother," Cameron said mildly, flipping to another channel with a bored little shrug. Compliments left and right tonight.

"You wouldn't have been out on the street if..." Kyle trailed off as Cameron chuffed. "I mean, you're between places, but that doesn't mean you...Right?"

"I'm saying sometimes things get tough."

"Tell me you wouldn't have been living out of your car."

"I don't know," Cameron said honestly.

"You don't even have a car," he tried to joke, but he felt stilled by the whole conversation.

"Look, I could record this show, and we could sit and have a long talk about how you're a great guy, and you can't get bogged down about these sorts of things, and it's not your fault that you're well off, that you're a responsible person, that your successes aren't cause to beat yourself up...But, brother, c'mon, I'm beat. I just want to watch TV. Can I just give you the Wikipedia version?"

"I...think you just did."

"Good." And then, patting himself on the back for rocking so hard as a brother, Cameron tossed Kyle a "good job, gold star!" smile.

. . .

[Donating Twenty Couches, So To Speak]

Riley slept for almost an entire day, swimming to a strange level of sub-consciousness only when he needed to use the bathroom. While his guest slept, Kyle Prince made phone calls. Many, many phone calls.

First he called work, which startled his assistant so much she asked if he needed emergency services. He'd never taken an unscheduled day off of work in the entire time he'd been with the company, and it took some time to explain the situation and assure her he was fine. Having regained her composure, she asked if she should call the baker's place of employment.

"What's his name?" she asked, and he could almost hear her readying her pen.

"Riley Harris." He'd finally learned *Not Kyle's* real name by nosing through his wallet and discovering his driver's license. Good, ol'-fashioned police work. He told her about the bakery in Midday South, and the thing was as good as done.

His next call was to his doctor—a man who did not normally make house calls, but who could be persuaded on occasion. Given the occasion coincided with a bad streak in his gambling, Kyle's price was right.

The examination was short, but thorough, the doctor being a gambler but no cheat.

"Well, he won't die of it," the doctor assured Kyle. "Fluids, bed rest, no more damn Christmas cake." He wrote Riley a couple of prescriptions, which Ms. Miller took to fill at the pharmacy down the street.

Kyle saved the last of his phone calls until that night, after Ms. Miller had gone home. Having loaned Cameron the car (something he never did when he was in his right mind), Kyle had to settle for searching the Internet for homeless shelters in Midday South. For a moment, he considered finding Riley a bed there, once he was feeling better, but a sudden, visceral protectiveness stopped him.

Now that he'd found Riley, and taken it upon himself to get involved, he couldn't really justify foisting him off on the city. Not his baker, not his standing date, not his *Not Kyle*. So instead, he wrote down number after number—disheartened by how many shelters there were. *Why were there so many?*

And then he began to call, pledging to donate—telling exhausted-sounding workers that he'd be sending the monetary value's worth of twenty of those couches. Most times he was met with snorts of laughter or derision. *They'd been promised things like these before*, he thought.

As soon as he hung up the phone, he began moving money between accounts, he made donations online, and when he couldn't do that, he wrote checks.

. . .

[Big Spoon, Little Spoon]

On the second day, Riley was weak but awake and very hungry. Kyle thought he seemed to be taking being in a stranger's house very well, but from his periodic protestations, there was a possibility that if Riley had the strength, he'd have snuck away with only a thank-you note to mark that he'd ever been in the apartment.

One of the first things Riley asked Kyle was, "Do I remember an angel?"

Kyle laughed and explained what had happened.

Riley apologized no less than seven times—once for every time Kyle popped in to check on him. He lamented repeatedly that he hated to be an imposition.

"I'm so sorry," Riley said, going for an eighth when Kyle came to sit on the edge of the bed.

"Please, just rest," Kyle begged, touching Riley's cheek gently and trying to hide his smile when Riley pressed back against his palm.

The truth was, Kyle didn't know how to take Riley's apologies. What was he sorry for? Living out of his car? Or getting caught? He made another flurry of donations that night, this time to a foundation for homeless youth, then to soup kitchens, clothes closets, and food pantries. It only slightly lessened the discomfort he felt.

How many people did he unconsciously smile at during the day that then went home to no electricity or no heat? How many went hungry? How many were living out of their cars? How many didn't even have cars to live out of? He wanted to do more, but he hardly knew where to begin.

By day three, Riley was able to eat breakfast at the kitchen table with Kyle and Cameron. He watched the brothers with an earnest gaze as they bickered over the right way to cook eggs: scrambled or sunny-side up. When

Cameron—spurred by his brother—cleared the table, Riley said quietly, "I think I like you both very much."

The words filled Kyle with warm happiness and, at the same time, a little pang of jealousy. It was one thing if Riley should like Cameron as well, but Kyle wanted to be liked as the better of the two.

"You said so before," Kyle smiled at him. "When we brought you here that first night—you told me that you liked me."

"I did?" Riley flushed deeply and Kyle wondered if his fever was returning.

"Sure."

"Well, what did you say to that?"

"That I like you too."

"I suppose it's good we like each other, Kyle...since we've been sharing a bed for the last three nights."

"It's a pretty big bed," Kyle mused. "But if you're uncomfortable, I can find alternative sleeping arrangements."

"I wouldn't kick you out of your own bed."

Every night, they started on opposite ends of the wide bed, and every morning, Kyle awoke to find Riley's back pressed against his chest. The whole sea of a bed and somehow they'd come to be sleeping like two spoons in the silverware drawer. Until last night...

"Though I should probably be going soon," Riley announced suddenly, looking up.

Could he read Kyle's thoughts? Did Riley know that Kyle knew the baker had awoken and not immediately pulled out of Kyle's grasp that morning? Was that anything to be embarrassed about?

"We should date." Kyle's face was serious, intense.

"Date?" Riley repeated, confusion blending with hopefulness in his expression.

"Well, it's all rather serendipitous, don't you think? That my brother's play is being put on right across from your bakery, and that I was there when you collapsed. We get along. You said so yourself, you like me. You and I, we should go out on a date together."

"Okay."

"Okay?"

"Yes, okay," Riley replied, flushing even more deeply red. "But I still need to go."

"There's no way you can go back out there. You can stay here with us."

"I couldn't," he said proudly. "I'm so grateful for everything you've done and if you really want to see me again—"

"I do," Kyle broke in.

"I'd like that very much, but I can't impose on you anymore."

"You won't be imposing," Kyle insisted. He wouldn't be able to sleep knowing that Riley was curled up in the back of his rusted car eating old cake. He'd crossed the wide chasm of shared mattress the previous night and pulled Riley close into his arms. It felt new and familiar at the same time, so nice. He wanted to keep Riley warm, always. "You can pay rent if you want."

"I couldn't afford a place like this," Riley explained without shame.

"We're dating now," Kyle flashed his most charming smile. "Right? Didn't we just decide?"

"We did."

"That makes you my boyfriend." Kyle secretly liked the sound of the word, the heady rush of a whirlwind romance and embarking on an unfamiliar adventure. "Now that I've found you, can't you stay here with me and let me get to know you even better?"

"Now that you're my...boyfriend," Riley replied, "that means even more that I can't take advantage of you."

"Then I'll break up with you," Kyle decided.

"That was fast."

He reached across the table and took Riley's hand, "Please don't go? Whatever trouble you're having, whatever debt, I'll help you."

"I don't know..." Riley trailed off. He seemed to choke on a lump in his throat. "We...aren't even dating anymore."

. . .

[Taking Responsibility]

It snowed the day Riley tried to return to his old life. How much he'd wanted to stay in the comfort of Kyle's spacious apartment with the motherly housekeeper, the comedic brother, the cable television, the doorman, the view of the city sprawled out beneath his window; and, most of all, the man who had become his prince. It would be a comfortable life with little to worry about. But all of these incredible factors made him even more determined to go out and stand on his own two feet.

He imagined Kyle awaking that fourth day to find the note of thanks and the apology, plus twenty-two dollars, and the empty space in his bed where Riley should have been.

He'd given Kyle almost all the money he had on him, painfully aware that it did not come close to covering the room and board and medical attention he'd received. He would treat the kindness as a debt and pay on it when he could. With what was left of his funds, Riley caught the metro back to Midday South and he walked through the flurry of snowflakes to the factory.

His supervisor caught him as he was clocking in and told Riley he could pick up his last paycheck from Payroll. He wouldn't even give Riley a chance to explain the special circumstances. Dejected, he walked over to Ravenswood, hoping to have better luck with his caroling job. The manager was much more understanding and listened sympathetically as he recounted the last four days, but the job had been permanently filled. By the time he made it to the bakery, Riley was soaked through, shivering, and certain that he'd be three for three.

"Are you feeling better?" one of the other baker's assistants asked him the moment he pushed through the door. He nodded and was about to explain himself when the store owner came around the counter to chastise him for coming back to work so soon. Riley insisted he was feeling better, but they could all see that the walk from the subway station had taken its toll on him. He was told in no uncertain terms to rest, but at least he still had a job.

That bit of good news was small comfort when he walked across to the parking structure to find that his car was gone, towed away for having been parked there so long. For minutes Riley stood there, staring at the spot where his car had been. He thought about the presents he'd purchased for his family and his change of clothes and how now, literally, all he had in the world were the clothes on his back and his job at the bakery. When he became so chilled that he could feel the cold in his bones, he began to walk back toward the art district. There was a run-down gas station with a pay phone there. It was finally time to call home. It would have to be collect, he only had a few pennies left; Riley just hoped they'd accept the charges.

. . .

[Let Go of Your Pride, Mr. Harris]

"Hi, Mom." He spoke into the crackling line, embarrassed, cold, sick, and just a touch defeated. For almost a full minute she cried—no words, just wracking sobs, and he realized they hadn't spoken since the phone company cut off the landline at his apartment. Riley was no longer feeling strong and proud, just small and foolish. He'd never even thought to call. He'd taken the whole of the burden on his back and started out into the world, leaving his mother to wonder where he'd gone.

When the tears dried, she told him in frantic little gasps that she and his father had gone looking for him in the city, contacted his old friends, his old landlord, everyone they knew to contact, but that he'd simply vanished. "I thought you were…" She couldn't finish the sentence before she was choked by a fresh batch of tears. "Where are you, Riley?" she finally managed.

He told her everything, pushing on even as she cried, hardly stopping for breath, and by the end he was left in tears himself as he admitted that he'd lost everything. "I'm sorry, Mom. They took my car. I-I lost the presents…"

At some point his father took the phone. He was hot with anger, and he laid into Riley for scaring them. Did he know what he'd put them through? And when was he coming home? And he loved Riley. Goddamn, he loved Riley. He said that no less than ten times. "I love you, son."

"I can't come home," Riley replied weakly, and he received a fresh round of lectures. He cradled the phone to his ear and listened as his mother tried to defend him in the background. He *would* come home, he was informed in no uncertain terms. He would come home and they would help him. They would get through it as a family.

"Tell me where you are, and I'll come and get you," his father commanded.

"Okay," Riley relented, squeezing his eyes tightly shut. His jacket was soaked through, and he wondered what Kyle was doing, and if he'd found his letter.

. . .

[The Baker and the Prince Miss Each Other Tremendously]

Home was a healing place. Riley had been so afraid of his parents' disappointment that he couldn't imagine finding comfort there—but the warmth of their hugs, even the love in the lectures they repeated *ad nauseam*, made it all seem a bit more bearable. There was no "if" they would help—they fully took control, relegating him to his bed to recoup, tearing apart his finances with practiced ease. They only had a little in savings, not much collateral, but his protests fell on deaf ears. His father took out a loan from the bank—one with sensible interest—and paid back all of Riley's creditors. The student loans were hefty, but his mother worked with the collection agency, and they negotiated a monthly payment. His parents would pay half of the student loans, and he would be responsible for the other half. Every hour or so, one parent or the other would pop in with a fresh glass of water or pills or something for him to read, and he would hear it again.

"We're so glad you're home."

And while they all tended to the mess he'd made of his life, Riley dreamed about Kyle, and how when Riley was all right again, he would go back to Kyle's apartment and knock on his door, with flowers and maybe a fresh Christmas cake from the bakery, and this time *he* would ask Kyle out.

Almost all of his pay would end up going to working his way out of debt—not just fighting the interest, but making significant headway into the debt itself—and what was left over he'd put into savings. His parents helped him get his car out of impound, though he took the bus to cut down on gas costs. And at his insistence, his parents accepted rent from him for his old bedroom, though they accepted just twenty-five dollars a month for it, with the mumbled consideration that they might renegotiate the terms once he was in a better position. And his stubborn pride conceded this was for the best.

Then, on Christmas Eve, a week after returning to the bakery, Riley simply couldn't stand it anymore. Kyle had been on his mind every second, distracting him at work, sneaking his way into the lulls in conversation, keeping him mired in lovesick thoughts. Every night when he closed, he scoured the parking lot for a sight of the man, even though the metro was in the other direction. But Kyle was not lingering near the back door of the theater. There was no smile. No wave.

Riley's need to speak with him unbearable, he gave in, looked up his number and called, hoping Kyle wouldn't say "Riley who?" when he introduced himself over the phone.

"I've missed you." Kyle Prince did not play coy as the words tumbled from his lips. "I've been trying to give you the space you need...but it's killing me." So, he'd been a bit lovesick, too? "I'm not a patient man, and I had no idea if you would ever...well, I just missed you."

"I've missed you, too," Riley whispered into the phone. His sisters were home for the holidays, and all three of them were nosey snoops who wanted nothing more than to pry into his business.

"Are you all right?" Kyle wanted to know, and Riley explained that he was staying with his parents until things improved.

"How are you, Kyle?"

"Lonely," he replied without shame or pride. "My bed's cold without you."

One of his sisters giggled from the other room, and Riley popped his head around the corner to make sure she wasn't listening in on his conversation. Even if they hadn't been around, all snooping, gossiping, giggles, he still couldn't have said what was on his mind—that he wished they could warm Kyle's bed together. It was too silly, too intimate.

"Tonight is Cameron's last performance, isn't it?" Riley asked slowly, lying to himself that he was just making conversation. "Are you going?"

"Well, I've got to pick him up."

"I haven't seen you there lately."

"No," Kyle replied without revealing more.

"If you're going to be there..." It wouldn't be a date if he was already there. "Maybe...maybe I'll see you after I close up tonight?"

"Could be," Kyle teased.

"And I was going to take the metro home, but…if you wanted…" Oh, pride be damned. "Well, seeing as you're my boyfriend and all…Wait, are we broken up still, or not?"

"Definitely not."

"Well then, would you like to drive me home tonight?"

. . .

[And They Started Their Happily Ever After…]

That night, two men smiled at each other from across the street, but instead of a brief, forgettable smile between strangers, it was an exchange between would-be lovers. Riley had no car to walk to, so instead, he headed toward Kyle, a freshly made Christmas cake in his hands. The light from over the theater's back door shone down over Kyle's head, making him look angelic.

He reached for Riley the second he was in grabbing distance and pulled him in close for their first kiss. It was both awkward and sweet. Kyle locked his arms around Riley's waist and refused to let go.

"Do I have to drive you home?" he murmured. "Or would your parents mind too much if I kept you for Christmas?"

That night the prince took the young baker to his bed, and instead of a sea of mattress between them, they held each other close and made love against the cool sheets. And—of course—they were happy together, always.

~ Fin

ABOUT THE AUTHORS

J P Walker

Jem Roche-Walker was born in Norwich and moved to the North West in order to attend Edge Hill University, studying Social Work Studies. After studying she began working in rehabilitation for patients with acquired brain injuries and has spent the last seven years writing her first novel, *Knights of the Sun*, published 2013 (Beaten Track). She lives in Burscough with her wife and baby girl and loves spending family time with them.

Website: www.facebook.com/jpwalkerknightsofthesun

Debbie McGowan

Debbie McGowan is an author and publisher based in a semi-rural corner of Lancashire, England. She writes character-driven fiction, covering life, love, relationships—the whole shazam. A working class girl, she 'ran away' to London at seventeen, was homeless, unemployed and then homeless again, interspersed with animal rights activism (all legal, honest ;)) and volunteer work as a mental health advocate. At twenty-five, she went back to college to study social science—tough with two toddlers, but they had a 'stay at home' dad, so it worked itself out. These days, the toddlers are young women (much to their chagrin), and Debbie teaches undergraduate students, writes novels and runs an independent publishing company, occasionally grabbing an hour of sleep where she can!

Website: www.debbiemcgowan.co.uk

Ofelia Gränd

Ofelia Gränd is Swedish through and through. She lives in a small west coast town with her husband and their three children. She has absolutely no time to write, so, naturally, that's what she wants to do. Have you ever tried to write something with one child in your lap and two more standing around wanting attention? Ofelia does all the time—try, that is. She could give up her glamorous life as a stay-at-home mom, and go back to her work as a teacher. But why not take advantage of the situation when she's living in a parental leave utopia? Enough about her being a parent, you think, and you're quite right. Ofelia is a No Poo practiser, a pescatarian who bakes her own bread and makes her own soap—now, you wished that we'd stuck to the children, don't you?

If you still want to know more, you'll find Ofelia here:

Website: www.facebook.com/ofelia.grand

Jonathan Penn

Jonathan grew up in The South. While new to the world of writing, he has been inventing tales for at least fifty years. He was probably also making stuff up during the two years prior to that but, as this was his pre-verbal period, there's no evidence one way or the other. An armchair linguist, he has taught himself to ask, "Where is the bathroom?" in seven languages. ~~He enjoys gardening,~~ He gardens, and enjoys red wines, cooking, theatre, and, of course, writing. Jonathan reminds himself every day how fortunate he is to have shared the best and worst of the last thirty-three years with the man of his dreams.

Website: www.jpennwrites.blogspot.com

Alexis Woods

Always an avid reader and colorful dreamer, it was only a matter of time before taking pen to paper, oftentimes literally. Every story I write has a song or theme, sometimes both, that encompass them because I'm a firm believer in every song tells a story and every story has a song. I sing under my breath, tap my toes and swing my hips, much to the delight of my co-workers and friends. I freely admit that becoming a romance author is the best mid-life crisis a girl could ever have.

I'm an: Anachronist, Coffee Lover, Daughter/Dancer, Friend/Fighter, Jewish, Khazar, Lover/Leader, Mother/Medievalist, Novice/Nightowl, Opinionated, Pharmacist, Romantic/Reenactor, Sister/Scout, Traveler, Visionary, Wife/Writer

Website: www.goodreads.com/AlexisWoods

Rick Bettencourt

Rick Bettencourt is the author of *Not Sure Boys*, *Painting with Wine* and *Tim on Broadway*. Rick hates to cook, and can often be seen eating out. He lives in the Tampa Bay area, with his husband and their dog, Bandit. You can follow Rick on Twitter @rbettenc, and you should also subscribe to his mailing list at rickbettencourt.com. You'll receive all sorts of good stuff, but never any spam.

Website: www.rickbettencourt.com

Amy Spector

Amy grew up in the Midwest. She spent far too much of her time in clubs—gay and straight alike—and far too little time in her university classes. That is, until she met a boy with cute hair and great taste in footwear. Now they live together with a number of small, rather noisy children and a dachshund named after her favorite horror actor of all time. She runs a number of sadly neglected blogs, and even though she has a lovely job that requires her to pick up a camera every now and again, she would still rather be writing.

Website: www.amyspectorauthor.com

Kathleen Hayes

Kathleen Hayes is a bit of an all around geek. She has mastered the art of procrastination, is owned by two crazy cats and is excited to have just added a fellow super geek to her clan. Kathleen loves to explore worlds – whether in her head or on page. She welcomes you into her worlds and hopes you have as much fun there as she does! She writes M/M Romance and poetry.

Website: www.khayes54.blogspot.com

Larry Benjamin

Bronx-born wordsmith and award-winning author, Larry Benjamin considers himself less a writer than an artist whose chosen medium is the written word rather than clay or paint or bronze. His passion is words.

His gay romance, Unbroken, is both a 2014 Lambda Literary finalist, and a 2014 IPPY (Independent Publishers Book Award) Gold medalist. Damaged Angels, a collection of short stories, first published by Bold Strokes Books in October 2012 (electronic edition), with a paperback edition published in 2013 by Beaten Track, is a 2013 Rainbow Award Runner-Up in the Gay Contemporary General Fiction category. His debut novel, the gay romance What Binds Us was released by Carina Press in March 2012.

He lives in Philadelphia, PA, USA with his partner and their Silky Terrier.

Website: www.larrybenjamin.com

Raine O'Tierney

Called "Queen of the Sweetness" (well, two or three people said it anyway!) Raine O'Tierney loves writing sweet stories about first loves, first times, fidelity, forever-endings and…friskiness?

Raine O'Tierney lives outside of Kansas City with her husband, fellow Dreamspinner Press author, Siôn O'Tierney. When she's not writing, she's either asleep, or fighting the good fight for intellectual freedom at her library day job. Raine believes the best thing we can do in life is be kind to one another, and she enjoys encouraging fellow writers. Writing for 20+ years (with the last 10 spent on M/M) Raine changes sub-genres to suit her mood and believes all good stories end sweetly. Contact her if you're interested in talking about point-and-click adventure games or about which dachshunds are the best kinds of dachshunds!

Website: www.raineotierney.com

CPSIA information can be obtained
at www.ICGtesting.com
Printed in the USA
LVHW030316220122
708923LV00002B/118

9 781909 192898